"Horse mothers put stage mothers to shame in this wildly entertaining thriller."
—*Publishers Weekly* (starred review)

"An engrossing read about competitive moms—and horse girls. . . . If in your youth you came across the intense energy of sports moms, then this book will certainly resonate."
—Shondaland

"I am obsessed with this fun and twisty read featuring gorgeous manes and dastardly deeds. . . . Come for the diabolical intrigue and stay for the vicious infighting. And the horses. Did I mention horses?"
—CrimeReads

"Irresistible . . . enough mean-girl drama and emotion to fill a horse barn . . . a blue-ribbon story of the haves and have-nots."
—*Kirkus Reviews*

"A wickedly delicious deep dive into the world of horse-crazy girls, whiskey-soaked barn parties, and high-octane show-jumping circuits. . . . But the cutthroat competition turns lethal when a corpse turns up at the summer show, and both mother and daughters must wrestle with what's truly important . . . a fabulous ride!"
—Kate Quinn, *New York Times* bestselling author of *The Diamond Eye*

"At turns hilarious and heartbreaking, *Girls and Their Horses* has Brazier's razor-sharp insight and blistering social commentary combined with a plot so subtly tense you'll hold your breath for whole chapters."
—Kiersten White, *New York Times* bestselling author of *Hide*

"Does for horse girls what Megan Abbott's *Dare Me* did for cheerleaders . . . A powerful, searing novel of hierarchy, desire, and desperation, told by a brilliant storyteller unafraid to take risks."
—Ashley Winstead, author of *The Last Housewife*

"Dark and deliciously twisted, this is the thriller of my equestrian dreams . . . or nightmares. You'll never look at horse girls the same way."
—Jessica Burkhart, bestselling author of the Canterwood Crest series

"Deliciously full of soapy, simmering tension; manipulation; toxic female friendships; power dynamics; and backstabbing aplenty . . . it's *Big Little Lies* meets *Dallas*, but even lustier and laced with Brazier's pitch-black humor. I couldn't put it down!"

—May Cobb, author of *The Hunting Wives*

"With stylish, incisive prose and laser-sharp commentary, this is a story that will draw readers in and hold them completely under its hypnotic spell . . . a reading experience as powerful, beautiful, and unsettling as the horses at its core."

—Laurie Elizabeth Flynn, author of *The Girls Are All So Nice Here*

"This recommended, well-written suspense poses questions about the cost of parents living vicariously through their children."

—*Library Journal*

"A slow-burn suspenseful read with plenty of drama."

—*Mystery & Suspense Magazine*

"Brazier's fine eye for detail and all-consuming passions does for the horse world what Megan Abbott's incisive behind-the-scenes novels did for ballet (*The Turnout*), gymnastics (*You Will Know Me*), and cheerleading (*Dare Me*)."

—*South Florida Sun-Sentinel*

"A deftly woven tale of families and horses, money and betrayals, emphasizes the constant abuse of young people and horses by those who seek money, fame, and power."

—*Fresh Fiction*

"Brilliantly mixes a coming-of-age with a crime thriller where every character is the lead."

—*Criminal Element*

ALSO BY
ELIZA JANE BRAZIER

If I Disappear

Good Rich People

GIRLS AND THEIR HORSES

ELIZA JANE BRAZIER

BERKLEY
New York

BERKLEY
An imprint of Penguin Random House LLC
penguinrandomhouse.com

BERKLEY and the BERKLEY & B colophon are registered trademarks
of Penguin Random House LLC.

ISBN: 978-0-593-43889-3

The Library of Congress has cataloged the Berkley hardcover edition
of this book as follows:

Names: Brazier, Eliza Jane, author.
Title: Girls and their horses / Eliza Jane Brazier.
Description: New York : Berkley, [2023]
Identifiers: LCCN 2022045492 (print) | LCCN 2022045493 (ebook) |
    ISBN 9780593438886 (hardcover) | ISBN 9780593438909 (ebook)
Classification: LCC PS3602.R3985 G57 2023 (print) |
    LCC PS3602.R3985 (ebook) | DDC 813/.6--dc23
LC record available at https://lccn.loc.gov/2022045492
LC ebook record available at https://lccn.loc.gov/2022045493

Berkley hardcover edition / June 2023
Berkley trade paperback edition / May 2024

Printed in the United States of America
1st Printing

Interior art: horse mane © OlesyaNickolaeva/shutterstock.com
Book design by Laura K. Corless

This book is dedicated to my mom and dad
for raising me to be a good horse mom.

DETECTIVE PEREZ

The police had to wait for the girl to finish riding her horse before they could take her aside for questioning. They assumed she hadn't heard what had happened, but she told them, "No, I know," as she took the seat across from them.

They were at the Southern California International Horse Show, an exclusive three-week event in the mountains. They had made an investigation room in one of the temporary horse stalls. The horse next door had returned, and through the wall they could hear it weaving and swishing its tail.

The girl was tiny, made of birdlike bones, dressed in sleek riding clothes. Her leg jiggled. She seemed distracted.

"Is this gonna take long?" she said. "Because I have another class."

Detective Perez hesitated. She came across a lot of people in her job, but there were no people quite like horse people. They shouted if you turned on sirens. They scolded you if you approached the horses. They claimed you were scaring the horses, but the animals were fine as long as people stayed calm.

They had horse shows like this one, intense competitions with a handful of the überwealthy. They spent all their time and all their money, dedicated their entire lives to animals they forced to serve their aspirations. Blue ribbons. Trophies.

Take the young lady in front of them. An unimaginable tragedy had occurred, and she was worried about show classes.

"We're just trying to understand what happened here. We were hoping maybe you could—"

"Oh, I can tell you exactly what happened." The girl sat back, crossed her neat black tall boots. "Do you have a mother?"

FOUR
MONTHS
BEFORE

MAPLE

Maple's mother had insisted she wear riding clothes to the horse stable, even though they weren't there to ride. They were there to feed the horses carrots. They had brought a big bag of them. The stable was only a mile away from their new house. It had been part of the promise of moving to California.

"Rancho Santa Fe has horses," Maple's mother had told her, like there weren't horses everywhere in Texas. "The first thing we're going to do is find you a new place to ride."

Heather sometimes seemed to genuinely believe that Maple loved horses just as much as she did. It wasn't that Maple didn't like horses; she just thought they were a little scary, especially the horses at this barn. They were huge and immaculate, nothing like the unkempt quarter horses in Amarillo.

Maple was turned out in breeches, a Cavalleria Toscana shirt and gleaming tall boots. Her mother had taken her to Mary's Tack and Feed yesterday and selected thousands of dollars' worth of riding clothes.

"Anything you want," she had kept saying.

Maple had had no idea what she was supposed to want. Her mom ended up picking, which satisfied them both.

But now Maple felt silly, dolled up in a stranger's barn—her hair was even in two French braids—like she was auditioning for the role of *rider*. What if someone saw them? Not only was she overdressed, but they were breaking the rules. There were signs everywhere that said not to touch the horses.

"Those are just for people who don't *know* horses," Heather said.

Heather herself wasn't exactly a pro. She had taken lessons in her youth. She had told Maple the story hundreds of times. How she had been the best rider, until her dad left and she was forced to quit. She'd had to sell her horse. She'd had to stop going to the barn.

Maple had been told that story so many times it had imprinted itself on her psyche, become an integral part of how she saw her mom—hair in two braids, shiny black boots, sitting outside the arena while the other girls rode their fantasy horses, out of reach.

It wasn't fair. The world owed Heather horses.

Maple's mother could have ridden herself now. She had even taken a few lessons, but she always ended up frustrated. It wasn't the same. It wasn't what she wanted. It didn't fix that event, as if the only way into her past was through her daughters' future.

Heather preferred to watch her daughters ride horses. First Piper, who had been a natural but who had quit when Heather pushed too hard. And now Maple, who was talentless and slightly fearful but willing.

Maple had always been a little captivated by her mother, who was beautiful, who was made even more beautiful by her strange, specific dreams. Heather wanted Maple to ride horses. She wanted her daughter to dress a certain way. She wanted Maple to have the right friends. She didn't care about the things other moms seemed to care about—grades and morality and even happiness.

"No one's happy," she had once assured Maple, offering a crooked smile-frown. "Don't worry about it." She had pressed her daughter's hair down. "I wish someone had told me that when I was your age. Then maybe I wouldn't have thought I was missing out."

Maple knew her mom had intended to make her feel better, to make her think about her own life, but instead it had made her think about her mom. When Heather kissed Maple's dad, when she grinned on vacation, when she had congratulated Maple at her elementary school graduation, Maple thought: *She's not really happy. She just seems happy.*

Right then Heather seemed happy, climbing up the rungs of a pipe corral to get a better look at a horse whose name was Desi, according to the engraved plaque outside his stall.

"You should ride this one," Heather said. "It would look so good with your hair."

Desi was huge, probably over seventeen hands—in horse measurements, a hand was four inches, or the width of a hand. He looked a little spicy, prancing around the far end of the stall, showing the whites of his eyes. He was wrong for Maple in every conceivable way except one—his golden palomino coloring—and that was all her mother saw.

Heather stretched her palm out, which seemed to make Desi more nervous. The gelding tossed his head, swishing his golden mane.

"He's perfect for you." Heather hopped down, startling the horse.

Heather adjusted her outfit and scanned the deserted aisle. She had dressed herself in discreet wealth. Everything expensive was slightly hidden: slivers of diamond earrings tucked beneath her hair, no logos on her leather purse. Her shirt was floral, simple. She could have gotten it from Walmart, but she hadn't. She had gotten it at a boutique in Santa Fe for eight hundred dollars.

"I thought more people would be here. It's Monday." Heather placed a hand over her perfectly made-up eyes and peered off toward a row of trailers. She had found a housekeeper who could also do her makeup. She loved telling people this, like it was somehow exceptional. "I'm going to see if I can find anyone to ask about lessons. You can stay with the horses, if you want."

Maple could tell that her mother wanted her to want to stay with the horses, so she nodded and dragged their enormous bag of carrots toward another barn.

Maple stepped into the cool shade of the breezeway. The horses stuck their heads over the doors and watched her. One noticed the carrots and whinnied. Then they all started whinnying, pacing around their stalls and tossing their heads. One even bucked and cantered a tight circle. They were freaking out. It was kind of scary.

Maple had a sense, always, that something terrible was about to happen now. *Right now*. She called it prophecy; her therapist called it generalized anxiety disorder.

"What are you doing?" A girl slipped out of a stall and into the aisleway.

She seemed older than Maple, but she was small and delicate. She was wearing a bright red coat, like a girl marked for death in a horror movie. But she had the face of the killer.

"You can't be here," the girl continued. "Didn't you read the signs?" She noticed the carrots. "Oh my God! Are you giving the horses *carrots*? Don't you know you can't do that? They could have Cushing's disease. Or bite you. I know this girl, and her mom got her finger bitten off by their horse, and the horse swallowed it. Seriously, I'm not fucking kidding."

Maple dropped the heavy bag on the ground. Her whole face burned. She wanted to run, but her legs felt weak. She was dizzy. She wished her mom were there.

Heather never seemed to be bothered by drama. In fact, she often seemed drawn to it. If there was a kerfuffle at a restaurant, if gunshots rang out, Heather drifted steadily toward it, clutching her purse and smiling benignly. *Can I help?*

"My mom—," Maple started.

"You need to leave," the girl said. "Seriously, you're actually trespassing. And why are you wearing riding clothes? It's Monday."

Maple burned up even more. She'd tried to warn her mother about this, when she had dressed Maple up like a doll.

A woman who must have been the other girl's mom appeared. She shared her daughter's red hair.

"What are you doing here?" she said. She also shared her attitude.

"My mom's here," Maple said, not answering the question. "I have to go get her." She took off like a lunatic toward the offices. She abandoned the carrots in the barn aisle.

"Hey!" the girl yelled after her. "You can't run around horses!"

M aple found her mom practically in the middle of breaking and entering. It would never have occurred to Heather that the office wasn't hers to open.

"Why are you running?" Heather asked, trying a combination on the lock. "I was thinking I could write them a note. I think this is the main office. I've already left seven voice messages."

Heather had been trying to contact this barn since before the move. Instead of giving up, she got only more determined.

Maple was breathing hard. She was on the verge of tears. "They said we can't be here!" Her voice rose precipitously. "They said we're *trespassing.*"

Heather perked up. "Who said that? Is someone here?"

Heather started in the direction Maple had come from, but then the red-haired woman appeared, matching daughter in tow. When she saw Heather, she smiled so fast it was like a quick draw in a shoot-out.

"Why, hello there!" Her eyes ran fast over Heather, like she was calculating the value of everything she saw—Heather herself included. "I'm Pamela and this is my daughter, Vida."

"I'm Heather. Parker. And this is my daughter Maple."

"I was just telling your sweet girl that unfortunately this barn isn't open to the public." Pamela was holding Vida's hand, their fingers laced, like they were best friends instead of mother and daughter.

"Oh, we're not the public," Heather said. They had been rich for a short amount of time, but Heather had adjusted beautifully. "We're here to sign up for riding lessons."

"It's Monday," Pamela said. "No one comes in on Mondays. And this isn't a lesson barn. They don't have school ponies or summer camps."

Heather stepped forward, crossed her arms neatly. Since she had become rich, Maple's mother had changed, although not completely. The root of what she had always been was still there. But she had become more herself.

"We just bought a house a mile from here," Heather said, as if that had anything to do with it.

But Maple could see Pamela's expression change. It softened a little, like the Parkers were closer to belonging not just there but everywhere.

"How lovely! That makes us neighbors," she said. "But I will warn you, this probably isn't the barn for you."

Maple knew the woman couldn't have tempted her mother more.

"There's a good riding school in Olivenhain. I can give you their number."

"No, thank you. I like this one. It's closer to our house. I want Maple to be able to walk to the barn if she wants to," Heather said. As if Maple would ever walk a mile. "Would you mind taking my number? Then you can pass it along to the owners for me. I've been trying to reach them."

"Kieran Flynn," Pamela said, like the name meant something to everyone. "He's the owner and the head trainer."

Pamela clearly didn't want to take her number, but Heather just waited. Pamela finally took out her phone. She typed Heather's number in quickly.

Then she added, "This is a show barn. Last year, we outperformed every barn at the Southern California International Horse Show. We demand total commitment to the program. We're a very tight community. You have to have your own horses, and your horses have to be in the training program. That means all of your rides are supervised by a trainer, and your horse is schooled by a Professional rider. It's really not a place for fun."

"Good," Heather said, taking Maple's hand like she was aping Pamela. "We don't want to have fun."

There was nothing Heather loved more than the word no.

two

PAMELA

Pamela kind of liked Heather. She didn't know what it was about her—possibly her real estate. She even liked Heather enough to Google her.

Pamela was sitting on a tack box in the A barn. She and Vida had commandeered the carrots Maple left behind. Vida was feeding them to all the horses that could have carrots.

No one, except the stall cleaners and the feeding crew, came in on Mondays. Pamela and Vida—who were at the barn every day of the week—loved Mondays for that reason. They could be alone with the horses. Just the dry California air and the smell of pine shavings and the warm animal bodies.

"Oh my God," Pamela said on Page One.

"What is it?"

Vida trotted over with the nearly empty carrot bag. Pamela held the phone out to her.

"Oh my God. Is that for real?"

"Her husband is loaded," Pamela said. "It has to be the same person, right? She said Parker."

"Yeah, Heather Parker. And they sounded like Texas people."

Vida hopped onto the tack box beside her mother. "What house did they buy?"

Pamela did a search of all the houses in a two-mile radius. One had sold three months earlier. She pulled up the listing.

Vida peered over her shoulder. "Holy shit."

Pamela had lived in Rancho Santa Fe since she was a child, but she hadn't seen every house. Most of the houses were hidden behind tall gates and down epic drives. The Parkers had purchased one such house for twenty-eight million dollars.

"It's like a resort," Vida said. "Look, it even has its own stables." She pointed at a cute wood barn on the far side of the property.

"Shit." Pamela hopped off the tack box. "We'd better go."

"Go where?" Vida hurried after her.

"To tell Kieran. I just found him a golden goose."

three

HEATHER

They were home so fast that Heather felt disappointed. She wanted to keep driving down those one-lane roads, peering over everyone's white rail fences at their tennis courts and orange groves.

Rancho Santa Fe was a different kind of money from any other that Heather had ever experienced. It was a cross between Hollywood Golden Age glamour and historic Spanish estates. The beach was fifteen minutes away. You didn't get traffic like you did in LA. The weather was perfect all year round. The light was better. There were only a few thousand residents, and they were wealthy beyond belief. Even Bill Gates had a horse property there.

Heather had felt special when she discovered the area, as if knowing of its existence was its own reward. It had been her push to move there. It was perfect. It had everything anyone could want.

"I thought everyone was leaving California," her husband, Jeff, said.

"Because they can't afford it," Heather said back.

They had kept their house in Texas. It was from the before times, pre-rich. It was modest but close to family. They had paid it off as soon as their fortunes changed.

Jeff owned seventeen companies, but he'd made most of his money investing. He had been doing it since he was a child. Just over a year ago, he had started to get lucky in a way that had felt like the magic you read about in books. It seemed like every month Jeff came home in shock to give Heather more good news.

I'm making two million this year.

I'm making six million.

Eighteen million dollars.

Thirty-five.

I have one hundred fifteen million dollars.

Then he stopped telling her.

It was scary to have so much money, to just keep making more.

The Parkers had become richer than they had ever imagined being. And suddenly they'd owed it to themselves to do everything they had ever dreamed of. It became almost a burden. Trips to Paris, the Bahamas, an RV they never used, "toys"—the best of everything.

And the kids! Think of the kids! Jeff and Heather needed to give their daughters the life they themselves had never had. Cars and clothes and bags and horses.

"Piper and Maple are going to have rich friends," Heather had insisted one night in bed. "Friends who get them places, the ones I never had." She meant the ones who had been taken from her.

Heather had grown up next to a horse stable. Every weekday after school, she would jump over her back fence and land in her dreamworld. Every weekend she would be there from sunup to sundown. Heather and her friends had called themselves the Barn Kids. They had spent practically every waking moment together, had sleepovers and pool parties. But when Heather had turned twelve, her father left.

He didn't go far. He stayed in the same town, just with a different family. New daughters, a few sons. He didn't pay child support, and Heather and her mother loved him too much to ask for it.

Heather's horse had been sold. For years after, well into her twenties, she wore a bracelet with the horse's name on it. It was like she was wearing her old life around her wrist.

Heather lost her barn friends. She never made good friends again. Perhaps she had been too afraid, not just of how quickly she could lose people but of how quickly they forgot her and moved on.

Her home life had changed rapidly. All the things that used to protect her family didn't work anymore: locks and friends and government officials.

And Heather felt herself change with it, become harder, more dissatisfied. She couldn't afford to be herself anymore. All her best parts had been sold off.

Heather used to imagine what her life could have been like if her father hadn't left. How she could have stayed in that halcyon childhood forever. How easy, how perfect things could have been. She could have kept her horse. She could have kept her friends and her barn and her family. It seemed to her that she'd been doomed to spend her life trying to get back to that place, to the paradise she'd lost.

Until she and Jeff ascended by accident. They had money, and suddenly they owed. They owed it to themselves to live every dream, to take everything that had ever been denied them. They owed it to their children to right every wrong ever done to *them*.

They owed it to everyone—even total strangers—to live the dream life. Beaches. Sunshine. Mansions. Horses. Sometimes Heather felt this alarming pressure, like a fist in her chest so tight she struggled to breathe. *You should be happier! You're not happy enough! Why aren't you fucking happy?*

Being rich, in some ways, was like being dead. You built your own heaven, and then you had to live in it.

Heather drove through their front gate. There was a man in a booth—three men actually, on a rotating schedule—just watching their gate.

As Heather sailed up the drive, she felt like she was visiting some foreign dignitary or a luxury resort, but this was her house. She wondered if it would ever feel like hers. Even the house in Texas—the ordinary one with the leaky roof and the seventies-style kitchen—had always felt like the home of the person she'd bought it from, an old woman who'd raised her kids there.

Heather didn't think she would ever be big enough to feel she owned this house, and looking at it now, she wasn't sure that she wanted to be.

She found Jeff organizing the books in the library. They had paid people to put everything away, only to realize with embarrassment how much space they had left to fill.

Jeff was very particular about where things went. It was part of how his mind worked. He could see things no one else could see, zero in and exploit them. But when he was "working"—a catchall term that seemed to cover everything he did—he was able to see only one thing at a time, so he could not see Heather, or the kids, or the world at large.

Right then he was working on the books. Because he had chosen to do that task, it was the most important one in the world.

He had spent their last night in Amarillo ruthlessly labeling the books in their boxes. He had neglected Heather's family, and his own family, and all their friends in favor of his self-appointed task.

Now, perched on the arm of a sofa, Heather watched him work. She was still looking for the right interior decorator. Maybe she would ask Pamela to recommend someone.

"We found the perfect barn," Heather said. "The stables are all stone with wood beams. And everything is so clean." Like those were the important points. "It's only a mile away, so Maple can walk if she wants."

Jeff frowned. "I wouldn't walk anywhere here. There are no sidewalks."

"She can use the horse trails." Heather had walked them herself to make sure. "It's called Rancho Santa Fe Equestrian."

That was Heather's favorite part about it. She looked forward to telling people the name, because they would know exactly where the barn was and what that address meant. Not like those other local barns, Sunset Hills or Moonrise Farms, which sounded like retirement homes.

"I don't think she should walk anywhere by herself," Jeff said, alluding to the other reason they'd moved to California.

Back in Texas, Maple had been bullied. It had started with one girl, and then escalated to half a dozen. First they teased her. Then they pushed her when the teacher wasn't looking. Another girl had yanked her by the hair and dragged her to the ground. She had pulled so hard that she'd torn the skin from Maple's scalp.

That terrorizing from girls barely in their teens had, over time, exposed the weaknesses in every member of the Parker family. Jeff insisted that Maple should ignore the bullying. Heather believed that her daughter should fight back. Piper said that Maple should kill the girls with kindness. All three were wrong. Nothing worked. There was nothing they could do. Until they realized that they could buy their way out of Texas, and their problems.

"We have to buy her a horse," Heather said. "They don't have school ponies."

"A whole horse? Can't we do a lease or something, make sure she's committed to this?"

Jeff was always warning Heather that Maple didn't seem to like riding as much as her mother did. His insistence irritated Heather.

If Jeff had his way, Maple would just stay home and hide. Heather was trying to make her tougher and braver and better—not better than Maple was, but better than Heather was. That was the goal of children.

"A good horse is an investment."

Heather lifted herself off the sofa and crossed over to Jeff. She found that the closer she got, the more convincing she was. Heather was a beautiful woman, and her knowing that was the most beautiful thing about her.

Jeff was fairly ambivalent about many things in life—friends, family, social norms—but he was always moved by beauty. He saw it as a number, something he could quantify. In the early days of their dating, he'd told Heather she was a 7.9. Negging had been all the rage back then, so Heather hadn't been as bothered by that number as she perhaps should have been, until he told her that her friend Jacinda was an 8.75.

Everyone had wondered why Heather married Jeff, except Heather's mother. Her mother had been so proud of her for marrying the smart guy.

"The smart guy will treat you right," she said. "The smart guy will never leave you."

People had a lot of wrong ideas about nerds.

The move to California hadn't been just a fresh start for Maple. It had been a fresh start for Heather, too. A way to keep Jeff from the eights and up. Because once he had become rich enough, Jeff seemed to have decided that affairs were a worthwhile risk. Heather knew that he could cheat in California, too, but getting him to move had still felt like a win.

Heather liked to ask Jeff for things. She thrilled at the friction, enjoyed pushing him, like she had with the house and the move. Jeff buying her things had become her only proof of his love. Sometimes his gifts made her feel better. Other times, she considered that the money might not mean as much to him as she thought.

Heather brushed Jeff's fresh-cut hair with her newly manicured fingers. "We have that stable outside. We have to have horses."

"How many horses are we talking?"

"Just one, to start." She smiled.

"It's a good thing I'm a rich man."

"Oh, it's a very good thing." And then she kissed him, parting her lips and inviting him into her want.

four

PIPER

Piper's new bedroom was bigger than her parents' master bedroom at the old house. And she had chosen one of the smaller ones.

When the Parkers had first arrived in California, Heather had driven the family to the property to choose rooms. Heather acted like she was hosting a reality show.

"Ready, set, go!" she said as she put the car in park.

Maple had broken into a little jog, but Piper just felt annoyed. This wasn't a reality show; this was her life.

Piper liked Amarillo. She had friends and a whole life there. Heather didn't like Piper's friends. She had constantly been trying to tell Piper who she *really* was.

"Don't you want friends who do fun things?"

"Don't you want friends who hang out with boys?"

"Don't you want friends who like to travel?"

What she meant was *Don't you want friends who are popular and rich?* Piper didn't give a shit about superficial things.

Piper was a worker. She liked to help people, to get involved. Back in Texas, she had been the busiest girl at school. She had played lacrosse and been class treasurer and the president of the debate team. She had built sets for the theater class and floats for the cheer team, and on weekends, she had brought pets from the animal shelter out to the local PetSmart to drum up adoptions. She had been known as the girl who got things done.

Now she was in California, with no friends and no clubs and no school.

Piper was eighteen. Technically, she could have stayed in Texas—although her parents wouldn't have supported her—but she was starting at UCSD in the fall, with the goal of eventually going to med school. Her mother had guilted her into cutting out of senior year early by insisting that Maple needed her. By telling her over and over, "This is our last chance to all be together. This is the last time." Piper seriously doubted that was true. Her mom was not the type to give anything up—especially not her daughters.

That first day at the house, her mom had followed behind her, asking, "Aren't you going to pick a room? Don't you want to pick a room?"

Piper, her eyes trained on her phone, came to a stop in the hallway. "Which room are you in?"

"The master bedroom, of course," Heather said.

"I'll just take the one farthest from you."

"Piper . . . ," her father cautioned.

"What? I'm almost in college. I need to have *privacy*."

Her dad looked around them. "I think you'll have that here. I doubt I'll even run into you most days."

Jeff tried to act down to earth, and Piper bought it some of the time. But he had agreed to the move, agreed to the house. Part of him must have wanted it.

Piper was constantly pushing her dad to donate more of his money. He did give generously, but it was never really enough for Piper. She was impressed by enormous gestures, huge sacrifices.

Was it really charity if it didn't hurt you a little? If she could have had her way, her dad would have given all his money to Feeding America, and the Parkers could have gone back to the way things had been before.

The new house scared her a little. Something about wealth didn't feel real, or safe. It was like they had been quarantined, cut off from the world, like in the opening of an episode of *Black Mirror*.

Back in Amarillo, Piper had known who she was. She'd had friends and school and clubs. That first night in her new room, she had lain back in her bed as the walls seemed to reel away from her.

Piper had insisted on keeping the family's old living room sofa. She had put it in her room. That night, she fixed her eyes on it to anchor herself, but it seemed impossibly far away, as if it were falling down a tunnel of space.

Piper couldn't explain her feelings to her parents. She couldn't confess them to anyone, because Piper was the worker, the one who solved problems—not the one who had them.

But, God, she felt so lonely in that house, so quickly and so deeply that she wondered if she had been lonely for years but had just been too busy to notice.

That was what she hated most about wealth. It solved all your outside problems and left only the ones you kept inside.

Piper was lying on her bed, scrolling through her friends' social media feeds, when Maple barged in. Her sister was dressed in immaculate riding clothes. She looked both adorable and embarrassing.

"Mom got yelled at!" Maple announced, bouncing onto the dingy old sofa.

Piper put her phone down. Her parents annoyed her sometimes, but her sister never did. Maple was sweet in a way that Piper didn't think anyone ever had been. She had always been immature, and at thirteen, she was still sewn through with sunshine.

"Why did she get yelled at?"

"She was trespassing. You should have seen her." Maple started to giggle. It was infectious. "The office at the barn was locked and she was, like, trying combinations." She paused, her mouth forming an "o." "Have you ever heard of Cushing's disease?"

"Yeah. People have it, too."

"We got yelled at for trying to feed carrots to the horses. There were signs everywhere not to touch them, but Mom said that was for *other people*."

Maple rolled her eyes, but Piper knew that when it came to their mom, Maple's rebelliousness was limited.

"Why did you even agree to keep riding? You're terrified of horses."

"I'm not terrified," Maple insisted. "I just think they're big. And they have teeth that go all the way back to their eyes." She pulled her own lips back with her finger in demonstration.

"So don't ride them." Piper picked her phone back up. "You don't have to just because *she* wants you to."

Maple straightened up. "You actually like horses, but you don't ride because she wants you to. So who's really the dumb one?" Although mostly sweet, Maple did have moments of cutting insight.

Piper fell back on her bed, and Maple crawled in beside her, propping her chin on her sister's shoulder as Piper scrolled. It was a family joke that Maple had no concept of personal space.

Maple would make comments every so often. "That's funny. . . . That's disgusting. . . . Oh my God, send that to me."

But mostly they just lay in the quiet, practically on top of each other in that big empty house.

five

VIDA

Vida's mom hadn't called Kieran before they went over. She probably hadn't wanted him to tell her not to come. He lived a mile away from the barn, in the opposite direction of the Parker property. Pamela's Mercedes pulled up to his gate. She reached out to plug in the gate code.

Kieran lived on one of the oldest estates in Rancho Santa Fe. He had inherited it from his parents after they died in a gas leak at that same house. The house always seemed imbued with death to Vida. The walls were yellowing. There were rows of Spanish arches and artfully crumbling fountains.

Vida loved it. The darkness spoke to her. She wanted to have a sleepover or a séance there. When Vida had been younger, she used to imagine herself in that house. She'd had a dream that her mother and Kieran would fall in love, and Kieran would adopt her. And all of the horses would be hers.

Pamela pulled into the porte cochere and got out of the car. No one came to greet them. The house was dead on Mondays, like the barn. It was the day of rest, the only rest they got all week.

"Do you think he's gonna be mad we're here?" Vida asked as they approached the Spanish Gothic door.

"Not when I tell him why." Pamela knocked smartly.

After a considerable delay, Kieran answered the door. He always looked older on Mondays.

"The fuck are you doing here?" he said, only slightly teasing.

"I have some very good news," Pamela said as he stepped back to let her in.

"I have a phone." He sighed as Vida followed them into the house.

The entryway was like something out of the old Hollywood movies Vida's mother made her watch. There was a twisting wrought iron staircase just waiting for someone to tumble down the red tile steps.

Vida and Pamela followed Kieran into the TV room. An old show-jumping event played on the enormous flat-screen. Douglas Dunn, a glorified intern and Kieran's top rider, was asleep on the sofa. He lived with Kieran as part of his job incentives.

"What is this big news you have?" Kieran asked, pulling an imported beer from his mini fridge. He cracked the top off with a horse-shaped bottle opener. It was early, but Kieran drank all day on Mondays. "Do you want a drink? I have one of your bottles somewhere."

"I'm fine," Pamela said, but she sounded anxious.

She often seemed nervous around Kieran, who had been her trainer for more than twenty years. Vida had grown up surrounded by the myth of her mother and Kieran. At one time, Pamela had been one of his most promising riders. Then her father died, and most of his money had died with him. Pamela could no longer afford to be great.

"We were just at the barn, and this woman was walking around with her daughter like she owned the place."

"That'd better not be why you're here," Kieran said. "You can tell people to fuck off yourself."

"I'm here because she just bought a house around the corner for twenty-eight million dollars—or rather, her husband did." Because she was a single mother, Pamela always liked to make that distinction, as if all her money hadn't come from her father. "I tried to tell her—before I knew who she was—that RSFE isn't a lesson barn, but she didn't seem put off." Rancho Santa Fe Equestrian—RSFE for short—was a place for elite riders only. "She doesn't even have a horse."

"Well, that's what we want." He looked over at Douglas, who hadn't moved.

He was like a corpse on that sofa, Vida thought.

"Exactly," Pamela said.

"I don't know why you tried to put her off," Kieran said.

"I told you, I didn't know who she was. She was wearing all this tacky Texas gear. But she's nouveau riche."

"My favorite fucking kind. Before they realize how dangerous money really is."

He dropped onto his ancient leather chair. Kieran had taste; he was old money. His family back in Ireland owned a castle somewhere. He had filled his own house with all the right things, the things that lasted forever, looked better with age and never went out of style.

"She's new in town, so she'll need friends. That's you and that woman you hang out with."

June, the woman in question, had been a client of Kieran's for six years, but he insisted on never remembering her name, even to her face. Vida believed this was because June, while exorbitantly rich, was also vocally antirich. She was constantly telling anyone who would listen how down to earth she was. She drove a Tesla, owned just two horses—one for her and one for her daughter, Effie—and showed only once a season, because "all this is really just for fun."

Vida loved June's daughter, Effie. She and her mom both agreed that Effie was all right, but even Pamela was constantly annoyed by

June. If it weren't for the barn, they would never have been friends, which was often how friendships worked. They were marriages of convenience.

"Of course," Pamela said, more than happy to help.

All of her life, Vida had been surrounded by people who revered Kieran. He was the true horse person. He was the head trainer, the final word on everything. The one who decided who rode what horses where and when. Everyone courted his favor. If Kieran thought you were good, then you were really, actually good. If Kieran thought you were bad, you were nothing.

Pamela was no longer in training or technically Kieran's student. But like everything at RSFE—the horses, the riders, probably even the dirt and the flower boxes—she belonged to him. That was the way it worked at a barn. You were a part of a *team*. And a team was a human amplification of a single voice: your coach's.

"Maybe we could bring her and her daughter to the barn for a lesson one day this week?" Pamela suggested. "Really show off. That way we can get her daughter signed up as quickly as possible, before someone tries to poach her."

"She doesn't have a horse to ride," Kieran pointed out.

"She can borrow one of ours," Pamela offered, "while she looks for one."

Vida groaned. "Which one? I don't want her riding one of my horses. She'll ruin them. You can tell she doesn't know *anything* about horses."

"Well, you'll just have to teach her, won't you?" Pamela said. "You can watch her like a hawk. We'll put her on Faustus. He's practically retired anyway."

"Ugh," Vida said. She hated being a team player sometimes.

"Excuse me, young lady," Pamela warned. "But this girl is going to be your *new best friend*."

six

PAMELA

Bright and early Tuesday morning, Pamela texted Heather and invited her out for coffee with June. They met on the coast in Del Mar, at a cute little place where they could have a table close to the water and away from everybody else.

June was her usual self, aggressively warning Heather about the snobs in Rancho Santa Fe like she wasn't one. Heather clung to her Kelly bag and nodded along.

Pamela had befriended women for Kieran before; even June was really one such friend. It was what you did to be a team player, to court Kieran's favor. Some women Pamela liked, and some she didn't. She wasn't sure about Heather.

Heather looked too much like a Texas beauty queen. She talked with an accent, which she tried to suppress. She seemed desperate to prove herself. It was Pamela's job to make her believe that the way to do that was by spending money.

"So, the training program runs ten thousand a month," Pamela explained, once June had stopped to breathe. "And then we do horse shows about once a month. Those are extra, of course. Your little girl can start training right away on one of Vida's string—we have the perfect horse for her—but she'll need to get her own horse as soon as possible. *If* Kieran agrees to let her train with us, he'll take you horse shopping right away."

Pamela sensed that it was important that she make it seem like Kieran *might* not take Heather. That was how you dealt with the new rich. People like Heather grew up believing they were somehow inferior to people with money. Exploiting that was crucial.

"Horse shopping is the most fun." June grinned. "There are so many cute ones."

They would not be shopping for a cute horse. They would be shopping for a Grand Prix horse, a horse that could compete at the highest level of the sport. A horse that neither Kieran nor Pamela could afford. That was what made Heather the golden goose.

"It's all so exciting," Heather said. "Maple will be thrilled."

"Kieran has time to watch her ride tomorrow morning," Pamela continued, "after he finishes a training session with Douglas Dunn. That's his top rider. If he agrees to let your daughter join RSFE, she won't be training with Kieran. He has this wonderful Junior trainer, Amy. But every client goes through Kieran first."

This was also a lie. Kieran didn't give a shit about the kids who trained with Amy, but the Parkers were special. He wanted to make sure they signed up, and maybe to show off a little.

Heather blinked her lash extensions. Heather was naturally beautiful, but all the add-ons made her beauty a little obscene. Pamela recognized lash extensions, hair extensions, Botox and lip fillers. She hated how women didn't seem to realize that this look had been influenced by porn stars, and that it kind of made them look like one. Pamela herself maintained a natural, horsey beauty, so she resembled a villain in a Jane Austen movie.

"Do the girls hang out at the barn all day?" Heather asked. "I used to do that when I was younger."

"Of course they do!" Pamela said. "My Vida is there all day, sometimes until after nine."

She didn't mention that Vida was there cleaning bridles for the training program until after nine. That was one of the special things about the horse industry: You paid through the nose and the barn still exploited your children for hard labor.

"This barn is *our family*."

Pamela considered herself the unofficial head barn mom, although lately her position had started to feel a little tenuous. To stay at the top of the pecking order, you had to be among the best, and to be among the best, you had to be able to afford it. She hoped that recruiting Heather would boost her profile.

"It's a place where we all come together *as a team*. A place where everyone *belongs*."

Heather's whole face lit up. She clung a little harder to her Kelly bag. She practically held her breath. She was such an easy target, Pamela almost wished that *she* had something to sell her. In a place like this, Heather was going to get eaten alive.

"You should stitch that on a pillow." June snorted.

June was constantly trying to undermine the barn, even though she was just as invested in it as anyone else. It was her way of feeling like she was in control.

"Will you both be there tomorrow?" Heather asked.

"Of course we will, dear." Pamela tilted her head, offering her softest smile.

Pamela had always thought there was a special joy in influencing someone. She had seen it with Kieran again and again: the way riders were transformed under his training. The change was both shocking and magnificent to witness.

"We'll be there with you every step of the way."

seven

HEATHER

Heather couldn't sleep that night. She tossed and turned on their thirty-thousand-dollar mattress. Her stomach was filled with butterflies. She'd had sex with Jeff twice, but eventually he'd begged off.

She was so thrilled about the horses. She liked June okay, but she really liked Pamela. She had a feeling that Pamela could be a riot once they got to know each other. Once they became friends.

Heather thought about her old barn friends. She wondered where they were now. She doubted they were as rich or successful as she was. She wondered if they ever thought about her. She hoped they did. She hoped they had looked her up; then she worried that they hadn't.

The next morning, Heather dressed Maple in a brand-new riding outfit. She had the housekeeper French-braid Maple's hair.

Maple's helmet was a little tight with the braids, but she looked adorable. Heather tried to get Piper to come with them, but she refused. Jeff was likewise not interested.

"I'm almost done organizing the books!" he said.

Heather and Maple made the quick trip to the stables and arrived fifteen minutes early. Heather had hoped that they would get to spend that time preparing the horse, but it was already tacked up and waiting.

Pamela zeroed in on them immediately, looping her arm into Heather's in a way that was intimate and intimidating. "The grooms do all that," she explained. "Sometimes, on Saturday afternoons, the girls will give the horses a bath or paint their hair bright colors just for fun."

Vida scooted right in with Maple, which made Heather happy. Vida was dressed in riding clothes today, and Heather made a note of all the brands she wore.

Pamela led them to the main arena. Brightly painted jumps set at unbelievable heights were scattered in the middle of the ring. It was surrounded by smaller arenas and, farther out, pastureland and trails.

Along one side of the arena, a wide patio was set with tables and chairs. Pamela took Heather to the table where June and her daughter were already waiting.

June's daughter, Effie, was stunning. She had wide-set dark eyes and sleek, beautiful hair. Vida and Maple sat down beside her. Heather was impressed by the effect of the three girls together. They just fit. They looked like best friends. She imagined their horse-girl future, which would be much like her own horse-girl past: sleepovers and trail rides and pool parties.

Heather automatically reached for her wrist, then remembered her old bracelet wasn't there anymore. She would have to get a new one, and get Maple one to match.

"Effie is fourteen, probably close to Maple's age," Pamela said. "But ages don't really matter with horse girls!"

"Maple is thirteen," Heather said. "How old is Vida?"

"Seventeen."

That surprised Heather. Not only was Vida tiny, but she had the spotlessness of youth.

Pamela pointed toward the arena. "That's the head trainer,

Kieran Flynn. Horses are in his blood. His great-grandparents moved here from Ireland nearly a hundred years ago. They were into horse racing. Kieran is one of the best show-jumping trainers in the world."

Heather nodded. Kieran looked Irish, and he looked like a horse trainer. He was muscular and distinguished, like a lord crossed with a bodyguard. He was training a male rider on an enormous bay horse.

Heather startled when the rider passed by and she saw his face. He was almost implausibly handsome.

"That's Douglas Dunn," Pamela said as if responding to Heather's little intake of breath. "He's Kieran's top rider. If you train here, he'll school your horse."

Heather remembered that "schooling" meant keeping the horse tuned up for its rider.

"He's really good-looking," Heather said, because not to seemed more suspicious.

Her eyes trailed him as he circled the arena. He was tall, athletic, vaguely European. He could sit a horse.

"Oh, yes," Pamela said. "You should see him at horse shows. Packs of girls just follow him around, sneaking pictures on their phones. It's just hilarious."

Heather couldn't blame them. She wanted to take a picture herself to show Piper, who would never believe her otherwise. "How old is he?"

"Legal," Pamela said, and Heather felt a little guilty.

"Dunn!" Kieran roared. He had just finished setting a jump that must have been over five feet. "Warm up over this."

Douglas followed Kieran's instructions.

Heather had watched show-jumping competitions on TV, but she had never seen a horse jump that high in person. It was a little unbelievable that such a large animal could launch itself into the air, tuck its spindly legs under its fourteen-hundred-pound body.

Once the horse had warmed up, Kieran laid out a course of

breathlessly sharp turns, of two and even three jumps in sequence, so the horse landed and took off again and again.

Kieran would scream at Douglas, and Douglas would take the abuse in stride, shortening his reins, rising up athletically when the horse took off, and then rocking back to stick the landing. There was something both controlled and perilous about it.

Heather felt her heart race. Sometimes she lost her breath. Halfway through the third round, she glanced over at Maple. Her daughter was covering her eyes.

"What are you doing?" she scolded.

"I'm scared he might fall," Maple said.

Vida just laughed.

"Douglas never falls," Effie said wistfully. "The horse will fall before he does."

Heather reached across the table to remove Maple's fingers from her eyes. "You need to watch," she said. "This is important."

Pamela seemed to note this interaction, and Heather felt a flush of shame. She had a tendency to get too invested in her daughters' riding.

Piper had hated how involved Heather was in her own riding. How Heather had chosen her clothes. How she had given her daughter advice. How she had interfered with Piper's lessons and her trainers and her chores.

It had all come to a head one afternoon at a schooling show, when Heather called out instructions to Piper during her round—which was against the rules—and got her disqualified. Piper had quit riding, even though Heather could tell she hadn't wanted to. She had quit because of Heather.

Heather was determined not to let that happen with Maple, but sometimes she couldn't help herself. She wanted what was best for her daughters. She was only trying to help.

Douglas pulled the horse up after a clean round and waited for

Kieran's instructions with a hand on his hip and a benign, dreamy expression on his face.

"Ice. Three rotations," Kieran said. The session was over.

"I'm not gonna have to do that, am I?" Maple asked, grimacing.

"Like you could." Vida snorted. "Even I don't jump that big."

Kieran vaulted smoothly over the arena rail, then approached their table. "So, what did you think?" he asked Heather, like they were already friends and he had done something special just for her.

"That was incredible," she said. "I didn't know horses could jump that high."

He frowned as if her reply had disappointed him. Then he fixed his eyes on Maple. "Is this the girl? You ever ridden a horse before, kid?"

Maple ducked her head and didn't answer.

"She's ridden hundreds of times," Heather said. "She took lessons back in Texas."

Heather wished that Piper was there. Piper was the better rider. Heather thought Piper could have impressed these people, and she had a feeling that Maple wouldn't. She tried to remind herself that she didn't need to impress anyone, but when had that ever been true?

"I want to hear her answer," Kieran said.

Heather's first impulse was to be insulted, but her second was gentler. He was a trainer. He was trying to train her daughter. It was good for her.

"You a rider, kid?" Kieran asked. "Or do you just dress like one?"

Heather was about to jump in again; she couldn't help herself. But she had a feeling that it wouldn't go over well with Kieran. Luckily, Maple spoke up.

"What my mom said: I took some lessons."

Maple sometimes put on a baby voice when she was nervous. She was doing it now. Heather wished she could tell her to stop.

Kieran perched on the edge of a table. "You any good?"

"Not really, no," Maple said. Her open, honest face was a little heartbreaking.

"Why not?"

"Um, I'm not really sure?"

"Do you want to get better?"

Maple looked at her mom. "Um . . . yes?" She looked at the two girls beside her. "I want to ride with Vida and Effie. That could be fun."

Kieran nodded, seemed to soften a little. "Okay. Why don't you grab Faustus and get in there?" He nodded toward the arena.

Maple hopped up from her chair, then hesitated. "Um, you're not gonna make me jump that high?"

"What if I did? Would you try?"

"I don't know."

Kieran sat back, exhaled slowly. "You know what, kid? I would never ask you to do something you couldn't do. Do you believe that? That's what it means to have a trainer. If you ride here, whether it's with me or Amy, you have to put your whole heart into it. All of your faith. All of your trust, into us. We're your family. All of us"— he made a circle with his finger—"are your barn family. Get it? And we will never ask for more than you can give."

Maple nodded, a little rapturous.

"Now, git."

She trotted off with Vida and Effie to collect the horse.

Heather's eyes felt a little teary, and she forced them away from the others.

All she wanted was for her daughter to be strong. Maple was such a good girl, but Heather and Jeff and Piper couldn't protect her from the world. Maybe a place like this could make her strong enough to protect herself.

eight

PIPER

The most unexpected thing about the new house was the silence. It was a species of quiet that Piper had never experienced before: no neighbors, no cars, not even the sounds of her own family. Piper had chosen a room on the far side of the house for privacy, but she hadn't anticipated the isolation she would feel.

It felt particularly intense because she was in a new place with no friends. She knew she would make friends in the fall, but her parents had pulled her out of school a month early. Her mother had insisted that the end of senior year was a waste of time. Heather wanted the family to get settled in California. She wanted to summer at the beach. She wanted them to spend time together before Piper started college.

Part of the reason the Parkers had left, Piper knew, was because her parents had already pulled Maple out of school. They had made this decision after weeks when the school seemed to do nothing as Maple was teased and pushed and humiliated. Her mother had finally pulled the plug.

Piper was proud of her mother for that decision, but she believed that leaving Texas had been too big a solution. Her parents could have switched Maple to a different school. They could have tried. But that wasn't the way her mother thought; Heather thought big.

Piper left her room around lunchtime. The silence had finally gotten to her. Back in Texas, her friends were all in class, so no one was responding to her messages.

She walked through the long hallways, peering into the great open rooms. As she walked, she heard the familiar sound of her parents shouting. It echoed through the mostly empty space.

"Ten thousand dollars a month? That's insane!" her dad said. "The last place was three hundred a month."

Piper hovered in the hall, wanting to listen but not wanting to be pulled in.

"This is different. It's a training program. You work with a trainer every day. They have a professional ride your horse. And then there are horse shows. They're huge events. The riders travel all over the country."

"How much does the horse cost if training it costs ten grand a month?"

"I'm not sure, but I'm sure it's a lot."

"So am I."

Piper spotted a crack in the wall. It was tiny, maybe two or three inches long, but it seemed exceptional in their perfect house. Piper had this feeling of wanting to protect it. It reminded her of home, her real home.

"How much do you spend on golf trips?" Heather said.

"You're kidding."

"How much was that RV you bought, the one we haven't used once?"

"Because you won't let me!" Anything he didn't do was her fault. And anything he did.

"How much do you spend on women?" That one shut him up.

Piper knew that her father had cheated on her mother. One night after a lacrosse match, Piper and her friends had all gone to Napoli's, and they had seen her father there with another woman.

Piper had gone to her dad first. He had insisted, "It's not what it looks like. I'm allowed to have female friends."

Then Piper had gone to her mother. She'd said, "I know, sweetie. Let's just ignore him," like it was all just a game.

Piper knew that Heather's father had left when Heather was young. Piper had seen him sporadically in her childhood—but mostly in the past year, because there was nothing like money to bring a family closer.

Piper had always thought he was a nice enough guy, until her mother revealed that he hadn't paid child support. That disclosure had incensed Piper, as any injustice would. She had been so angry she had stopped speaking to Heather's father.

Heather had actually confronted Piper about her decision. Heather had explained that because *she* wasn't mad and because Piper's grandmother wasn't mad, Piper wasn't allowed to be mad.

"But it's *wrong*," Piper told her. "He owed you that money. He's your father."

Her grandfather wasn't exactly impoverished. He and his wife lived in a nice house, had a handful of classic cars.

"I don't need the money now," Heather said, as if Piper's grandfather had known she wouldn't.

Heather's reaction had angered Piper, but what sometimes angered her more was that her mother's behavior seemed to be contagious. Sometimes Piper could feel Heather seeping into her, like something toxic in her blood, changing her mind, bending her will.

Piper should have punished her father for cheating on her mother. What he had done was wrong. She should have stopped speaking to *him*. But instead, she mostly followed her mother's advice. She ignored the cheating, just like her mother had ignored her own father not paying child support. Just like everyone seemed miraculously capable of overlooking all the many varied flaws in other people so they wouldn't have to be alone.

Now Piper stayed frozen in the hall as Jeff recovered from Heather's question. Eventually he said, "That RV was a present for the family," like he could just skip over the cheating accusation. And it worked. The conversation continued.

"So is this," Heather said. "Maple's at the pool with her new friends right now. Do you know how long it's been since she's had a playdate?"

Piper knew. It had been since Maple's twelfth birthday, the summer before she started junior high. They had thrown a big party, and one girl showed up. Upon realizing she was the only guest, the girl had very clearly wanted to leave. Piper had joined them, tried to force the girl to have fun, but instead she seemed to expose how childish the party was. Even the bounce house wasn't fun with only three people in it—especially when one of them was an older sister. Their one guest had texted her mom to pick her up within an hour of arriving, leaving Piper and Maple to watch the magician alone.

Junior high was excruciating for everyone, but it seemed far worse for Maple. Maple was immature, innocent and naive. She still played with toys, pretended to be animals, and made up stories about wizards and princesses. In junior high, all those qualities fell under the umbrella of "weird." Back in Texas, one mean girl had selected Maple as a target, and like sheep, everyone had fallen in line behind her. Then Maple's life became a living hell.

Piper couldn't help but feel happy that Maple was at a pool party. Couldn't help feeling that maybe her mom had done a good thing. And to reward her, Piper walked toward the fight.

Heather and Jeff were in the library. Her dad had finished organizing all the books, but there were still many empty shelves.

"What are you guys talking about?" Piper asked, like she hadn't heard them yelling.

Heather smiled. "Your sister's at a pool party with her new friends. Isn't that great?"

"Yeah." Piper nodded, adjusting a new lampshade. "That is great."

Her mom looked relieved. Piper could be pretty mean to her mom sometimes—she knew that—but she was always on Maple's side. And maybe Maple *did* need this barn. Piper used to ride herself, and she had heard her mother's stories. She knew deep friendships could be made over horses. Ten thousand dollars a month was a lot of money, but her dad did have hundreds of millions.

"Do you think this is a good idea?" he asked her in the way he had, like he genuinely valued her input.

Piper shrugged. "We have months until school starts. She needs to do something."

There were other options, other sports, but there was no sport as immersive as horseback riding. You didn't hang out at the soccer field all day. You didn't spend the weekend at a dance recital hall.

Her mother couldn't resist saying, "You could ride, too, if you want."

"No, I'm good," Piper said automatically. She couldn't help it. Her mother's dreams for her were so specific they sometimes made her own ambiguous goals scatter. "But I think if Maple is making friends, that's a really big deal, right?"

Heather beamed. "And these are nice girls."

nine

PAMELA

Pamela was pouring herself a glass of wine when she saw Maple with blood running down her face.

"Shit," she cursed, leaving her wine on the counter and grabbing a hand towel.

She forced the glass door open. It always stuck a little at the bottom. Everything in her house didn't work quite like it was supposed to. That was what it meant to be single and not rich.

"What happened, sweetie?" Pamela said, pressing the towel to Maple's temple.

She couldn't help feeling a little annoyed. Of course an injury *would* happen the first time she was watching the girl.

"I hit my head on the side," Maple told Pamela. Her face was pale and grave.

"We were doing spins!" Vida shouted from the hot tub, where she was crouching with Effie, totally unbothered that her new friend had head trauma.

Vida had a tendency to invite "accidents," much more than other girls did. Pamela had heard the complaints before, the gossip from other moms, the pointed comments.

"Have you ever noticed that whenever something bad happens, Vida is right there?"

"Some girls just love drama."

"Anytime there's chaos, you can bet she's at the center of it."

Personally, Pamela didn't believe this reputation was Vida's fault. Vida was just tougher than other girls. She could do things other girls couldn't: climb fences, talk back to police officers, jump horses over four-foot fences faster than anyone else at a horse show.

Pamela was proud of everything her daughter did. Even the truly wicked things were proof that her daughter was strong. Stronger than Pamela. Stronger than the world that had made them both. And that quality, Pamela was sure, could only be a good thing.

Still, it was a pain in the ass dealing with the collateral damage.

"Nice one!" Pamela scolded Vida. Then she shepherded Maple inside. "Come inside and let me have a look at it, okay? Does it hurt?"

"No, it's fine," Maple said, her words unexpectedly rough. "I did a spin from the Jacuzzi into the pool, and I got too close to the edge."

Pamela sighed. "I really don't understand the point of leaping around in a pool."

"Vida showed me."

"Of course she did. Here, sit down."

Pamela directed the girl to a barstool. Pamela had acquired most of her furniture on trash days. People in Rancho Santa Fe were always throwing stuff away. They were too paranoid to sell things—*I don't want anyone coming to my house! Then they'll know where I live!* So they often just left nice furniture out with the trash. The barstools were her favorite, thick and Gothic, like something Kieran would have owned.

"I'm sorry," Maple apologized.

"It's not your fault, dear." Pamela wetted the hand towel under the sink and soaked up the blood. "Are you a bleeder?"

"I don't know. A girl once pulled my hair out by the roots. See the scar?" Maple pulled back her hair to reveal a small jagged scar on her scalp.

"That's not very nice. Why would she do that?"

"She said I was weird."

"What a little bitch." Pamela dabbed the wound, which was thankfully starting to coagulate. "Do you know what?" She pulled Maple's barstool around so the girl was facing her. "If you start riding with us, next time some girl tries that, you'll fuck her up."

Maple laughed at the swearword.

"You think I'm kidding?" Pamela sat down beside Maple. "Horse girls are the toughest girls around. You know why? They make a thousand-pound wild animal do whatever they ask." She pointed at Maple's heart. "I can tell you're tough in there. You didn't even cry."

"I used to cry for everything," Maple admitted.

"But you stopped."

"It just makes them hit you harder."

Pamela hugged the girl. She couldn't help it. She felt terrible for her. She actually felt, in some fucked-up way, that she and her daughter could help Maple.

ten

MAPLE

Maple stopped bleeding. She went back out to play. Heather was worried when she picked her up and saw the bruise, but Maple told the story of how brave she had been and how Pamela had said the f-word—which Heather didn't seem to approve of, even though Maple had heard Heather say it a million times.

As soon as they got home, Maple raced through the house to find Piper. She told her sister about the jumping demonstration and her lesson with Kieran.

"He said I have a natural eye."

"What does that mean?" Piper asked.

"Not sure," Maple said so fast that Piper laughed.

Maple had been kind of relieved when Piper hadn't gone to the barn. Despite his comment about Maple's natural eye, Kieran hadn't seemed particularly impressed with Maple's riding. Her lesson had lasted only seven minutes—she knew because Heather told her so afterward. And most of it had just been Kieran asking about her experience, then seeming mildly disbelieving of her answers.

"Well, kid," he said at the end of the lesson, resting a hand on Faustus's shoulder, "you've got a lot of work to do."

He seemed to be waiting for her to volunteer something—some kind of cheer, some show of strength—but she honestly just felt like crying. She'd risked a glance at her mother in the audience and caught Heather before she had wiped the disappointment off her face.

If Piper had been there, Heather would have been smiling.

If Piper had ridden, Heather would have been proud.

Piper was better than Maple at every conceivable thing, so even when something good happened to Maple, she couldn't help thinking it *wouldn't* have happened if Piper had been there.

If Piper had ridden, Kieran would have looked up at Piper with awe. Instead, he had looked at Maple with something like frustration.

"I'm going to need your full commitment," he told her as if he were the devil casually bargaining. "Mind, body and soul—can you give me that?"

"Uh . . ." Maple fiddled with her reins. "Sure?"

She could tell that her weak response had annoyed him, but then Douglas cantered past, and Kieran seemed to transfer his annoyance to him.

"You call that a counter bend?" Kieran had roared across the arena. Maple flinched.

Heather had met Maple at the gate. She didn't say, "Good job." Instead, she said, "You'll do better next time."

And Maple felt a tremendous pressure, like "next time" was a death sentence.

Back in Piper's bedroom, Maple told her sister all about the pool party. She tried not to think about how if Piper had gone to the barn, Vida would have invited *her* instead.

Maple had made a friendship bracelet at Vida's. Although it felt a little unearned, Maple put her name alongside "Vida" and "Effie." The bracelet was like a promise. And as she lay in bed that night, she spun it around and around her wrist, feeling the beads and the grooves of the letters, seeing the names all twisted together.

Maple had never thought she could just leave the bullying behind. It had been so intense, so relentless, that she was sure it would follow her forever. But it hadn't. And if circumstances could change, maybe she could change, too. Maybe she could be tough like Vida. Maybe she just had to learn how.

eleven

PAMELA

Everyone in Rancho Santa Fe knew that Pamela had been a teenage junkie. That was the downside of living in the place where she had grown up. Pamela would always be known as the girl who had gone to rehab when she was in high school.

Even as a mother, she had a reputation for being a little too edgy, freethinking, irresponsible. The other mothers *loved* her, but they didn't always like to send their kids to her house. Pamela was fine with that. She wasn't a babysitter. And a long time ago she had rejected the real world in favor of the horse world.

In rehab as a teen, Pamela had participated in equine therapy, which basically involved taking care of horses for free. She had mucked stalls, cross-raked breezeways, picked hooves and fly sprayed the horses. The patients weren't allowed to ride; that wasn't the point. The point was to take care of another living thing, to learn responsibility. And Pamela had loved it.

She loved horses. How perceptive and kind and willing they were. How trusting. Animals were like people who had never been ruined. They could love you with their whole heart. They never tricked you, or manipulated you, or hurt you with malice.

Pamela was sensitive. The real world had always been too hard for her. But the horse world felt safer, more controlled.

When Pamela had left rehab, she relapsed—not after days or weeks but in four hours. Her dad, who worked, hadn't known what to do. Her mother was gone. She had left them both for heroin.

That night, when her dad got back from work and found Pamela high, he asked her, "What can I do? I'll do anything you want."

Pamela, who had no intention to stop using but also no intention to miss the opportunity, told him, "I want a horse."

That Saturday, her dad drove her to RSFE. He introduced her to Kieran. Back then he was just starting out, glowing with his own brilliance.

Kieran took Pamela horse shopping. They drove up and down the coast in his rattletrap truck, arguing mostly, because young Pamela had loved to provoke people any chance she got. Eventually, they had a horse shipped from Florida, an eight-year-old mare with a serious attitude problem.

Kieran said the horse was made for Pamela, and he was right. She kicked a hole in her stall. She escaped every chance she got. She was the only horse Pamela had ever met that set the other horses free, too, throwing the barn into chaos.

Pamela trained with Kieran, and then she showed, buying more horses and competing at higher and higher levels. She still did drugs. Even now she always kept a little coke hidden in her house. Bottles of Xanax and OxyContin. She knew that if she didn't have them on hand, she would obsess about scoring, but she no longer had the time or the energy to take drugs.

When Vida was born, Pamela had transferred her love of horses to her daughter. Vida was a natural. Pamela used to set Vida's car seat on the fence so her daughter could watch her ride. Vida took her first steps at RSFE. Before that, she had ridden her first horse—not a pony, but a full-sized horse—with Pamela holding her in the saddle while one of the grooms led.

When Pamela's father died, he had left her his fortune. It hadn't been as much as she'd expected. She withdrew large amounts in those early years—for the house, for fun, for things Vida and she needed, but mostly for horses. Without her father to make money, Pamela's bank account dwindled. The interest shrank.

Pamela cut out the fun. She cut back on her house and her hair and her clothes. Her whole life became a process of downsizing. Soon she had to cut back on horses, too. She couldn't afford to support her career and her daughter's, so she quit riding. She put everything she had into Vida. All of her horses and all of her dreams. She was happy to do it.

Pamela's goal had always been to be the mother she never had, to make up for the love she had lost. She spent all of her time with Vida. They were closer than a mother and a daughter. They were best friends. They were sisters in that fucked-up barn family. But Pamela couldn't afford to give Vida the horses or the training she deserved.

That year would be Vida's last as a Junior. Next year, she would become an Amateur and have to compete against adults. She would need better horses—horses Pamela couldn't afford. In a way, that year felt like the last one in which Vida even had a shot at winning. Pamela wanted to make sure it was her daughter's best year yet.

Vida wanted to become a Professional rider—to ride for money—but Kieran had never expressed an interest in hiring her. He had reduced and reduced their rates, out of kindness, maybe, but also a little out of duty. And still they struggled. Still they were barely hanging on.

But now they had Heather. Pamela was more than happy to befriend Heather for Kieran, but she wanted to make sure she was in some way compensated. She wanted to make clear that what she was doing was for her own benefit.

The night of Maple's first lesson, Pamela found Kieran walking from stall to stall, doing his nightly check of the horses.

"So, what do you think of the Parkers?" she asked him.

Kieran snorted. His response slightly tickled Pamela, who often felt she was in competition with everyone, especially at the barn, where she kind of was.

"But they have money," Pamela noted. "And they seem especially eager to spend it."

"We'll see."

There had been many nights like that one, with Pamela and Kieran alone at the barn. Vida had gone to Effie's for a sleepover. Pamela should have gone home, but she hated to leave. She never wanted to leave at the end of the day. Her home felt empty without all the horses and horse people.

She hopped onto a tack box and watched Kieran go from stall to stall, letting himself in, running a hand over every horse, feeling for injuries or irregularities. Seeing Kieran with horses always warmed her.

He was a true horse person. He listened to horses. He learned from them. It was something he drilled into every student, every person who worked at the barn. *It's always the human's fault. You never blame the horse. You never hurt the horse.*

She had seen him yank riders out of their saddles for using spurs incorrectly. At horse shows, most trainers looked the other way when they witnessed animal abuse, but Kieran always reported it, or worse. He delighted in human confrontation. One of his proudest moments, Pamela knew, was when he'd broken another trainer's jaw for snapping a whip in half over a horse's back.

He and that trainer still saw each other at the shows. They greeted each other cordially. That was how the people in the indus-

try worked sometimes: They protected their own. Even the unde-
serving. Even the downright dangerous.

Pamela had seen a lot of crazy things in the horse world. Most
of those things had happened right there at RSFE, because while
Kieran was adamant that no one ever hurt a horse, he was less strict
when it came to human beings.

Still, there was a lot she could forgive a man for when he loved
horses.

When Kieran finished in that barn, Pamela hopped off the tack
box and followed him to the next one. "Do you have a horse in mind
for them?"

She knew that he did, knew that he had the exact horse already
picked out and a complicated plan for ensuring they bought it. That
was how Kieran operated, with such precision that everything
seemed like an accident or fate.

"Huh," he said, which was his way of saying *Mind your own
business.*

"Well, I'm glad I brought her in," she said, wanting to remind
him that if it hadn't been for her, Heather might not have come. As
if Heather hadn't been calling for weeks. As if Heather hadn't shown
up looking for Kieran.

Pamela waited for him to thank her. She waited for him to reward her. She would probably be waiting a long time.

DETECTIVE PEREZ

Amy Bracken was the last person Detective Perez would have expected to see involved in a situation like this one. She had a bright, hopeful expression. She spoke like a schoolteacher.

"I think everyone is in shock," she said, clasping her hands together. "You can't really judge anyone's reactions too harshly. We're just in shock! We're all such a tight-knit community. We're really like a family. I don't think anyone could have seen this coming. . . . I don't think they could. . . ." Her neatly threaded eyebrows arched in worry, as if she were considering that last part again.

"You teach the younger students. Is that correct?"

"Yes. I teach the Juniors. The way it works is they count the year of your birth, not the actual date. So I train students up to their eighteenth year."

Detective Perez had ridden horses as a child, although her barn had been a backyard operation in the mountain community where she grew up. It was nothing like RSFE. "Would you say the mothers are a little more invested in this sport—more so than, say, soccer moms?"

"You could say that— Not that it's a bad thing!"

"Why do you think that is?"

Amy sat up and dutifully gave the detective the PR spin, as if she had done so before.

"Well, a lot of our mothers are former riders. And having a horse is a daily responsibility. They need food and water and exercise and socialization. They're not meant to be cooped up in stalls all day."

Detective Perez had noticed that the easiest way to get horse people talking was to get them talking about horses.

"Having a horse is a little like being a parent, isn't it?" Amy said. "I think a lot of our job is just fixing the problems that we actually cause. . . ." She drifted off, as if she might have said too much.

But the police weren't there because someone had hurt a horse. They were there because someone was dead.

twelve

HEATHER

That weekend Heather and Kieran and Douglas went to look at horses. Heather was surprised to learn that Maple wasn't invited.

"There's no point dragging a kid around on a trip like this," Kieran had explained. "We'll be in the truck for hours. And it wouldn't be safe to throw an inexperienced rider on a strange horse. You can't trust anyone selling a horse. Douglas will try the horses first."

"And then Maple, if we find a good one?" Heather asked.

"No need," Kieran said. "Douglas and I are experienced horse people. We can find her the perfect horse."

Heather thought that was a little weird. She wanted Maple to pick the horse or at least to be a part of the horse-buying process, but Kieran had an answer for that, too.

"A kid will pick a horse based on looks or how sweet it is on the ground. She won't know what she's looking at. It's better for everyone if we pick for her. Don't worry. A girl will fall in love with a mule if it's all hers."

That was how the three of them had ended up in Kieran's truck that Saturday afternoon. Heather was riding shotgun. Douglas was in the back.

His appearance was distracting, Heather thought. Her eyes were constantly drawn to him, the way they might have been to a model in an advertisement or to a beautiful photograph.

Douglas was charging his phone, and he kept reaching over the seat to check it for messages. She could feel the warmth emanating from his muscular arms, smell the peppermint in his mouth.

"So, Douglas, where are you from?" she asked when he sat back down again.

"Rancho Santa Fe," Kieran answered.

Heather was surprised. She would have thought if he were from there, he would have lived with his parents and not with Kieran.

"How long have you been riding?" she asked.

This time Douglas answered. "Since I was a baby." He had a very soothing voice—a voice that was designed for calming horses.

"I started riding when I was five," Heather twittered, feeling a little awkward in the truck with two men she didn't know well—two men who didn't seem to be paying her much attention. "But I had to stop because my family couldn't afford it."

Douglas's dark eyes met hers in the rearview mirror. "I know what that's like."

The truck juddered as Kieran switched gears. "That's the funny thing about horses," he said. "There's money everywhere, but no one's making it."

The horse at the first barn was a beautiful bay gelding. He was also a complete lunatic. Douglas stayed with him for longer than Heather understood. He even jumped him as the bay bucked and reared and spooked.

"Why are we still looking at this horse?" Heather finally said to Kieran in front of the owner, who she felt had lied to get them there.

"I know he's a little rough around the edges," Kieran said, "but you give Douglas a month on that horse, and you could strap your grandma on him."

Still perplexed, Heather nodded as Douglas hovered quietly in the stirrups while the horse bucked six times in a row.

By the third horse, Heather was starting to panic. All the horses had seemed wildly inappropriate for Maple. Yes, Heather was inexperienced compared to Kieran and Douglas, but the horses they were trying seemed dangerous.

Heather had issues with control, no doubt stemming from abandonment, and right then she was feeling very out of control. She was in a hot truck that bounced too much. She wasn't driving. The seat belt kept hitting her lap in a funny spot. She was being ignored.

She could feel the beginnings of a panic attack as the three of them trundled along through Kieran's jerky shift changes. The two men just talked unintelligibly about the horses.

Heather felt a silent buildup of emotions swelling under her skin, inside her skull. She wanted to go home. She wanted to take a bath. She wanted a makeover and a glass of wine, but most of all, she wanted that exact moment to end.

Heather excused herself as soon as they arrived at barn number four. Breath pounding, palms sweating, lips numb, she walked down a horse trail and had a full-blown panic attack.

She just wanted to help her daughter. She was just trying to do the right thing for her daughter. But what if she was wrong? What if a horse wasn't what Maple needed?

She had expected a cute little pony, but Kieran insisted that Maple would grow out of it too quickly. Heather had expected something soft and cute that the entire family could spoil and feed carrots. Not these heavily muscled, threatening animals.

"Hey."

Heather turned and saw Douglas standing a little up the trail. He was watching her with the gentle but direct eye contact he might have used on a frightened horse.

"Everything okay?" He took a step toward Heather, no sudden moves, as if not to spook her.

She brushed a hand along her cheek, wiping away a stress tear. Her makeup was melting in the California sun. Her hair had gone limp. She felt overly done up and completely out of her depth.

"I'm just worried that this isn't the right . . . This isn't what I was expecting."

"I'm sorry."

Heather, who wasn't used to men apologizing, was startled. "Well, it's not your fault."

"It's really stressful, looking at horses," he said. "All the ads are exactly the same." He recited: "'Available due to no fault of their own.' 'No buck, no bolt, no rear.' I once went to . . . um"—he stepped a little closer—"try this horse in LA County. A paint. Beautiful in the photos, but when I got there, the horse was in this tiny barbed-wire pen under a highway in Alhambra. Hooves all overgrown. The halter had been left on so long it had rubbed the hair off his face."

Heather flinched. "That's terrible."

"Yeah. I told them they'd better give that horse to someone who could take care of it. Then I reported them. Point is"—he was even closer now—"it can be really stressful. We try to vet the horses as much as we can, but you never really know what a horse is until you see it for yourself."

Heather took a deep, calming breath, then squeezed her arms tight around her middle. "I understand."

The sun broke through the trees, lighting the perfect planes of Douglas's face. "You know, you don't have to come with us for this part. We can find one and then, you know, invite you out to see it."

"I just want to make sure it's a good horse for Maple."

He nodded slowly, thoughtfully, the way he did everything. "What do you think a good horse for Maple is?"

"One that keeps her safe."

"See, I disagree. People are broken, even young girls like Maple. You want a horse that matches the broken pieces, that will make her whole."

Heather's heart swelled. She wanted a horse like that. "And you think you can find that horse?"

Douglas smiled. "It might take a few tries, but sure."

When Heather got home that night, she was dizzy and coated in dry sweat, but she felt oddly satisfied. The three of them had bounced from barn to barn in that hot truck. Douglas had kept brushing her shoulder with his arm when he reached over the seats to check his phone. Kieran had listed boring, inexplicable details about all the horses they saw.

Deep into the afternoon, they stopped at a taco shop in Temecula, drank Mexican colas with crushed ice. It was like they were on a family road trip. Kieran—although probably as close in age to Heather as she was to Douglas—was like the daddy, with his oddly specific rules about the radio or where they could stop and go to the bathroom.

Later, they pulled off at a scenic viewpoint to watch the sunset. Kieran didn't even explain why he stopped. He just did it, like the sunset was something you shouldn't miss. On the way home, Douglas slouched in the back with his legs spread and complained to Kieran about how sore he was.

The horse-buying trip had been an adventure. It spoke to Heather's Texas roots and her little-girl heart. All her life, she had wanted a horse to fix the broken pieces. That was all she had ever wanted or dreamed of or needed.

Heather found her family having dinner. Their new favorite Korean food was spread across the kitchen island.

"Did you find a horse?" Piper asked, fighting to appear uninterested.

"Not yet."

Heather brought her loaded plate over to the too-small table they'd shipped from the old house. She took a seat between her daughters. Then she told her family about everything: the bay who wouldn't stop bucking; the gray horse that kicked the groom; the immaculate jumper barn way out in Menifee, where a Grand Prix rider kept his horses; the little colt she'd seen running around a turnout.

Maple gasped at all the right times. Piper laughed and asked for explanations. Even Jeff seemed interested, drawn into the mysterious, complicated horse world.

Even though Heather had gone alone, sharing the story made them all a part of the search for the perfect horse for Maple.

Heather had a feeling that one day she would look back on that moment as the start of an incredible journey. Months from then, there would be horse shows that the Parkers all attended, and years from then, they would retire the horse and move it into their backyard, and every time they looked at it, they would remember that very night.

The night they became horse people.

thirteen

VIDA

Vida had ridden horses for as long as she could remember. In fact, her first memory was of her mother holding her on top of a horse while it walked beneath her. Sometimes when she shut her eyes, she could feel that swaying motion beneath her, like horses ran through her blood.

Horseback riding was a lifestyle. Your barn was your family. Every day after school, Pamela and Vida went to the barn. Pamela would gossip with the other mothers and owners, do Mary's Tack and Feed runs or pick up tacos for everyone.

Monday became the worst day of the week, because the horses had the day off. Summers were the best, because the sun stayed out until eight.

Vida became a "working student"—a horse world tradition that provided free child labor for the barn and free childcare for parents. Vida mucked stalls, groomed horses or sat around gossiping until she was given another list of chores.

Her favorite job was cleaning bridles for the training program, because she got to be right in the middle of the action. She could see the most exquisite horses being led in and out of the crossties, and she could call to the top riders, "Have a good ride!" and "Did you have a good ride?"

Sometimes Vida stayed until well after dark to get every last bridle done; then she swept the crossties. She loved the work. She loved all the people and the drama. She loved getting yelled at. She loved setting goals and achieving them. She loved her friends, with whom she spent so much time that she sometimes felt like they were one unit.

Vida felt like the horse world had been designed for her. In the real world, Vida was too cold, too stubborn, too attracted to danger. But in the horse world, all of those attributes were assets.

Fear was contagious around horses, so her coldness kept them calm. Her stubbornness helped her spend months perfecting a single aspect of her ride. And her attraction to danger meant she always wanted to jump higher.

Vida dreamed of becoming a Professional rider. Of traveling the world and riding the best horses in the best shows. She had it all mapped out. That year her dreams would start to come true, beginning with the Little Palm Cup at the end of the summer. She was going to win, and when she turned eighteen, Kieran was going to ask her to be one of his Professional riders.

She would be like Douglas, riding a dozen horses a day, training with Kieran, seeming at times to become something more than just a rider—because when a horse and a human truly came together, they created another being. Something holy and untouchable.

One evening, after everyone else had gone home, Vida found Douglas asleep in the break room. He had fallen asleep standing up, like a horse.

Vida crossed to the freezer to get an Otter Pop. When the cold air hit Douglas, his eyes flew open.

"What time is it?" he said.

"Almost ten. At night," she added when her answer didn't seem immediately clear.

He let that sink in, then slid to the floor.

"You should go home," she pointed out.

"I can't walk," he said, grinning charmingly at her.

Everyone had a crush on Douglas. Effie was obsessed. She had pictures of him all over her bedroom walls: cutouts from horse magazines and Polaroids taken by espionage.

Personally, Vida didn't understand the attraction. She and Douglas had grown up together. He was like a brother to her. He had been there when she got her first period. Vida had even made him find her a tampon. He had not only procured her one but had later convinced Kieran to install a tampon dispenser in the restroom—an act of pure heroism he would probably never live down.

Only Vida seemed to see his behavior for what it was: overkill.

Douglas's mother had been involved in a serious riding accident. Before the accident, Douglas had been a different person: passionate, forthright, even arrogant. In fact, he had been a lot like Vida. But after the accident, Douglas had become suffused with a neediness, a desperation to be liked at all costs. When he was younger, he had been obsequious. As he got older, he slept with a lot of women.

"Do you want an Otter Pop?" Vida asked him.

"Sure. Orange."

"No one likes orange," she said, but she still tossed him one.

"I like the picture, see?" He pointed at the dog next to Little Orphan Orange on the wrapper.

"That's a stupid reason to pick a Popsicle." She perched on the massage chair as they quickly devoured their Otter Pops. "Every time I see you lately, you're asleep. Except when you're riding."

"Oh, I've fallen asleep on a horse before. A couple times. I usually catch myself before I fall off." He tipped his Otter Pop back to suck out all the juice.

"I wish Kieran would give me some of your rides."

If Vida wanted to become a Professional rider, she needed to get experience riding all different kinds of horses, riding client horses, but she couldn't do that unless Kieran let her. She hoped things would change when she turned eighteen, but the closer that day got, the more things stayed the same.

"So do I." Douglas tossed his wrapper in the trash and let his head fall against the wall.

"I wish I could trade places with you."

He scowled at her as he sat on the floor, too tired to walk to his truck. "No, you don't. You have your mom."

Vida sighed. "I guess. . . ."

"No, you don't guess." He shoved himself up suddenly. He charged toward the exit, then paused at the door. "You have no idea how lucky you are."

He left her in the break room alone. She stayed there awhile, thinking how the air had changed. It was buzzing with something invisible, electric, a little scary.

fourteen

PAMELA

P amela was surprised to find herself enjoying Heather more and more. Heather wasn't like the other rich mothers who came only for horse shows and came distracted, stood on their marks and waited to be directed by their husbands.

Heather came to the barn every day, even when Maple wasn't riding. She bought everyone lunch and watched training sessions ringside. She latched onto Pamela and followed her everywhere, learned all the culture and the trade secrets of barn life.

In exchange, Heather told Pamela the truth about everything: how her husband had cheated, how her older daughter hated her and her younger daughter had been bullied. Pamela loved honesty, especially when it was salacious.

Heather gave Pamela things.

"I bought the wrong halter. Do you want it?"

"These breeches would fit Vida, right?"

"They got the rose gold helmet in, so I don't want the silver one anymore."

Vida hated that Pamela took these things. "It's embarrassing! I'm not wearing my friend's castoffs!"

But she seemed placated when Pamela reminded her that the Parkers were borrowing Vida's horse for free. "Consider them thank-you gifts."

Meanwhile, little Maple was less enthusiastic about the barn than her mother. Amy had her taking private lessons to fix her seat. She would plop Maple on a lunge line—a thirty-foot rope—so that the girl could circle around her and not have to worry about controlling the horse. Amy made Maple do endless exercises to fix her foundation.

Heather was embarrassed. "She's been riding for years," she told Pamela, dropping into the chair beside her on the patio.

Heather had just been at the round pen watching Maple's latest lesson. She always had a perturbed expression after she watched Maple, like she couldn't for the life of her figure out why Maple wasn't the best rider there. "I don't understand why she has to be on a lunge line."

Pamela understood why. The girl was a terrible rider. She was tense in all the wrong places. She was a ball of anxiety. She struggled to pay attention. If she wasn't shutting her eyes, she was holding her breath. She had no balance and seemingly no control over her limbs.

If the Parkers hadn't been so rich, even sweet Amy probably would have told Heather that riding just wasn't for Maple. But they *were* rich, and money meant never having to hear the word no.

"All of the girls went through the same thing," Pamela said. It was sort of true. Effie had been on a lunge line for a few lessons when she started. So had Vida, when she was five.

June contributed, "Effie was only on the lunge line for two or three lessons." A lot of help she was.

Heather deflated.

"But Amy still makes Vida and Effie do seat work," Pamela argued. "You want to make sure Maple starts with the proper foundation."

"But she's not *starting*," Heather complained. "That's my point."

Most people didn't understand what good riding looked like. They only ever saw horses in movies, in which stunt doubles flapped around, or in high-stakes competitions, in which riding was more abstract.

Good riding was like ballet. It required precision. What Heather didn't understand was that Maple had been riding for years with a bad trainer. Someone who had let her canter and jump when she hadn't even learned how to sit. In fact, all of Maple's previous experience was working *against* her.

"You don't have to ride here," June said. "RSFE is not the only barn in the world. I once took Effie to this great place in San Marcos—I can give you their number."

June loved to tell anyone how RSFE was overpriced and cliquey, and yet she never considered leaving. She seemed to think she could be down to earth in opinion only.

"Any luck with the horse search?" Pamela asked, thinking it was time to change the subject.

"No," Heather said, drooping in the sun. "It feels like we're going from bad to worse."

"You should just keep her on Faustus for six months," June said unhelpfully. "Then see if Maple still wants to ride."

Heather wasn't even paying Pamela for the privilege of using her horse, because Kieran hadn't told Pamela to charge her, and now it seemed too late to ask for money. Pamela certainly didn't want Maple riding her horse for six months. And it was obvious to everyone that Maple didn't like riding, but it was rude of June to point it out.

Heather withered and Pamela frowned. Kieran was going to have to be careful that Maple didn't quit—at least not yet. Most riders quit eventually.

Horseback riding had an extremely high turnover rate. People showed up on a whim, fed carrots to the prettiest horses and signed up for lessons. They arrived on day one in brand-new, extremely expensive equipment. Six hundred dollars for a Samshield helmet. Four hundred dollars for Equiline breeches. A thousand dollars for Parlanti tall boots. They took a couple lessons on school horses that had the terrible distinction of being unflashy, of looking old and ugly in Instagram photos.

Then they bought a horse. They were advised to buy an older horse, a colder horse, a horse that would suit a beginner. They did not. They imported beautiful, delicate, hot horses from Europe. They signed them up for the training program on the assurance that one day, maybe, they would actually be able to ride them.

They stopped taking lessons on school horses, waiting for their horses to be ready for them. When they had waited long enough, they hopped on and inevitably fell off. They promised to come back, to ride again one day. They did not. Almost half the horses in the training program had been abandoned that way. They were in training for riders who would probably never return.

Pamela had no doubt that the Parkers would meet the same fate. In fact, she invited it. She had started to formulate an idea of how she could get a horse good enough for her daughter. Vida was already taking Maple's cast-off breeches and helmets, so why couldn't she land her cast-off horse?

Pamela knew that Kieran wouldn't like the idea. He would want the horse for himself, but Pamela was doing all the work. Now that the Parkers were officially signed up, Kieran hardly spoke to Heather or her daughter.

Heather might even end up *wanting* to give Pamela the horse. They were becoming friends. Maple was spending a lot of time with Vida. Pamela was looking out for them both. Pamela had never thought of herself as naive, but part of her wished that Heather would recognize how talented Vida was and try to help her along. What Vida really needed was a benefactor.

Pamela watched as Heather sighed hopelessly. "This just isn't what I had in mind when we came here," she said.

Pamela was starting to learn that Heather wanted the appearance of a thing more than the thing itself. Pamela could give her that.

"I have an idea," Pamela said. "What if we have the girls go on a trail ride together next weekend—wouldn't that be fun? We can get Amy to go out with them. Maybe they can even bring a picnic."

"I'll probably be horse shopping," Heather complained, but Pamela could tell she was warm to the idea.

"We can borrow a western saddle. How cute would Maple look in a cowgirl hat?" Half of convincing Heather to do anything was selling her on the outfit.

Heather sat up and gripped the armrests of her chair. "I could buy her a western saddle—do you think she might use it?"

"Oh, sure, the girls use them on trail. Vida has one." Pamela had found it at Goodwill. "And you can get such pretty ones. Leather tooling, silver accents."

"Effie doesn't have one," June said. "Waste of money."

But Heather's eyes were bright. "We should go to Mary's tomorrow. We can get the girls matching hats. My treat."

Pamela sat back. "That would be *so* cute. We'll have to take pictures."

Heather nodded, spellbound. Seeing the pictures. Seeing the life.

fifteen

HEATHER

After another fruitless weekend of horse searching, Kieran called Heather with bad news: She would not be able to find Maple a horse in California.

"But California's huge," Heather protested.

She was becoming increasingly frustrated with RSFE. Amy still had Maple on a lunge line. She wouldn't even let her hold the reins.

Heather had watched Vida's and Effie's lessons. As far as Heather could see, there wasn't any difference between them and Maple—or at least not *much* of a difference. At Maple's last barn, she had been jumping. At RSFE, she spent most of the lesson walking in a tiny circle around her trainer.

The horse shopping was a disaster as well. Every weekend it seemed like Heather was being shown worse options, crazier horses with more and more problems. This was not at all how Heather had pictured the search for the horse. She felt like an outsider and a loser. She was embarrassed.

"The West Coast is not a respected place for show jumping," Kieran explained, like he was talking to an idiot. He barely acknowledged her at the barn, even though she was there every day. He was more focused on his Professional and Amateur riders jumping their insane jumps while Maple walked. "All of the good horses are on the East Coast. Or in Europe, if you really want to get down to it."

"How good a horse does Maple really need?" she said. Amy would barely let her trot.

"I can't let you buy her a bad horse. It devalues our program. And don't forget that once we start competing, this horse will actually earn you money."

That was a big factor Kieran had floated, one Jeff was especially keen on. The Parkers would buy a Grand Prix–level horse that Douglas could compete with, winning them money back. The glory of being rich was that you could afford to make money on everything.

"I just think it's taking a *very long time*," she said, because she had run out of excuses.

"Mrs. Parker— Can I call you Heather?"

"Yes."

"Heather, can I be honest with you?" He didn't wait for her response. "I don't think the issue is the horse. I think the issue is that you are not the one in the driver's seat. I see it a lot in this sport. People are drawn to horses because they're easy to control."

"I don't think I'm like that," Heather said.

In fact, she knew she was. She just hated when other people noticed it.

"If you want to train at this barn, you need to relinquish control. To me. I promise I will take care of everything. The problem, you see, Heather, is not that you don't have control. The problem is that you want it."

Heather reminded herself to be patient. Her attitude was starting to rub off on Maple, which was the opposite of what she wanted. Maple, she knew, was happy with her easy lessons. And Amy *was* helping her confidence.

After her lessons, Maple would brag that Amy said that she

wasn't squeezing with her knees as much or that she'd done a good job keeping her shoulders back, and Heather would have to bite her tongue. She knew she was being unreasonable.

Heather sometimes felt like she *was* Maple, trapped on that lunge line, going round and round while everybody else jumped and pirouetted and flew around her. Heather wanted everything— all of her dreams—*now*. She felt like she had waited long enough, but she always seemed to need to wait longer.

"So, how do we get a horse *outside of* California?" she asked Kieran.

"Well, there are two options. We can pick a horse online and have it shipped over here on trial—we'd have to pay for the ship-ping. Or we can fly you and Douglas out to Florida or Kentucky to try some."

Heather considered those suggestions. Douglas was the one thing about the barn that she liked all the time. Since he had com-forted her that day, he had taken to checking on her, asking her how things were going, then nodding along quietly as she vented.

He reminded her of the cute boy in high school who used to hook up with her in secret. Because she'd been a teenager, Heather had never questioned the boy's motives until she met his girlfriend. Heather hadn't blamed the girlfriend. She hadn't even blamed the boy. She had just blamed herself. For years afterward, that early experience had convinced her of her own deficiencies.

Douglas didn't look like that boy, but he had that same cute-guy energy—like he had been given the power to decide a woman's wor-thiness. If he liked you, you were likable. If he didn't, you were just a woman.

The idea of going to Florida or Kentucky with Douglas was probably too appealing. The more time she spent with him, the more she wanted to convince him of her value. *I'm still pretty! I'm still young! I'm still sexy!*

But she was married, and she could keep her hands to herself. It might be kind of fun. It reminded her of the kind of thing she used to do in college, last-minute road trips to Cloudcroft or Palo Duro Canyon. The long drives with her friends in which they talked about life's deep questions. And wouldn't it make a great story?

She didn't like the idea of Florida, but she would have loved to tell people that she'd bought her daughter's horse in Kentucky. She could even bring Jeff back some bourbon.

"Kentucky might be nice," she mused to Kieran.

"Excellent. I'll start building a lineup right now," Kieran said. "Oh, and Heather? There's one other thing. Horses outside of California are quite a bit more expensive. We haven't really had much luck inside your budget. You might want to consider raising it."

"How much?" Heather said, a little terse.

"Add another zero," Kieran said, completely cool.

Heather called Pamela to discuss the possibility. More and more she was relying on her friend's advice.

"Kieran's right," Pamela said. "I got my first horse in Florida."

"This just seems crazy."

"The horse world is crazy. You can Google it. The East Coast is better for horses. And Europe is even better."

"Should Douglas and I go to Paris?" Heather joked, and Pamela laughed.

Heather Googled while they were on the phone.

"You're right," she admitted.

The whole West Coast had a bad reputation for show-jumping horses. And even though Heather still sometimes felt like she was in over her head, she loved the idea of having the best.

She loved knowing that she was at a much better barn than the one she'd been banned from as a child. That she was giving Maple the best chance. Sometimes she watched Vida or Douglas or the other riders and thought that she actually *could* see the difference in the way they rode, and that one day, if she was patient, Maple would look as good as they did.

Sometimes Heather imagined Maple's horse. With how picky Kieran was being, they couldn't help but end up with the best horse in the world, a horse that could fly to the moon. A horse that would match her broken pieces.

But first she would have to get Jeff to agree to let her go to Kentucky.

It sometimes seemed the more money he got, the more he was obsessed by it. He definitely worked more, and he was even more stressed about money than he was when they didn't have it, which was something she didn't understand. He didn't have to work at all—that was something *he* constantly said.

"I never have to work again," and then, five minutes later, "I'm under a lot of pressure with work right now."

He would say both of these things all the time—often in the same conversation—and never acknowledge that they were opposites.

He worked long hours, locked up in his monastic office. He worked obsessively, storing up future joy. He claimed he was being practical.

"Now is the time."

"I'm on a winning streak."

Their marriage was crumbling. Heather had thought moving would help them, but so far they were the same people in California as they had been in Texas.

Part of the reason Heather had selected California was to get Jeff away from the woman he had been seeing. She was twenty-three. Her name was Amber. She was at least an eight, maybe even a nine. Everyone in Amarillo seemed to know about her.

Jeff was still going back to Amarillo for work all the time. Heather was sure he was seeing that woman, but the important thing was

Heather wasn't. That was how she dealt with things she couldn't control.

Unfortunately, it was how Jeff did, too. One night, he had told Heather he wanted his own bedroom.

"It just doesn't make sense," he said. "Couples sleeping in the same bed. I'm not really sure how it became popular. Kings never did it." As if he were taking on history and not just telling her he didn't love her. "Every time you move on the mattress, I feel it."

She now walked down the long hall to his bedroom to ask about Kentucky.

His bedroom looked exactly like her bedroom—same mattress at the same height with the same pillows and blankets. The only difference was she wasn't in it.

She stood in the doorframe. He was in bed on his laptop.

"I wanted to ask you something," she said, "about Maple's horse."

"Did you find one yet?"

"We were thinking of Kentucky."

"Now you want to move to Kentucky?"

"No, just a trip to look for the horse. Would that be okay?"

He tilted his head, running the options. "All of us?"

Heather's heart lifted. She hadn't thought of that, but why not? They could make it a family trip. She had been dying to get Piper more involved. Heather was sure she just spent all day on her phone.

Piper had recently joined Jeff on one of his Texas trips. He hadn't seemed too happy about her coming with him. The night they had returned, Piper announced at the dinner table that her friend back in Amarillo had offered to let Piper come live with her for the rest of the summer.

Piper kept saying, "But her parents are cool with it," like that was the concern.

"I want you to spend time with *us*," Heather said.

And Piper said back, "All you do is hang out at the barn."

"Then come to the barn."

But Piper had refused. It broke Heather's heart a little.

Heather had always dreamed that one day her adult daughters would be her best friends, would respect her, but most of all would want to *be* with her. Go on trips with her. Call her when they were worried. When they were falling in love.

Mom, you're closer to me than anyone in the world.

Heather had always loved Piper, but more than that, Heather had always admired her. Piper was more intelligent, more likable, more confident and more secure than Heather had ever been.

When Piper had gone through her teenage phase and suddenly seemed to hate her mother, Heather had been sure it was because Piper recognized the flaws in her personality. Her daughter made her feel like she was somehow wrong in the world.

Regaining Piper's favor seemed like the most important thing. Piper loved horses. Heather had ruined it. She knew that. She had been too invested. She had pushed too hard. But she had changed. Heather was trying to be the right kind of supportive. She was trying *so hard* with Maple, but what did it matter if Piper wasn't there to see?

Heather wanted her daughter back. She knew once the family got the horse, Piper would not be able to resist it, which only made this never-ending search more frustrating.

Heather waited while Jeff considered the Kentucky trip.

"Thinking about it," he finally said, "I'm not sure how well that would work. Piper doesn't want anything to do with the horse stuff, and even Maple would probably be bored."

Or scared. Heather didn't say the words out loud. Some of the horses they'd seen in California had frightened even her.

"You're right," Heather admitted. "Maybe it's too complicated."

"And I'm really slammed with work."

Jeff rubbed the bridge of his nose. He was his own boss, could work whenever he wanted, but he seemed to love to slam himself with work.

"Why don't we plan an RV trip for when I get back?" Heather asked.

She hated the idea of being trapped in an RV with Jeff and the kids, pissing in a plastic container, but she wanted to spend more time with them. She wanted to be a family.

"We could go to Pismo Beach," she said. "Or somewhere on the coast?"

Jeff nodded. "Let's plan on it."

He would never set a date. Heather knew that, and maybe he knew it, too. Something would come up at work. Probably something that dragged him back to Amarillo. He would make sure of it.

"There's one other thing," Heather said. "Kieran said we might want to consider raising our budget."

"I bet he did," Jeff said.

Jeff's response irked Heather. He hadn't been involved in the horse-buying process. He didn't understand anything about the horse world.

"We've seen dozens of horses," she said, "and none of them have been good enough for Maple. Kieran is a professional. He knows what he's talking about."

Jeff took off his glasses and rubbed the bridge of his nose. He was always overwhelmed by any display of emotion, especially when he incited it.

"This is for Maple," Heather said. "This is for our daughter."

Once again, Jeff didn't respond. He turned his attention back to his laptop and his work. It was only when Heather had turned away and started down the hall that she heard him mutter, "Could have fooled me."

sixteen

PIPER

One night, Piper walked to RSFE. She didn't tell her mom. She just wanted to see it. Her resolve to never go there, to never participate in this dream her mom kept foisting on her, was starting to erode.

Piper hadn't made friends in California. She wasn't sure how she could. She was too young to go to bars. She didn't want to go to concerts by herself. She sometimes went to the beach with Maple or her dad and passed by packs of kids her age, all tan and blond like prototypes for the idea of California. She couldn't approach them. She couldn't say hi or stand on the edge of their crowd. That would make her look insane.

It was ridiculous how hard it was to make friends outside prescribed situations: at school, at work, at sports practices. Should you ever approach anyone outside those activities, you would be cut dead.

Her mom had been right about RSFE. It was gorgeous. All stonework and arched wood. Piper walked along a row of stalls at the edge of the property. The horses were nothing like the horses in Amarillo. They were tall and shiny and athletic. If horses could be snobby, these horses were. They seemed nervous when she tried to pet them, although with patience she won them over.

She went from horse to horse, learned their language, respected them like she'd been taught to, loved them until they loved her back.

Piper knew it was stupid, this death match she had with her mom over horses, but she had been fighting Heather on it so long that giving in now felt like losing, even if it might feel like winning, too.

She sighed, gazing down the barn aisle. It would be so easy to solve all her problems. All she had to do was give in.

seventeen

VIDA

Vida was polishing bridles when she overhead Kieran and Douglas arguing. This was why Vida loved the cleaning bay. It was perfectly situated for hearing all the gossip about the top horses and top clients.

Barns generated more gossip than other places, because you had spoiled rich riders, hot horses and megalomaniac trainers under pressure. The pressure was self-generated, a product of the dream. Everyone wanted to be one with their horse, but nobody could be.

Kieran arguing with Douglas was a particularly juicy piece of gossip because Douglas was usually quiet and well-behaved.

"I don't understand why I have to go with her alone," he said to Kieran.

"If you're that clueless, I can't help you."

Kieran was not a particularly fun person to argue with. He had an answer for everything, and it usually hurt.

"I just think you should come with us," Douglas said. "What if something goes wrong?"

"Then you'll handle it. Like you've been handling it. I wouldn't ask you to do something you couldn't do."

Vida knew they were talking about Heather's trip to Kentucky.

It was all anyone could talk about. How *great* Kentucky was, all the pretty horses. Vida had become insanely jealous when she heard. She was actually surprised that Douglas was protesting. Vida would have been more than happy to take his place.

"Douglas," Kieran continued, his voice gentling.

Vida peered carefully around the tack room until she could see them: Kieran resting his hand on Douglas's shoulder; Douglas leaning against the wall like he couldn't stand up unsupported.

"This is going to be *our* horse. He's going to lift the entire team. He's going to change *everything*. He's all picked out. He's perfect. She's tired of looking. She'll buy anything. She'll pay anything. All you have to do is smile at her."

Douglas pouted. "What if it doesn't work?"

Kieran dropped his hand, stepped away. "Then you can stay in Kentucky."

Vida laughed in surprise, perhaps a little too loudly because Kieran started walking in her direction. She hurried back to her bridle.

He stopped outside the cleaning bay, leaned over the side of the crosstie, watched her. "Eavesdropping?"

"Cleaning your bridles." She held up a set of reins in demonstration.

He chewed something over. "You like your new friend?"

Vida shrugged. "Not really."

"Why not?"

"Maple's kind of immature. Plus, she's, like, *way* younger than me."

"How old is she?"

"Thirteen."

"How old are you?"

Vida was a little insulted that he didn't know. This was her big year. "Seventeen."

He squinted slightly. "Are you sure? You're so small."

"Riders are supposed to be small."

"Are you suggesting that you're small by will?"

He smirked, and Vida felt like she'd won.

"Yes, sir."

"When do you turn eighteen?" he asked.

Her heart soared a little, as if she could see him calculating her future, calibrating the arrival of her dreams. She would turn eighteen, and he would make her one of his elite riders.

"November."

"This is your last year as a Junior," he said.

Her heart was in her throat. "I'm gonna win the Little Palm Cup."

He cocked his head. "Are you, now?"

"Yes."

She wanted to say, *And then I'm gonna go pro*, but she was afraid of what he might say back. *With who?*

Eighteen was young to become a Professional rider. Most people did a few years as an Amateur first. But Douglas hadn't. And Vida couldn't afford to. She was planning to ride Nikita in the Cup, but Vida knew that this was Nikita's last big season. She was getting too old. Vida was outgrowing her. She needed a new horse.

Kieran nodded, let a hand rest briefly on her shoulder. "Good for you, kid." Then he stalked off, to make other people's dreams come true.

Vida sometimes liked to believe that Kieran didn't affect her the way he did everyone else. That she didn't *need* his approval. That she didn't think they had a *special connection*. But other times she knew that was a lie.

Kieran had a way of making her feel *right* in the world. All of the things other people saw as flaws—her cruelty, her aggression, her strength—seemed to delight Kieran.

She sometimes let herself imagine what it would feel like to be part of his team. In those dreams, she was so wholly herself that it was like a superpower.

eighteen

HEATHER

Douglas Dunn slept for the entire flight. Heather let him have the window seat, and he passed out immediately, face against the glass, and didn't wake up once.

Kentucky was all grass. The horses were better than any Heather had ever seen. The barns were more beautiful. It was like horses were an art that Kentucky had perfected. Heather and Douglas found two contenders on the first day, and they would be there for three more days.

They had separate rooms, of course, but by the end of that first night, they had spent hours by the pool, talking over the horses they'd seen and drinking bourbon brewed at one of the barns they'd visited. The blue light from the pool lit Douglas's face. He got tipsy chatty, telling her what he loved about a good horse. How there was no better feeling in the world than being on horseback.

"The whole world just falls away," he kept repeating until the words were so embedded in her brain, she heard them that night in bed when she shut her eyes.

Heather felt as if she were on one of the high school trips she'd gone on with the football team when she was a cheerleader. Sixty teenagers abandoned at a strange hotel by a bunch of inattentive chaperones. It was kind of a dream, to be able to do something like that again, when she'd thought those days were over. It made her think anything was possible. It made her think her life was just beginning. She wasn't just a mom to two moody teenage daughters. She wasn't just a wife stuck in a dead-end marriage. She was human again.

They found The Horse on day three. They both knew he was the one. He wasn't the most beautiful horse they'd seen. He wasn't even the most expensive—although he was priced at 1.5 million dollars—but he was The Horse.

Heather saw it first in Douglas's face, which she was taking the temperature of all the time. Then she saw it in the arena. The horse moved the way water flowed from one place to the next. He was calm, not like some of the frantic horses they'd seen. He loved jumping.

He was huge, powerful, quiet. He reminded Heather of her own heart.

If she was broken, that horse could fix her.

His name was Commotion.

nineteen

MAPLE

Maple was actually enjoying her lessons with Amy. She had been worried that Amy would push her too hard, but Amy did the opposite. She didn't push Maple at all. As the weeks passed, Maple felt the thrust of her own self pushing, wanting to be better, wanting to do more. It was a cool trick.

Maple loved the other girls: Effie with her neat beauty; Vida with her tiny intensity. Maple could hardly understand what they saw in her, but as time passed, she started to believe she was at least worth seeing.

They hung out at the barn all day, mucking in with everyone. Maple became the best bridle cleaner—after a rocky start when she got yelled at for soaking the leather with water. Now she sometimes cleaned thirty bridles a day. No one could believe it. Maple was so proud.

Her mother wasn't always, Maple could tell. Sometimes Maple would watch Heather laughing with Pamela and think that she had done it—she had finally made her mother happy, proved to her that happiness did exist. Other times Maple would catch Heather's crinkled expressions of disappointment.

That weekend her mother was away. Heather had gone to Kentucky with Douglas Dunn. Maple could have gotten away with not going to the barn. She could have told her dad that she was tired and stayed home, but she found she didn't want to. She and Effie and Vida were going to ride together for the first time. They were going on a trail ride and bringing a picnic. It would be fun. Heather had bought Maple a western saddle, so she would feel extra safe.

With Amy in the lead, the four of them went out into the trail network. There was enough space for Vida and Effie and Maple to ride side by side. Amy took pictures to send to Heather.

They passed by Maple's house, and farther along by Vida's and Effie's. Maple liked being out in the open air. She liked being with her friends. She even liked being on horseback. It was actually fun without the constant criticism of a lesson.

Maple had this big, wide feeling that she had snuck into someone else's dream. This surely wasn't a life that Maple deserved. She had stolen it, borrowed it—maybe from her mother.

She had nice friends and good horses and beautiful, endless trails. The ride was magical, even if it didn't feel entirely real, entirely hers: the smells of leather and oranges; the crisp dryness of the air; the gray-green eucalyptus trees; the pale estates; the swaying motion of her hips and her heart, like she was underwater holding her breath, never wanting to come up.

Maple and her friends talked about all their horse goals. Effie wanted to be in the Olympics, which seemed unlikely, but no one said so. Vida wanted to go pro, which seemed totally possible. Maple just wanted to have a cute horse in her backyard.

"And not take lessons," she added quietly, making sure Amy didn't hear. "And just do whatever I want."

"Exactly!" Vida said. "Once I turn eighteen and go pro, I'm gonna do whatever the fuck I want!"

Vida was slightly more exuberant than Maple, but Maple still agreed rebelliously, "Totally."

"Why wait?" Vida shortened her reins. "Ask Amy if we can canter."

Maple glanced at Amy's back, up ahead on the trail. Maple didn't want to canter. She wasn't even allowed to canter in the round pen, so she doubted Amy would let her canter on trail, but it was hard to turn Vida down.

"Yeah," Effie agreed, watching Amy's back. "*You* have to ask."

Maple took a deep breath. She thought it was pointless to ask, but her friends wanted her to, and she wanted to have friends. Besides, Amy would just say they couldn't. There was no harm in asking.

"Amy, can we canter?"

Amy seemed alarmed. "Let's just walk for now."

"But we can canter later?" Vida said.

Amy caught her eye and seemed to understand the question better.

"We'll see," Amy said, seeming unable to say no to Vida either. "Let's just have our lunch first."

Amy was carrying the lunch. Sandwiches that no one wanted.

Vida was carrying the sodas. She pulled a can out of her saddlebag and cracked it open.

"Vida," Amy scolded.

"I'm thirsty," she said, then passed one to Effie. "Effie's thirsty, too."

They fell into haunting girl giggles. Amy rolled her eyes and slowed down, so she wasn't too far in front of the girls.

"Do you want one, Maple?" Vida asked.

Maple didn't want one. She wanted to keep both hands on the reins, but she was afraid of Vida. Afraid of her disapproval. She was afraid that one day her new friends would realize what a loser she really was.

Secretly, Maple was still convinced that those kids in Amarillo had been right. To call her weird. To push her. To pull her hair.

Moving to California and realizing that she could leave the bullying behind had meant so much to Maple, but as time passed, she couldn't get over the feeling that she had escaped only momentarily. She had feinted away from the bullying, but it would come back.

When Maple said something dumb and caught Vida shooting Effie a significant look.

When Vida made one of her seemingly innocuous comments: "I can't believe you don't know that" or "Is that how they do things in Texas?"

When her mom said, "Still on the lunge line?"

When her dad asked why she wasn't jumping yet.

When Piper gave her a pitying look.

Maple was wrong in the world, and everyone else knew it. She would never, ever fit.

"Okay. Give me one." Maple awkwardly placed the reins in one hand and reached toward Vida.

Amy's back twitched, but she didn't turn.

The cold soda landed in Maple's hand. She sat back, trying to steady herself.

"You have to open it, silly," Vida said after four or five steps.

Maple tilted the soda can up. She clenched the reins in one nervous fist. She cracked the can with her thumb. It exploded, shooting soda everywhere.

Underneath her, Faustus spooked and took off at a gallop.

twenty

HEATHER

S hould we even bother looking at other horses?" Heather said to Douglas when she met him at breakfast the morning after they saw Commotion. "We know which one we want."

Heather had memorized Douglas's breakfast order, which was staggering: black coffee and as much food as he could fit on his plate. He ate only breakfast. The rest of the day, he just sucked peppermints.

He finished chewing, swallowed, washed his food down with coffee. "It might be good to have an alternative. In case Commotion doesn't vet."

Kieran was flying his vet out that morning to examine the horse. Kieran didn't trust anyone else, and the owner of the horse was being a little difficult. He claimed to have other offers. Kieran had advised Heather not to give the owner her name until after he had accepted the offer, but the owner seemed to know she was rich. He wasn't budging on the price either.

Heather didn't care. She would pay the whole 1.5 million. Part of her even wanted to. What was the point of buying something if it didn't cost just a little too much?

"We're getting that horse," she said. "I'll sell myself if I have to."

Douglas's eyes flew up. He was so easily shocked.

"Don't you want him?" she pressed.

He sat back. His chair scraped the floor. "If he's sound," he said, meaning if the horse didn't have any lameness.

"He's The Horse. I know it. And you know it. He's the right horse for us."

He tilted his head. He seemed a little unsure of her sometimes. He would look at her like she was a horse spooking at nothing, like he was wondering why she was acting the way she was.

Sometimes she felt the same way. They had one more day in Kentucky. One more night.

"Okay," she said as if responding to his unspoken rejoinder. "We can keep looking. But we should do something fun tonight. For our last night." Like they had been out there together for eons.

twenty-one

PIPER

Piper had gone back to the barn during daylight hours. Her mother was out of town, so there was no chance of Heather seeing her. She might hear later that Piper had been there, which would annoy her, but Piper was okay with that.

Piper walked the barn aisles, observed the crossties with a dozen grooms working like clockwork, taking horses out and putting them away. She drifted toward the main arena, where the jumps were set to absurd heights, to the tops of the standards that held them. Piper couldn't believe horses could really jump that high.

Inside the big arena, a woman not much older than Piper was taking a lesson on a large gray horse. The woman listened quietly as the trainer laid out the course. Piper watched in awe as the horse circled, squared up to one of those ridiculously tall jumps, cleared it with ease, made a rollback to a combination and leapt long over a water jump.

The rider was transitioning to a walk when Piper heard a kerfuffle. People started hurrying—not running but walking fast—toward the far side of the property.

"Loose horse! Loose horse!" people shouted.

Piper followed the crowd, anxious to help. Then a bay horse came barreling past the trailhead, its reins flapping, stirrups banging, saddle empty.

Piper helped form a wall of people. She and the others spread their arms wide to create a barrier as they approached the horse in unison, boxing it in.

"That's Vida's horse," someone said.

"Faustus," said another.

"Where's Vida?"

"She hasn't been riding him. That little girl was."

Piper knew in an instant that they meant Maple. She took off toward the trailhead, not running but walking very, very fast.

Her heart was pounding. She imagined Maple in pieces on the ground or impaled on a fence. Broken legs. Broken back. Paralyzed.

With a burst of speed, Piper blamed her mom for forcing Maple to ride. When Maple was scared. When Maple was immature and innocent and breakable.

Piper reached a fork in the trail. She wasn't sure which way to go. She scanned the dirt, saw the hard pattern of galloping-horse hooves and darted in that direction.

"Slow down!" someone yelled. "You're scaring the horses!"

Piper heard giggling as a horse came along the trail. Two girls were riding double on the horse's back. The first had red hair that burned in the sun. The second was Maple.

Piper stopped in her tracks.

"Piper!" Maple squealed. "That's my sister! She rides, too!"

"Hop on!" Vida joked, transitioning to a stop beside Piper.

Two more horses pulled up behind Vida.

"No!" an older rider who must have been their trainer, Amy, said.

"Did you fall off?" Piper asked Maple.

"She *flew* off," Vida corrected Piper.

"Launched," Effie agreed.

"Like a soda pop," Maple said, and they all laughed.

Piper couldn't believe it. She had never seen this Maple. She had never known that this Maple existed: vivid, giggling, fearless.

"I think they caught your horse," Piper said. "Are you okay?"

"I've never seen Faustus gallop like that," Vida noted.

"I landed on my feet," Maple said.

"Did she ever," said Vida.

"It doesn't count as a fall if you land on your feet," said Effie.

"We're really proud of her," Amy said, stopping alongside Piper as the other girls moved off. "I'm Amy. I'm Maple's trainer. You must be Piper."

Piper nodded. She had heard about Amy and all of Maple's new barn friends.

She felt left behind as she watched the girls ride ahead. It was an icky feeling, but she envied Maple a little. She missed friends and inside jokes and getting the giggles. LOL-ing over text messages wasn't the same.

"Yes," Piper said, falling in beside Amy.

"Is Piper thirsty?" Vida said, and the three girls exploded into giggles again.

Amy ignored them. "Your mom said you might want to take lessons, too?"

Piper's first reaction was annoyance, but her second was confusion. "I don't know. Maybe?"

She found herself wanting to tell Amy about her mom and the pressure she had put Piper under, but Heather was Amy's client. Heather spent all her time at the barn. It felt a little gossipy to bad-mouth her. So Piper said nothing.

"Well, if you ever want to give it a try," Amy said, "you just let me know. We have a lot of fun."

Up ahead, the girls were practically hysterical now.

Amy made a face. "Sometimes a little too much fun."

twenty-two

HEATHER

Once Heather had established that she and Douglas would do something special that night, she was hard-pressed to find anything that made sense. What did people do at night? They went to dinner, which Douglas didn't eat and which would have felt like a date. They went to bed, and they went to bars. The former was inappropriate, so she chose the latter.

In her youth, Heather had understood the appeal of bars. They were places where she would go head-to-head with her female counterparts for male attention. Late at night she would go home alone and count up all the men she had rejected. She didn't think going to a bar with Douglas would be like that.

She selected a dive bar off the beaten track; that choice should have been her first clue about her own intentions. She selected a private booth, bought drinks and shots and picked the next ten songs on the jukebox.

She clinked his glass as she slid into the booth beside him. "Thank you for taking me out here," she said as her music crooned from the jukebox. "I'm sure you have better things to do."

"It's my job." He sipped his beer. "Anyway, I like looking at horses."

"You're sweet."

The records clicked in and out of place. A limp disco ball spun from the ceiling. She bought them another shot.

"You're gonna get me drunk," he said.

"Is that a bad thing?"

He looked at her. She looked at him.

"Do you have a girlfriend?" she said.

"No. Just horses." He was running his fingers up and down his bottle absently, sending the condensation down in tears.

"But you're so good-looking."

"I don't really have time for, you know, a lot."

Heather didn't know what was wrong with her, but she often found that she couldn't stop pushing. She would pick the scab. She'd say the thing that she shouldn't have said. She'd worry the issue, create a fight out of nothing. Sometimes she wished she could stop it. Sometimes she wished she could let it fly.

"Pamela says you have a reputation, at horse shows."

"Huh."

"That you fuck women. In the backs of trucks, in trailers, in horse stalls." She was a little drunk, which made her feel cruel and alive.

"Huh."

"Is that true?"

He nodded, just marginally, and finished his beer.

"Do you want another shot?" she said.

His dark eyes locked onto hers. "What do you want?"

Heather sometimes wished she could live more than one life. She had chosen her path, it was true, and she mostly thought it was the best path, the luckiest path in the world.

But other times she wanted more. Not more money, not more

stuff. She wanted more chaos, more mess, more disaster. She wanted to roll to the brink, ride the edge, come up hot and sweating and begging for more.

Harder.

Rougher.

Deeper.

Fucked.

twenty-three

PIPER

Piper did a quick scan of the barn aisle, then let herself into the horse's stall. It was after dark, and she was alone. The horse was Faustus. He wasn't *her* horse, and she didn't have the owner's permission, but her sister was riding him. There was some connection.

She just wanted to be close to a horse again.

Sometimes she felt it in her blood. Like love but stronger, deeper. That need to be near horses.

Faustus ambled over to Piper, sniffed at her elbow, then nudged her, so she laughed in surprise. She stepped closer to him, finding the spot on his crest where horses groomed one another. She massaged it until he wriggled his lips in pleasure.

She pressed her face against his neck, breathing in his horsey scent. And then she was crying, pressing her face into the horse's neck to hide her tears, feeling bougie but also like it was better crying on a horse than it was crying by herself in her room.

Piper was so lonely. She didn't know what to do. She told herself that once school started, everything would change, but sometimes she was afraid that her staying alone for too long would alter her permanently, that she would never be able to fit with people again.

And the worst part was her aloneness was her own fault. In seeking not to be controlled, Piper had isolated herself from everyone. She sometimes thought she could just *go* to the barn. She could just show up.

She could say, *Surprise! I changed my mind. I was wrong. You were right.*

You know me better than I know myself because you are me. I am you.

We want the same things.

We make the same mistakes.

We break the same way.

twenty-four

HEATHER

Heather was in Douglas's hotel room. She was on Douglas's bed. He was in the process of mounting her when she told him, "I can't do this."

He collapsed beside her on the bed, gasping at the ceiling.

"I'm sorry," she said.

"It's totally fine," he said, in about the tone you would have expected.

She waited for him to leave, and when he didn't, he reminded her, "So, this is my room."

Her own room was two doors down. She walked there, feeling unexpectedly deficient.

She wanted to cheat on Jeff. She desperately wanted to be that kind of person. It seemed like such a joyful, reckless thing to do, to cheat on her cheating husband. To cede control in the most incendiary way possible. To let go of everything. To surrender to lust.

But she couldn't. She couldn't switch off. She couldn't stop thinking about what would happen next.

The hardest thing about cheating was knowing what to do afterward. There was no manual on extramarital affairs. In movies, one or both parties became obsessed—stalking, hunting. They couldn't get enough. Heather doubted she would feel that way about Douglas. She knew he wouldn't feel that way about her.

Would she have to get a divorce? Would she have to sleep with Douglas again? Would she have to sleep with someone else?

She didn't want to do any of those things. She wanted, really, for her husband to love her. More than that, she wanted to love him.

She went to bed alone. She thought sometimes about going back to Douglas's room, asking him to just sleep beside her—no sex—but she had a feeling that would not appeal to him. Still, she longed to ask him, a practical stranger, *Aren't I good enough to share a bed with? Don't I deserve to be loved?*

The next morning when Heather knocked on Douglas's door, an unfamiliar girl answered. Heather checked the door number when the girl said, "You must be his mom."

Perfect.

The girl opened the door to reveal the bed stripped of covers and the comforter in a mass on the floor. Presumably Douglas was somewhere inside it.

"Our flight is leaving soon," Heather said. "I just wanted to see if he wanted to go down to breakfast."

Heather was a little impressed. She had left Douglas's room well after midnight. It was now six in the morning. In that time, he had somehow acquired this girl, who stated with total ownership, "We'll be down in a minute."

The girl, Tabitha, sat with them at breakfast although her friends were one table over, sometimes giggling, sometimes outright staring.

Heather was glad she and Douglas were leaving, because she had a feeling that otherwise Tabitha would have been absorbed into their fucked-up little family.

Tabitha explained to Heather how she and her friends were on a road trip. How she had left her room last night to get ice from the machine when she ran into Douglas.

"And we got to talking. . . ." She gazed at him with love in her eyes.

The whole situation was dizzying, but it did make Heather feel better about her decision not to sleep with Douglas.

"Maybe I can convince my friends to take a detour to California," Tabitha mused. It was just a sixty-hour round trip.

Douglas was very sweet about the whole thing, letting Tabitha come with them to the airport so they could make out in the back of the rental car. Her friends picked her up at departures.

Heather paused to watch Tabitha and her friends drive away. She didn't regret not sleeping with Douglas. She did regret not being nineteen.

twenty-five

PIPER

Piper's mom came home prepared to do battle. She'd found The Horse, the one they'd been looking for. She got Maple on her side first, showing her pictures and videos.

The Horse taking a treat from her hand.

The Horse nodding his head.

The Horse whinnying at her.

"His name is Commotion," Heather said, looking up as Piper came in.

Heather and Maple were folded into the corner of the sofa—Maple practically in Heather's lap. Heather ran her fingers along Maple's French braid.

"Isn't he beautiful?" she breathed into her daughter's ear. "Isn't he like a unicorn?"

Piper perched on the arm of the sofa chair across from them. Piper could appreciate the picture they made. She loved them both intensely of course, but sometimes it was easier to do that from a distance.

"Do you want to see?" Heather held out the phone.

It seemed stupid not to look. Piper stretched her neck.

Heather selected a video and pressed PLAY. The horse appeared. He was gray, but he looked white. He cantered across the screen. Heather swiped. The horse whinnied, stretching toward the camera. Swiped. The horse jumped alone on a lunge line, arcing into the air with a perfect bascule.

"What do you think?" Heather asked, bringing the phone to her heart, like his image could keep her warm.

Piper shrugged, not wanting to, but wanting to.

"Piper came to the barn," Maple volunteered, mutinously snuggling into their mother's chest. "When you were gone."

"What did you think?" Heather asked—same question, different subject.

"Maple fell off," Piper countered, getting her sister back.

"Nuh-uh," Maple said. "Doesn't count 'cause I landed on my feet."

Maple explained to their mother about the trail ride, how she had gotten to ride double with Vida.

Heather brushed Maple's hair back and kissed her forehead. "I'm so proud of you, my little horse girl."

Piper felt flimsy. She felt flimsy all the time in this new world. She felt weaker than herself, more needy. She didn't know how to get her strength back—didn't know where it had ever come from. She wanted to go to the barn. She wanted to see the horse—their horse.

"I can't wait until he's here," Heather said, swiping through the videos again. "He's going to be part of our family."

DETECTIVE PEREZ

Y ou see, RSFE is like a cult," the woman—June Far—told Detective Perez.

She was sitting across from the detectives in the horse stall. She hadn't even been on their list of people to talk to. She had just waited patiently outside until they brought her in.

Now that they had, she seemed to have nothing important to say. Still, she spoke at length about the barn. What Detective Perez found especially odd was how much she seemed to dislike it.

"And you and your daughter have been riding with Rancho Santa Fe Equestrian for . . . ?" she asked.

June seemed to see where she was leading. "*All* barns are like cults. These are horses we're talking about. They take up all of your time. Drain all your money. There's a reason they say 'horse girls' but not 'soccer girls' or 'ballet girls.' Horses consume you."

Detective Perez found June's superiority a little grating. June seemed to be occupying the detectives' time for no other reason than to have a captive audience to air all her horse-related grievances.

"Detective Perez, can I level with you?" June sat forward, with the air of someone who watched too much true crime. "Every horse trainer is a megalomaniac. Every coach, if you want to get down to it. Every man, if you want to get serious. I let Effie train at RSFE because I want her to learn: This is a toxic man. Don't let him fuck with you."

twenty-six

PIPER

Piper went to the barn the morning Commotion arrived. Her mom was going. Her sister was going. Her dad was in Texas. She wanted to see the horse. Needed to. At night, she had dreams about it—dreams of a gray horse in the dark, like a beacon guiding her home.

Commotion came storming out of the trailer, prancing, whinnying, wild.

Kieran passed by on his way to the arena. "It will take him a while to settle in. Sometimes it even takes months."

The head groom put Commotion in a stall next to Vida's horses. Commotion was frantic, weaving and bobbing and racing back and forth, blasting air from his nose in a panic.

"This is totally normal," Pamela assured Heather. "Imagine if one day someone took you from your home and drove you across the country. Plonked you in a totally new place."

"I can imagine that," Piper said, and Heather rolled her eyes.

"I feel bad," Maple whined as the horse paused to sniff her, then rocketed away. "Maybe we should send him back. Maybe he wants to stay there." Her face crumpled with worry.

Pamela put a hand on her shoulder. "He was for sale, dear. He would just end up somewhere else. You'll take good care of him. He just needs to get used to the barn. To know he's safe here. He doesn't know he's home yet, but he will."

Vida watched the horse with an appreciative eye. "He's huge."

"Bigger than your horses," said Effie.

Kieran reappeared with one of the grooms in tow. The crowd parted as he marched up to the stall. He observed the horse, his hands on his hips.

"Well, let's get him out into the arena."

Heather jumped up. "Today?"

Piper could tell she was nervous. Maple looked ready to make a run for it.

"Yes," Kieran said. "It will help get his energy out, give him something to focus on."

The horse bobbed up and down, then reared a little.

"But isn't it dangerous?" Heather said.

"That's what Douglas is for." Kieran nodded to the groom to fetch the horse.

"Everyone, stand back," the groom ordered, unlatching the gate.

"Go find a seat by the arena," Kieran instructed Heather. "Clear the aisle."

Maple was the first to move, rushing toward the arena as if afraid Kieran might throw her on the horse instead. Piper and Vida followed, pausing to look back as Commotion charged out of the stall.

The groom lost control of the horse for a second; then he pulled Commotion in a tight circle.

Commotion looked beautiful but wild, like horses in movies Piper had seen. She wanted desperately to put her hands on him, to calm him down, to make him love her the way riders did in those stories—*The Black Stallion, Heartland, Free Rein.*

Already Piper thought she could feel a special connection, as if she and the horse belonged to each other. She couldn't help it. He was beautiful and he was in a new place, far from home. He needed to be saved, and Piper was specially tuned for saving.

"I wish I could afford a horse like that." Vida shot Piper a bitter look, then followed the others toward the arena.

The crowd for Commotion filled the entire seating area. Not just the Parkers and Pamela and June, but a handful of grooms, the barn manager and two dozen owners had all gathered to get a look at the new horse.

They all went quiet as Douglas rode out. Piper hadn't seen Douglas before, although she knew he had gone to Kentucky with her mom. She had a feeling her dad had no idea Douglas looked like *that*.

The horse, which had been frantic not twenty minutes earlier, now seemed serene. He walked out boldly, with his head bowed and his back lifted.

Kieran stepped into the ring. Piper watched them warm up. The horse was so athletic. He moved with precision and flow. Douglas seemed to disappear, like Commotion was moving of his own volition or reading Douglas's mind.

Once they had warmed up, Kieran called the girls in to set jumps. Vida and Effie and even Maple scurried around the arena and put the jumps up high, according to Kieran's specifications.

When they were finished, Douglas picked up a canter, and Kieran directed him to warm up over a fence. Piper could see Douglas grin when the horse made the first jump; Commotion had cleared it by at least a foot.

"This horse wants to jump big," Kieran said, grinning, too. He laid out a course. "Just take it easy. Listen to him. We want to set the foundation."

Douglas rode Commotion smoothly from one fence to the next as the crowd oohed and aahed, talked about the horse.

"Now, that's impulsion."

"See how he flicks his back legs up?"

"Jesus Christ. I've never seen a horse like that."

It was like a religious experience. *On the seventh day, God created horses.*

After he finished jumping, Douglas cooled the horse out. He let him walk up and down the barn, showing him everything, getting him comfortable. Then the grooms untacked Commotion and put him away. Back in his stall, the horse still paced, but he seemed mildly less frantic.

Piper watched him from a tack box. Her mom and sister had stayed by the ring. The other owners had surrounded Heather and congratulated her on her accomplishment—she had bought a good horse.

Piper did not want to fall in love with Commotion. That was not in her plan. But he was a living, breathing animal, and he belonged to the Parkers, and it seemed impossible not to.

Impossible to stop her heart from going out to him. His eyes were enormous, so worried and sad. He was smart and he was lonely, and he was looking for someone to love. And so was she.

twenty-seven

VIDA

Vida was surprised that Kieran had put Commotion in that stall. It was the best stall in the barn—centrally located, a few feet longer than the others—but it was also a little cursed. Vida made sure to tell Maple that right away.

"You know, two of the riders who had their horses here had horrific accidents," she said when the three girls met outside the stall the next morning.

"It's true," Effie said when Maple's jaw dropped. "One even died."

Vida nodded vigorously, looping her arms around Commotion's neck. "Do you want to know what happened?"

"No, thank you," Maple said, proving she was no fun.

The three girls spent the morning hanging out in the barn aisle to help Commotion adjust. Maple sat on a tack box across from her horse, scrolling through her phone. She wouldn't even get close to him. Vida had seen her feed him a treat only once.

Vida knew Maple's reticence was none of her business, but it annoyed her. She would have killed to have a horse like that. Maple's eyes just grazed over Commotion, like he was a toy she hadn't asked for.

"Don't you want to bond with him?" Vida said, reaching up and scratching the horse's neck as he nibbled her shoulder.

"I will," Maple said.

All morning she had been saying that—*I will*—in a silly singsong voice. What was she waiting for?

"You can't just ride Faustus forever," Vida complained.

Maple looked up, alarmed. "When do I have to stop?"

Vida paused. It wasn't really her choice whether Maple rode Faustus or not. It was her mom's choice, which meant it was Kieran's choice. And Kieran didn't give a fuck if Maple ever rode her own horse. In fact, he probably would have preferred to keep her off him, as long as her parents kept paying for it.

"We should trade," Vida said.

"I wish I could," Maple said, and then added, "I mean, I like Commotion, but I really like Faustus, too."

Vida knew they couldn't actually trade. They weren't in control of their own horses, but still she said, "Since you're riding my horse, I should get to ride yours."

"Yeah," Maple agreed. "Totally."

Vida imagined herself riding Commotion into the arena for the Little Palm Cup. His powerful head bowed, his muscular shoulders reaching, his tail streaming behind him like a white flag telling the whole world to surrender.

It's over. I won.

Later that afternoon, Vida told her mother that she wanted to ride Commotion.

"Let's just let the horse be here for a week before we start getting into all that," Pamela said as she drove Vida and Effie to get smoothies.

Maple had gone home. She was spending less time at the barn now that her horse was actually there. Vida could tell that Maple felt pressured to want him, to love him; that she felt like everyone was watching her. And everyone was.

The whole barn was talking about Commotion, what an amazing horse he was. Kieran even said Commotion was the highest-quality horse he'd ever had at RSFE. Vida could already see that Kieran's plan was working. People were excited to be on a winning team, but that wasn't enough for Vida. She needed to be the one winning.

Vida was naturally competitive and all of her riding life had been dedicated to sharpening that inclination. She needed to be the best. If she didn't win, she didn't exist.

"But Maple is riding *my* horse," Vida insisted to her mom. "It's only fair that I get to ride hers. And she doesn't care! She would let me!"

"The horse is in the training program," Pamela said. "It's Kieran's decision what she does with him."

Vida knew that. All of the horses at RSFE were in the training program, which meant that Kieran made all the decisions for them, which essentially meant that all the horses at RSFE belonged to Kieran, although he didn't technically own any of them.

"It's so dumb!" Vida said, thrusting her back against the seat. "She doesn't even want him. She's afraid of him."

"Let's just wait it out," Pamela said as she turned into the parking lot. "Let's stay friends with little Maple and just keep our eyes peeled and see what happens."

Vida was already miles ahead. Sometimes her mind and her heart were like wild horses running away with her. She knew what she wanted, and she was seized with bright, impulsive ways to get it.

Sometimes she thought she could have anything if she would just stop holding herself back.

She had this sense that she wasn't like other people in that way, that she could truly let herself go—not care about the rules or society or even human decency.

Sometimes that made her feel powerful.

Other times it made her feel scared.

twenty-eight

PIPER

Piper had taken to sneaking out at night to visit Commotion. Hidden as she was on the far side of the Parkers' enormous house, she could easily disarm the security system and walk out the door. She would walk through the yard, past the pool and the tennis court and the basketball court and the putting green and the guesthouse and the barn, until she reached the fence.

She would pass through the gate and, using the flashlight on her phone to illuminate the way, walk the mile to RSFE.

Piper wouldn't leave the house until around ten or eleven, when she was pretty sure her parents were in bed at least. It had to be late enough that no one was at RSFE either. That had been the scariest part.

There was a family who lived on the property as caretakers. One night the father, Nash, had caught her. Extra petrified in the dark, Piper had explained how a horse there belonged to her family. Nash told her that the barn was closed to boarders after ten, but when he realized which horse she meant, he backed down. Now he waved when he saw her.

Piper would sit with Commotion for an hour. Sometimes she

would let herself into his stall and pet him, rubbing his poll or massaging his withers, and feed him treats from her hands. Sometimes she would rest her head against his shoulder. Sometimes she would cry, wish that she could go back to Texas, back to the person she had been before they'd moved and she'd realized that she didn't know herself at all.

She was on the verge of tears again that night. She was at the point of sadness where tears would have felt like a relief, like freedom from the oppression of not being able to cry.

She was leaning into the horse's shoulder, willing the tears to come, when Commotion heard something in the aisle.

Piper craned her head, searching for what had captured the horse's attention. Her eyes landed on Douglas Dunn.

"Hey," he said. The horse reached for him and he reached back. "Sorry. I didn't know anyone was here."

It was after eleven, late for either of them. Piper felt like she was in trouble, but she had more justification to be there than he did. The horse belonged to her family.

"It's fine," she said, debating whether she should let herself out of the stall.

The horse was preoccupied with Douglas. There was nothing that broke her heart more than fighting over the preferences of animals.

"You're Piper, right?" he said, rubbing the horse's poll.

"Yeah."

"Your mom said you used to ride," he said.

She nodded.

"Why'd you stop?"

"I don't know."

The truth—that her mother had pushed her too hard—seemed silly, as if Piper had lived her whole life opposing her mother's dreams.

"You like horses, though? I mean, you're here. It's pretty late."

"I couldn't sleep."

"Yeah." He stepped back. "Well, I'll let you . . . I mean, I don't want to be in your way."

"No, I'm leaving."

"Did you drive? I didn't see a car."

"I walked."

"Oh . . . In the dark?"

"I have a flashlight on my phone."

"By yourself?"

Piper hated when people pointed out that she was alone. "It's fine."

"Let me drive you back."

"No, I . . . My parents don't know I'm here," she confessed.

"Well, I can't let you walk by yourself. What if something happened?"

"It's a mile on a horse trail."

"I mean, either I walk with you, or I stay here and worry about you."

He shrugged, like she had trapped him in this spot. Like only she could rescue him.

So she agreed.

He was so well put together, he kind of seemed like a hallucination. All muscled limbs and tight clothing, and that extraordinary face sliced neatly into perfect planes. He was a cute guy, and he was going to walk her home, and no one else would know about it or ever could, so maybe this night was a close cousin to a dream.

They started on the horse trail.

"Man, this is *dark*," he observed.

Her flashlight was a little bead of light on the ground. "I've done it before," she said. "It's flat the whole way. No monsters."

"That we know of."

He smiled a little, seeming amused by her. He was nothing like the other boys she knew, so in a way, he made her feel *more* alone, like it was crazy to think they even existed in the same space.

"So, how do you like living here?" he asked.

"I don't," she said too fast. "Sorry. I mean, I start college in the fall, so I'm sure then it will be okay, but right now it's . . ." She trailed off. She had been on the verge of admitting she was lonely, which seemed tantamount to admitting she deserved to be alone.

"You should come out to the barn," he said. "I mean, in the daytime. You don't have to ride if you don't want to. You could just hang out."

"I don't know. I like to do my own thing."

He tilted his head at her. He must have thought she was weird, coming to the barn after dark when everyone was gone. "You shy or something?"

"No," she said, and then, because being shy seemed worse, she admitted, "It's just my mom. She puts all this pressure on me. I used to ride, and it was like she was breathing down my neck."

He nodded, taking it in. "Have you told her this, maybe? Asked her to give you space?"

"My mom doesn't take direction very well. She just does whatever she wants."

He nodded again. "Huh. Well, there are arena lights, if you wanna come ride one night. Here, let me give you my number."

He reached for her phone, his fingers brushing hers, and then her phone was in his hands. His breath smelled of peppermint.

"What's your passcode?" he asked.

"Five-six-eight-three," she said, feeling a little light-headed. She wondered if he knew the numbers spelled "love" on a keypad.

He plugged his number into her phone, then handed it back to her. "Don't tell anyone, okay?"

"Would you get in trouble?"

"Not if we don't get caught." He smiled a slightly uneasy smile. Piper felt the horrible sense of responsibility that came from talking to a cute boy—the feeling that she would now be liable for keeping him happy, for keeping him interested, forever.

"Is it worth the risk?" she asked.

"Horses are always worth the risk."

She could see her house up ahead, but she didn't say anything until they reached the back gate. He paused when he saw the estate, trying to take it all in.

"It's big," she said, and she felt stupid until he agreed.

"Yeah."

She plugged in the gate code. "Thank you for walking me."

"No problem."

She hovered at the gate, watched him walk back alone in the dark.

twenty-nine

HEATHER

Commotion was the right horse. Every day Heather felt more certain of it. Everyone at the barn was in awe of the horse. Little crowds formed whenever Douglas took him out. Sometimes they even formed around his stall.

No one seemed able to derive the source of his perfection—was it his legs? His hindquarters? His head? His heart? The horse had charisma. He was a star. The only person who didn't seem taken with him was his rider, Maple.

Heather could tell Maple was afraid of Commotion. Her fear was the thing that could ruin everything. What was the point of having the best horse if Maple didn't ride it? It was embarrassing. Heather needed to push Maple in that direction, so she tried an array of tactics.

First, she tried ignoring Maple's anxiety. That was always her go-to. Maple would come around eventually. There was no use trying to force her.

Then, very quickly afterward, Heather tried force, because maybe there was *some* use to it.

She made Maple lead the horse to a sun pen. Maple, holding the lead rope and facing Commotion, walked five feet away from the horse and jumped every time he moved.

"You have to look where you're going!" Heather scolded. "Don't look at the horse!"

The horse stopped.

"See? He doesn't know where to go, because you're looking at him! He'll go where you look! Maple, you know this! Look where you're going!"

When Commotion nibbled Maple's sleeve, she yelped and dropped the lead rope. Heather leapt in, caught the horse before the whole seven figures took off across the barn.

"Maple!" she scolded.

"I'm sorry," Maple said, distressed. "I thought he was gonna bite me."

"This horse doesn't bite," Heather said. "Only cheap horses bite. Come on," she directed. "At least stand next to me, so I can show you."

Heather was trying so hard not to be controlling, but it was frustrating. Especially because Maple had seemed to be making progress at the barn. She had turned her fall on the trail into a joke. She was getting bolder. She spent most of her lessons trotting now. But her horse's arrival had triggered a massive backslide.

Maple had stopped paying attention in lessons. She was jumpy. She always seemed on the verge of tears. Heather and Jeff had spent over a million dollars on a horse that seemed to terrorize their daughter.

Heather was petrified of Jeff finding out. Luckily, he was too busy to come to the barn. Heather didn't push.

Heather wished that Piper would come out to help. She had thought they were making progress there, too. She had thought that Piper wouldn't be able to resist, but Piper was, leaving an exasperated Heather and an insecure Maple alone with a confused horse.

After a couple of frustrating weeks, Heather confessed her concerns to her fellow barn moms, as if they hadn't noticed. They had just watched Douglas school Commotion, and they were now sitting ringside.

Heather said, "I'm not sure what to do with Maple. She seems a little scared of the horse."

"I know," June said. June was never one to make anyone feel better about anything.

But Pamela was. "That's totally normal," Pamela said.

Pamela was always assuring Heather that Maple was normal, but Heather never noticed the other riders struggling as much as Maple did.

"These things take time," Pamela said.

"I feel stupid," Heather confessed. "I bought this horse for *her*. What if she never rides him?"

"You can always sell him," June said.

Heather wondered if June realized she was constantly encouraging Heather to give up. Did she actually not want to be friends?

"It's a little early to think this way, but"—Pamela leaned forward, generous and confidential—"I know Vida just loves the horse. So if you're ever really stuck, maybe we could work out a lease? It might be a good tactic, too." Pamela settled back in her chair. "There's nothing a girl wants more than whatever her friend has."

Heather felt a strange prickle. She had asked Pamela for help. Pamela was probably a little right, but the horse was for Maple. She didn't want Vida riding him.

After all, there was nothing a mother wanted more than for her daughter to have the best and to be the best.

thirty

PIPER

Having Douglas's number was a little surreal. Piper would look at it sometimes, the shapes of the digits all in a row, and think about how he had typed them into her phone, as if he had designed them himself just for her.

She memorized the numbers. Years from now, on her deathbed probably, she would still know them by heart. It was a heady thought. Like she owned a part of him.

She thought about texting him every night. Debated. Maybe he wasn't serious! Maybe it wasn't his real number! Maybe he was setting her up! She never considered the good possibilities. That would have been vain.

After three days, she decided to wait a week.

After seven, she decided not to text.

The next day, she texted.

She wanted to see the horse but had been afraid to go to the barn in case she ran into Douglas. What if he asked her why she hadn't texted? What would she *say*?

She finally typed out a message, then hit SEND before she'd even had a chance to read it. It had a typo. She thought that was a good thing. It showed she didn't *really* care. The message said:

Were u serius?

He typed back right away, which made her panic, regret everything.

About what?

She sat up in her bed. Forced the breath from her lungs in one short pump.

That you would watch me ride?

She pressed SEND before she realized that her question sounded weird—was that even what he'd said? He'd said something about riding, something about turning on the lights at night. He hadn't used the word "watch." She felt humiliated.

Sure.

She hated that word. She had never hated it before, but now it seemed purposely obscure, possibly sarcastic. She exhaled again, more sharply.

When?

Now?

The question mark could have crushed her.

———

Piper had planned to walk to the barn alone, but Douglas met her on the horse trail.

"Is it bad for Commotion to go out this late?" she asked, feeling anxious.

"Naw, it keeps him on his toes," he said, falling into step beside her. He was wearing a cloth ranch jacket. He had his fists stuffed into the pockets. "Commotion doesn't sleep until after midnight usually."

"How often do you visit him at night?"

He shrugged. "You haven't been coming out." Had he been waiting for her?

She asked him mundane questions. He was from around there. He said he was almost twenty, like he couldn't admit to being nineteen. He had been working for Kieran since he was fourteen years old.

"What about your parents?"

"Ah, they're not really around."

When they got to the barn, Commotion was already groomed and booted. All of his tack was ready. Douglas adjusted the saddle and tightened the girth.

"Do you have a helmet?" he asked.

She shook her head.

"You should always wear a helmet, every time you're on a horse."

They broke into the tack room to borrow one. He checked it over before handing it to her.

"Sorry," she said. "I need to buy one."

"It's okay."

On the way back to the stall, they startled when they heard a branch break. Douglas seemed nervous, too.

"Are we okay to do this?" Piper asked.

"Nash knows we're here. Besides, it's your horse." His expression went a little dark.

Piper wasn't exactly sure why Douglas was helping her. It seemed unlikely that he had fallen in love with her after one small interaction. Helping her seemed a little rebellious.

He slipped the bridle onto the horse and handed her the reins. "Let's go."

She followed him out of the stall.

Douglas switched on the arena lights.

Piper swallowed her apprehension. She hadn't ridden in a while, but Douglas was experienced. He wouldn't let her ride Commotion if he thought the horse was dangerous.

He held Commotion at the mounting block while she climbed up the steps. He kept Commotion still as she slipped her foot into the stirrup and swung onto the horse's back.

"Nicely done," he said.

She passed by Douglas on her way to the arena. He shut the gate behind her, and then she was on the horse on her own. The floodlights seemed to hold the darkness at bay, contain her whole world in one golden circle as she rode along the rail.

The night was like something out of a movie—a secret midnight ride with a cute guy—but it felt more intense, less lighthearted. She shortened her reins.

Douglas climbed onto the fence. "Do whatever you want."

She walked in both directions, then tried circling. Douglas didn't say anything, but he was watching her—or at least watching the horse.

She asked the horse to trot. It took her a few beats to adjust to his long, athletic stride. Commotion was different from the horses she'd ridden before, more intimidating. She turned a circle, and he bent so smoothly, dropped his head and lifted up through his back. She felt like she was floating, riding a cloud.

"Wow," she said. "This is a good horse."

"He's a very good horse," Douglas agreed.

Piper let the ride flow. She trotted, did circles and figure eights and serpentines. Then she transitioned to a walk and prepared to canter. Cantering had always been her favorite. She loved the smooth, rocking feeling.

Douglas sat up a little, as if sensing her anticipation.

She picked up a canter. It was like nothing she remembered. It was like the horse was made for her, like the moment was made for her. She swung through the dark, and the whole world fell away. She smiled.

Anyone who didn't believe in magic had never ridden a horse.

thirty-one

MAPLE

Maple did not want to be afraid of her horse. Every night in bed she promised herself that tomorrow she would not be scared. But every day when she arrived at the barn, her body expanded into a cavern of nerves—dancing, playing, ricocheting through her.

She couldn't eat. She couldn't sleep. Sometimes she couldn't catch her breath, would feel it pounding, explosive, through her hollowed-out chest.

She wanted to cry. She wanted to hide. Most of all, she wanted to be someone else. Someone better. Someone braver. She just didn't know how to be that person.

She did know who that person was: Vida.

Vida was fearless. She had a severe coolness. Maple had once seen Vida fall when her horse refused a jump. The horse had spun and Vida had flipped over its side, then hit a wooden pole.

Thwack!

Vida had untangled her limbs. She had calmly stood up and dusted off her breeches. Her liberated horse had sprinted round and round the arena until Douglas finally caught it.

Vida had just walked right to Douglas, taken the horse back and led it to the fence, where she got back on—swiftly, abruptly—and picked up a canter and aimed her horse at that same jump.

Maple just *stared* at Vida sometimes, trying to discover the source of her power, only to conclude that Vida had an emptiness, a bottomless implacability, as if hers was a coldness on which the world could rely.

Maple had crowded herself into Vida's and Effie's company. More and more, she felt the strain of friendship and belonging. They would spend all day at the barn, always together. They would argue over whose turn it was to pick where they had lunch, organize sleepovers and watch shows of escalating terror—*Stranger Things* and *Breaking Bad* and *Euphoria*.

Maple felt stronger, crueler, braver with her friends. But she felt weaker around her mom, like she had used up all her nerve.

Her relationship with her mother started to feel strained, shrill. When Maple was around Heather, her voice whined. Her posture sank. Her heart felt thick and tight.

She wanted deeply to be the daughter her mother wanted. To be strong and brave and vaguely soulless—*untouchable*—but the more she couldn't, the weaker she became.

If she could just ride the horse, everything would be okay. If she could just ride the horse, she could be saved. It was like the horse had become proof of her worthiness.

The harder her mother wished, the more Maple crumbled.

Finally, it was Pamela who pulled the trigger. She put Faustus up for sale. If Maple didn't ride her horse, she wouldn't have a horse to ride.

Desperate, she turned to Vida. They were all hanging out in Vida's bedroom, talking about all the different shapes of penises they'd seen. Well, Vida and Effie were—Maple had never seen a penis in real life. She sort of doubted Vida and Effie had either.

Maple interrupted to say, "I don't know how I'm gonna ride Commotion. I'm, like, in my head about it."

"Why are you so scared?" Vida said, cross-legged on her red-and-white bedspread like the queen bee in a high school movie.

"I'm not *scared*," Maple said. "It's a mental block."

"You should go to therapy," Effie said.

Maple did not tell them that she already went to therapy. Her mom had scheduled her sessions for Mondays, because no one was at the barn then. The previous week, her therapist had drawn a circle and made Maple list all her fears. She'd had to draw a bigger circle.

"What do you think is gonna happen?" Vida asked.

Maple flinched. She felt that girl in Texas yanking her hair. Felt her body hit the ground. Tasted dust. "I don't know. . . . That I'll fall, maybe?"

"Everyone falls," Vida said. "It's, like, six feet. On soft ground."

It wasn't just the falling that scared Maple. Once she got on her horse, she would prove to everyone that she didn't deserve him. He was a great horse, and she was a bad rider. As long as she stayed off him, she could pretend that one day she would climb on Commotion's back, and the pair of them would fly off like a girl and her Pegasus.

"I just feel awkward. I don't know. I'm not ready."

"You'll probably just walk for a month like you did with Faustus," Effie pointed out. "Amy's not gonna make you jump or anything."

"Yeah, but I can't control how I feel."

"Take a Xanax." Vida looked up from her phone. "Oh my God, do you want a Xanax?"

"You have Xanax?" Maple asked.

Maple was already on medication for anxiety, but it didn't seem to do much. It certainly didn't make her brave enough to ride her horse.

"My mom does." Vida stretched her legs, suddenly energized.

"Do you want one? Let's go to the drugstore." She swung her legs over the bed.

"Vida's mom used to be a drug addict," Effie explained as they left Vida's room.

Currently, Pamela was in the hot tub drinking a margarita. As the girls walked along the hall, Maple could see the top of Pamela's wide hat through the window.

Pamela's bedroom was huge and littered with junk—makeup and handbags and beauty products.

"My mom is such a hoarder," Vida said, making a beeline for the bathroom.

She opened the medicine cabinet and removed a bottle of Xanax, which she threw at Maple. To her own surprise, Maple caught it.

"Take as many as you want," Vida said.

Maple took one, which she thought was the smallest amount she could take without getting called out. She didn't actually want to be a drug addict. She set the bottle on the counter.

"Won't your mom notice?" Maple asked.

"Doubt it. She doesn't do drugs. She just has them." Vida started rifling through drawers. She dug past floss and Crest Whitestrips and a pink Taser. "It's like an ex-junkie thing. She has to have them around, or she gets anxiety. If she finds out, I'll just tell her you stole it." Vida found a bag of gummies, then poured out three heart-shaped candies. "Come on, let's microdose."

Maple had no idea what Vida was offering her, but it looked like candy, and these were her friends, and they were older and cooler.

The girls locked eyes with one another as they put the gummies into their mouths. Maple felt a thrilling flip-flop in her stomach.

"I wish we could smoke a cigarette," Vida said, stuffing the gummy bag back and banging the drawer shut. "Let's go watch a cartoon."

Maple didn't feel anything at first; then she felt everything at once. She started panicking. She kept asking Vida if she thought Pamela might call the cops, if they might get caught, if she could ever go home.

Finally, Vida convinced Maple to take the Xanax, and she felt herself spiral down. They were watching *Finding Nemo*, and she thought, *I wonder if my mom would look for me if I was lost.*

thirty-two

HEATHER

Heather was at the end of her rope with Maple and the horse. She was getting desperate. She had gotten it into her head that it might help to talk to Kieran about the situation. He was supposed to be the horse expert. Plus, she was a little annoyed with him. She felt like he had been ignoring them since they purchased the horse, as if his work was done. Or worse, as if they weren't worthy of his attention.

Pamela advised her not to. "This really isn't Kieran's forte. Talk to Amy. She's Maple's trainer."

But Amy wasn't even letting Maple canter. She had just started to let the girl off the lunge line when Maple's backsliding triggered a return to the round pen.

Amy wasn't pushing her, and Maple was barely and rarely improving. It was time, Heather thought, for a stronger hand.

It happened with horses sometimes. They needed to be pushed. Heather remembered that at her old barn, whenever the lesson horses acted up with one of the students, trainers would jump on them and force them to behave.

Heather was trying to be less controlling, but the truth was

sometimes you had to *make* someone do a thing. Maple would realize it wasn't all that scary. Heather knew her daughter. If Maple
wasn't pushed, she would *never* ride the horse, and all of Heather's
efforts would have been for nothing.

Heather went to Kieran's office when Pamela wasn't looking.
She knocked on the door, and he snapped, "Who the fuck is that?"

Heather walked in, drawn toward conflict as usual.

"Oh." He seemed to back off. "What do you want?"

His office was dusty and dark. The yellowing blinds were drawn.
A fat gray computer sat in one corner. Piles of sloppy paperwork and
crushed horse show ribbons were littered across the cabinets.

Kieran sat behind a large desk, filling out paperwork.

Heather was a little shocked by how grimy his office was. "I
wanted to get your thoughts on something," she said.

Kieran grunted but seemed open to the exchange. Pamela had
been wrong.

"Sit down." He directed Heather to a black office chair that
creaked when she perched on it. He raised his eyebrows. "What's
the issue?"

"It's just . . . my daughter. I think she's a little scared of the
horse."

"She's not scared of the horse." He turned to his desk, went back
to filling out forms.

"I'm sorry?"

Heather was annoyed. Obviously, he hadn't been paying attention. Maple was terrified of the horse.

"She's not scared of the horse. She's scared of you."

"I don't think—"

"You just dropped seven figures on a horse for her. You're here
watching her all the time, commenting every time she does something wrong. Do you know the kind of pressure that is for a kid?
She's scared of *you*."

Heather shouldn't have been surprised by that accusation. It was basically the same thing Piper had told her back in Amarillo: Heather was too invested, too wrapped up in her daughter's life.

"I don't . . . well . . ." Heather scanned the room. "What should I do?"

"Stop wanting it so bad." He scooped up the paperwork and swiveled his chair, then started making copies on an ancient machine. "You know, people think we make horses do things. They think we force them to let people ride them, to jump over fences. But the truth is you can't *make* a horse do anything."

He finished his copies, then spun back to face her. "I had this horse once. It was my dream horse. I sank everything into it. I was gonna win on this horse, you know? I was gonna go all the way. We were nearly there. I was so happy. We were partners in every sense of the word.

"Then one day, I took him out on a course, and he refused one jump. I could force him over, but it was a fight. I thought, *Okay, bad day*, right? Next day, same jump. And the day after. And the day after. Every day, it was a battle to get him over that *one* jump, until it wasn't just that one jump. It was this other jump, too. And that one. And then he didn't want to go into the arena. He would plant his feet and fight me for hours.

"I had him vetted, six different vets. It wasn't physical. It was mental. He didn't want to do it anymore. I fought that horse every damn day. I didn't want to give up. *This is a good horse*, I said. *This is the best horse I ever had.*"

He stood up, preparing to leave.

"You coming?" he said at the door.

Heather was mystified. "What happened to the horse?"

"Ahh. He's in a field somewhere, being an asshole."

Heather wasn't sure what was happening, but Kieran seemed to want her to follow him, so she did. They went to the head groom.

Kieran had a private word with him. Then he went to Amy, said her lesson with Maple was canceled.

"Why?" She glanced at Heather, seemingly afraid she'd done something wrong.

"Because I'm teaching her," Kieran replied.

Heather felt her heart spread. This was a good thing. This was what she wanted. So why did she feel scared?

They found Maple in the cleaning bay, working on a bridle. Vida and Effie were with her. They all jumped to attention when Kieran approached.

He walked up to Maple. He looked her in the eye. "You ready to ride your horse?"

She opened her mouth and said nothing. Her eyes, tinged with mutiny, drifted to her mom.

"Don't look at her. Look at me."

She did. "Okay." Her response wasn't exactly rousing.

Kieran told Heather to sit on the far side of the patio. He told her she could watch, but: "You cannot talk. Not a word. Or it's over. Do you understand?"

Heather nodded and did as he had directed. Pamela grabbed a seat beside her. June grabbed another. At first, Heather wasn't sure if she was even allowed to talk to them.

"I heard Maple is having a lesson with Kieran?" Pamela said. Heather nodded. Word had gotten around fast. A small crowd was forming. Heather wished the other boarders wouldn't watch. She felt somehow that she was the one on display. Even Douglas was there, straddling the fence.

Maple mounted the horse and walked into the arena. Kieran closed the gate behind her. There were two other horses already in the ring. Heather wondered if they were trapped now.

Commotion took five steps into the arena, then came to a stop. Heather thought she could see Maple shaking, even at that distance. She could feel her daughter's panic inside herself, feel her pain, but her empathy didn't help Maple, she realized. It didn't make her daughter feel less.

Heather took a deep breath.

Everything is going to be okay, she told herself. *Just let go.*

"Walk," Kieran instructed.

Maple played with her reins.

"Why aren't you walking?"

"I'm . . ." And then Maple drifted off. Said nothing. There were tears in her eyes.

Heather looked around her, embarrassed. That was her kid.

"You're not scared of riding a horse." Kieran climbed onto the fence and sat down. "You're scared of people watching you ride a horse. But do you know what none of these assholes will tell you? They're scared, too. All the time. Everyone's scared. Not of horses. We love our horses.

"We're scared that we're shit at riding them. Shit at taking care of them. Monsters for using them. We love our horses, but we're scared they don't love us back. Just walk."

Maple started walking.

"What every horse person is looking for— Maple, are you listening?"

Her eyes had drifted over the crowd. They snapped back at his word.

"What every horse person is looking for is proof that their horse loves them. If he picks up a trot when I ask, he loves me. If he stops when I say stop, he loves me. If he jumps when I say jump, he loves me. Now pick up a trot."

Maple did. The horse trotted serenely beneath her. She rose up and down with the motion.

Heather felt a gush of relief, sending fireflies through her skin. Maple was doing it. She was riding her horse.

"Faster," Kieran said.

Maple trotted faster, all the way around the arena.

"Change direction."

Maple trotted twice around the arena in the other direction.

"Now walk."

She walked.

"Pick up a canter."

Heather felt her breath dive inside her. Maple hadn't been allowed to canter once since she'd started riding at RSFE. She'd been doing so good, but this would be too far. Now was the moment it would all fall apart.

Maple collected the horse. She turned his head to the inside. She put her outside leg back. The horse picked up a canter. Maple flew past Heather, looking like Queen Boadicea.

Kieran made her canter in the other direction. The horse was perfect. The audience was rapt. He let her walk.

"Now tell me: Does your horse love you?"

interview 3

DETECTIVE PEREZ

The detectives interviewed Elodie Thomas, the groom who had found the body. She was pale and nervous—couldn't have been much more than eighteen. Her leg was jiggling. She stood slightly every time horses passed, as if drawn to them.

"When you found the body, you called Kieran Flynn. Is that correct?"

"Yes."

Elodie had her hands clasped between her knees. Next door, the horse shifted in its stall.

"Not the police."

Detective Perez hated when people didn't call the police first, but so many people didn't. She never ceased to be amazed by the stupid things people did in emergencies. The way they acted, like animals but with less sense.

"It was in the stall with the horse. I wanted to make sure the horse was okay. Kieran said he would call the police."

Take that girl. Her first thought, when she had found a body slumped in a horse stall, was to call her boss. Like she was more worried about trouble from him than a death.

"And then they moved the body?"

"Yes. Like I said, it was in the horse's stall."

"Why didn't they just move the horse?"

That question gave Elodie pause. She cocked her head. "I suppose it could have upset the horse. Some of them get very stressed at these events. It can have terrible consequences. In 2022, a horse went neurological at a show and caused an outbreak that shut down the whole circuit in California. The horses get stressed and then—"

"All right. You were worried about the horse."

Elodie nodded.

"Who moved the body?"

"Kieran. And Dominic. He's the head show groom."

"Was the needle in the stall?"

"Yes. Kieran bagged it."

Detective Perez had been annoyed by both those moves. Kieran seemed to think that he had done the police a favor, that he had assisted them, when he must have been told by the 911 operator not to touch anything.

Kieran and the others should have left the body and the needle where they had found them. They should have moved the horse. But they seemed to have a reason for everything, and the reason came down to this: They were protecting the horse. Never mind the body. Horse people were crazy.

"And you found the body slumped against the wall?"

"Yes. Sometimes people sit with the horses, to help them relax. At first, I didn't realize anything was wrong."

"And you haven't told anyone?"

"No. Kieran said we should wait until you gave us the all clear. In case there was foul play."

That Kieran should have been a cop. He seemed to have everything covered.

The detectives hadn't spoken to Kieran yet, but his name had come up in every interview—so frequently, in fact, that Detective Perez was beginning to feel that she knew him. His name had almost always been followed by "said."

Kieran said it was suicide.

Kieran said not to worry.

Kieran said not to say anything.

Kieran said everything would be fine.

"Do you think there was foul play?" Perez asked.

"No. Of course not, but . . ." Elodie drifted off into the dead end of her suspicions.

"But?" Detective Perez coaxed.

"It just doesn't feel . . ." She pressed her toe into the stall mat. "I guess it's hard to believe? But maybe death is hard to believe? But, like . . . why would you do it like this? Late at night. In a horse's stall. And why Ace?"

Acepromazine was a mild horse tranquilizer. Detective Perez had learned it was kept on hand during horse shows, but Elodie was right. If suicide had been the victim's intent, there would have been much more effective drugs.

"It doesn't make sense. But maybe suicide doesn't make sense?" Elodie was asking the questions now, and they were very hard questions to answer.

Suicide was hard—maybe impossible—to understand. But then, so was murder.

THREE
MONTHS
BEFORE

thirty-three

PIPER

Piper had been cautious about texting Douglas after that first ride. She didn't want to seem too eager, be too demanding. When she finally did text him, he said he couldn't meet her that night and she felt humiliated, like she had created the night herself.

But after Maple had ridden Commotion, Piper felt itchy with longing. She wanted to ride. She wanted to ride that horse. Yes, it was Maple's horse, but Maple didn't *really* like horses. Except lately she seemed to.

Maple seemed different so fast it made Piper's head spin. It reminded her of the time that her former best friend had gone to summer camp. Her friend was gone for two weeks, and she came back with a heart full of secrets and a wildly different personality. She and Piper fought. They even stopped being friends for a while, until Piper gave up and reshaped herself so they fit together again. They lasted another couple of years before finally going their separate friendship ways.

Maple seemed more mature, more present, more assured. She walked with better posture. She spoke with more authority. She had deeper thoughts.

Piper missed her sister, the one she had known. She didn't want to hold Maple back, but she also felt like she was losing something important.

The day Maple had ridden Commotion, Douglas texted Piper. When are you coming out?

Piper texted back right away. Now?

Piper took a shower, which was pointless. She was only going to get dirty at the barn. But she hadn't washed her hair, and it was greasy; it had been for days. She didn't want Douglas to see her like that.

She met him at the gate to her family's property. They walked on the unlit horse trail. It was too dark to see his face.

"No riding tonight," he said when they had arrived at RSFE. "I think Commotion needs a break. I rode him. Maple rode him."

Piper felt an odd flicker. Why was she there if she wasn't going to ride? But it was too late to go back now.

She followed Douglas to Commotion's stall. They sat on tack boxes on either side of the door.

Douglas looked exhausted, Piper thought. He rested against the wall, as if casually, but his body was limp. His eyes were hooded.

Commotion stuck his head over the door to greet Piper. When the horse pulled away, Douglas's eyes were closed. She didn't want to disturb him, so she stood carefully and let herself into the stall. She massaged the horse's favorite spots, played games with him. Eventually Douglas woke up.

"Sorry," he said. He started to let himself into the stall but then stopped, leaned against the door.

"You seem tired," she said.

"Sorry," he said again.

"No offense, but I'm not sure why you wanted me to come out. You should just go home and sleep."

He frowned as if puzzling out her suggestion. "I wanted to talk to you. About riding."

She cocked her head, leaned against Commotion's shoulder. "Are you trying to convert me? Is this the hard sell?"

The accusation woke him up a little. "No, it's something you said. It got me thinking. About your mom."

That was an unexpected direction. "What about my mom?"

"About how she pressures you to ride and everything," he said. "The thing is, you know, I understand. My mom was like that." He seemed to struggle to speak for a moment, as if the topic made his tongue thick. "If it wasn't for her, I would never have ridden horses. I mean, what little boy wants to ride a horse, right?"

"Sure," she encouraged him, wondering where his mom was now. She could tell by his manner that it wasn't somewhere great.

"But she used to push me. Our whole life was designed around horses. We were at the barn all day, every day. We were gonna go live in Europe and train there—that was the dream. She used to say, you know, *Horses are in your blood. One day you'll understand.*"

"Did you?"

"When she was gone." He swallowed hard, looking at Piper like he had entrusted her with something, his reason for something. Like he was afraid of what she might do with it.

"I'm sorry," she said, not sure what she was sorry for.

"It's not your fault," he said. He moved closer to the door, as if needing her to understand. "I just wanted to tell you because . . . I guess because I wish I had understood back then. Before it was too late."

Piper found her mother alone in her room. The room Heather had to herself.

"You're still awake?" her mother said, putting down her phone.

Heather had found a decorator, and now her life was a barrage of emails, of hunting for the exact right furniture, for the perfect lights to create the perfect shadows.

"Yeah, I was just . . ." Piper wished she could tell Heather about Douglas. Piper wished she and Heather had a relationship like that.

It was Piper herself who had built the wall between them, with no thought to how she could disassemble it. Or if she even could.

"I was thinking, maybe . . ." Piper drifted off, as if afraid of making her mother too happy. "Maybe I could come to the barn tomorrow?"

Heather's lips rose into a smile so fast and so full it was like Piper had given her everything. It was like she'd given herself to Heather.

"That would be wonderful, darling. I know you'll love it. We're all just one big happy family there."

"But you have to—" Piper stopped, struggling to put her feelings into words.

Piper was so good at everything. She got good grades and did well in sports; she was pretty well liked by everyone. But she always seemed to fail when it came to her mother. Why was that? Why did everything with Heather feel so hard?

"I need you to give me space, you know?" She used Douglas's words. "I want to make my own choices. Have my own life."

"Of course," Heather said so fast that Piper doubted her sincerity. "I've been learning. I understand. I do. I had to back off with Maple, too. I was putting too much pressure on her, like I did with you, but I'm trying. I'm trying not to be too involved."

Heather was saying all the right things, and maybe she was learning; maybe she could change.

"Okay." Piper started toward the door, then hovered uncertainly. "Mom?" She turned to face Heather. "I love you."

"I love you, too."

Maybe it would take time, or maybe it would crash down all at once, but right then Piper believed there wouldn't always be a wall.

thirty-four

PAMELA

P amela made sure to go to Kieran's house when she knew he would be there, and after Vida was asleep. Pamela knew better than to call Kieran on the phone; he would just hang up.

Kieran's property was different at night, as if it had only ever been intended to appear after dark. In the day, it was bleached by the sun, revealing all the cracks and imperfections.

At night, it might have been a place where treaties were signed— a place where knights crossed swords or enemies attacked. The fountains hummed with the history of all the things that had never happened there, but could have.

Pamela stood under the eaves, rubbed the beaded bracelet that Vida had made her, and knocked on the door.

She could hear the scuffing of sneakers from a basketball game on the big-screen TV. It masked the sound of Kieran's approach, so she kept knocking and ringing the bell right up to the point when he finally answered.

"Are you kidding me?" he said, catching her hand, which was halfway to the buzzer.

"I didn't hear you."

"I heard you." He didn't immediately step back to allow her in.

"I need to talk to you."

"It's after midnight."

"You're awake."

"Someone rang my doorbell ten or fifteen times." He finally stepped back and let her into the house.

The basketball game was an old one. Everything Kieran liked was old—the old way of doing things. His preference was sometimes charming, sometimes suspicious.

He muted the game and sat on a chair. He did not offer her a drink. "Can you make it quick? Some people sleep at night."

"I just wanted to ask you about—" She stopped when the front door opened and Douglas came in. She could see him through the arches in the hall. "You're out late."

Douglas said nothing but hovered under one of the archways, possibly to listen in.

Pamela turned back to Kieran. He was massaging his temples with his knuckles.

"I'm confused," Pamela said, "about the motivational speech we all witnessed today."

Kieran hated being questioned on his methods, but Pamela didn't like the way things were going. She thought the idea had been to get the Parkers to buy a champion horse, and then to let them drift away.

The old leather creaked as Kieran sat back in his chair. "There are three things that people want in this life: God, family and romantic love. At my barn, we provide all three."

Pamela glanced at Douglas. She could tell he was thinking the same thing she was—was Kieran providing those three things to them? And perhaps he didn't like the answer either.

"I don't understand how you got the horse to behave like that," Pamela said.

The horse had been perfect. It wasn't that Commotion was a bad horse, but he was an advanced horse, and Maple was not an advanced rider.

"He Aced him," Douglas volunteered to Kieran's annoyance.

Acepromazine was mostly used for injured horses, especially for bringing them back to work slowly, but Pamela had heard of people using it for silly reasons. Even Pamela had once Aced a show horse so Vida could ride it in a Halloween parade.

"I issued a small sedative, as a precautionary measure." Kieran pointed his beer at Douglas. "You look tired."

"I'm learning," Douglas said back.

Just lately Pamela had noticed that Douglas was developing an attitude. She kind of liked it. He used to worship Kieran. They all had when they'd first met him.

"So, what?" Pamela asked. "You're just going to drug the horse every time the girl rides?"

"Do you really need a play-by-play?"

"I'm just a little confused about what I'm getting out of this."

If anything, the Parkers' presence seemed to have moved Kieran further away from Pamela, as if she herself had cleared the path for her own exit. She didn't have the money to compete.

"I'm the one doing all the heavy lifting," Pamela said. "Vida and I. You barely interact with the Parkers."

Kieran sat forward, square with Douglas. "What do you think about all that?" When Douglas said nothing, Kieran added, "Tell her where you were tonight."

Douglas looked unsure, his eyes moving from Kieran to Pamela. "At the barn . . . with Piper."

"Piper, Heather's daughter?" Pamela was confused.

"She showed up the other night," Kieran explained. "Nash saw her. She's been visiting the horse. How did it go?"

Douglas slouched. Pamela felt a little bad for him. Douglas wasn't a duplicitous person—at least he hadn't been—but there was certainly an air of moral erosion that she recognized in him. Her own erosion was far more apparent, when she looked in the mirror.

"She's coming out tomorrow morning," Douglas said.

Pamela was not at all pleased with this new development. It would mean twice the money from the Parkers, and twice the competition for Kieran's attention.

"Why do you want Piper joining the team? Isn't it hard enough teaching her sister?"

Kieran exhaled, as if he were the most overburdened man in the world. "We're a family. All of us are family. What benefits one benefits all."

"But mostly you," Pamela noted.

"You want the horse for Vida, but that was never part of the arrangement," Kieran said, always knowing exactly what Pamela was thinking without her having to say it.

Pamela stammered. "She . . . she likes Commotion quite a lot. I— Heather and I were talking about a partial lease."

Kieran laughed. "You fucking treacherous bitch."

"I don't see why—"

"Because I didn't say so. That's fucking why." When Douglas started toward his bedroom, Kieran's voice rose. "No. You don't leave now."

Douglas stopped in his tracks. When Kieran looked back at Pamela, she could see the rage throbbing in his temples.

"The way this barn works is, I am God, I am the father and I am the one who fucks. My name is on the door, and you can walk out right now if you want to. I promise I will not miss you."

Pamela said nothing. She felt a kind of cool elation. She had always liked rattling cages, and rattling Kieran's still had a peculiar kind of bewitchment.

Of all emotions, someone's anger was the one you could feel the most. More than love. More than sadness. Angry people always felt particularly moving, particularly compelling to Pamela.

"Now." Kieran's chair groaned as he sat back. "As I was saying . . . uh . . ." He drifted off, seeming unmoored by his own ferocity. "The Parkers. In addition to having nearly a billion dollars, they also have *two* daughters."

He picked up his phone, tapped and swiped, then held it up to Pamela.

"What is that?" she asked, drawing closer.

Douglas did, too.

"It's in Stockholm. Out of— What was that horse I liked that won the Grand Slam?"

"Magic Maker," Douglas said, his voice slightly reverent, the way it got around good horses.

"That's the one," Kieran said.

Pamela observed the horse, a blood bay mare priced at a reasonable three million dollars.

"Or we could do your plan. Push them out now, and let Vida ride a partial lease for six months until they decide to sell it out from under her." Kieran snatched the phone away.

"I would make them sign a contract," Pamela said, but she knew her words sounded flimsy. She knew she was wrong.

"For ten years?" Kieran shifted in his chair, exploded into a sigh. "God, I hate being questioned on things. God, I hate it." He rubbed the wrinkles from his forehead. "I am an artist. I'm making music here. I'm making these people *sing*. And you come in and ask me to explain myself? Just sit back and enjoy the fucking music."

thirty-five

MAPLE

Initially, Maple was excited for Piper to go to the barn. She even texted Vida and Effie to say, My sister is coming today!

The next morning, Heather and Piper and Maple all went to Mary's as soon as it opened.

That was when Maple's excitement started to dip. Piper, although caving on the horse issue, was still Piper. And as far as their mother was concerned, everything had to be a battle.

"I'll just get the cheapest ones," Piper insisted, grabbing a pair of ratty breeches. "There's no point wasting a bunch of money on me."

"The nice ones last longer," Heather said.

"That's just what they tell you."

Piper looked at Maple; she seemed to want her sister to take her side. In the past, Maple would have, but Piper was being kind of annoying. She reminded Maple of June, who everyone secretly made fun of.

Plus, it seemed to Maple that Piper just wanted attention. Lately, Maple had taken to considering what Vida would think in any given situation, even when she wasn't around. Vida would have thought that Piper was being a drag.

The Parkers had a shop assistant who was supposed to help them. Piper was making the assistant's job harder.

After nearly an hour of back-and-forth on every item—breeches, shirts, boots, gloves—Maple finally said, "Piper, just get the damn gloves. You're being so immature."

Piper looked like she'd been slapped. It was a particularly pointed insult because Maple was known as the immature one.

Heather, who was being defended, was speechless.

Piper finally said, "I just don't think I need the most expensive thing in the store for the sake of its being expensive."

Maple clapped back, saying, "Well, all of us would like to leave the store at some point, so maybe you could stop arguing about every little thing." Maple was so heated that she added, "I'm gonna wait outside."

Maple stood next to the wheelbarrows and water troughs as the sun rose in the sky. She had a sinking feeling that Vida was not going to like Piper going to the barn.

thirty-six

VIDA

Vida did not like Piper coming to the barn. Piper had a smoky voice and preternatural confidence. She was less than a year older than Vida, but she seemed *much* older. She acted like a front desk receptionist at a dental office—boring and yet somehow unjustifiably smug.

Piper got involved immediately, practically became a volunteer groom. She cleaned bridles faster than Maple. She helped tack and untack horses, which none of the other girls were allowed to do. She was constantly telling people where things were—like she had invented the entire barn system. Even Douglas would watch her ping from one task to the next with staggering efficiency.

"Your sister's really smart," Vida pointed out to Maple. She didn't mean it as a compliment.

They watched as Piper disassembled a running martingale while walking one of the owners through all the treatment options for osteochondritis dissecans.

"Yeah," said Maple, who went slightly limp whenever her sister was nearby.

Kieran had said that Piper would need to get her own horse, but she seemed more interested in Commotion. When she wasn't managing the entire barn, she was bonding with Maple's horse.

Piper took Commotion for walks, did ground work with him and taught him tricks. She would explain her methodology in excruciating detail to anyone who would listen.

Worst of all, Kieran seemed to love Piper. Of course he did. She was working for him for free—better yet, she was paying him to work.

Vida did not intend to include Piper in her friend group. She was looking forward to icing her out, but she never got a chance. Even on that first day, Piper turned down Maple's lunch invitation.

"I said I would lunge Storm for Moira," she told Maple.

At that point, Piper had been at the barn for three hours. Owners already trusted her with their horses. The owners still didn't trust Vida, which sometimes made her worry about her future. How was she supposed to ride their horses when they didn't trust her?

They claimed she was too intense.

"I don't know what it is about her. . . ."

But in Vida's dreams, the world was imbued with an unnatural fairness, and her skill as a rider was more important than her likability. She would win the Little Palm Cup at the end of the summer, and then she wouldn't have to apologize for being herself. Winners were allowed, even encouraged, to be unlikable.

Maple asked Piper out to lunch again the next day, and the day after that. When she refused a fourth time, Vida couldn't take it anymore. She insisted to Maple, "Don't invite her again."

One afternoon, they were hanging around Vida's bedroom in their damp bathing suits when Vida asked Maple, "When is Piper gonna get her own horse?"

When they'd left the barn, Piper had been teaching Commotion to bow. She was *so* annoying. Commotion was a show-jumping horse, not a circus nag.

Maple bristled. She had been making small steps with Commotion, but Piper was already far ahead of her. Vida could tell it drove Maple crazy. It would have driven Vida crazy, too.

"I don't know," Maple said. "She keeps telling my mom that she doesn't want one because of college. Like she won't have time or something."

"But she's . . ." Vida considered tactfulness, but it wasn't her strong suit. "I mean, she basically stole your horse."

Maple's shoulders tensed. "I know," she said darkly.

"You should make her fall off or something. Remember that time I made you fall off?" Vida said to Effie, who looked up from her phone. Vida explained to Maple, "She was doing around the world, and when she was backward on Gunther, I waved a crop in his face. He took off bucking."

Maple raised herself up with her elbows. She looked nervous, as if talking about something bad could make bad happen. "Why would you do that?"

Vida shrugged. "I was just being random," she said, but even she knew that was a generous way of putting it.

"It was kind of mean," Effie pointed out.

"I didn't *know* you would fall," Vida said. "It just happened."

Effie made a face but seemed to accept that explanation.

"I don't want to make Piper fall off Commotion," Maple said.

Maple seemed scared, as if Vida might do it without her permission. Vida felt hurt, as she always did when people believed the bad things she told them about herself.

"You should tell your mom it's not fair," Vida said. "You don't want to share your horse with Piper."

"I . . . ," Maple started, but she drifted off. "It's just hard because she's my sister."

"She's taking advantage of you because she's the old one and the smart one and the good rider."

Vida watched every one of those points hit. She felt a little bad, but she was just being honest. Maple already knew all these things. She knew they were true. That was why they hurt.

"It really is unfair," Effie agreed. "Piper should actually know better."

Maple wrapped her arms around her middle, as if feeling exposed.

"True," Vida said. "She's the one who's being a bitch. Everyone knows not to take their sister's stuff. Especially not their sister's horse."

thirty-seven

PIPER

Piper loved the way Commotion's breath blasted from his oversized nostrils, how big his heart was, how his lower lip quivered when she rubbed *that* spot on his crest, how he bowed his head to let her rub his poll. His enormous eyes always seemed worried, as if he needed her, as if he wanted her to stand close and protect him. As if they were friends. As if they were partners.

He was beautiful and smart and powerful. He learned things quickly. She had taught him to shake hands and follow her like a dog.

One afternoon, she was in the round pen with him when Douglas appeared. The horse stretched to greet him.

"He's such a good horse, right?" she said.

Piper had been struggling to manage Douglas in the daylight hours. She didn't know what it was, but some boys made girls feel responsible for their emotions. Douglas was one such boy. So even though Piper knew she was being illogical and self-obsessed, she often worried that Douglas's mood was the consequence of her actions. Like she had been assigned to keep him happy.

"He's a great horse," Douglas said.

His mood seemed to lighten when he was around Commotion. "I love him," she said.

Douglas rubbed the horse's crest, observing Piper thoughtfully. "You know, you don't have to do everything the grooms ask you to do. They actually get paid to do the work they have you doing."

"I heard you don't get paid at all," Piper pointed out.

"I mean, I get housing and stuff. But I like working."

"So do I." She slid the halter onto the horse.

Douglas fell into step beside her as she led Commotion toward the A barn. "So, when are you gonna get your own horse?"

"I don't think I need one. I'm starting college in the fall and . . . I mean, it's kind of working now."

It wasn't really working. Douglas rode the horse three days a week. Piper and Maple split the other three days. Maple rode first, and Piper rode second. Piper could tell that Maple wasn't happy with this arrangement.

The truth was college wasn't the issue. If Piper didn't have time to ride once her classes started, Kieran had plenty of people who could ride the horse for her. She could ride on weekends. Or holidays. Or not at all.

But Piper didn't want another horse. She liked Commotion, and she thought he was too advanced for Maple. What she wanted, really, was for her sister to get a more suitable horse, but she didn't know how to convey that without hurting her sister's feelings. She hoped Maple would eventually figure it out on her own.

"Do you really think this is the right horse for Maple?" she asked Douglas.

"You want this horse." Even he seemed a little surprised, like he could taste her betrayal.

"I don't know. I just feel like we're a better fit."

"What does your sister think?"

Piper felt awful. "You think I'm a bad sister."

"I think there are a lot of nice horses out there—"

"But this horse is special," Piper said.

"But he's not yours."

His Adam's apple throbbed. He seemed tense, as if he were defending himself, too. She suspected *he* wanted the horse, but he was a lot further from getting him than she was.

"I just think Maple might be happier on another horse, that's all," she said. "And I think you know that."

"I think a lot of people would be happier on other horses, but people buy the horses they can afford, not the horses they deserve. I mean . . ." He drifted off, realizing he probably shouldn't have said that to her, but it was too late.

"You're probably right," she said. His eyes flew to her. "But this horse belongs to my family and I'm a better rider than Maple. And if he were my horse, I'd let you ride him whenever you wanted. Not just when you were supposed to."

He lit up immediately, and she felt herself light up with him, as if they were both tied to his path. She led the horse into the barn, and Douglas followed her, resting his hand on the horse's side.

thirty-eight

HEATHER

After Maple's lesson with Kieran, Heather was so proud. She was in awe of Kieran. He had knocked something loose in the girl and the horse. He had saved them with a snap of his fingers, like it was easy.

Then, the next day, Piper had announced she wanted to go to the barn.

Magic had happened, and everyone wanted to be near it. It was like the Parkers' money. One day their luck had turned, and it was like Jeff couldn't stop making it.

Everyone at the barn loved Piper.

"She's so smart."

"She's so helpful."

"You're so lucky to have a daughter like that."

One evening, when Heather was walking down the barn aisle, she spotted Piper and Maple cleaning in the bridle bay, and she thought, *This is exactly what I wanted. This is what happiness feels like.*

Heather had always believed that no one was ever really happy, that the concept of happiness was just something concocted in a lab to make people perpetually dissatisfied, probably to make them work harder, because they'd always believe they were missing out.

But lately, when Heather looked around her, she thought maybe she had been wrong about happiness. The more time she spent at the barn, the more she thought that happiness was just seeing everything that you wanted and nothing that you didn't.

Within the boundaries of the barn, the real world ceased to exist. When she passed through those gates, when she drove by those pastures of green grass and clean horses, she was safe.

She wondered if her childhood barn had ruined her for the world. If being at that barn every day, if those halcyon summers before she had been expelled from paradise, had left her unable to exist outside it. As if all her life she had been unhappy because she could never go back. But now she could.

Sometimes at night, when she watched the girls play games in the dark—jumping over fences or acting out horse shows—she thought she *was* back.

She saw her friends. She saw herself home at last.

When do I get to come watch?" Jeff asked one morning, as if he had been forbidden.

The family was in the kitchen, the girls packing snacks and drinks for the day, their mother helping them. All three of them looked at him like they had just realized that he lived there, too.

"Whenever you want," Heather said, but it sounded like *Do you really want to?* When you had everything that you wanted, there was nothing worse than being confronted by something you *should* want.

"How about today?"

"Well, today is . . ." Heather drifted off.

It was Saturday. Maple and Piper both had lessons with Amy in the afternoon. They would be at the barn all day, helping out, hanging out. It was hard to see how Jeff could fit.

"I want Daddy to come," Maple said, hanging on his arm.

"Yeah, you can watch us ride," Piper agreed.

Both daughters tended to side with their dad, because he was so rarely moved to engage. It was a participation trophy.

"I said he can come whenever he wants," Heather said, defending herself. She wanted to add that there might have been a better day, but would there be? Every day at the barn was the same; that was part of the magic of it.

Heather did manage to convince Jeff to wait until their daughters' riding lessons. At least she thought he'd agreed. But then he showed up hours early, aggressively searching for her until he found her on the viewing patio with June and Pamela.

"Ah! This is the mysterious husband!" June said.

"I was looking everywhere for you," Jeff said to Heather, his tone accusatory.

Elodie—the groom who'd helped him find Heather—wandered off.

"Thank you," Heather called pointedly to the retreating groom.

Jeff dragged over a chair from one of the other tables. He was loud enough to slightly spook a passing horse.

"I thought you were coming this afternoon," Heather said.

"I was bored," he said.

Heather had a feeling he had come early to catch her out. He had a way of doing that sometimes. Jeff loved being right about everything but especially about *her* things. He took particular pride in enlightening her on her shortcomings.

"You'll be bored here," Heather pointed out, and then wished she hadn't. She was just teeing him up for a successful destabilizing.

"Where are the girls?" He scanned the arena like they might be riding someone else's horses.

"I told you, their lessons aren't until later. Maple is cleaning tack, and Piper is lunging a horse," Heather said, proud they were working.

"They get paid for that?" Jeff asked. Of course.

"They're learning responsibility," Heather said.

"There's no better preparation for life than working your ass off for nothing," Pamela said, and Heather loved her a little.

Pamela had an admirable hatred of other people's husbands. She had disliked Jeff immediately on hearing of his existence, and she was constantly pestering Heather for any horrible facts about him, which Heather was normally pretty readily able to supply.

June also tended to hate husbands, but she had one. No one had ever seen him, and the running joke was that he didn't exist. Heather wished Jeff were as mysterious.

Jeff was currently scanning the yard, taking in everything with his laser focus. "Is this what you do all day, sit here?"

"Sometimes we sit there," Pamela said, scoring more points with Heather.

Jeff just frowned at her. "Where are the girls? I'd like to see them," he said, like Heather was holding him hostage.

"I told you not to come so early."

Heather sometimes wondered why she had been so eager to immerse herself in the horse world. Having Jeff there really brought it home. He was one of the things she was trying to escape.

"Can you bring me to them—and my horse? I'd like a full tour."

He stood up. Heather had never seen him relax for ten minutes. He genuinely believed that everyone wanted to work as much as he did, but only he could.

"All right."

Heather frowned at Pamela. She wished Pamela could come with her, but even best friends didn't subject each other to walking tours.

Heather and Jeff found Maple in the cleaning bay, which didn't impress him, and Piper in the round pen, which did. Then they went to see Commotion. Heather let Jeff into the stall and showed him all the places the horse liked to be pet. Jeff did not pet him.

Instead, he let his eyes rush over Commotion and asked, "Does the value depreciate over time?"

Heather took Jeff out to lunch just to get him off the property. He was smothering her dreams, like he always did. It would take days to restore order, for all the blood to come coursing back through her veins.

When they returned from lunch, they watched Kieran train Douglas. That session deeply impressed Jeff, as did anything involving men working together.

"Does Kieran teach the girls?"

"No," Heather said. "Well, sometimes. He taught Maple once. It was *incredible*." Heather still got slightly breathless thinking about that lesson. "He really understands people. And horses. That's what makes him such a great trainer."

"Why doesn't he teach her all the time? I'm paying enough." It was the thirteenth time since his arrival that Jeff had mentioned he was funding the operation.

"Because . . ." Heather drifted off. It was hard for her to argue, because she wanted Kieran to teach the girls, too. She thought Amy was too easy on them. "That's just not the way it works. He teaches the advanced riders. Maybe in a few years."

"I'm paying for it."

Fourteen.

Jeff squinted at the riders in the arena. "Is that the guy you went to Kentucky with?"

"What guy?" Heather said.

"The guy riding the horse." He pointed at Douglas.

"Yes," Heather said because she didn't know what else to say.

"Did he look like *that* in Kentucky?" Jeff asked.

"Everyone looks better in Kentucky," Pamela said, which wasn't very helpful.

Heather had rarely thought about her nearly sleeping with Douglas. Being reminded of it set off a minor earthquake in her belly. Even though she had made the right choice in the end, she couldn't help sometimes thinking she had failed.

She stood up. "Should we watch the girls get the horse ready?"

It was still an hour before Maple's lesson, but Heather needed the girls as backup. For having been *so* excited to have their dad visit, they had volunteered for none of the heavy lifting.

Heather and Jeff collected both their daughters so they could all four tack up the horse together.

While the girls weren't especially enthusiastic at first, there were moments when Heather was glad Jeff had come, even glad for bigger things, like that she had married him and had his children.

Piper took over, demonstrating every grooming tool and explaining what each did, which Jeff loved. And Maple kept exclaiming or giggling over every little thing Jeff did to help.

"You brushed his mane! Dad! You picked his hoof!"

There were still moments with her family when Heather felt so secure, so positively grateful, that she blamed herself for all the times things went wrong. Her family was perfect. She must have been the problem.

Those good feelings vanished during Maple's lesson. Amy seemed to have missed the memo that Jeff was the one to impress. She had Maple doing seat exercises in the round pen.

"Why is she in this tiny arena?" he asked. "Why is she going so slow? I thought she was jumping at the cheaper place?"

Heather tried to explain about seat and leg and hand positions, but she didn't really understand what she was saying. She just knew that Maple was naturally bad at all the things the other riders were good at.

Piper's lesson was a little better—at least she cantered. But Jeff thought she should have been jumping, too. And he somehow got Kieran's name in his mouth again.

"I should talk to him. I need to talk to him. There are some things— I'm sorry, but there are some things where it's better if a man says it." Jeff pointed at himself, chest swelling with sudden onset manliness.

Heather couldn't stop him, and maybe she didn't want to, because she, too, wanted Kieran to train the girls. And even if Jeff couldn't get what they both wanted, she would love for someone to tell Jeff no. It was kind of a win-win.

Heather watched from a distance as Jeff approached Kieran outside the arena. Kieran was in the middle of teaching a lesson, which was the worst time anyone could approach him.

Heather wished she were closer, but she wanted to keep herself separate from the event so Kieran would know it was all Jeff—not Heather—asking the questions, making the demands.

Luckily, Pamela was conveniently near Kieran. Heather trusted Pamela to tell her all about the conversation. Heather hid, ducking into the barn aisle with the girls to help untack the horse.

To Heather's surprise, Jeff returned beaming.

"Great guy," he said. "Love that guy."

When Heather pressed for details, he said, "We're looking at a horse in Europe for Piper. And Maple's going to show at the end of the summer. It's some big thing in the mountains. SCI. The Southern California International Horse Show."

Heather already knew both of those things. Jeff didn't mention anything about Kieran teaching the girls. Heather was afraid to ask about it, in case Jeff realized his question hadn't been answered.

Heather later asked Pamela about the conversation, and Pamela told her, "Kieran shut him down fast."

thirty-nine

PAMELA

The Heather situation was pushing Pamela past reason.

It was true—Kieran hadn't promised Pamela anything. And the Parkers' money *was* good for the entire team. Everyone would rise. But it wasn't fair.

Commotion was way too good for Maple. Pamela saw this every time Douglas rode him. He was faster, stronger, more athletic than any horse Pamela had ever seen. He never touched a rail. He could turn on a dime. He had perfect balance, impulsion, rhythm. He was the horse everyone was looking for, the Aristotelian ideal of a horse. And Maple could barely ride him.

Pamela wasn't sure if Kieran was still drugging the horse before Maple rode, or if the strategy was to exhaust him before she got on. Commotion was lunged intensely before Maple's lesson. They let her ride in a round pen for only half an hour; she spent most of that time walking. Then they shepherded the horse away before she could ruin it.

That was what no one talked about—how easily good horses could be ruined. If you hung on their mouths. If you fell out of balance. If you flapped your legs against their sides. Things Maple did all the time. Pamela was pretty sure Amy had been specially instructed to minimize these risks, because she hardly let Maple breathe, but sometimes Pamela believed she could see the horse's perfection slowly corroding.

It was wrong. It wasn't fair to the horse. The horse deserved a better rider. And Vida was that rider.

Vida, Pamela knew, would never get the chance to own a horse like that. Pamela didn't have that kind of money. They had lived off a trust, but it had evaporated. This had led to more and more complicated efforts in making and saving money—but the trickiest part was that Pamela had to appear to be rich. She had to sell off all the possessions that she'd been told would never lose value—and she subsequently discovered that those possessions would have kept their value only if she hadn't *needed* to sell them.

Pamela had resorted to label swapping and contractor shopping and a number of purchases made across the border. But a horse was not something she could skimp on. There was only one person who had ever turned a plow horse into a show jumper, and that was why everyone knew about it.

Pamela wanted Vida to have Commotion. It would take so little. Maple could still ride him here and there, although Pamela doubted she really wanted to. And Maple and Vida were best friends.

But Pamela could not ask for the horse. When she had floated the idea to Heather, she could see the other woman's look of distaste. Pamela had liked Heather at first, and Pamela still liked her enough to constantly ask herself if they *really* were friends. But other times, she did not like Heather.

RSFE was becoming the Parker Show. Everyone *adored* Piper, seemed shocked to discover there was such a thing as a nice teenage girl.

They courted Heather's favor, tried to sit at her table, asked her horse-related questions as if she knew the difference between a canter and a cantle.

They gossiped about Maple: how she was in over her head with that horse, how she was turning into another Vida. In some ways, that was what Pamela envied most. She was so used to being in peril—first as a teenage junkie, then as a teenage mother—that she had a real thirst for negative attention.

Meanwhile, Pamela was practically raising Maple, who was at her house at least three times a week—the girl seemed to prefer it.

Thanks to Pamela's and Vida's influence, Maple was actually showing some spunk for the first time in her life. Did Heather appreciate it? No. In fact, she seemed to take credit for it. Serene with her money and her Elon husk of a husband and her two overly solicitous daughters.

That Saturday afternoon, the three girls were sitting in the pool drinking "mocktails." Pamela was pretty sure they'd spiked the drinks when she wasn't looking.

Pamela didn't care if her kid drank a little—in fact, she encouraged it. It was normal. At Vida's age, Pamela had been smoking meth out of light bulbs. A little vodka was practically a win.

Pamela was currently drinking tequila, parked out on a lounge chair beneath an umbrella. She was keeping a close watch on the girls because they were drinking, but also because Vida was starting to get annoyed with Maple. When Vida got annoyed, bad things tended to happen.

The three girls were crowded onto a ledge in the deep end, sitting shoulder to shoulder and holding their pink fruity drinks up out of the water. They were talking about Commotion, which they often did—Vida eager and enthusiastic while Maple became increasingly reticent and uncomfortable.

"What classes is he doing at SCI?" Effie said. "With Douglas."

Vida answered, probably because Maple didn't know. "They're doing the Sunday Grand Prix every weekend."

"Shit," Effie said.

The Sunday Grand Prix were the most prestigious classes, with the biggest purses. The prize money for the final week was six figures. And it couldn't have gone to a family who needed it more.

Douglas had already won a Grand Prix on the horse the previous weekend. It had been a last-minute decision, to start earning points. The team trailered the horse in that morning, won the Grand Prix that evening, and were safely back at RSFE before midnight. It was that easy when you had money.

"What classes are you doing?" Effie asked Maple.

Maple crinkled her nose; she was a ball of nerves even when she was tipsy. "I'm not sure."

Vida gave her a long look. "You'll probably have to do Walk/Trot. Or Lead Line." She exploded into giggles. Vida was not always the best kind of friend.

Lead Line was a class for little girls on tiny ponies. Even Walk/Trot on a horse like Commotion would have been humiliating. And Maple wouldn't even have had a shot at winning such a low-level class. Her equitation—the way she moved on the horse—was still terrible. Some days she seemed to ride better, but so marginally it wasn't worth talking about. Then, the following day, she was right back where she had started. Or worse.

Pamela was beginning to think it was Maple's head that was the problem. She didn't need a riding instructor. She needed a better therapist. But Heather was totally oblivious, especially now that Piper was at the barn. Piper was not an exceptional rider, but at least she wasn't a total basket case.

"I'm not doing Walk/Trot," Maple insisted. "Or Lead Line."

Vida discreetly rolled her eyes at Effie. "What do *you* think you're doing?"

Maple took a robust gulp of her drink. "I'm gonna ask Amy if I can do Jumpers."

The suggestion was so ridiculous that it made Pamela gasp.

Show jumping was the goal for everyone at the barn. It was the pinnacle of jumping on a horse. But all riders started in Hunter classes. They worked their way up over the years.

Hunters were judged by form. Jumpers was a speed contest. Riders had to get around a course the fastest, without knocking down rails. It was one of the most dangerous things you could do on a horse that was still legal.

Even Vida, who had been riding since she was born, still mostly competed in Hunter classes. The goal was to do Jumpers. The goal was to go pro. The idea that Maple—who had been at the barn for five minutes, relatively speaking—would even suggest that she might be allowed to compete in Jumper classes was patently offensive.

Vida was made momentarily speechless by the assertion, which was a real feat.

"But you don't even canter," Effie pointed out.

"Yes, I do," Maple said. "I cantered with Kieran."

That was the problem with Kieran giving Maple a lesson, Pamela thought. It made her think she was better than she was. She didn't deserve it. She could just afford it.

"One time," Effie reminded her, splashing a little in the water.

Vida's blood eventually returned. "Are you fucking crazy? You can't do Jumpers."

Maple squared her bare shoulders. "Commotion is the best horse. You all said so. All I have to do is stay on."

Maple sometimes sounded just like Vida. It was at these moments that Pamela liked her the most.

"You're terrified when he trots fast," Vida accused.

"Yeah, you are," Effie agreed, resting her head on Vida's shoulder, ganging up.

"No, I'm not." Maple kicked at the water, slightly spraying the other girls. "I'm gonna ride Jumpers."

"Ha." Vida stabbed at the ice in her drink with a straw. "You're insane."

It was kind of remarkable how mean young girls could be to one another. Pamela sometimes found it fascinating. She sometimes envied it. She would have loved to tell Heather that she was insane.

Maple set her empty drink on the edge of the pool, then left the ledge and dog-paddled out into the water.

"I might even enter the Little Palm Cup," she said when she was five feet away from the other girls, safe.

Or not, because Vida leapt off the ledge. She didn't even set her drink down. It spilled into the water, diffusing pink liquid and crushed ice. She landed on top of Maple and forced her down. She held her head under the water.

Effie got out of the pool in alarm. Pamela swung off her lounge chair and marched over.

She stood at the edge of the pool as Maple fought, gasping for breath every time she popped out from under the water.

Pamela crossed her arms. "Too far, Vida."

Vida gave Maple one last shove before paddling merrily back to the ledge.

Maple was gasping, clutching her throat like she'd been choked. Pamela waited to see if she would cry, demand to call her mom or be taken home.

Effie dropped back on the step beside Vida. They all watched as Maple pulled herself together, blinking like a little lost fawn.

When Maple had finally caught her breath, she swallowed hard and swam meekly to the ledge. Pamela reached down and offered her hand, then lifted Maple out of the pool. Her wet bathing suit, yanked out of shape, hung crookedly on her small body.

"Come here, dear. Let's see if you bruise easily."

Vida watched mutinously from the ledge as Pamela led Maple toward the pool bar.

"Lift up your neck," Pamela directed. She could see little bruises forming—bright red but they would turn purple, Pamela knew. "Great. Just fucking great."

Maple's eyes were still wide, as if Pamela blamed her. Maybe she did a little.

"Next time she does that, just kick her off."

Maple gasped a little. "What?"

"You think I care if you push my daughter? You have my permission to slap her if she deserves it."

A laugh cracked Maple's lips.

"Here, sit on the stool," Pamela directed. "I'll make you a better drink."

Maple did as she was told. Pamela made her a cocktail with a heavy pour.

"I don't think you should tell your mother about this," she suggested, sliding the drink in the girl's direction. "Other mothers don't always get it. Girls fight. It's normal. I would just tell her you were playing. All of you. Not just Vida."

Maple shrugged. Pamela didn't think she would tell Heather. Maple probably knew what would happen if she did. Heather would not want Maple to go to Pamela's house anymore. She would not want her daughter to hang out with Vida. People would talk, and then stories might come up, of other fights, accidents, *drama*.

Maple took a sip of her drink, then flinched at how strong it was.

Pamela leaned over the bar, rested her chin on her fist. "Do you know what I think, Maple? I think you're too sweet."

Maple tried to stir her drink to dissipate the alcohol. "I thought it was good to be sweet."

"Not when no one else is. If everyone is tough and you're sweet, then you're at a disadvantage, don't you think?"

"I guess so."

Pamela crossed over to the barstool beside Maple's. Violence always made Pamela feel closer to people. There was something extra bright about the moment it ended. The relief of making it out okay. The thrill of still being alive.

Pamela had felt that way many times on horseback. After a close shave, after a fall or a spook or a freak-out. When she'd looked herself over, looked her horse over, and seen that everything was still intact. And she'd always thought, *How? How did I survive that?*

Pamela could see it working through Maple now, the ecstasy of surviving. The joy.

"You know"—she nudged Maple—"when I first started riding, I was a little like you."

Maple forced herself to take a big sip of her drink. "Really?"

"Yep." Pamela nodded vigorously. "All money and no talent."

Maple didn't seem too pleased with the assessment, but it was better to get real, Pamela thought. Everyone tiptoed around the fact that Maple was a bad rider, but how did that help her?

"I came to riding late. I was sixteen—almost seventeen—when I started. Completely missed any chance at making a name for myself as a Junior. Everyone thought I was the crazy girl, the wild child. No one thought I would ever amount to anything." Pamela gazed at the light dancing on the surface of the pool water. "But you know why that was a good thing?"

Maple shook her head.

"Because no one saw me coming."

T he next morning, Pamela was taking her daughter on their traditional Starbucks run when Vida said, "I don't know why you had to, like, baby Maple yesterday. It's annoying when you do that."

Pamela shot her a look. "It's annoying when you choke-out your friends."

"She was being a bitch. Did you even hear what she was saying?"

Vida leaned forward in her seat. "Apparently, she's gonna enter the Little Palm Cup now. She only knows what it is because it's my fucking dream. And you know what the worst thing is? I bet Kieran will let her. He'll let her do anything as long as her parents pay for it."

Vida was right, and Pamela believed that she should say it.

Pamela had always believed that if she was patient, Kieran would eventually take an interest in Vida. That year was Vida's last as a Junior. The following year, she would move up to one of the adult trainers. Pamela had always assumed Kieran would train her, like he'd trained Pamela, but now she wasn't sure. He was so busy, busier than ever with the Parkers and all the new business they were already bringing in with their phenomenal jewel of a horse. And Pamela didn't have money anymore.

She hadn't paid her taxes in three years, which she was a little proud of. Last month, she hadn't paid her mortgage. She actually owed RSFE thousands of dollars in training and board. That debt wasn't in itself unusual. Kieran knew that her money was subject to the whims of the trust, and it couldn't always be readily extracted. What he didn't know was that this time it couldn't be extracted at all, because the trust was gone.

Sometimes late at night, Pamela fantasized about discovering that her father had set up another trust—one that he'd kept secret, knowing things might turn out the way they had. As if he were still out there somewhere, watching, looking after her. As if his love and his money could have defied death.

But she knew that was wishful thinking. She couldn't rely on her father anymore. She couldn't rely on Kieran. Maybe it was time to take matters into her own hands.

"Would you like to have her horse?" Pamela asked.

Vida sighed. Her eyes drifted hopelessly back to her phone. "Of course I would. But they're never gonna give it up. And now her annoying sister is riding it."

Vida was uncreative with her insults, but never did the word "annoying" sound as damning as it did from her fresh lips.

Pamela flicked the turn indicator, then veered easily toward the parking lot as she did every morning.

"Why do people quit riding?" she mused.

Vida's eyes met hers in the mirror. "They get scared. Or fall off."

Pamela nodded. "That's right."

DETECTIVE PEREZ

You helped move the body?" Detective Perez asked Dominic Orlando, the head show groom.

"Yes."

"Do you remember how it was positioned?"

"Seated. On the stall floor. Against the near wall. You could not see it from the outside." He spoke quickly and precisely.

Before Detective Perez had time to ask another question, he said, "Is that all? I have three horses to prepare before noon."

"Not quite," she said. "You've worked here for twenty years?"

He shook his head. "I am here to talk only about the body. I don't have time to talk about anything else." He started to rise from his chair.

"Do you think it was a suicide?"

He hovered as if he was uncertain, but his words were sure. "Yes. I don't understand why you are asking so many questions. I thought you would only ask me about the body. I don't know anything else."

"We just need to—"

He put his hands up and backed toward the door. "I'm sorry.

Please understand. I have to go. These people are so demanding. I can't just spend all day talking to you."

They had been talking for approximately two minutes.

Detective Perez looked at her partner, started to rise. "If we could just—"

But it was too late. He slipped out of the investigation stall and slid the door shut behind him.

forty

PIPER

W ait. Here, so . . . look at this one."

Piper was sitting in the front seat of Douglas's truck. He leaned over the console to show her a video of a horse on his phone.

They were parked on the beach, where they had eaten their lunch and then stayed parked, looking at horses.

Piper could smell his peppermint breath, could see his muscles straining beneath his polo shirt. It was overwhelming, being in such a tight space with him. Even at the barn, he seemed surrounded by a sexual halo, a mind-bending fog. In his truck with the windows rolled up, it was like aura asphyxiation.

"Nice," Piper said, trying to focus on the horse, a delicate chestnut, as she flung her little horsey hips up after every jump.

"And she's a mare. You could breed her."

He took his phone back. Piper sighed. His eyes flicked in her direction.

"I know you like Commotion, but you could like another horse, too."

"That's easy for you to say. You'd still get to ride him." Piper started to sigh but stopped herself, so she made a slight strangled sound.

When she was alone, she hated how much she liked Douglas. When she was around him, she could not even think. His mere presence blotted everything out, made her thick with the sense of him.

"As long as Kieran lets me," he muttered.

Piper didn't know exactly what it was about Kieran, but she didn't like him. She didn't like how everyone revered him, how everyone watched for him and listened to what he said. Sometimes it occurred to her that perhaps it wasn't Kieran she disliked but the way everyone treated him. Especially Douglas, who was so obedient, so tuned to his frequency, that he sometimes appeared robotic, soulless, trapped.

"Did I show you this one?"

He held up his phone, but she looked at him. She tried to see past the delicate curves of his lips, his dark eyes and horsey lashes. She tried very hard.

"How did you end up with Kieran? You were fourteen, right?"

He put his phone down, seemed to deflate. Outside the windshield, the waves flowed steadily in and out.

"Yeah. My . . . um . . ." And then he drifted off.

"You don't have to say," Piper said.

Douglas had a real air of tragedy about him. It was one of his most compelling qualities. Piper was a problem solver, so her weakness had always been boys who needed to be saved.

Douglas squared his shoulders, but they dropped immediately. "No, it's fine. Remember I told you my mom used to ride with Kieran? She had an accident. She's in a . . . uh . . . residential-care facility. Brain damage. Kieran pays for it." The story was brief and mixed up, as if he were trying to get it out as quickly as possible. "I would never find another trainer who would do that. And he lets me stay with him. He's a good guy, really." The story seemed more about Kieran than about anyone else.

"I'm sorry. That must be really hard."

"I go to see her on Monday mornings." He stared straight ahead, under the spell of his own sadness. "She's at that place, you know, it's kind of by Mary's?"

Piper nodded, although she didn't know the place. She wanted to make it easier for him. "I bet she'd be so proud of you."

"I don't know. . . . She used to have all these dreams for me: that I would train in Europe, do all these big shows. But I can't do any of that because I would have to leave her." He reached for the keys in the ignition like he was going to start the truck, but didn't. "I used to think that one day we would bring her out to watch me ride and she would come back. Like in a movie. Like I could just see her again."

Piper wanted to be a doctor, and she was pretty sure that couldn't happen. He seemed pretty sure, too.

"Does she ever watch you ride?"

"Not since the accident. I guess I couldn't take the disappointment."

They were both quiet, for longer than was comfortable. He was watching the ocean, and Piper thought there was no emotion more beautiful than sadness. Not happiness or love or anger. And being pragmatic, she considered that this was a survival mechanism, a way for sad people to get what they needed.

She reached for his phone. "Let me see that mare again."

forty-one

MAPLE

Sometimes Maple appreciated how mean Vida was to her. Vida was teaching her to be tough. When she held Maple's head down in the pool, when she pulled Maple's hair, when she told her what a bad rider she was, she was showing Maple how strong she really was.

Afterward, they were always still friends. It wasn't like back in Texas, where the girl who had bullied Maple never smiled at her, never invited her over, never relented, even for a second. Maple was always quietly convinced that she was kind of impressing Vida. That she was hanging in there.

Yes, Maple was a bad rider. Yes, she was annoying and a brat. But she had friends, and that was the most important thing. Sometimes friendship hurt, but that was how you knew it was real.

It was like that with horses. Sometimes you fell off. Sometimes horses bit or kicked you. Sometimes they didn't listen. Sometimes they seemed to hate you. But that was all part of the relationship, part of the journey. Your horses might not love you, but at least they tolerated you. They let you on their backs. They let you brush them and braid their hair and pick up their poop. And every once in a while, they nudged you with their noses and looked you in the eyes as if to say, *Hey, you're okay.*

Maple was trying so hard to connect with Commotion. Douglas had seemed to connect with him instantly, the way he did with all the horses, as if they had been waiting for him to come along.

Piper had also connected with Commotion—maybe not as intensely as Douglas had because she wasn't as experienced as he was—but on the ground, they played games and knew some of each other's secrets.

Maple found Piper in Commotion's stall all the time. Every time it made Maple feel bad, as if she should have been there. She should have been stealing every moment she could to love on her horse.

Instead, Commotion made Maple feel guilty. The horse seemed scared whenever Maple was around, even though she rarely got close and was always super careful.

Amy had tried to explain. "You make him nervous because *you're* nervous. A horse can feel a heartbeat from four feet away. He knows you're scared, but he doesn't know what you're scared of. His instincts tell him that it must be a predator. So every time he feels your fear, he's sure there's some monster hiding in the bushes to devour you both."

Maple was nervous. Of falling, yes, but mostly she was scared of not being good enough, particularly not being as good as Piper, who everyone liked, even people who still hadn't learned Maple's name.

Piper had taken their mother's attention, too. Heather seemed relieved, flush with compliments on what a nice girl Piper was, what a hard worker, what a good rider. Meanwhile, everyone at RSFE gave Maple a wide berth, packing her off with Vida and Effie—the bratty little girls, the ones you couldn't quite trust.

It frustrated Maple. It seemed to her that so much of her life had been decided for her by nothing more than other people's opinions. She was immature. She was weird. And now she was a brat. When was it going to be her turn? When was she going to have a say? When was she finally going to get to decide who she was? Who she would be?

In preparation for SCI, Maple graduated to having her lessons in an enclosed dressage arena on the far side of the property. There was a long wall of mirrors on one side so riders could watch themselves. Amy seemed to think it would help Maple to see what she looked like on Commotion, but every time Maple caught her reflection in the mirror, she was shocked by how terrible she looked, how much worse than everyone else.

At the start of each lesson, Maple's mom sat at the top of the arena with the same hopeful expression. And at the end of each lesson, without fail, it had crumpled.

Hope was the hardest part. Maple herself still hoped. That she would be good enough. That she would be different at least. That she would finally be someone else.

One morning, Maple was having her usual lesson when a woman appeared at the side of the arena. She was watching Maple ride. Maple didn't know who she was.

At first, Maple assumed the woman was an owner she hadn't met. But then why was she watching her? Why didn't she leave?

Then she thought the woman might be a friend of Amy's, but she was standing on the far side of the arena, away from everyone. She was hidden from Amy's view by the wall of mirrors.

She was wearing a bright red shirt, and she was holding a long black umbrella, even though it was a sunny day.

As Maple traversed the arena, first at a walk and later at a trot, she watched with growing discomfort as the woman stood stock-still, her expression hidden by a pair of oversized sunglasses. Who was she?

Maple passed along the wall of mirrors and avoided looking at herself. At the top of the arena, she trotted past her mother and Amy. Every time she turned toward the far side of the arena, she craned her head to see if the woman was still there.

She was—waiting, expressionless, surreal—as Maple passed by again and the woman disappeared behind the mirrors.

"Is there something in that corner?" Amy asked the next time Maple passed. "What do you keep looking at?"

Maple started to answer as she came around the corner again and the woman came back into view. She was holding her umbrella like a spear now. Maple's mouth went dry.

The woman opened the umbrella. It made a loud popping sound. Spread like a black sun.

Commotion spooked sideways. Maple flew through the air. She could see the dirt rushing toward her. Could feel the fall, but was pulled up short by her ankle.

Her foot had slipped inside the stirrup. Her mother had insisted that they buy those stirrups—rose gold to match her helmet—instead of ugly rubber-band-edged safety stirrups.

Maple swung beneath the horse as he took off. A galloping hoof whacked her helmet. The edge of a horseshoe cut into her face.

Commotion raced toward the gate, which was closed. But the fence was only five feet tall. Commotion could clear it with ease.

forty-two

HEATHER

Everyone heard the sound of Maple going through that fence. Thank God it was vinyl and not wood or metal.

Heather had been watching Maple's lesson, of course. Half watching at least; lessons could get a little boring. But she had seen the spook. She had seen the fall. She had seen the horse heading for the fence, seen Maple's limp body banging alongside him like a doll. It was easy to forget that underneath the leather and the polish and the ShowSheen was a fourteen-hundred-pound animal with metal shoes nailed to his hooves.

One moment her daughter had been beautiful, and the next, she was a crash test dummy.

Commotion charged the fence, gathered himself and jumped. He cleared the fence, but Maple didn't.

She slammed through the rail, then made a grab for it, wrapping her arms around the fence for a moment until the force of the galloping horse tore her away.

The horse was racing toward the upper barn with Maple twisting, flailing behind him.

Heather jumped to her feet as Amy yelled, "Don't run! Someone will catch her!"

Heather thought, *Fuck you*, and took off. In her panic she believed she could run faster than the horse.

In all the arenas, horses stopped and riders dismounted. People shouted, "Loose horse! Loose horse!"

All the grooms trooped out with their arms spread to box Commotion in, but he charged right through them, causing the grooms to scatter.

It was Douglas who finally caught Commotion. He cantered down the barn aisle and rode up alongside the horse—which was not the protocol at all.

He held the horse steady as one of the grooms undid the girth and another shepherded Maple to the ground. They laid her in the dirt and instructed her not to move until the ambulance arrived.

Maple's face was bleeding, but she wasn't crying.

She had a mouthful of dirt, and she was looking up at the sky, her chest pumping.

forty-three

MAPLE

Everything happened so fast that Maple couldn't feel it happening. Now, lying in the dirt, waiting for the ambulance, it all replayed in her mind, all the ways she had fucked up.

She should have told Amy about the woman.

She should have told the woman to fuck off.

She should have known Commotion might spook.

When the woman started to open the umbrella, she should have told her to stop.

She should have shortened her reins.

She should have sat back.

She should have put her heels down.

She should have relaxed.

She should have stayed with the horse.

When she fell and was dangling, she should have tried to climb back up.

She should have grabbed the horse's neck.

She should have tried to grab the reins.

She should have stayed calm.

She should have done anything else, but what she actually did was fall. What she actually did was scream. What she actually did was dangle as the horse dragged her across the barn, in front of everyone.

She didn't know if she was hurt. She was too shocked to feel anything.

Her mother was kneeling beside her, delicately holding her wrist like a bracelet.

Standing off to the side with one of the grooms, Piper was analyzing the situation. "It doesn't *look* like anything is broken, but you never know. I had a friend once who fractured her olecranon. . . ."

Waiting dutifully on a tack box, Vida and Effie were slightly bored but annoyed that they had missed the excitement. They didn't want to miss anything else.

Pamela was listing all of the falls that she had witnessed. "And this poor woman broke her back. . . ."

On his way to teach a lesson, Kieran paused briefly to mention that having Maple laid out in the middle of the barn aisle was a safety hazard.

Everyone else, at one point or another, asked Maple stupid questions.

"Do you know what day it is?"

"Can you wiggle your toes?"

"Can you feel this?"

Or they diagnosed her.

"She definitely has a concussion."

"She *for sure* cracked a rib. Probably more than one."

"Look at her ankle: broken."

The pain was the last thing to arrive, right after the ambulance. Maple heard the siren, and her whole body lit up, as if now it was safe to catch fire.

Maple screamed when the paramedics moved her onto the gurney. She wasn't even sure if she felt pain or irritation or frustration.

As they loaded her into the ambulance with all their ridiculous equipment, Maple felt a burning sense of injustice. Why did it have to be her? Why did it always have to be her? She was always the one every bad thing happened to. She just wanted to be like everyone else. It wasn't fucking fair.

forty-four

VIDA

Vida was so disappointed that she'd missed Maple's fall. Falls were events in the horse world. Everyone talked about them—for days and weeks and even years afterward. Vida remembered good falls better than she remembered good rides. They were battle scars. Stories told at horse show campfires.

Maple's fall had been a *great* fall.

Not only had she been dragged, but her horse had jumped out of the arena! Over a five-foot fence! Then he galloped through the barn! Until Douglas had ridden up alongside Commotion like a cowboy and saved her!

And Vida had missed the whole thing. She and Effie had been in the wash rack, giving Faustus a bath so they could clip him. The wash rack was enclosed by stone walls, so they hadn't heard the yelling, hadn't heard everyone racing toward the panicked horse. She hadn't even realized something was wrong until she led Faustus out of the wash rack and saw Maple lying in the dirt in the barn aisle with a small crowd around her.

Vida sometimes pretended she had seen the fall. She would re-count the story and add little lies.

"Oh, yeah, I heard her scream! She ran right past us! It was crazy!"

Vida was a little jealous of the fall. She would have loved to at-tract that kind of attention without actually being injured. She wished she could have a cool scar.

Her mother saw the whole thing rather less romantically. She drove Vida and Effie to lunch that day. When they got back to the barn, she made Vida stay in the car.

Vida watched Effie hover near the steps, waiting for her.

"I want you to ask Kieran if you can ride Commotion," Pamela said, reapplying her lipstick.

"By myself?" Vida said in surprise.

Everyone thought Vida was fearless, but Kieran scared her a little—except she called it respect. She wanted his approval. Her dream was to ride for him professionally one day. To be part of his team of elite riders. So she *respected* him, but mostly from a dis-tance, afraid that if she made the wrong move, her dream would go up in smoke.

"Yes. He likes you."

Hearing Pamela say those words made Vida's stomach flip.

"What should I say?" Vida's voice curled down anxiously.

Her mother knew how much riding Commotion meant to Vida, as if she had given birth to the dream in her daughter's mind. The dream she'd had the day Commotion arrived: Vida riding into the arena at the Little Palm Cup on that horse, the white flag of his tail.

You won! You're a winner. There is nothing wrong or bad about your mind.

Pamela snapped the mirror shut. "Just say that with Maple out for a while, you'd love to take a turn on the horse. Douglas doesn't have time to ride him every day."

"What about Piper?"

"I'm sure she won't want to ride him either, after what happened to her sister. Just let Kieran know you're available. And that you *want* it—that's important."

Vida knew that her mother had been training with Kieran for over twenty years, longer than almost anyone else at the barn. That should mean that Pamela knew him best, but she didn't always seem to. She had blinders on, like everyone else.

Vida opened the door but then held it partly closed. "Should I wait until he's in his office? Or maybe we should go to his house later?"

"No. The important thing is we get in first, before someone else does."

Vida nodded and got out of the car. She expected her mom to follow, but to her surprise, Pamela drove out of the parking lot. She was abandoning Vida. To ask Kieran to make their dreams come true, on her own.

Vida brought Effie with her. She knew her mom wouldn't like it, but she had to. They went everywhere together. It wasn't like Vida could just instruct Effie to stand thirty feet away while she asked Kieran. Plus, Vida kind of needed her. She was nervous, and Vida was rarely nervous.

This was not the way she had planned to achieve her dream, but it would guarantee her dream's success. If she could ride Commotion in the Little Palm Cup, she would win.

She had always imagined her life would change when she made it inside the Winner's Enclosure. She and her mother and Kieran would all gather there, like they had a dozen times when Pamela used to ride and win. He would look up at her and say, "You're riding for me now," or something equally confident, as if he had always wanted her, as if that had always been the plan.

She approached Kieran, who was sitting on the rail. He was training Douglas, so she hoped that he wouldn't mind the interruption as much as he would have if he were with a paying client.

Kieran saw them coming. "Hey, you two! Go set some jumps."

Vida and Effie scurried into the arena and set jumps to Kieran's specifications. Vida thought maybe their helping him would put him in a better mood, but it didn't seem to.

After they had finished setting the jumps, Vida approached again. Effie followed. They hopped out of the arena and stood beside Kieran, who was still on the rail.

He looked over his shoulder, then glared down at them. "What are you two hanging around for?"

Out in the arena, Douglas started his course.

"I wanted to ask if I could ride Commotion," Vida said too fast.

"I beg your pardon?"

"I thought maybe if . . . um . . ." Vida felt very small.

"Maple fell off," Effie said helpfully. "And Piper will probably be too scared."

"I just thought maybe if you needed someone . . ." Vida lifted her chin.

"You thought I might need you?" Kieran said.

"Yes . . . I don't know." Vida huffed. She got a little indignant when she was nervous.

"Did your mother put you up to this?"

"Yes."

Vida had no problem throwing Pamela under the bus. She wasn't even there to help.

"Right, well, you tell your mother that she needs to buy you a better horse, not try to poach horses from my other clients."

Vida's eyes darted toward Effie. She was embarrassed, but she still admitted, "I don't think she can afford a better horse."

Kieran raised his eyebrows. "Well . . . them's the breaks, kid."

It was just as Vida had feared, the pin that could pop her swollen dreams. Kieran didn't intend to let her ride Commotion. He didn't want her. And she couldn't afford a new horse. Another trainer might not understand her the way Kieran did.

She would be forced out, banished from the horse world, and what would be left for her? That world was the only place she fit, the only place her weird, mean, unlovable personality made sense. She would probably end up like her grandmother—it was actually a bit of a horse girl cliché: moving seamlessly from riding horses to injecting horse.

Vida could not let that happen. She thought about her power—her sometimes fearsome power—to let go of everything except her own desire.

Vida stood square. "Will you ever let me ride other people's horses?"

Kieran scanned her up and down, running a quick analysis. "You're a good rider, but the clients don't like you."

Vida burned.

"I didn't say *I* don't like you."

That made her burn in a different way.

"Maybe tone it down on the ringleader bit. People like us have to learn to suppress our instincts." He leaned toward Vida. "You can still torture people. Just don't be so obvious about it."

Vida laughed. She felt seen and, more than that, appreciated. "You got it, coach."

He clapped a hand on her shoulder, gave it a quick shake, then turned to Douglas. "What the fuck happened on that last line?" he roared across the arena so loud that Vida and Effie both winced.

forty-five

HEATHER

Maple had stitches in her cheek, bruised ribs and a lot of soreness. Still, Heather was thankful her daughter had suffered no serious injuries.

"Kids are so bendy," Pamela said.

Heather had returned to the barn to make sure Commotion was okay and to let everyone know that Maple was going to be fine. Heather hadn't gone home right away. Instead, she and Pamela were sitting ringside after dark sharing a bottle of wine. Heather was trying to come down from the events of the day. Poor Maple was in bed asleep.

Piper had come back to the barn with Heather. She was responsibly disseminating the news about Maple to everyone.

The barn had finally gone quiet. The trees were still, and the air was tinged with the bitter scent of eucalyptus.

Heather felt terrible. She couldn't stop seeing the moment her daughter had transformed in front of her eyes into something fragile, something *so* vulnerable. There had been falls before but never one like that. Maple had been dragged through a fence. The horse was huge. His hooves had hit the girl's helmet several times.

"She could have been seriously injured," Heather confessed to Pamela. "My God, I can't believe . . . I can't believe she's okay."

"I'm so sorry. What a terrible thing to have to witness. Vida's had falls but never anything like this."

Heather let her eyes drift over the darkened arena. "I don't understand what happened. She said there was a woman with an umbrella, but no one else saw—"

"It might have been a hallucination," Pamela suggested.

That seemed a little extreme to Heather. The doctors had said that Maple's head was fine, thanks to her six-hundred-dollar helmet.

"Or sometimes people just wander in off the street," Pamela said. "To look at the horses."

That didn't seem likely either. They were in Rancho Santa Fe. "The street" was at least a forty-minute walk.

Heather shook her head.

"That's the thing about this sport," Pamela continued. "There are so many freak accidents. I thank my lucky stars every day Vida doesn't get hurt. The falls I've seen at horse shows! I saw a man get paralyzed once. And two women die. And that's nothing on the number of horses I've seen injured or euthanized. We tell ourselves it's a civilized sport, but it's really one of the most dangerous sports in the world. Do you realize riding a horse is more dangerous than riding a motorcycle?"

Heather frowned. Pamela wasn't exactly making her feel better.

"It's my fault," Heather said. "I should have bought the safety stirrups."

"Safety stirrups don't make a difference," Pamela countered. "They're a crutch."

Heather knew Pamela was trying to make her believe that the accident hadn't been her fault, but Heather had specifically chosen the rose gold stirrups because they looked better.

Heather exhaled. "It's safety stirrups from now on. Or those cute ones with the cutaways. Or have you tried the magnetic ones? Those might help."

"She might not want to ride right away," Pamela said. "And Faustus is still available. That last buyer fell through."

Pamela had been having trouble selling the horse, which was near retirement age. Heather had heard the price was too high, and sometimes she thought Pamela was hoping *she* would buy the horse.

"The first rule of riding is to get back on the horse," Heather recited. "It was the stirrups, and that was my fault, not Maple's."

"The horse didn't take off because of stirrups. It didn't jump a five-foot fence with little Maple dragging alongside because of stirrups." Pamela straightened up in her chair. "Even if there was a woman with an umbrella, what do you think is going to happen at a horse show? There will be hundreds of things Maple has never experienced. Have you ever seen a warm-up ring? It's like a three-ring circus in half a ring. Frankly, I'm a little shocked that you would even consider going forward at this point." She slid a calm hand over Heather's. "Think about what Maple would want."

Heather narrowed her eyes. She hated being questioned on things, especially things pertaining to her daughter. But most especially things she herself was unsure of.

"Maple is tougher than you think."

Heather stood up. The wine bottle was empty. It had been for a long time.

forty-six

PIPER

That night, Piper found Douglas talking quietly to Commotion. He was telling the horse how much water he had drunk, which Piper found patently adorable. Douglas seemed very impressed that the horse had drunk half a trough, and then he said that Commotion had drunk so much because he was scared, and then he admitted that he was scared for him. Then he realized Piper was there. He was actually embarrassed that she had heard him, which made him all the more adorable.

"I think I'm losing my mind sometimes," he explained.

She could tell he was exhausted. Between all his rides, he had squeezed in saving her sister.

She let herself into the stall. "You're the hero of the day."

"Yeah, right. You know how much trouble I got in for that?"

"But you saved her."

"Yeah, but it's not what we're supposed to do. I should have dismounted and stood there like an idiot."

"I thought it was pretty cool."

Piper had been in the cleaning bay when Douglas and Yellow-jacket cantered past, like something out of a movie. Once she had made sure her sister was going to be okay, she had found time to be impressed.

"I'm glad she's okay, anyway," he said as she reached across him to pet the horse. "And I'm glad he's okay."

"This is really too much horse for her," Piper said. "It's getting dangerous."

Everyone at the barn was talking about Maple. They had even talked about her in front of Piper, because they trusted her. She was one of them. But no one ever said a word in front of Heather.

"Maybe," he admitted, which she was pretty sure he wasn't supposed to do.

"I'm gonna talk to my mom about it. See if we can come up with something. Hopefully she realizes how serious this is."

Piper was running her hand down the horse's shoulder. Douglas was standing right beside her, watching her do it. His breath smelled of peppermints. Dried sweat had licked the ends of his hair into curls.

Piper imagined the horse was hers. Imagined a whole future life with her own barn and dogs and mini horses. She didn't care that it was unrealistic and immature. Dreams were supposed to be like that.

No matter how old you got, your dreams stayed young.

forty-seven

MAPLE

Maple saw the accident again and again, whether her eyes were open or shut. The ground she had never hit. The fence she had split. The underside of her horse. The sharp edge of his shoe.

She saw these things over and over through the sharp filter of her panic, as if in an emergency her mind had seized on certain obstacles, and she was doomed to see them forever barreling toward her.

But the worst part was being sure that it had been her fault. It hadn't happened to someone else; it had happened to her. Just like that girl in Texas had singled her out, bullied her so bad that Maple's whole family had to move. Just like every bad thing happened to Maple.

Maple was weird. Maple wasn't good enough. Maple deserved everything she got. She asked for it. It was all down to something wrong with *her*.

She didn't want to be that person anymore, but she wasn't quite sure how to stop. Could she just change her mind? Could she just become someone else?

She wanted to be tough, like Vida. She wanted to be the person no one could touch. She thought about how the light in Vida's eyes went out when she was angry. She wanted to be *that*. She wanted to turn her own lights out. To feel nothing.

Not pain, not sadness. Even happiness didn't seem like something she could trust.

She lay back on her bed, feeling too much. Frustration. Disappointment. Fear.

Hunger, which she could fix. She got out of bed. She convinced herself that food might help her sleep.

That was how she ended up outside the kitchen. Her mother, her father and Piper were all crowded around the counter, talking about her.

"I'm sure she'll be happier," Piper was saying. "I'm sure she'll be relieved. We can find her some nice horse—even Vida's horse. She likes that one, right?"

Maple couldn't believe Piper's nerve, taking this opportunity—Maple's accident—to try to steal her horse.

Maple's heart contracted as her mother spoke. "I just don't know. . . ."

"Piper's probably right," Jeff agreed with his preternatural man authority. "They barely let her walk on that thing. They obviously know it's wrong for her. I can't begin to imagine why they pushed you to buy it." That last bit was sarcastic.

"I'm sorry, but it needs to be Maple's choice. It's her horse."

Maple's heart sang. Her mother was on her side. She had started riding for Heather, stuck with it to impress her, and her mother was supporting her.

Maple chose that moment to enter the ring. There was a time when she would have turned around, hidden, gone back to bed. But maybe she had changed a little.

Piper sat bolt upright on her barstool when she saw her sister.

Their mother and father moved toward Maple but stopped when they saw her expression.

The kitchen was dim, with only the small overhead lights switched on. The whole house was incredibly dark, because they were having custom fixtures made to perfectly illuminate every corner. In the meantime, the space was gloomy and hollow.

"How are you feeling, sweetie?" Jeff smiled hopefully at her, like he hadn't just been talking about what a bad rider she was.

Jeff had always liked Piper better than Maple. Piper was like him, smart and analytical. She was the worker. Maple was the baby. She was cute in small doses, but a little pathetic.

"I can't believe you're talking about giving away my horse," Maple said. "My body's not even cold."

It was something Vida would have said, a little shocking, a little inappropriate. There was power in the right words.

"It's not like that." Piper tilted her head, had the audacity to offer a worried look. "I thought you might want to. It's an option. . . ."

All Maple could see were all the times she'd supported Piper: watching her lacrosse games, debates and events. She'd even gone to plays that Piper wasn't in just because Piper had built the sets. Piper didn't support her sister in the same way. It was assumed that because Maple was bad at everything, it wasn't necessary. Piper had never watched one of her lessons. Never tried to help her with riding.

It had never occurred to Maple to ask Piper for that, but now it occurred to her that she shouldn't have had to. It was always taken for granted that Maple was the second sister. The lesser sister. The extra one.

Commotion was the first thing that Maple had been given first. And the moment that the horse arrived, Piper had appeared, had risen up to take what had always been meant for her. She was the good rider. She was the one Heather wanted to buy the horse for.

Maple had volunteered as tribute, but now Piper was back to take her rightful place. Unless Maple did something to stop her.

Maple crossed her arms. She looked her sister dead in the eyes. "I don't want you riding Commotion anymore. Get your own horse."

It was a gauntlet. Both their parents were right there to stop it, to tell Maple that she needed to share.

Maple wondered why they didn't. She wondered if they weren't a little impressed by her. If Maple was finally tough enough.

If she was the daughter they'd always wanted her to be.

forty-eight

HEATHER

That night Jeff followed Heather into her bedroom to talk. He stood near the door, as if he didn't want to intrude too far into their shared past. "What do you think about all that?"

"I don't know," Heather said.

She was about to prepare for bed—take off her jewelry, brush her teeth, wash her face—but she felt awkward going through her nightly ritual with Jeff watching. She would have to go into the bathroom, and she wasn't sure if he would follow her. Would they just end up shouting from separate rooms to hear each other?

"It was just a fall. Kids fall off horses. They've both fallen before. *I've* fallen dozens of times."

It was true. Heather remembered, from her own reckless-rider past, that there had been a period when she would fall at least once a week. But Maple wasn't the same kind of rider Heather had been, not at all.

"This was a little more than a fall."

Heather could tell Jeff was genuinely worried, and she begrudged him his concern. She was so mad at him about other things that she didn't want him to ever present as human, much less as the father of her children.

It was so hard being married. It was so complicated. They slept in separate rooms. He cheated. And yet they had to stand in the semidark before bed and make big decisions for their children.

"Look, it's a beautiful horse," Jeff continued. "But I think it's a little out of her league. I'm not even sure if I want Piper riding it."

The worst part was Heather kind of agreed with him. Commotion did seem like too much horse for Maple.

When Heather looked back at the horse-buying process, now with distance and a clearer head, she could see that she had been caught up. Kieran and Douglas had been so determined, and so convincing. They seemed to know so much more about horses than she did. She could even admit that Douglas had had a slightly mystical effect on her brain. She had thought that turning him down had broken the spell, but she could have also argued that he was no longer casting it, had stopped paying attention to her once she'd bought the horse.

She sighed, releasing the pressure of the memory. What were their options, really? Neither Piper nor Maple would let them sell the horse. They both loved the barn. Heather loved it.

"They love that horse," Heather said. "We can't just take him away from them."

Heather realized with a start that forbidding her daughters from having the horse or going to the barn would be almost like doing what had been done to her—exactly what she had been set on righting.

"Kids fall. That's just the way it is. They're learning. What message are we sending if we tell them to give up?" She knew her argument wasn't convincing Jeff, so she had to think about what would. "Did you see Maple tonight?"

"Yeah, it was a little scary." Men were always secretly afraid of girls.

"But she stood up for herself. She set boundaries. Two months ago, Maple would never have done that. I know it's a little scary. And yes, riding is dangerous, but I still believe it's good for her. For both of them. Piper seems so happy. So much more settled."

She knew he couldn't disagree. Lately, Piper had been on cloud nine—smiling, helping, polite—nothing like the girl her parents had dragged from Texas. She hadn't even asked to go with her dad on his next trip to Amarillo. Piper was falling in love with the place.

Jeff slouched against the wall, worrying his lip. "It's all just very intense."

Heather sighed. "Of course it is. It's girls and horses."

forty-nine

PIPER

Piper met Douglas at the gate. She hadn't known why she had wanted to meet him, but when he'd agreed, she couldn't stop herself.

It wasn't about the horse, although if she were honest, she still wanted him. It was about being alone, about feeling alone. With her family. At the barn. With everyone except for him.

They started walking toward the stables.

"Is everything okay?" he asked.

"Yeah. I guess I'm just— Is it okay that I texted you? I hope I'm not bothering you."

"I like hanging out with you."

She stopped. "Really?"

"Yeah," he said. "I like you. You're a nice person."

Piper had heard that before, but usually people cringed when they said it, like they were worried for her. Like she would probably be punished for it.

"Well, you don't really show it. You don't really show much emotion at all," she admitted, even though it scared her.

You weren't supposed to challenge the boy you liked. You

weren't supposed to call him anything but perfect until you had him married with children. Then you could call him anything you wanted.

"I just think it's easier to shut everything down," he said matter-of-factly.

"What do you mean, 'shut everything down'?"

She looked at Douglas. He seemed sometimes to have a darkness, an adornment of shadows, drawn around his edges. But that darkness didn't scare her; it drew her closer, like it was something she could dispel.

"I mean, not let myself be controlled by my emotions," he said.

"You mean, not feel things? Not be alive?" Her voice was teasing, but her words felt serious.

"I'm still alive. I'm just alive the way I want to be." He lifted his chin, like it was something to be proud of. "I used to be too sensitive. I felt too much, and it was painful. I was angry. I was sad. Honestly, I was afraid. But Kieran taught me it's easier to switch everything off. The whole world, all the people in it. I don't even have to shut my eyes, and all I see is horses."

"Don't you get lonely?" she asked.

"I'm not alone."

They reached the barn, and all of the horses were waiting in their stalls, their ears pricked.

Piper swallowed. "I don't think there's anything wrong with feeling something."

They stopped outside Commotion's stall. The horse put his head on Douglas's shoulder.

"Maybe not for you," Douglas said.

Piper stepped closer, thinking she was moving toward the horse, but she found that she was moving toward Douglas. She wove her fingers through his. She drew him toward her, and she kissed him. He tasted first a little of dirt and then deeper of peppermint.

She pulled away, her heart racing. "Did you feel that?"

"I . . . ," he started, but then he stopped.

He turned away. She let him. She watched him slip into the stall, run his hands along the horse like it was part of the magic he used to shut himself down.

She followed him inside.

"Which horse do you think I should get?" she asked, crossing into the stall and leaning against Commotion's shoulder as he nibbled at her neck.

"The mare from Stockholm. The blood bay."

He leaned against the horse, like he was exhausted or relieved, but it seemed seductive.

She moved to pull a shaving from the horse's mane. Seeming to misread the action, he slipped his fingers around her wrist.

"Do you want to kiss me again?" she asked.

He nodded, his eyes bright beyond the barrier of control.

Piper had never understood why people lost themselves when it came to love, or lust. It had never made sense to her. It still didn't. But as she kissed Douglas again, she could sense a rising tide not inside her but inside *them*, as if something in their coming together could overpower either of them alone.

He said he felt too much.

He said it was painful.

And she could feel it when she kissed him.

DETECTIVE PEREZ

I hate to say this. I really, *really* hate to say this. . . ." Alicia Williams seemed to relish the pause. "You need to talk to Vida."

"The little girl?"

"The little demon. Sorry." Alicia seemed to think that saying "sorry" was enough to excuse any hyperbole. "I know it's horrible—just horrible—to say this about a teenage girl, but she's . . ." Alicia made a fist. "She *punched* my daughter. Not hit. Not slapped. Punched. I could have pressed charges. I should have." She bounced on her seat, seemingly jazzed by her dramatic retelling.

"I'm embarrassed to admit that we used to go there all the time. To *Pamela's*. With the antique pool and the heavy-pour cocktails. She had one of those signs: *It's Five O'Clock Somewhere*. Or maybe: *It's Always Wine O'Clock*? If that isn't a red flag . . . Not that I blame Pamela. Her daughter is something else. No one even knows who the father is, but it's pretty clear why it's kept a secret."

Detective Perez shifted in her chair. She hated gossip, but it was a big part of her job. One of the more tedious parts, because gossip was usually a very complicated way of saying something simple: *I don't like her.*

Alicia leaned forward conspiratorially. Detective Perez's new best friend. "Everyone says that Vida's father was a psychopath, that the reason you don't hear about him is because he's in jail. For murder." She sat back, swelling with certainty. "I'm just saying, these things tend to run in families, don't they? You would know."

Sometimes interviews could leave Detective Perez with less clarity than she'd had before. She'd learned to sense when someone was clouding her mind.

Alicia opened her mouth again, so Detective Perez hurried to say, "Vida was at the hotel when it happened." It was a small town. Detective Perez knew the owners of the hotel. They had seen the girl come back that night. "They have her on camera. She couldn't have been involved."

"Well"—Alicia blinked—"isn't that neat? Still, I wouldn't put anything past her. She's a very devious little girl. . . ."

TWO
MONTHS
BEFORE

fifty

MAPLE

The next morning, Maple woke up regretting what she'd said to Piper. She'd been angry—mad that she always had to be the one who struggled—and now she had signed herself up for more struggling.

She was scared of Commotion, more scared than ever after her fall, and now she wouldn't even have Piper to ride him.

Vida texted her in the afternoon. You dead?

Maple wrote back, I wish. She deleted the text, but then typed it again and pressed SEND before she could stop herself.

Why? Vida's answer surprised her.

Maple couldn't think of a good enough answer.

Everyone hates me.

There's something wrong with me.

I suck at everything I try.

Maple couldn't even come up with a good reason to be dead, so she finally settled on: I don't know.

Come to the barn, Vida texted.

Maple wanted to go, but she said, I'm too embarrassed. It was true.

K. Lemme know if you change your mind.

Maple was a little surprised that Vida was being so nice, but she had noticed that Vida tended to dig in when bad things happened. She had never been nicer to Maple than right after she had hurt her. Maple figured Vida was probably a little in awe of her accident, a little breathless and lusty with the violence of it.

Vida texted Maple again that night, after eight o'clock.

You should come now. It's just me and Dunners here and he's asleep. x

Maple had been on her phone all day, scrolling through TikTok for hours. It had done very little to improve her mental health. And Vida wanted her there. And just being wanted felt like enough.

K, she texted back.

I t was incredibly easy to sneak out of the Parkers' house. A whole other family could have been living there, and they probably wouldn't have noticed. Their property was enormous, endless.

Maple crossed the yard for ten minutes before she reached the gate that led to the horse trail. She punched in the security code. Then she walked the mile to the barn.

RSFE was eerily empty. It felt lonesome without the chaos. The horses were all quiet—some lying down, some standing with a hoof cocked.

Maple found Vida waiting for her inside Commotion's stall.

"Holy shit! You got stitches!" Vida said, her voice thick with envy. "Let me see."

Vida dragged Maple close. She analyzed the stitches, then gave a big sigh.

"You're so lucky. I wish I had a scar like that."

Maple had definitely not thought about the scar that way. It was right on her cheek, under her eye. It looked like a hook. She could've been blinded.

Vida stepped aside, and Maple saw that Commotion was tacked up.

"Why is his saddle on?" Maple asked.

"I thought you might want to ride him." Vida smiled at her own audacity. "Get back on the horse."

Maple was confused. Vida had never gone out of her way to help Maple before, so it immediately felt like a setup.

"Um . . . I don't know if that's a good idea," Maple said as Commotion ambled over, then stuck his nose over the gate.

"Would you rather wait and do it in front of everyone?" Vida said. She had a valid point. "Besides, I'll watch you. I'll be your trainer. And Dunners is passed out in the break room, if you die or something."

Vida lifted a bridle from a hook outside Commotion's stall. "Get your helmet."

Maple's heart, previously suppressed somewhat by the cocktail of drugs she'd been prescribed postaccident, now knocked politely on her chest, as if to say, *Please don't do this.*

"Umm . . ."

"C'mon," Vida said, slipping the bit easily into the horse's mouth. "My mom always says you need to get back on as soon as possible. The longer you wait, the worse it is. Don't you trust me?"

Maple didn't, but that seemed less important than other things, like impressing her.

Vida opened the stall door. Commotion nudged Maple, probably playful, but Maple jumped a little. Vida rolled her eyes and handed Maple the reins.

They led the horse toward the big arena. Vida paused to let

Maple mount. Vida shut the gate behind Maple for safety, although Commotion had already proved a fence couldn't hold him.

Seeming nervous and uncertain, the horse lifted his head and blasted air through his nostrils. Part of Maple wanted to back down, to run, but Vida was watching her, so she felt like there was no way out.

Maple let the horse walk first as she tried to cool her nerves, to get used to the feel of him.

"Do something," Vida ordered. Perched in Kieran's spot, she leaned forward like she was waiting for something terrible to happen.

Maple shortened her reins and picked up a trot, thinking that the action would at least distract her from her thoughts.

As usual, Commotion didn't seem to know what she wanted. He trotted bigger and bigger. He tossed his head nervously because she was nervous. Then he started to canter. Maple didn't know what to do. She didn't think she could stop him even if she wanted to. He bucked, throwing Maple forward. She just barely caught herself on his neck, then shoved herself back in the saddle.

At the rail, Vida laughed.

Then the horse—seeming to realize Maple had no control over him—took off at a gallop, faster than Maple had ever gone. He was totally out of her control. Maple rose out of the saddle, trying to stay with him. Trying to stay on.

Maple couldn't even see Vida anymore as Commotion whipped round and round the arena. The sharp air stung her eyes and her nostrils. She couldn't feel anything but the pounding of the horse beneath her.

She was going to die. She had wanted to die, and she was going to get what she wanted *now*, that night.

It took her a few rotations to realize she didn't feel scared. To understand that she was more afraid when nothing was happening than she was when something bad was actually happening.

Commotion ran until he tired himself out, and then, uncertain, he slowed to a trot and finally to a walk.

The ringing in Maple's ears dissipated. She heard Vida laughing. Vida had set her up.

Maybe that was what did it. Maybe that was the moment Maple finally snapped.

Or maybe it had started with the fall, the realization that she had faced the worst.

Or maybe it had been that text, those words spelled out: I wish.

If she wished she were dead, what did she have to be afraid of anymore?

Maple's eyes were drawn to the jumps at the center of the arena. She shortened her reins. Before she could think too much, she asked Commotion for a canter. She pointed the horse at a jump. It was one of the smaller jumps in the arena, but it was still bigger than anything she'd ever tried.

She went into two-point early, rising out of the saddle to get out of the horse's way. Commotion arced beneath her, lifted off like a rocket. She could feel all the power in his hindquarters. They launched toward the stars in the sky.

They landed, a little hard, on the other side. Maple let him canter to the rail.

"Nicely done."

She gasped. The horse shied a little, but she was able to quiet him. Her eyes found Douglas standing behind Vida at the fence.

All of the girls had a crush on Douglas Dunn. It was practically a requisite of riding at RSFE. He was handsome. He was the best rider. All the horses loved him.

Maple had never said a word to him before. "Are we in trouble?"

Douglas shrugged, then climbed onto the fence beside Vida, who looked surprised. "It's your horse."

"Okay. I'm gonna jump again." She thought he might stop her, but he didn't.

She took the jump in the other direction. Then added another one. Then she took a deep breath and did a whole course. With every jump, she felt stronger. She felt different. Like she could be someone else—but not if she tried. She could be someone else if she stopped trying.

"I'm done now," she told them when she'd finished her third course.

Vida was scowling. "How come you don't ride like that when people are around?"

Maple loosened her reins. "I don't know."

"You should figure it out," Douglas said. And then he hopped off the fence and walked away.

fifty-one

VIDA

Vida ran into Douglas in the parking lot, just as he was getting into his truck.

"Hey," Vida said, "can you give me a ride? I'm staying at Effie's house."

Vida had lied to her mother about where she was going. She'd told Pamela she would be at Effie's house; then she had gotten an Uber to meet Maple. Now she had to go to Effie's to make her story true.

"Sure," he said, stretching across the passenger seat to open the door for her.

She climbed in beside him. Even his truck smelled like pepper-mints.

"So," he said as they turned out of the parking lot, "what was that all about?"

He shot her a suspicious look. She supposed she couldn't blame him. They had grown up together, and in that time, Vida had been known to do naughty things, to do dangerous things. To cause chaos of varying degrees. Never enough chaos for her. Always more than enough for everyone else.

She stretched forward and stuffed her hand in the tub of

peppermints he kept on the floor, digging deep as if they weren't all the same.

"I was just trying to help her. *Get back on the horse.*"

"Huh."

She extracted a peppermint, unwrapped it and popped it on her tongue. "You saw how good she did. I should be a trainer probably."

"Sure." He stretched back in his seat, uncomfortable.

"Doesn't it annoy you," Vida asked, sliding closer, then resting her elbow on the console between them, "how they just get everything we've worked our whole lives for?"

Douglas made a sound, like he wanted to agree but couldn't. But she knew how to get to him. She always knew how to get to people. It was a gift she hadn't asked for—a gift that didn't exactly give so much as take away.

"She's gonna fuck that horse up. She already is. Every time you hop on him, it takes him longer and longer to figure out what you're asking, to get his head straight, because she's confusing him. She's *ruining* him."

The truck hopped when Douglas switched gears too late. He had a peppermint in his mouth. He turned it over on his tongue. "That's the way it goes, Vida. They're not our horses."

But she sensed his bitterness, could see it throb in his temple.

They hit a red light. The streetlights cut shadows across his face.

"*Anyway*"—he exhaled, forcing his frustration out—"it's not their fault. They're nice. Piper's nice. . . ." He ran his fingers down his key chain.

His neck flushed slightly at the mention of her name. Of course he liked her. She was a Basic Bitch Dream Girl. She was boring as hell, but to damaged people, boring was exotic.

"I'd be nice, too, if everyone liked me," Vida said.

Douglas smirked. "Pretty sure it's supposed to work the other way around."

"I thought Kieran assigned you to her mom?" That wiped the smile off his face.

The light turned green, but the truck didn't move.

"I don't do everything because Kieran tells me to," Douglas finally said.

Vida was often surprised by how deluded people could be about themselves. It sometimes seemed to her that people understood themselves even less than they understood other people.

Vida knew what Douglas wanted her to say, knew what she was supposed to say in this kind of situation. *Of course not! That's not what I meant!*

But she didn't. She said, "The light's green."

The truck jerked forward. They turned onto Effie's street.

She could tell Douglas was upset, and she did feel a little bad. He was doing her a favor. And even if she didn't want to like him—mostly because *everyone* liked him—she had to admit that he had always been happy to accept that, to accept *her*, chaos and all.

She swiveled to face him. "Look, I get it. You're afraid of being alone. Kieran is all you have, just like all I have is my mom."

"But I don't *just* do what he says," he repeated. His jaw clenched. His eyes swirled with his desperate darkness.

He really wanted her to lie to him, but she wouldn't. That was the gift of Vida.

fifty-two

HEATHER

Heather had never really recovered from Maple's twelfth-birthday party. She had felt personally responsible when none of Maple's friends showed up.

Heather should have made it cooler. She should have told Maple she couldn't have all the childish things that she wanted. She should have befriended the other mothers who had children in Maple's class to make sure their kids came. She should have served booze and trays of cigarettes to all the little brats in Amarillo.

Maple's fourteenth-birthday party was going to be an altogether different affair. Heather had invited everyone from the barn—even Kieran and the grooms. She was holding the party at the new house.

Maple had wanted the party to be at Vida's house, which irritated Heather. The girls spent all their free time there. Pamela's house was old and a little gross. It was not a good fit for the kind of party Heather needed to throw.

Heather didn't want people *inside* her house because, between delays on the imported marble and the chandeliers she'd sent back because they were too heavy, it wasn't quite ready yet. But her pool was way better than Pamela's pool. It had an oversized Jacuzzi, a basketball hoop and a rock feature with two slides and a secret grotto.

Heather had hired caterers and bartenders. She had included nothing vaguely childish—not even a stray balloon could be found. It was a pool party, so the guests all arrived in swimsuits and caftans far too stylish to ever get wet. Only the littlest kids even touched the water.

Piper wouldn't stop helping—directing people to the bathroom, taking out the trash, assisting the caterers. She had at least agreed to wear a swimsuit, but she looked ridiculous serving people in it.

Maple and her friends sat in a corner, whispering and laughing sinisterly.

At one point, Jeff went over to Heather and told her, "I think they're drinking."

Heather thought so, too. She didn't especially want her fourteen-year-old child drinking, but she also knew that it was what the cool, mature kids did, so she was a little torn.

"I know, but I don't want to make a scene at her party," Heather said. "Why don't we take turns walking over there every fifteen minutes? Annoy them with dad jokes, so they know we're watching."

Parties always made Heather feel better about her relationship with Jeff. They both knew—a little too well, maybe—how to look like a totally healthy couple. He spoke to her more, and he seemed to listen when she talked. He stood beside her and introduced himself at all the right times. Seeing themselves as a perfect couple in other people's eyes was more than a little confusing.

Kieran had come to the party. He was holding court with all his top riders, but all they talked about was boring horsey things. Still, it was a real coup to have him there.

He had brought Douglas, who sat alone and looked exactly as Heather would have expected a nineteen-year-old boy to look at a fourteen-year-old girl's party.

Pamela and June had gone to the bathroom and come back nearly half an hour later, both a little tipsy.

"My God, we got lost in your house!" Pamela squealed. Heather was sure they had not gotten lost by accident. They had just wanted to snoop. "It's like the fucking pyramids."

June nodded vehemently. "Very empty!"

"We've had some delays on furnishings. I'd be happy to show you around once everything's perfect," Heather said pointedly.

It annoyed her that they had taken a tour when the house wasn't ready. It felt like a personal attack.

"How do you find your girls in a place like that?" June wondered. Her own house was a modest ten thousand square feet.

"I think the girls are drinking vodka," Heather said, redirecting the conversation.

She was pretty sure they drank at Pamela's house—that was probably why they liked hanging out there so much. Pamela seemed the type to be very lax on drinking.

"It's good for them," Pamela said, basically confirming Heather's suspicions. "I noticed you have two master bedrooms."

Even June seemed surprised by Pamela's audacity.

"Jeff works late. He wakes me up." Heather's lie was odd in that it was basically on par with the truth, but Heather preferred that they think the separate bedrooms were her idea.

"How Continental," Pamela said.

Pamela seemed to be in a nasty mood. Had been, really, since Maple's fall. She seemed annoyed that Maple hadn't quit, which Heather thought was a little odd. She kept thinking of the suggestion Pamela had made weeks ago: that Vida should part-lease Commotion.

Heather knew Pamela well enough now to see that she wasn't as well-off as Heather had originally thought. Heather had assumed that Pamela had a slightly ramshackle house and worn clothes and a vintage Mercedes because she was preoccupied with horsey things, but she was beginning to think that Pamela actually didn't have the money to repair or replace them.

Especially because of Vida's horses. They had three horses, all allegedly Vida's, but all of them had once belonged to Pamela. And while Pamela was constantly reminding everyone that Vida had *three* horses while all the other girls had one, what did the number matter if none of them were very good anymore?

Heather wondered if Pamela hoped that Maple would quit riding so that Vida could ride Commotion.

It was a terrible thought to have about a friend, especially someone Heather spent so much time with, but people were people, and they were bound to want things they didn't have. Heather just hoped that Pamela would get it under control.

Commotion wasn't her horse. He would never be her horse. Heather understood envy better than most, but there was no chance in hell that she would ever give Maple's horse to Vida.

fifty-three

MAPLE

Maple tried not to think about her old birthday on her new birthday, but she couldn't help the constant comparisons.

There were tons of people at the pool party—even if they were mostly adults from the barn. There was an open bar, which was easy to steal from. There was a glamorous pool, and there was fancy food. Douglas Dunn was there, and he was really cute.

Maple took tons of pictures. She rarely used social media except to post heavily curated images from her new life, specifically aimed at making her bully jealous—as if she were the only person on the Internet.

Maple was with her friends, and they were drinking spiked mocktails, which were basically cocktails, which seemed incredibly mature and cool. Maple had even posted a picture of one with a winky face. It was perfect, almost.

To shore up her courage, Maple was drinking a little more than she should have. Kieran was there, and Maple needed to talk to him. She kept an eye on him from the special birthday-girl table she was sharing with Vida and Effie. When he left to go to the bathroom, she excused herself—which was a little harder than she'd expected, because best friends did everything together—and then she followed him.

She caught him in the hallway between one unfinished room and another.

"Happy birthday, kid," he said as she blocked his path. "Sorry you took a tumble." Like her fall had in any way been cute.

"I wanted to tell you something," she said.

She hadn't wanted to start like that. She had intended to just tell him. She was tired of apologizing and asking permission. It seemed to her that she had tried to be a nice girl her whole life and what, what, *what* had that gotten her?

"I want to ride Jumpers."

That got his attention.

Maple was currently training in Hunters, like all the girls were. Ideally, people learned to ride properly before they attempted show jumping. But Maple didn't care.

She wanted to ride Jumpers. She actually wanted to compete in the Little Palm Cup. Maybe she had been bluffing when she said it in Pamela's pool, but the more she thought about it, the more it seemed like the proof she needed—a way to make everyone understand she was not who they thought she was.

As if winning could change her. As if she could become Vida by beating her.

"Everyone keeps saying how much I suck," Maple started.

"Who says that?" he asked.

"Well . . . Pamela," Maple said honestly, which made Kieran laugh.

"Why don't we have a chat?" He scanned the area. "Are there any chairs in this house?"

"In the kitchen," she said.

They made the long walk there. They each took a stool by the kitchen island.

Maple had been so geared up to talk to him, had been thinking about what she'd say all week. She started to ramble. "I know I have terrible equitation." Equitation was the classical method for riding a horse. "But you don't need good eq in Jumpers. You just need to be fast. It's at least half the horse, right? And I have the best horse."

"And what's your . . . um . . . your time scale on this proposition? Shall we find you a Grand Prix this weekend?"

Maple knew he was teasing her. He didn't understand what it was like to be everyone's loser. The weaker daughter, the bad rider, the one who got bullied. But she could prove herself. She could be tough and fearless. She could be someone else. She just needed someone to give her the chance.

"If you want. It would be your decision, because I want you to train me."

That got him. He looked at her like she was a child, but perhaps his child. "Only the best ride with me."

Maple wasn't the best. She knew that. It was like Pamela had said: She was all money and no talent. But wasn't money an advantage?

"What makes you think you're the best?"

"My parents' money?"

That made him laugh again.

fifty-four

PIPER

Piper was a bundle of nervous energy. First because Douglas might come to the party, and then because he did.

Piper didn't know how to approach him. After they'd kissed, he had told her that nobody could know.

It was a very obvious red flag that Piper was keen to overlook. Maybe he wasn't allowed to date clients. Maybe it was a rule. Maybe he was scared. Maybe he was so deeply in love with her that he was afraid other people might ruin it.

An abandoned cocktail glass finally brought her into his vicinity. His eyes stayed trained on his phone. There was a line of sweat between his pectoral muscles. It dropped like an arrow from his heart.

"Do you want anything to drink or, like, food or something?" she asked.

He flipped the peppermint on his tongue and smiled drowsily. "What are you, the waiter?"

"I'm just trying to help."

"Cute," he said, too quiet for anyone else to hear. His eyes dropped to his phone.

"What are you looking at?" she asked.

He held out the phone, and she got closer, did a quick scan and sat down beside him. He had been looking at horses. He stayed consistent. She could smell his sunscreen, feel heat coming off his skin like the sun's rays had converged inside him. On his phone screen, a rider was taking a horse through a jumping course. She recognized the horse, and then she recognized the rider.

"You're watching yourself on Commotion. Congratulations, by the way. I heard you won."

He had ridden Commotion in another Grand Prix the night before. The Parkers hadn't gone to watch. They had been too busy with all the preparations for the party.

"It's easy on Commotion," he demurred.

"Why are you watching yourself?"

"I always watch myself ride. It's a good way to learn. You should try it." He frowned at the screen. "But it's funny, you know. I can always tell what I did wrong, but it's harder to see what I did right."

"Maybe you just got lucky."

"Probably."

He glanced at her again, then shifted slightly. She couldn't tell if he had shifted closer or farther away.

He was back in rider mode. It was almost scary how he had seemingly trained himself to switch off. Sometimes Piper couldn't sleep at night because she was torturing herself with questions about him. Why did she even like him? Why did she need to turn him on?

Piper wasn't a particularly spiritual person, but lust had a way of making her suspect dark magic; it settled in her belly like a curse. She wanted, very much, for him to come to her bedroom. She wanted to close the door and lock it so they could be alone together, so she could stop helping with the damn party so much. She wanted to kiss him again, and it was painful, like a bruise blossoming over her heart.

"Do you want to see my room?" she asked quickly, her words all running together.

He looked up suddenly. It was like headlights over her heart, and everything was illuminated.

"What would we do?"

She felt a little dizzy. "I could show you my Breyer horse collection."

He cracked a smile. Between them, his hand slid toward hers. He brushed her knuckle with his pinkie, faint as a wish.

He scanned the party, but his eyes dimmed as they drifted over her parents.

"We'd better not."

He flipped the peppermint in his mouth. Then he pressed PLAY and watched his ride again.

fifty-five

MAPLE

Kieran had agreed to teach Maple, but he had conditions.

"I don't want your mom to watch. You come early, six a.m., before anyone else is there."

Maple wondered if Douglas had told Kieran about seeing her ride, how she had done better when her mother wasn't there.

"I don't understand why Kieran wouldn't want me to watch," Heather complained. "I've never said a word during any of your lessons. He can ask Amy."

"It's not my rule," Maple said, although she supported it.

Her mom dropped her off at the barn at quarter to six. Heather claimed she would just wait in the parking lot, but Maple made her leave.

"What if Kieran catches you?" Maple asked. "I don't want to mess this up."

When Maple walked down to the barn, she was surprised to see Commotion jumping in arena one. Douglas was riding him. The horse had already worked up a sweat. Maple figured they were trying to tire him out before she got on, which she was okay with.

Kieran was at his usual spot on the rail.

"Come over here," he directed her. "I want you to watch Douglas."

Maple stood beside Kieran. She already had her helmet on, so she felt a little stupid watching Douglas ride. She didn't know exactly what she was supposed to be watching for. Douglas was so much better than her that everything he did, right or wrong, was imperceptible to her.

Kieran stretched back and said, "Do you know what your problem is?"

"No," Maple said, trying to be obedient.

"You're not invested. At all. In any of this."

The accusation stung, but Maple wanted to prove herself. She knew that if she backed down, she wouldn't get another chance.

"That's not true. I'm here every day. I'm here all day."

"Doing what? Hanging out with your friends. Cleaning bridles."

Maple was embarrassed that he had noticed. Her whole face burned up. Douglas waited on the horse, but even though he was far away, she thought he could probably hear Kieran.

"You never watch the other riders. Never try to ride other horses or even work with them. You want to suck."

That got her. "No, I don't!"

"Of course you do," he said.

"I don't. . . . Why would I want to be bad?" The accusation was ridiculous. It didn't make sense.

"Because even if you were good, even if you were the best that you could possibly be *right now*, in this moment, you still wouldn't be good enough. And you know that."

It wasn't exactly the inspiring lesson she'd hoped for.

Kieran called out to Douglas. "Dismount and give her a leg up."

After what Kieran had just said, Maple honestly thought the lesson was over. Why would he even bother teaching her if he thought she would never be good enough?

"Go," he directed.

She went. She stood beside the horse as, behind her, Douglas counted in her ear and then lifted her up into the saddle. They adjusted the stirrups. Maple took up the reins.

"How high was she jumping the other night?" Kieran asked Douglas.

Douglas had told Kieran that he'd seen her. She wondered if that was part of the reason Kieran had agreed to teach her. She hoped it was. Hoped that she was secretly gifted, secretly good enough in a way that would soon be revealed to everyone, the way things happened in horse movies.

"Meter thirty," Douglas said.

"You're kidding," Kieran said.

Maple wanted to ask what that was in feet, but she was afraid to know the answer. Kieran directed Douglas to set jumps. Maple's eyes widened when she saw how high they were.

"They look bigger in daylight, huh?" Kieran said, but Maple privately wondered if Douglas was wrong about the height. "All right, let's not waste any more of my time. The green vertical, to the red oxer, to the blue line in six."

Maple's mouth went dry. He wanted her to jump a whole course *now*, without even warming up. If she backed down, he might never teach her again.

Maple shortened her reins. She picked up a canter before she even looked to see where the first jump was. She had to cut across the arena and change directions to line herself up for it, which was a little embarrassing, but she did it as quickly as she could.

She took the first jump and then the second. She lost a stirrup in the line and was so preoccupied with getting it back that she forgot to count strides.

It was a pretty sloppy ride, but she had done what he'd asked. She hadn't fallen off or knocked anything over. She hadn't died. For someone who had spent most of her lessons walking in the round pen, she thought her riding had actually been pretty impressive.

After she finished, she transitioned the horse to a halt and waited for Kieran's response.

"Like I said, you want to suck."

"No, I don't! I just wasn't ready."

When Kieran hopped down from the fence, the horse spooked a little under her. "You weren't ready? Did I not tell you that we had a lesson at six o'clock this morning?"

Her palms were slick with sweat. Her voice quavered when she said, "You told me."

"Then why the fuck aren't you ready?"

Maple had heard Kieran swear at other riders. It was scary secondhand, but it was terrifying having him swear at her.

"I'm sorry."

"Sorry? What does that do for me?"

"Can I try again?"

"No, you can't *try*. You do it properly, or you get the fuck out of my arena."

"Okay." She shortened her reins.

This was going worse than she had imagined, which somehow made her feel calmer, more in control.

She picked up a canter in the *right* direction. She felt the horse's strides, tried to make them the correct length, the perfect distance to meet the jump at the exact right point, so she . . .

Hit the first jump perfectly, already looking at the next one, gauging the strides on the bend, so she hit that one perfectly, too.

She kept her chest out and her heels down, and she followed her natural eye through the line. She executed exactly six strides, so she found her distance on the last jump, too, and then she cantered quietly away before she transitioned to a halt.

Anxious, she turned to Kieran.

"Better," he said.

She did it again. She did it three more times, until the horse was in a lather, until Maple's muscles ached, until everyone started to arrive: Vida and Pamela and Effie and June.

When the lesson was over, Kieran approached Commotion, laid a hand on his shoulder and gazed up at Maple.

"Stick with me, kid, and maybe one day you won't suck."

fifty-six

PAMELA

Maple's fall had unexpected consequences. Pamela and Vida arrived at the barn on the Tuesday after Maple's birthday party to find Maple jumping a course in arena one. Kieran was screaming, his voice already warmed up at that early hour.

"Eyes up! Look where you're going!"

Pamela couldn't believe it. She'd had this dream before, but in her dream, Vida was riding.

"Mommy, what's happening?" Vida asked, stopping on the stairway from the parking lot.

"I don't know, honey, but I intend to find out." But not right away. They watched the rest of the lesson. Everyone did.

Maple wasn't jumping small jumps. She was clinging to that horse like a monkey, her face so tight that her stitches started to bleed, a single red tear beneath her eye.

The only person who wasn't watching was her mother. Heather wasn't there. Pamela knew she should text her, should tell her what was happening, but she didn't. She couldn't bear the jealousy of Heather getting to watch Maple ride with Kieran.

They all observed breathlessly until Moira rode into the arena for her lesson. Maple was done.

"Walk him out around the property," Kieran instructed Maple, even though she had never walked the horse anywhere alone. "And tell the grooms to ice his legs." Then he put his hand on the horse's shoulder and said the most hideous thing Pamela had ever heard. "Stick with me, kid, and maybe one day you won't suck."

Vida drifted after Maple. She knew which way the wind was blowing.

It took Pamela several minutes to even approach Kieran, she was so overcome with feeling. Moira was warming up. Perched on the rail, Kieran was watching her ride as Pamela approached.

"What on earth was that about?" she asked.

"What?" he said.

Pamela had known Kieran for more than twenty years, and she had never in her life witnessed something like the scene with Maple. Was he softening in his old age? Had he lost his mind?

"Maple," she said, but he was going to make her spell it out. "The lesson . . . Why? I don't understand why you're giving her a lesson."

"I like her. And I think people underestimate her."

"She had a horrific accident *last week*. She's in over her head. She could get—" Pamela didn't say "killed," but the word was implied.

"Horseback riding is a dangerous sport. I've seen people impaled in crossties. Kicked in the head picking hooves . . ."

Pamela folded her arms and went to the bone of the matter. "I don't understand why you never teach Vida like that. She's a much more talented rider."

Kieran stretched back. "What do you say to me every time Vida loses at a horse show? *But it wasn't fair, the other kid had more money.*"

He was right. She did say that.

"So you do understand. But you're still asking questions. I think you're just trying to wind me up." He turned to give her his full attention. "This isn't a sport about who's the best. There's a kid in a field somewhere who can ride circles around every overdressed prat on this property. If racing is the sport of kings, then this is the sport of princesses. And all of us are the minstrels, so you'd better start fucking dancing."

"But Vida is your—" She was on the verge of saying something that he had convinced her never to say. Kieran had said it was best for everyone so long ago that she couldn't remember why. "Best little rider," she finished too fast.

He dropped from the rail, entered the ring. "I said we'd work on bending lines today, right?" he called to Moira. "Why don't you warm up over the green vertical?"

Pamela watched him stalk away from her and wondered, not for the first time, how she had ever had sex with him. It wasn't that he wasn't sexy, but he seemed to exist on a different plane—the horse plane. Where Buckley had an abscess; where Cobalt's topline had been improved, so now his saddle needed to be re-flocked; where Firenze got his best impulsion through transition work, so how could they replicate that on course?

If she had to define a reason for how they had ended up smashing over a tack box, she would have said Kieran was worried about her switching to another trainer. Back then Kieran had been the closer. He was the one who drew clients in, and sometimes in and out. Like most men, he never seemed to equate sex with making babies—only horses had sex for that.

She sometimes wondered if Kieran really was Vida's father. The secret was so deeply kept that she questioned her own sanity, wondered if Vida might belong to someone else even though Pamela had been sleeping only with Kieran.

Still, there was something impenetrable about Kieran's insistence, like his mind was a force field pushing every unwanted thought out. For all she knew, Vida might have been a child of some other god.

fifty-seven

VIDA

Vida was having trouble keeping the Parkers' names out of her mouth. It had started with Heather, who she loved to carefully pick apart in front of Maple.

"Your mom is so pretty. . . . Like a cheerleader . . . like a beauty queen."

Her comments seemed like compliments, but the trick was they weren't. Not in Vida's capable mouth. She never said Heather was smart. She never said she was cool. She never said she was nice. She was just beautiful—a valueless, artificial trait. Something she hadn't earned or deserved, a distortion.

And when Maple let her say those things, it escalated.

"She's always here. . . . She's so annoying. . . . She has no chill."

Until Maple said, "I like my mom." And Vida had to stop.

Then Piper came, and Vida found the perfect target.

"So annoying."

"Bossy."

"Such a know-it-all."

At first Maple didn't agree, but she didn't stop Vida either. And after repetition eroded her resolve, Maple admitted, "I know."

And after weeks, Maple contributed:

"She's always been like that."

"She's just so helpful."

"It really irritates me actually."

And Vida felt relieved.

Vida had in herself this urge, this need, to tear people down. It made her feel slick and powerful. It made her feel like herself. She needed friends who would allow it, even participate in it. Or else she would resent them. Or else she would feel like a freak.

In essence, she trained her friends to be her little mirrors, to assume the worst aspects of her personality and thus reinforce it, cleanse it, redeem it.

Effie was good most of the time. Maple was better. Maple was, in fact, becoming a little too good. Because the point of training her friends to be like her was to place herself at the center, and sometimes Maple seemed to become too much like Vida—more Vida than Vida was. She seemed to pull the focus to herself.

And then Maple had that lesson with Kieran.

Vida was walking down the steps with her mom when she saw them. She swayed on her feet. She felt deliciously sick. A wave of nausea. A numbing sensation. She caught herself on the stair rail.

"Mommy, what's happening?"

She watched the whole lesson. Barely breathing. Someone was choking-out her heart. It was like she was watching her own dream come to life, only in this dream, she had someone else's face.

After the lesson, Vida flew to Maple's side. She hated herself for it. She walked beside her, hovered just under her right stirrup as they cooled the horse down.

"How did that happen?" Vida asked when she found her voice again.

"What? The lesson?"

Yes, the fucking lesson.

Maple shrugged. "I just asked him."

"Why did he say yes?" Vida's voice had a little edge to it.

Maple loosened her reins so that Commotion could stretch his neck. "I don't know. I guess because he knew the horse could do it."

"He probably felt bad for you. After what happened last week," Vida snapped, super supportive.

"He told me I was tougher than everyone thought." Maple scrunched her face, as if thinking about that marvelous revelation.

"He once told me I had soft hands," Vida said, and then she hated herself for being pathetic.

Effie came trotting up. "What happened? I heard you were jumping with Kieran?"

Maple beamed. "I was."

"Congratulations!" Effie said.

Vida had skipped that part.

They all walked together, but now they were silent. Effie seemed to recognize that she shouldn't keep praising Maple, and Vida wasn't about to praise Maple. In fact, Vida was so miserable she didn't even want to say mean things about anyone. No, that wasn't true. She wanted to say mean things about Maple.

She wished they could go their separate ways, but of course they couldn't. They were friends, so they had to do everything together. Maple had to go to the bathroom, so they all went.

And when she was locked inside, Vida exhaled and said fast, "I can't fucking believe she had a lesson with Kieran."

"My mom said it's because people were talking, after her fall. About how she shouldn't be riding that horse," Effie said quickly. "Kieran's just trying to prove something."

Vida immediately felt better. Effie was a good friend. Maple was a total bitch.

Maple came out of the bathroom too soon, and they were all tied together again. Vida felt a terrific pressure. All day long she couldn't help relieving it in short, cruel bursts.

"Those pants fit weird. It's not you! It's just the pants!"

"I think you have something in your teeth."

"You should let Effie fix your hair."

At the end of the day, Vida got into the car with her mom. As soon as she had shut her door, she exploded.

"I can't believe she's riding with Kieran now. She's the worst fucking rider at the barn. Did you see her lose her stirrup? How she grabbed mane over the oxer? She nearly fell off! And she looks like fucking Scarface with her stitches," Vida said, although she actually envied the scar.

"I know, sweetie. It's ridiculous," Pamela agreed. "I'm very, very unhappy."

Vida kicked the glove compartment. "A lot of good that does. You said she would quit!" At the end of the day, everything was her mother's fault. All roads led to Pamela. "You said after last week, she would quit!"

"I thought she would. Her mother is clearly a fucking lunatic."

Vida sagged in her seat. "At least she's a rich fucking lunatic."

She knew their financial situation was her mother's sore spot. Pamela was perpetually disappointed at not having as much money as *everyone else*—at least, everyone around them.

"Talent trumps money," Pamela sang.

"That's bullshit! All the top riders are the children of fucking billionaires."

Pamela kept her eyes trained forward. "I didn't mean talent at riding."

fifty-eight

PIPER

Piper went to the barn every day, but she had no horse to ride. She wasn't experienced enough to ride horses for the training program. She was still allowed to help with other things, but she was starting to feel a little pathetic. It was embarrassing. Douglas was riding fifteen horses a day, and she couldn't even ride one.

Worse, Maple had started policing Commotion, hanging around on the tack box outside his stall, stopping Piper from even getting close to him.

"What are you doing?"

And "I was just about to take him out."

And "Why are you here?"

It was ridiculous and bratty and not at all like the sister she knew. But Maple had just had a major accident, and Piper figured she was extra stressed. She would get over it. She would let it go. Except she didn't. If anything, she got worse. More blatant. Ruder.

She made mean comments under her breath or to their mom.

"I don't know why you're here if you don't even want your own horse."

"Who are you trying to impress?"

"It's not like you're friends with anyone."

She was being a total brat, and Heather did nothing about it. Jeff did nothing about it. They both seemed a little shocked by Maple's attitude, but they also seemed protective of it, as if a bad attitude were a delicate thing.

As if being a brat was better than being a victim.

As if they preferred Maple that way. Piper was losing her sister, and everyone else seemed to think it was a win.

Piper complained to Douglas about Maple's behavior, but he just said, "I thought you were getting your own horse."

She had found him in the break room. A slightly primitive instinct kept her near the door, the only possible escape route.

They hadn't been alone since they had kissed. In fact, Douglas had taken a big step away from her—no more lunches, no more late-night meetings.

At first, Piper was proud of her ability to be patient. Douglas liked her. She liked him. Of course they would be together. Of course it would work out.

But days passed and his eyes kept slipping over her, like she was something sharp to avoid. He still spoke to her. He had to; they practically worked together. But he was disconcertingly adept at making her feel invisible.

In time, she learned that she wasn't the only girl he had made disappear. It was allegedly his MO, to sleep with girls, then ghost them, only he did it live and in person, a full-on zombie.

She promised herself she was different; then she realized she was. He hadn't even had the courtesy to sleep with her before he shut her down.

She felt angry, and then she felt sad, but she convinced herself those emotions weren't fair—to her or to him. Just because someone liked you didn't mean they owed themselves to you. Maybe she was wrong to feel entitled to Douglas, in spite of what either of them felt.

Maybe.

Then he texted her at two in the morning.

I can't sleep.

It was unclear why he was telling her that, but after reading his text, she could not sleep either, and she told him so. Then he started texting her other things.

Good morning, in the morning.

Good night, at night.

Why aren't you here? Since she was at the barn, she texted him, I'm in the feed room, and expected him to come find her, but he didn't.

She felt very cautious about these text interactions, like she was capturing a wild animal.

Did you have lunch yet? When she told him she hadn't, he didn't suggest that they eat together.

Where are you? But he wouldn't meet her.

Did you ride today?

There's a cake in the break room.

I fell off. Did you see?

And she texted, No, so he told her what had happened. They texted back and forth about it until she said, I'm glad you're okay.

Then he said nothing for over forty-eight hours.

He probably forgot. He probably got distracted. He probably wasn't even thinking about her.

But then he finally texted her back, at three in the morning: Thanks. And she was overcome with the certainty that he *had* been thinking about her all that time.

And now she was alone with him in the break room. He was holding his phone limply, like a gun with no bullets.

"I am getting my own horse," Piper answered him. "Probably. I haven't decided yet. Anyway, I don't want to talk about horses."

He immediately looked uncomfortable.

"You said you liked me." Piper felt exposed, childish. She was back in the third grade, when feelings were openly used as weapons. *You like me. You hate me. You're mean.* "But it kind of seems like you're avoiding me."

"I text you all the time," he said, like this was a spectacular concession.

She took a step toward him. He took a step back. She wasn't even sure if he realized it.

"It's like you're afraid of me."

"I am afraid of you," he said a little bravely.

"Why?"

"You don't understand what it's like. You have parents and money. You could never really fall." He shook his head, tired, frustrated. "Kieran is my boss. He's supporting me. He's supporting my mom. No one else would do that. I don't have other options. This is the only thing I'm good at. And this is the only place I can do it."

"So Kieran doesn't want you to have a life?"

"It's not about Kieran. I can't lose focus. There's too much at stake."

"Did you ever consider that passion might make you a better rider?"

His eyes darkened. "It would make me a more dangerous one."

She could see it then, in a flash: the point of his fear curved around the word.

"What do you mean, 'dangerous'?"

"You don't know what I used to be like. Before . . ." He exhaled, eyes dimmed with pain as if it pulled him from the moment, pulled him from himself. "I used to get so angry at my mom. I'm embarrassed to admit it."

"I totally understand. Believe me. But you didn't make her fall. It's not your fault."

He shook his head, as if she didn't understand. As if he secretly knew everything. As if he held the whole world in his hands, under his control, except for that one moment, except for that one little slip.

Piper could see him shutting down, and she wanted to catch him, to help him. She tried to think of something he would understand. She thought of horses.

"Have you ever heard of 'learned helplessness'?"

It was a term people used to describe horses that had shut themselves down. Horses that did everything they were asked to do, did it perfectly, as if they were machines and not living things.

"Yes." He seemed to suspect what she was getting at.

"If you were training a horse, your own horse, would you train it like that? Would you force it to bend to your will? Would you take away its personality? Its soul?"

"Of course not."

"Then why do you train yourself that way?" Piper started toward the door. It was like working with a horse. She had to feel out when to ask and when to release. "You know what I think? I think your mom would want you to be happy way more than she would want you to be a good rider."

"Piper."

She turned. She could see his chest pumping, could maybe see his heartbeat in his throat.

She had caught him, and then she released him. She walked out the door.

DETECTIVE PEREZ

H ave you talked to Douglas Dunn yet?" Emma Moreno asked. She was another mother who had volunteered her services but seemed more intent on airing her complaints.

"Who's that?" Detective Perez asked.

"Oh, you would know if you saw him," she assured her, glowing with the light of that certainty. "The one who rides the horses."

"Why would we talk to him?"

Emma tossed her neat blond hair, as if preparing for a starring role. "I saw him leaving this barn aisle around midnight last night. Alone."

Detective Perez tried not to lean forward. Up until that point, she had been assured that the barn aisle would have been empty so late at night. Everyone would have already gone home.

Preliminary signs placed the death at around midnight, shortly after the deceased had last been seen alive. The body had been found the next morning, around six. The 911 call had been made about half an hour later, after the body had been moved and the needle bagged.

"Around midnight, you say?"

"Yes. I was with Tracy Hicks's team," Emma confirmed. "You can ask. My daughter Cassidy and I are considering switching trainers."

"And what is Douglas Dunn's relationship to the deceased?"

Emma smirked, almost girlishly, before sobering up. "Well, I would assume it was the same as his relationship to any other client— Sorry. Any other *female* client."

"I'm not sure I follow." Detective Perez kind of thought she did.

"He doesn't just ride the horses."

Detective Perez wished everyone she interviewed would stop letting their personal feelings color their evidence, but she knew that was impossible. People ran on feelings, not facts.

"Is that why you want us to talk to him?"

"No. This is not sour grapes," she said. "I think you should talk to him because they say he killed his mother."

"I beg your pardon?"

Emma paused, as if pleased to finally have had some effect. "Sorry," she admitted. "My mistake. She isn't *dead*, not exactly. But she might as well be. I heard she's practically brain-dead."

"And you think this Douglas Dunn is responsible?"

"They were arguing right before the accident," Emma said. "She wanted to move to Europe. He didn't want to go. She was riding a green horse that he had trained. And when she fell, her helmet strap somehow snapped. He was the only one with a motive. I think he's a very dark person. Nobody notices because he's so attractive. But underneath? I think he's very *damaged. Intense. Passionate.*"

The conversation was veering wildly off track. All of the barn moms had a lot to say, but none of it seemed relevant to the situation at hand.

Detective Perez took a centering breath. "All right. So you're saying he was here last night, and you think he had some kind of sexual relationship with the deceased. Why would he have killed her?"

Emma smiled. "I heard he got a girl pregnant."

SIX
WEEKS
BEFORE

fifty-nine

PIPER

That night, Douglas texted Piper two words: Come over.

Piper pulled up to Kieran's house after dark. Piper had never seen the house, and it was honestly creepy. It looked like something from an old Hollywood horror movie.

Douglas answered the door in sweatpants. The house was dark behind him except for one light, down a distant hall, that cast a burnished yellow glow.

"Hello," she said, peering over his shoulder.

"He's at the horse show in Burbank," he said, answering her unasked question. "Do you want to come in?"

"It's so dark," she said, and then wished she hadn't. She didn't want Douglas to think she wasn't totally comfortable. That was the game you played with boys. "I mean, it's fine."

She followed him into the house, past the Gothic entryway, past oil paintings of galloping horses.

"This house is huge," she said.

It wasn't nearly as large as her parents' house, but the fact that it was old made it seem bigger. New houses were always enormous, but a big old house felt epic.

"Yeah, it gets really cold," he said.

The house was cold, California cold, as he led her through a network of hallways to his bedroom.

His room was smaller than she had expected. It was also extremely bare, like he had just moved in. There was nothing on the walls. No shutters on the windows.

He folded himself onto his bed. There was no chair or couch of any kind. Piper should sit on the bed, right? It would be weird to sit on the floor.

"Here." He scooted over on the bed, making room for her.

Now she had to sit down. She reminded herself that they had already kissed, but the thought didn't have the relaxing effect she had hoped it would.

She sat down. His bed was softer than she had expected. He had a nice mattress.

"Oh," she said, scooting back against the wall. "This is comfy."

"It's, like, a memory thing."

"Sure."

She couldn't look directly at him. Her breath seemed trapped in the web of her throat.

She looked out his shutterless window. She could see the moon. She thought to point it out but felt her throat closing. She was going to die. What if she died right there? Would that be weird?

He moved so he was sitting in front of her. He gently took both of her wrists, pressed his fingers to her pulse, looked down like he was reading it. Approximately fifty million beats per minute.

"I need to tell you something." He gazed up at her through the shield of his eyelashes. "I was lying when I said I wasn't lonely. I didn't used to be. Until I met you. I miss you when you're not around. Not just now, before we even met. Like you should have been here all along. Like I *missed* you before I even knew you."

"I know exactly what you mean," she said.

It was crazy. Of course it fucking was. Falling in love never made sense until you did it, until you *had* to do it. And then the whole world rearranged itself, as if revealing that it was designed explicitly for just you two.

"You're smart," he said. "And you're beautiful."

Piper knew that being beautiful wasn't important, but she had never been called beautiful before. Her mother had always been the beautiful one, so Piper's first instinct was to correct him.

"And you're so kind. That day at your sister's party, I knew that I would never meet anyone as good as you. I mean, it was a party, and your family is so fucking rich, and you were walking around taking drink orders, picking up glasses."

"So you like me because I'm servile?" she teased.

She couldn't help herself. She had always believed that she was confident, but nothing made her feel more exposed than kind words.

"I like you for every reason."

The swelling in her heart dimmed only when she realized it was her turn, and he hadn't left much on the table.

She laced her fingers in his, drawing him out. "I was thinking about what you said the other day, how you changed after your mom's accident. How you switched yourself off. I don't think that's true. I've seen you with horses. You're sensitive and you're passionate and you're loving. You put your soul into your horses because it's safer there. But you're safe with me. Your heart is safe with me."

His eyes were locked on hers, and inside them, she could see all the passion that she had known was there all along. She had the immense feeling that she was dying. That she would never be the same again after that night. And running underneath everything was the delicious guilt that she had encouraged this. She had pushed for this, never considering that he might be right: It might be dangerous to feel too much.

When he shifted closer, her eyes grazed over his sweats. Did he have a hard-on? She hadn't looked closely. This was a nightmare. This was terrifying. But it was also the most exquisite, wonderful thing that had ever happened to her.

"What do you want to do?" she said.

He was hovering over her, eyes drifting downward, so it was fairly obvious, but he was polite enough to answer, "That's a question for you, I think."

"Well, I am a virgin." She hated that she'd had to volunteer that information, but it was *what you did*. To explain why you might not be a superior performer. "But, like, not by choice."

He broke into a smile. "What does that mean?"

"I mean, like, I just haven't met the right person, but I've wanted to not be a virgin for a long time. *Really long*," she said, like she was eighty-one instead of eighteen.

It was the truth, and she was glad she had waited—which she hadn't expected to be. She had been waiting for someone exactly like Douglas, but she had also told herself so many times that someone like Douglas didn't exist. Someone handsome and talented and kind. Someone who really liked her. She had told herself this so frequently that she had started to believe it, but she had still held out, and she was so glad she had, because this was going to be exactly right.

"I have done some stuff," Piper said. "Just not the whole shebang." She immediately regretted the use of that word.

"Okay," he said, nodding like he had been given an assignment, like he did in the arena when Kieran laid out a course. And then he executed it, to the letter.

He kissed her, so delicately it was like he was slowly unwrapping her. He pressed himself against her, hard inside his sweatpants. Then he directed her down onto the bed.

He moved carefully down her body. She was still dressed—pretty stupidly, she now realized—in her riding clothes. He took off her tall boots—something she normally found extremely difficult, but he did it easily. She undid her belt and her breeches, then lifted her hips.

He hooked his fingers through her belt loops and slipped off her pants and underwear in one smooth move. Then he put his mouth over her and warmed her up like a good rider.

She could tell he had done this before—what was more, he thought about it. Every boy she had fooled around with up until then had been shockingly inept. They stumbled around like cops at a crime scene, sticking their fingers everywhere, making a mess.

Douglas was disconcertingly adept. He had the air of someone who had done research—possibly in the field—and he used his mouth and his tongue and his fingers and his breath. He used, really, everything at his disposal, in such a way that Piper was simultaneously so overwhelmed and happy and scared that all she could do was try not to moan, try not to writhe.

Enjoying sex so much seemed obscene, and Douglas kept having to stop so she could calm down—which, incidentally, did not help her calm down.

"How are you so good at this?" she said, gasping as he came up to kiss her lips and let her taste herself in his mouth. "Wait," she amended. "Don't answer that."

"I want you to come," he breathed in her ear, almost pleading. Then he slid back down her body and got to work.

The very things that made Douglas a good rider made him good in bed: He had perfect cadence, he created impulsion, he understood how to correctly apply his aids and he wanted—seemingly with his whole body, his whole self—just to please you, to give you exactly what you wanted.

Piper was trying *not* to come, because she was afraid that she really might lose control then, might moan so loudly even the horses and ponies would hear her, but eventually she couldn't stop herself and she covered her own mouth as her orgasm racked through her again and again and again, because naturally Douglas knew how to make it last longer.

As the final wave settled, he came back up to kiss her lips, called her a "good girl" like she was one of his goddamn horses.

Then he started to move away from her, like his job was done, but she wasn't going to let him go. She wrapped her fingers through his. She pulled him closer. She made him look her in the eyes, so she could make sure he was there with her.

"I want you to . . ."

She couldn't even say the word; she was so dizzy and sex bright she had lost the ability to form a thought. So instead, she slid her fingers under his waistband.

He swallowed, looked hard in her eyes like he might say no, but he didn't. He started to get up to look for a condom, but she pulled him back down. With a completely straight face, she told him he could ride her bareback.

He helped her remove his sweats and his boxer shorts; then he guided himself into her.

They had sex. It was perfect. They had the same rhythm because they rode the same horse.

Afterward they talked about horses, cuddled up, still undressed in bed. They slid through pictures on his phone, like a Tinder couple looking for a third. Sometimes he would shift, and she would flush with the awareness of his penis. She knew where it was and what it was doing at any given moment.

"You can tell this one has a lot of heart," he said, showing her a little mare leaping over a water jump.

"Which one do you like the best?" she said, still slightly breathless.

"You know, I . . ." He shifted away from her. "That night we met at the barn? It wasn't an accident. I knew you would be there."

"Okay," she said, holding on to his eyes, waiting for him to finish.

"Sometimes, it's kind of my job to . . . encourage people. To buy horses. And spend money."

"I know." Piper knew all kinds of things about Douglas—things that were probably true and things that probably weren't. She was practically a groom, and grooms talked. "I hate to burst your bubble, but you have a little bit of a bad reputation."

"You don't have to buy a horse if you don't want to," he said.

She knew he wanted the horse a little for himself. He would get to ride them. He would get to compete on them. It felt strange to have that kind of power, the power to give someone something so expensive. Part of her knew it was a little bit dangerous. But she trusted him.

She knew she shouldn't. How could she trust someone who was asking her to lie about their relationship? But he shifted again, and she trusted him all the way down to her toes.

When she finally crawled into her own bed, Piper kept thinking about the night, letting it climb over her like a dark-haired boy.

She thought breathlessly of the sex, felt the echoes of it still burn in the hollows of her soul, but then one persistent thought kept bobbing up from beneath the waves of her contentment.

Piper didn't know a lot about sex. She certainly didn't know as much as Douglas did. But she had suggested they not use a condom—probably to impress him, she could now admit. Because she'd heard it felt better. Because in her postorgasm glow, she'd thought it was more romantic.

She had also suggested, in the brief moment when either of them had had control, that he come inside her—which he did immediately upon request. He had probably assumed she was on birth control. In fact, *she* had assumed she was.

But lying there now in bed, she remembered that she hadn't taken birth control pills since she'd moved from Texas. It had seemed too depressing, when she didn't have friends, to even think she might have sex.

Still, it was *one time*, and it didn't feel remotely baby-making. She'd had an orgasm. It ought to be a rule that you couldn't get a girl pregnant if you made her come.

sixty

MAPLE

Over a month into Piper's exile from the horse, she appeared at Maple's bedroom door.

"Hey," Piper said in her cool-girl voice.

"Hey." Maple didn't look up from her phone.

Piper walked slowly into the room; she was distracted by the decor: a Polaroid wall filled with pictures of Vida and Effie and Maple and their horses; a collection of blue ribbons that Maple hadn't won. They were faded and wrinkled and crushed.

"They're just for decoration," Maple explained, slightly embarrassed at how long Piper looked at them.

"I just wanted to say hi."

"Hi."

Maple started texting. She wanted Piper to leave. It was so fucking awkward. And Maple could tell Piper wanted something; she was probably still after the horse.

"Who are you texting?"

"My friends," Maple said.

"I heard you've been doing good in your lessons."

"Are you being sarcastic?" Maple snapped. Vida had taught her that most compliments weren't actually meant to be nice.

"No."

"You don't think I should be jumping."

"I don't know. I'm not a professional."

"You're better than me, though."

"I don't know if it works like that. . . ."

Maple could tell Piper was lost, overwhelmed by her younger sister's anger. Of course she was. Probably no one had ever been angry with her before. Piper was too perfect. Piper was too nice. Piper was the girl Maple would have been if it weren't for Piper.

"I'm just worried about you getting hurt, is all."

"I already got hurt. And I'm fine," Maple said.

Maple knew that Piper didn't really want to help her. Piper had never helped her before.

When the bullying had started, Piper had seemed furious but completely powerless. Maple was in junior high. Piper was in high school. Piper wasn't the type to call people up and threaten them, but sometimes Maple wished Piper would have. Wished Piper would have fought for her.

More than that, Maple wished her sister understood. Maple wished that all the bad things didn't just happen to *her*. Wished that just a few bad things could happen to Piper. To make Maple feel less like a freak.

Piper had no idea what it was like being her sister. What it had *always* been like. Sometimes Maple felt like she wasn't even a part of the family. Like it was Piper's family and she was just there. Piper was the smart one and the talented one and the one everyone liked. She had no idea what it was like not to be her.

"Maple—," Piper started.

"I don't understand why you're here. If it's about the horse, like, get over it. Get your own horse."

"I am getting my own horse," Piper said. She held up her phone to prove it. "I came here to show you."

Maple felt a little loosening. Enough to take a breath.

"Do you want to see her?" Piper asked.

Maple wanted her sister to leave, but she allowed, "Okay."

Piper came into the room, walked over to her sister's bed and climbed on. Maple felt weird having Piper so close, not because she hated her—she didn't—but because she'd been so mean to her, because she didn't know if she could stop. She didn't know if she could ever be a nice girl again.

Piper slid alongside Maple. She had showered, but she still smelled horsey. "Look." She held out a photo of a little blood bay horse. It looked like the horse on one of Maple's book covers: *King of the Wind*.

"Wow."

"Yeah. Look at her jumping." Piper played the video. The horse was fast and light. "Her name is Queenie. We're going to have her vetted next week, and then they're going to fly her out. But she has to be quarantined for two weeks. So it will probably be another month before she's at the barn."

"Cool."

Queenie was a cute horse, but Maple felt a kind of dread. When Piper had first gone to the barn, she kept saying she didn't want a horse because of college. Back then, Maple had been relieved that there was an expiration date on her sister's being there.

It wasn't that Maple disliked her sister—she didn't—but it had been nice when the barn was Maple's own universe. With Piper there, Maple was constantly being compared to her sister, and she constantly came up short.

Sure, Maple was jumping now. She'd had lessons with Kieran. But Piper was still the better rider. And now she always would be. Queenie would probably even turn out to be the better horse. Maple would probably ruin Commotion.

"Are you still mad at me?" Piper said.

"I was never mad at you," Maple said. She needed Piper to agree, to let her off the hook.

Piper didn't. "You seem like you are."

"I can't help what I seem like."

"Because you don't want me to ride?"

Piper shoved herself up. The mattress bounced. Maple wished her sister would get off her bed.

"Because you don't want me to come to the barn?" Piper asked. "I've been riding for longer than you."

That was a pitch, and Maple had to hit it.

"Yeah, but you quit. You made a big thing about not wanting to do it anymore."

Maple started to slide off the bed, then stopped. Piper should get off. It was Maple's bed.

"And you told me it was dumb, remember?" Piper said.

Maple remembered. Way back when they had first come to California. A thousand years ago.

"And you were right. I love horses. I love being at the barn. I'm seriously— I'm honest-to-God glad we moved here. I wouldn't go back to Texas even if I could."

Maple was surprised. She wanted to be a nice sister. She wanted to be a good sister. But she would never be as nice or as good as Piper.

"I just want *one* thing that's mine," Maple said.

"It's not a competition."

Winners were always saying things like that.

"We can both ride horses," Piper said.

"I know that," Maple said, because what else was she supposed to say? Piper was not making it easy at all. She was making it hard.

"Good. So is it okay if I just ride Commotion until my horse gets here? It's one month."

"Not really."

"I'll ask Mom."

Maple was punctured by her sister's sudden treason. "It's not Mom's horse."

"C'mon, Maple. I mean, technically, it is." Piper got off the bed.

That was why Piper had come. She'd pretended that she wanted to make up and be friends, but really she'd just wanted Maple's blessing—not her permission, because Piper was going to ask their mom anyway. And they both knew that Heather would never turn Piper down.

Piper was leaving the room. It was Maple's chance to say, *It's fine. Of course you can. Knock yourself out.*

But she didn't.

Maple knew that she was being ridiculous. Somewhere under her pumping teenager blood, she knew that she had to give in. She wouldn't have a choice. It was one month. She was being silly. But it was so hard sometimes.

Being a younger sister was just about the worst thing that could happen to a person.

sixty-one

PAMELA

Pamela had gone to a rooftop restaurant on the beach in Del Mar to meet friends from high school. Her friends had all left early, but Pamela stayed late. Pamela always stayed late; it was one of her biggest flaws—a propensity to close down every bar, to never give up on a night out. Most people quit too early. Pamela stayed until the bitter end. When she had been younger, she would stay out for days, doing drugs on drugs, trying to find the end of the night.

She had bummed a cigarette off some guy in a suit, and now she was standing at the edge of the balcony. Beyond the railing, the waves were gushing noisily.

Pamela was thinking, as she often did, about her daughter. How important it was that Vida didn't end up like her. How vital it seemed that twenty years from then, Vida was not smoking a cigarette at some bar, drunk and alone.

It was becoming less clear how Pamela would prevent that eventuality. Pamela was broke. She had thought that she was making strong choices: to be independent, to be a barn mom, to be determined and bold and uncompromising. But it now seemed to her—at the edge of the balcony—that she had only been deluding herself.

She needed money. She needed a partner. She needed her father. She needed the same things as everyone else.

"Excuse me?" A woman with a bright face approached. "Do you ride horses?"

Pamela often dressed in horsey clothes in public. Why not? They cost so much that just wearing them at the barn was a waste. She didn't wear a helmet or breeches, of course, but she did sometimes wear a hunting jacket or knee-high boots. A horse-person indicator of sorts.

"Not anymore," she said. "But my daughter does."

"That's awesome!" The woman beamed, then edged closer as Pamela tossed her cigarette over the ledge, onto the beach below. "I've always wanted my daughter to ride horses."

Pamela often had conversations with other mothers in which she was the cheerleader for the sport. She had pat answers about how horseback riding was great for mental and physical and emotional health. How it taught empathy. How it taught young girls to care for other living things. But she did not use them tonight.

"Horseback riding is great." She smiled her best cheerleader smile. "It teaches girls the two most important things they need to learn in life: how to be tough and how to keep secrets."

"Oh," the woman said, confused. Her smile hung limp on her face. "What do you mean, 'keep secrets'?"

Pamela put a finger to her lips, winked cheekily. She swayed a little on her feet and clutched the railing to steady herself.

The woman was polite enough to ignore her unsteadiness. She stepped forward and gazed dreamily over the ocean. "I've always loved horses."

"It has nothing to do with horses," Pamela muttered, past the point of understanding herself.

"Sorry. What?" The woman was trying so hard to like her.

"Horseback riding," Pamela snapped. "It has nothing to do with horses."

sixty-two

PIPER

Piper went straight to her mother's room. She should have just gone there in the first place. She was getting her own horse because of Maple. But she couldn't just snap her fingers and make the horse appear. It was one fucking month. Maple was being a brat, and Piper was tired of everyone acting like her sister's behavior was a good thing.

Heather was watching *Real Housewives*. Piper knew her parents had separate rooms. Her dad had explained the arrangement to Maple and her one morning: about how old-timey couples had separate rooms and how people now shared rooms just to save money. It was basically a very boring way of saying that her parents' marriage was moving from unconventional to unsalvageable.

Before she had found out about the cheating, Piper used to kind of blame her mother for her parents' estrangement. Piper had always been a daddy's girl. She and Jeff had more in common. Her mother always seemed so superficial. But Piper's relationship with Douglas was opening her eyes a little. She was beginning to realize that men had a way of making women seem responsible for *their* actions. It had been weeks since Douglas and she had first slept together, and he still wanted to keep their relationship a secret—but a secret from whom?

"Everything okay, sweetheart?" her mother asked, pausing her show as Piper stepped into the room.

"I wanted to ask you something." Piper walked to the edge of the bed. "As you know, my horse won't be here until after SCI. But I want to ride before then."

"I know," Heather said. "I wish Pamela would just let you ride Faustus. She's being so silly about it."

Pamela had said she didn't want anyone riding the horse while she was trying to sell him, because he might be off when people tried him. But no one ever came to try him.

Piper did not want to ride Faustus. Once her horse came, she might never have an excuse to ride Commotion again. She still hoped that Maple would relent, but at this rate, it didn't seem likely.

"I wanted to ask you if I could ride Commotion. Just until my horse comes."

Heather frowned. "Have you asked Maple?"

"Yes. She said no, but . . . it's not fair. It's just a few weeks. She's being such a brat."

Piper stopped herself, realizing she should not employ that tactic. She took a deep breath and climbed onto the bed with her mother. She was being a little manipulative maybe, but she was doing it for the horse, and horses were always worth the risk.

"I just love being at the barn so much. I'm honestly— I'm so happy we moved here. I love it. I wouldn't go back to Texas even if I could." She wasn't lying, but it was the first time she'd admitted it to her mother. She licked her lips. "You were right."

Heather gasped. Surrounded by the white clouds of her pillows, she looked like a ghost. Piper had killed her.

"Thank you," Heather said. "That means so much to me."

"It's just a few weeks," Piper nudged.

Heather sighed. "You're right. She needs to share."

Before Heather could change her mind, Piper started to slide off the bed.

"I'd like to do the horse show, too," Piper said. "Just one or two classes?"

She might not have another chance to show Commotion. And she loved Commotion. And Douglas loved Commotion. And her family loved Commotion. And there was something about that horse and all the things he had brought her—the new life he had brought her. It was just one little show. And then it would all be over.

"That's fine, sweetheart. It'll be nice. All of us together. The whole family."

sixty-three

MAPLE

Maple was waiting in the hallway when Piper came out of their mother's room. Piper caught her eyes and shrugged, and Maple knew everything.

She stormed past her sister, found her mother on a throne of pillows.

"Did you say Piper could ride Commotion?"

Heather put her phone down. "Just until her horse comes." Sensible.

"But I thought he was my horse." Ridiculous.

It wasn't just about the horse. It was about the question *Who do you like better*—a particularly heavy question when you were growing up and not sure if you even liked yourself—*my sister or me?* Who is smarter, and nicer, and more talented? Who do you love the most? Who is your *real* daughter? And who is the extra?

"It is your horse, sweetie. Of course it's your horse."

"Then shouldn't it be my decision?"

Heather crossed her arms, annoyed. "It is your decision."

"I don't remember making it."

Heather scowled. "You're getting an attitude, little miss. Your sister just needs the horse for a month."

"But I'm jumping now. And we're getting ready for the show. And Douglas is riding in all these Grand Prix. Can't Piper just ride some other horse?"

"There isn't another horse right now. And Piper wants to do the show, too."

"On my horse?"

"It's one show, Maple."

Maple resented the whole situation, but most of all she resented how Piper and Heather were turning her into the bad guy, the crazy girl who couldn't share.

They didn't recognize how much things were changing, how seismic it was that Maple was jumping with Kieran, that Maple was getting ready to show.

It was like she had finally become someone else, escaped the weak person that she used to be, and now they were taking it all back. They wanted her to be weak. They wanted her to be pathetic. They wanted her to be bullied. *Poor Maple.* They wanted her to go back to how she had been before.

"I just don't think it's fair," Maple said, and then she left before she started crying.

Her mother didn't follow her. Maybe she didn't realize Maple was crying. Maybe she didn't care.

Maple had become a whole new person for her mother. She had ridden horses. She had become stronger, tough.

She had changed, but nothing else had.

sixty-four

PAMELA

When her Uber pulled up in front of Kieran's house, Pamela was confused.

"What are we doing here?" she said. "This isn't my house."

"This is the address you gave."

"This is Kieran's house," she said, like the driver knew who that was. Then it slowly dawned on her that she had wanted to go there.

"If you pay me cash, I can take you somewhere else," the driver said.

"No, this is fine." Pamela sighed and made a big to-do to cover up the fact that she had chosen that destination.

She wandered toward the door. She'd had this idea that she could confront Kieran. She was drunk, but Kieran always had a way of sobering her up. There had been many times in the past when he had sobered her up—with a yell, with a directive, with a fuck.

She stood outside the front door, gazing up into the eaves. She could hear the television, so she knew he was inside the house. She didn't think that bursting in drunk was her best option. But it was that or go home, and she hadn't yet found the end of the night.

Kieran answered the door in the clothes he'd been wearing earlier that day, but he'd clearly been asleep. She had woken him up, but he didn't seem angry to see her. He stepped back to allow her in, then said, "I'm watching Ocala," which was a horse show going on in Florida.

She followed him into the vaulted TV room, took a seat on a sofa.

She hadn't been at Kieran's house alone in a very long time, she realized. Not since her money had dried up. Her money and her horses and her shot at anything. Now she was on the outside, and so was Vida.

Unless Pamela could find a way to get her back in.

Kieran hissed as the horse on the screen hit a rail in the jump-off. "Did you see that?" he said.

"No." She had been looking at him. "I missed it."

He pressed PAUSE and hit REWIND. "He comes in long and then goes for the three—what a fucking idiot. Watch him hang his horse out to dry."

Pamela watched, steeling herself. "Ouch," she noted, and Kieran seemed relieved. She was playing nice. But not for long. "So, how's it all going with the Parkers?"

Kieran smirked. "She just pulled the trigger on the mare from Stockholm. I think they'll buy more, too. In six months, a year. I think we can get them a whole string."

"Jesus."

"Yeah. Do you want some of your wine?"

She did, but she had a feeling he was about to kick her out, because she wasn't there to watch a horse show.

Pamela was worried that Kieran was squeezing her out of the barn. Vida's horses were getting too old. She was outgrowing them in ability. Pamela couldn't afford better horses, and Kieran wasn't offering Vida client rides.

Pamela had a feeling that Kieran was intentionally pushing them out without being direct about it, which was how Kieran did everything. They would be out. And Pamela wouldn't be able to give her daughter the things she deserved, to give her a better life. To give her a father.

"I wish we could do something for Vida," she said. "I mean, with all these expensive horses coming in, it would be nice to give her an opportunity."

"I make the decisions," Kieran said lightly, as if he were gauging the field.

She didn't think he was just talking about horses. He had never forgiven her for having his child, as if she had wrenched Vida from his very marrow. He had told her not to have the baby. When she had told him that it was *her* decision, he had said, "You can't force me to be a father." She'd always believed he was a little wrong.

He was Vida's father already. He was the patriarch of the barn family. He made the rules. He offered the guidance. He inspired the breakthroughs. He was everyone's father.

But lately, things had shifted. Or maybe things had been shifting for years. Or maybe things had always been bad. Maybe Pamela had been padding reality with her dreams, making excuses, promising herself that Kieran would step up. When Vida was old enough. When Vida was good enough. One day, he would be proud to call her his daughter.

Pamela was beginning to question if he even could. Kieran had never gotten along with his own father. They had fought and argued over every aspect of the business right up until the gas leak.

Kieran had told her once, years before she got pregnant, "Some people should never be parents. I wish more people would admit that."

At the time she had thought he was talking about *his* parents, and she had been inclined to agree with him. Her own mother had been one such person. Her father had probably been one, too. Pamela's whole life seemed to be an exercise in unraveling their mistakes.

But now she was inclined to believe that Kieran hadn't been talking about his parents. That he had been talking about himself.

"I just don't think it's fair," she said.

"Pamela."

"Vida is your daughter."

It felt so good to say it, in the worst way. Because immediately following the relief was the feeling that she had done something incredibly stupid, as if she had destroyed something she had spent years making—so carefully, so delicately, so intricately: the appearance of a relationship with Kieran, the appearance of intimacy and friendship, even fatherhood.

Kieran paused the horse show. His chair creaked as he sat up. "I think it's time for you to go," he said, as if it was because she was drunk. As if she was being unreasonable.

Right then the front door opened and Douglas walked in. It was as if a match had dropped on gasoline, the way Kieran's eyes lit up, the way he seemed to know that Pamela could say anything. She could say so many things right now.

"Night," Douglas said, bleary-eyed, exhausted, like he always was. Too tired to see that he walked like Kieran. He stood like him at the fence. He watched horses with the same light in his dark, magnetic eyes.

Douglas's mother had been involved in a particularly brutal accident that had been made worse because a strap on her six-hundred-dollar helmet snapped. After the ambulance had carted her off, Pamela had seen Kieran pick up the helmet and inspect it. She had never seen the helmet again.

Kieran had stepped up for Douglas. He was a father to him in everything but name. He had taken over the care of Douglas and his mother, never admitting that he owed them that and more. He did it for Douglas.

Pamela didn't know if Kieran loved Douglas. He seemed incapable of an emotion so devoid of power. But he took care of Douglas because he was easy.

Douglas was made up of all of Kieran's best parts: his charm, his attention, his skill with horses. Vida had not inherited the easy parts of her father and so Kieran seemed always slightly afraid of her, as if he recognized the child who could consume the parent.

But secretly Pamela loved those parts of her daughter. Secretly she cherished them. Because in her heart those were the parts that made her believe Vida could slay all the dragons that Pamela could not.

Kieran's eyes never left Pamela as Douglas walked along the hallway, appearing and disappearing beneath the arches. Kieran watched her, as if waiting for her to make a wrong move, almost as if hoping she would.

"Good night," she said as Douglas passed beneath the final arch.

"Good night, Pamela," Kieran said to her and only her.

DETECTIVE PEREZ

The news of Douglas Dunn's appearance had not been exaggerated. He was classically handsome, taller than expected, with lean, horsey muscles. However, what struck Detective Perez most was the pervasive aura of guilt that seemed to surround him, as if he was waiting all the time for you to punish him for something.

"Do you know why you're here?" she asked.

Douglas perched on a chair. "No."

"Really?"

"I just rode five classes back-to-back. I'm working. I have no idea what's going on."

"Were you working here yesterday?"

"I work every day."

"What time did you leave?"

Douglas flinched. He seemed sensitive, and sensitive people could be tricky to read because they overreacted to every little thing.

"I'm not really sure. . . ."

"Could you make a guess?"

Douglas didn't respond. His arms were crossed, and his eyes drifted as they followed the sounds of every horse that passed through the barn aisle.

"Five? Six?" Detective Perez prompted. "Sundown? Later?"

"Midnight. Maybe later."

The detective scooted forward a little; she couldn't help herself. Sometimes she wanted to catch people at anything. Could sense a *Gotcha!* like blood in the water.

"What is it that you do again?" she asked.

"I ride horses."

"And you were riding horses at midnight last night?"

"No," he answered after a slight delay, looking more and more uncomfortable.

"What were you doing here?"

"Do I have to say?"

Detective Perez glanced at her partner. "This interview is not compulsory."

"I don't even know what this is about." He kept looking from one detective to the other, as if hoping one of them would tell him what to do. "How can I answer if I don't know what it's about?"

"Your answers should be the same no matter what," Detective Perez cautioned him.

It was clear that Douglas was guilty of something, although it could have been something else entirely. He would have to be pretty naive to volunteer to speak to them if he had actually killed her. Or else he had to be *acting* pretty naive.

"What were you doing here last night?"

"I'm sorry. I can't say."

"Did you see anyone in this barn aisle? Speak to anyone?"

He bit the inside of his cheek.

"We'll be able to confirm these things," Detective Perez said, which wasn't exactly true.

There weren't cameras. Horse shows weren't heavily attended, and the clientele were not paying attention to anything besides their own horses.

"Um . . . I guess my trainer? Kieran Flynn. And Heather. Parker."

sixty-five

PIPER

Piper had never truly understood the meaning of the word "dickmatized." She had never looked it up or really thought about it. She had assumed it meant that even though a guy was an asshole, you still liked him. But she was learning it had nothing to do with the guy.

Douglas had a pretty dick. Piper hadn't seen a lot of dicks, but she was sure of it. She wanted to take a picture of it so she could show her friends back in Texas, ask them, Isn't this a pretty dick? Isn't this the nicest dick you've ever seen?

But she also knew that appearance wasn't the most important thing. It was what he did with it that really mattered. And the things he did with it.

In the back of his truck.

In an abandoned horse stall.

On the trail outside her house, after dark, on dirt soft and rough at the same time.

They used condoms, which assuaged her earlier anxiety. It was such a virgin thing, to think you could get pregnant on the first time. Although to be fair, if someone told her she could get pregnant looking at Douglas, she would halfway believe it.

The only slight snag in the fabric of her feelings was the fact that he was still unwilling to share their relationship with anyone.

He made some vague arguments: Her parents might not like it; he wasn't really supposed to date clients. And when she pushed him, he mentioned the horse show and all the pressure he was under, so she got the idea that maybe they would tell everyone *after* the horse show.

Still, worrying about that red flag kept her up at night, when his dick didn't.

She knew from a logical standpoint that guys usually kept girls a secret when they were seeing more than one girl, but Douglas was with her at the barn all the time. The only time she didn't see him was on Monday mornings, when he visited his mother. She had asked him once if she could go, too, but he seemed uncomfortable.

"It's not really nice. It's not fun," he said.

"I understand, but I would be going to support you."

He just shook his head and walked away.

She hoped that one day he would let her go with him. His refusal was yet another red flag. It was a sign that he didn't trust her and that maybe he wasn't serious about her. And even a pretty dick couldn't fix that.

M aple had been icy with Piper over the past few weeks. Now the horse show was nearly upon them. Piper's own horse would be arriving soon. And maybe once she did, they could patch things up.

The week before the show, Kieran started training Piper after he trained Maple. The day before they left for SCI, Piper made a point of being nice to Maple as she handed Commotion over after her lesson.

"How was your ride?" Piper asked.

"Fine." Maple avoided her eyes. "I already adjusted the stirrups for you."

Piper had longer legs than Maple, so she set the stirrups longer. Maple usually adjusted them for her, because the saddle was *Maple's*, and she didn't want Piper touching it—even though she rode in it. Piper's saddle would be custom-built once her horse arrived.

"Have a good ride!" Maple called, possibly sarcastically, as she walked away.

As Piper mounted the horse and rode toward the arena, she tried not to feel irked.

Inside the main arena, Douglas was being screamed at over fences. Sometimes Kieran trained them together, directing her over a smaller course while Douglas waited, then directing him over something tall and treacherous while she looked on.

Kieran would point out to her things that Douglas did, as though she might not be absorbing his every move.

"See what he did on the corner? How many strides was that? See how he backs off? See how he pushes?"

Yes, sir.

That day Kieran was setting a course for her while he screamed at Douglas. "Wake up! Wake the fuck up! Where is your head?"

Piper's and Douglas's eyes met as she came into the arena. She felt a little bad for him, but she also slightly hoped that he was distracted by his overwhelming love for her.

Kieran was already in a mood at six thirty a.m. "Piper, are you ready for a course? Take a lap," he said to Douglas, which meant that Douglas should stay on deck while Piper rode her first course.

"Yeah, I'm ready," Piper said, shortening her reins and adjusting her seat.

Lately Kieran had been diving right in. It was dizzying but exciting.

Kieran laid out a complicated course of rollbacks and bending lines. "If you wanna win this weekend, you need to be able to think on your ass."

Piper wasn't sure what that meant, but she circled and picked up a canter, preparing for the first jump. Kieran had set the jumps pretty high—over four feet. Something Commotion could get over easily, but higher than Piper had ever jumped. Her heart rate picked up a little.

"Ride to the bottom of the jump. Don't shit yourself when you get close."

Piper did as she was told, holding Commotion in until they hit their distance. She went into two-point as he arced high in the air. Then she heard a *snap!* She felt her left stirrup drop out from under her, and her whole body was thrown out of balance.

The horse landed crooked, and Piper listed sideways. She made a grab for Commotion's neck, but it was too late. She fell sideways into the dirt.

Douglas was above her in a flash, his face creased with worry. "Are you okay?" He ran his hands up and down her body, searching for an injury.

"I'm fine." She started to sit up, but he held her down.

"Don't move. You could have a concussion. Something might be broken. You can't always see it."

She felt his hands quivering as they moved over her.

"Douglas, give her some fucking air." Kieran was still on the side of the ring. When Douglas didn't listen to him, he yelled, "Dunn!"

"She might be hurt," Douglas snapped back.

"I'm fine," Piper repeated.

Kieran hopped the fence to approach them. "It's a wonder she can fucking breathe with you on top of her." He pulled Douglas up by the shoulder. "Get back on your horse."

Commotion had been caught by a groom who was holding Douglas's horse, too.

Douglas hesitated. Piper saw a cool line of fury in his eyes, thought he might actually stand up to Kieran. But then Douglas took a deep breath, and he swallowed it.

"Can you move?" Kieran asked Piper.

Piper sat up, dusted the dirt from her shirt. "My stirrup just snapped," she explained.

Piper could see her mother approaching, walking fast so as not to scare the horses.

"What happened? Is everything okay?" Heather called.

The stirrup was in the dirt. Piper scooped it up; then she noticed the leather had split. Maple's saddle had brand-new stirrup leathers—the best money could buy. The cut was mostly clean, except one jagged little end that must have torn when Piper put weight on it over the jump.

"Oh my God," Piper said. "It looks like someone cut it."

sixty-six

HEATHER

Heather knew that riders fell. She herself had fallen dozens of times. She had many great stories. The time a horse had taken off on her and galloped twenty circuits around the arena before she got him back under control. The time a horse had bucked her out of the arena. The time a horse had pulled a dirty stop, and she had flown over a jump without him. The time a horse had fallen *on* her.

But it was different when your daughters fell. First Maple, and now Piper. And both under slightly suspicious circumstances. The woman with the umbrella. The broken stirrup leather.

Both Pamela and June waved off Heather's concern.

"Effie used to fall all the time," June said. "It's a rite of passage. It's good for them."

Heather thought that was pretty insensitive.

"It's not just that they fell. It's *how* they fell," Heather insisted.

The groom who had tacked up Commotion that morning had been fired. Heather had protested, but she thought the decision was right. Even if someone else had sabotaged the stirrup, the groom should have noticed.

Practically the instant Piper had fallen, Kieran claimed he had seen the exact same thing happen before.

"They make all this crap in sweatshops," he said, which Heather didn't think was strictly true.

To escape all the drama, the barn moms had lunch at a cute lounge on the beach. And by lunch, they meant cocktails, which were more than necessary.

"Is this normal?" Heather asked Pamela and June.

It was scary, how breakable her daughters were. Daughters seemed more breakable than anything, more delicate than life.

Heather considered that she hadn't done enough to protect them. She wanted them to be horse girls. She wanted them to be tough. But she did not want them to break.

"Totally normal," June assured her.

"Horseback riding is a dangerous sport," Pamela said. "Accidents happen all the time. You can't blame anyone."

June agreed. "Show jumping might not be the sport for you. I still have the number for that lesson barn in Olivenhain. I think they do trail riding."

"Much safer," Pamela agreed.

After lunch, Heather went to Kieran. She found him walking down the barn aisle, stopping to check all the horses before they were trailered to the show.

"I'm worried about the girls," she said. "All these falls."

He stepped smoothly into a stall, ran his hands first down the horse's legs, then along its back, pressing down in places so the muscles compressed. "What did I tell you that you need to learn, Heather? What did I tell you that you need to do?"

Heather sighed, remembering that conversation, which seemed to have taken place so long ago now. And she *was* doing better. She was pulling back. She kept quiet about Piper. She supported Maple. She was doing what Kieran had told her to do, what he'd trained her to do.

"Leave it with you."

He ran his hands over the horse's face, peered into its eyes. "Exactly. Relinquishing control doesn't mean that bad things won't happen. But do you know what it does mean? It's not your responsibility when they do."

"I just don't want them to get hurt."

"I won't let them get hurt." He stepped out of the stall. "You just have to trust me."

sixty-seven

PIPER

I'm so glad you're okay," Douglas said for approximately the millionth time since Piper's fall.

They were parked in their usual spot looking out over the beach. He was kissing various obscure parts of her body—the hollows of her eyes, the base of her neck, her inner elbow—as if worried he had never appreciated those parts of her enough, might never be able to appreciate them again.

Piper understood that her accident had probably been a massive trigger for Douglas, but it was a little hard for Piper to think straight when he was burying her in affection.

She was thinking about the stirrup leather. She wished she had brought it with her. But amid all the chaos after the accident—with her mother and her sister and all the rubberneckers needing to know what happened—she had lost track of it.

"Didn't it look like someone cut it?" she said.

"I don't know. . . ." Douglas was kissing between each of her knuckles now, but he paused. "I don't think Angel should have been fired, though."

"I'll talk to Kieran about it," Piper said, because she was inclined to agree.

Maple had ridden in the same saddle, and she hadn't noticed anything wrong. Kieran hadn't noticed anything either. Maple had even adjusted the stirrups for Piper.

Piper went cold so fast that Douglas looked up.

"What is it?"

"Maple adjusted my stirrups before I got on Commotion."

If the stirrup leather had been cut before Maple rode, it would have snapped on her. Standing in two-point would have forced a break, like it had with Piper.

Piper's first instinct was to think that Maple would never do that, but her second instinct was less sure.

"Why would she cut your stirrup leather?" Douglas said.

Piper shook her head to clear it. "She's mad at me about the horse. I . . . It's a really silly sister thing." But it had turned into something else.

"I hope that's not true. You could have been seriously hurt." He gripped her hand tighter.

She could have been killed. And all because Maple hadn't wanted her riding Commotion for one more day?

Piper wondered if the bullying had changed her sister more than she realized. If what had been done to Maple was now somehow embedded in her, shifting something essential in who she was. Ruining her.

"I need to talk to her," Piper said.

That was the hard part. Piper didn't want things to blow up worse than they already had. It didn't seem fair to punish Maple, but didn't she need to be punished? She was lucky her prank hadn't had far worse consequences.

Piper knew Maple saw a therapist once a week, but maybe she needed to go more often. Maybe she needed to see someone else, because right now Maple seemed kind of dangerous.

sixty-eight

MAPLE

Everyone was in such a tizzy about poor Piper that they didn't even realize Maple had been the target. It was her stirrup leather that had been cut.

Maple's own accident had been much worse, and she couldn't help comparing people's reactions.

They seemed more upset about Piper. More worried. They asked after her. Bought her lunch. One of the owners even had flowers delivered, like Piper was dead, when she barely even had a bruise.

The barn was a constant chorus of *Poor Piper! She's so nice! I hope she's okay!*

It seemed to Maple that no one had cared about her when she fell; all they had cared about were the gruesome details, the violence. She was the inferior sister, so they'd had no sympathy.

Vida put it more succinctly. "She's even better at falling than you are."

Maple, Effie and Vida were hiding in Vida's bedroom because Pamela was downstairs drinking with June. Every now and again, the girls could hear the ferocious roar of the women's laughter rising from below.

The girls were drinking, too, but their moms were so drunk that it kind of took the fun out of it.

Maple was pretty sure that Vida had cut the stirrup leather. She had been at the barn early that morning. Maple had been suspicious of her ever since she'd revealed that she once made Effie fall off her horse. Yet when Vida had invited Maple to sleep over, Maple agreed without hesitation. Because they were friends. Because Vida had asked.

Back in Texas, Maple had been friends with her bully all through elementary school. Not *best* friends but pretty good ones. Even after the hair-pulling incident, if that girl had turned around and invited Maple over, Maple would have gone. It was what you did. If you were included, you went, no matter what your friends said or did. You just had to. Or else you wouldn't have friends. Or else you'd be alone.

Being alone sometimes felt like death to Maple—or worse, because at least dead people were mourned. She would do anything to belong. And now she belonged at the barn, and it was worth everything to her—the lady with the umbrella, the cut stirrup leather.

Loosely, Maple thought, these were almost attempts on her life. But the part of her that wanted to belong thought, *But I'm still here. I'm fine. I've had worse.*

She wasn't going to be scared off again. She wasn't even going to be scared. She was going to look Vida's cold implacability in the eye and keep on rising.

"She can be the *best* at falling," Maple said, taking the flask from Effie. "I'm happy to lose that competition."

They were drinking vodka neat. It tasted like broken glass.

"Don't you want to know who did it?" Effie asked.

Maple wondered if Effie knew. If it was a test.

"No."

Maple's eyes crept toward Vida, but she was looking out the window. Downstairs her mother's laughter roared.

Effie dropped back on the carpet. They were all in a circle on the floor, although there were more comfortable places to sit. The vodka made the carpet soft. Effie sighed at the ceiling. "Aren't you nervous about the show? What if another accident happens there?"

"I'm not nervous about anything," Maple said. Normally, she was anxious about everything. But just lately, she didn't feel it. She knew she was still nervous, but she couldn't feel it anymore.

Instead, her thoughts were consumed with rides, jumps and distances. Sometimes when she shut her eyes, especially when she was drinking, she could feel Commotion underneath her, the steady rock of his canter stride. She could see a jump on the approach, feel the lift as he took off.

She heard Kieran yelling at her in her sleep, egging her on.

Every night, she dreamed of entering the Little Palm Cup and showing everyone who she really was.

Sometimes she dreamed she won. Sometimes she dreamed she died.

sixty-nine

PIPER

Piper texted Maple, but Maple left her on "read." Piper went to Maple's room to find her, but she wasn't there. She could see the evidence of hasty packing, preparations for the horse show the next day. There were clothes scattered on the floor, a box of tampons on the bathroom counter.

Piper felt a shot of hard panic. How long had it been since she'd had her period? She tried to do the math, but her calculations had to be wrong. She pushed her concerns aside and kept searching for Maple.

She checked all the rooms her family actually used. First she went to the entertainment room, and then she headed to the kitchen, where she found her father making a microwave dinner.

For someone with unlimited resources, her dad had horrible taste. When Heather wasn't around, he ate Lean Cuisine and frozen burritos—anything that was fast and easy.

"Everything okay, Pipes?" her dad asked.

When the microwave dinged, he removed his dinner and shoveled it onto an Hermès dinner plate, like that would make it more appetizing.

"I'm just looking for Maple."

"I think she's at a sleepover."

"You're kidding," Piper said.

Piper sounded more annoyed than she was. She couldn't stop thinking about the math. The period math. Piper had always been good at math, but for the first time ever, she hoped that she was worse than she'd thought.

"Is there a problem?"

Piper wasn't about to tell him about the math, but she found herself telling him about the stirrup leather. She knew she shouldn't. It was a horse world problem. It couldn't be solved by an outsider.

Heather hadn't even told Jeff about Piper's fall, so right away he wasn't happy. In fact, the more Piper explained, the more he seemed to be directing his anger toward Heather, which had not been Piper's intention.

"This whole thing just feels like a scam!" he said. "And meanwhile, I'm out millions of dollars."

That was not at all Piper's point. She also didn't think he was taking into account the considerable amount of money that RSFE was actually winning him on Commotion every week—as the owner, he kept most of the Grand Prix winnings—but Piper knew Jeff wasn't really complaining about money. He was complaining about Heather.

"I just think someone needs to talk to Maple," Piper said, trying to redirect their conversation. "I mean, for starters, I don't think she should be at a sleepover."

"With those creepy little girls," he said, taking it too far, farther than Piper wanted. "And that druggie-looking woman, your mom's friend—what's her name again?"

"Do you mean Pamela?"

Jeff nodded. "I really don't like her. I don't know what your mom sees in her."

Piper honestly should have known better than to trust her dad to understand anything that involved her mother. "Okay, but this isn't about Mom."

"Yes, it is. Why is Maple even at that barn? Why is she riding that horse?"

"Maple does like horses. She's coming around to it. But I just think . . ."

What did Piper think? What did she actually want?

"I could have been seriously hurt," she said, repeating what Douglas had said.

"Maybe we all need to take a look at this horse thing," Jeff said, not listening to her. "All of you spend way too much time there. It's a little weird." This from a guy who worked around the clock.

Jeff started toward the front door, abandoning his congealing dinner.

"Where are you going?" Piper said.

She didn't feel like she'd done anything wrong, but she did feel like she'd done something that was about to go wrong.

"I'm going to get your sister."

Maple was going to be pissed.

seventy

PAMELA

Pamela and June had drunk three bottles of champagne and a few cocktails, which was a lot even for Pamela. But Pamela was under a lot of stress with everything happening at the barn. Even June was feeling it. Things were different now, because of the Parkers. The barn had once been an escape, but now there was constant tension, a sense of escalation, as if they were all heading somewhere dark, moving faster all the time.

"What do you really think about all this stirrup business?" June asked, spinning her straw through the crushed ice in her mojito royal. "And Mary Poppins?"

Mary Poppins was the name they'd coined for the woman with the umbrella, because she was probably a figment of Maple's imagination.

"I don't know what to think," Pamela protested, like she was under suspicion. "I *do* think that things are different with the Parkers around. And not in a good way."

"I agree," June said, and Pamela was surprised.

Pamela was usually so busy being annoyed by June, she had never really considered how the other woman felt about the Parkers.

But looking back, Pamela did see how June had constantly been encouraging Heather to leave. Pamela had assumed that June had just been acting contrary, but maybe she did actually want Heather and her family gone.

"I almost wish they would quit," Pamela mused, testing her friend.

"Oh, I wouldn't worry about it," June said. "I have a feeling they won't last long."

Pamela's phone started ringing. She answered. "Hello?"

"I'm coming to pick up Maple."

It took Pamela a second to realize that it was Heather's husband, Jeff.

"Is there a problem?" Pamela said.

It was late for him to be picking the girl up. Pamela was also pretty sure the girls had been drinking, so she wasn't exactly happy about turning Maple over.

"It's a family issue," he said—pretty brusquely, Pamela thought. Then he hung up.

Pamela hurried upstairs and pulled Maple out of Vida's room. Maple was furious, of course. They went into the kitchen, where Pamela and June gave Maple coffee and strawberries to take the alcohol off her breath.

Jeff rang the doorbell almost instantly, so he must have called from his car. Pamela felt an almost teenage burst of fear, like she had been caught breaking curfew. She stuffed the coffee and the strawberries into a cupboard. June got the giggles.

As she answered the door, Pamela had to remind herself that she was an adult. She straightened her top, then put on her best game face.

"Is this where you live?" Jeff said, like he couldn't believe she lived in such squalor. He strode into the house like he'd been invited, took one look at Maple and said, "I thought so."

"She's all ready to go," Pamela said, hating that her voice dipped a little.

She wasn't scared, not really. Just one tiny bubble of fear had slipped out, more from surprise than from anything else.

"She's loaded," Jeff said.

"She's a *child*," June scolded.

"Well, I'm glad you know that."

Jeff thought he was some big deal. All men did really—especially *husbands*. They were so goddamn proud of themselves. Everything they did, everything they said, was followed by a round of applause in their heads.

"Why are you picking me up?" Maple said, her voice ripe with teenage irritation.

"Because you're in trouble, little miss."

"Why? What did I do?"

"Your sister said you made her fall off her horse," Jeff said.

Pamela perked up. This was an interesting turn of events.

"Are you fucking kidding me?" Maple quickly realized the f-word was a mistake. "I did *not* make her fall! That's completely insane! She probably cut her own stirrup!"

"I think we need to take a break from the horses," Jeff said.

Pamela almost smiled, just from surprise.

"I'm gonna kill her!" Maple ranted. "She's such an evil bitch! She's just trying to steal my horse!"

"Hey, hey, hey, take it easy," Jeff said. Like most men, he couldn't handle any display of emotion—except violence. Violence was always acceptable. "This is all getting a little silly."

"I hate her. I hate her so much." Maple ground her fingernails into her palm.

Pamela felt a little bad for her. It surprised her, but she liked Maple. She understood what it was like to be passed over. To not be the chosen one. She understood what that could do to a person over time.

"You do not hate your sister," Jeff insisted. "I think all this horse stuff is getting out of hand. Everyone's getting just a little too passionate for my liking." He pulled at his shirt collar, totally out of his depth.

"We're leaving for the horse show tomorrow," Maple said. "I'm riding Jumpers."

"This is your *sister*. That's more important than a horse."

"Nothing is more important than a horse," Maple vowed, like a good little rider disciple.

"Don't talk back," Jeff snapped, then looked uncomfortably at his audience. "Let's go home."

"I don't want to go home," Maple said.

"She doesn't have to," Pamela put in.

Jeff's eyes lit on her. "Oh, yes, she does. And she's not coming back here either."

Her house wasn't good enough for him. Pamela wasn't good enough for him. Pamela hated him in that moment, but more than that, she knew she had power over him. She had his daughter. And she knew things about him, all kinds of horrible things that Heather, under the blood pact of friendship, had confessed.

It was Kieran, really, who had ruined men for Pamela, but she was more than happy to punish all of them for his sins.

"Shouldn't you be in Texas fucking some teenager?" Pamela said neatly.

It was amazing how fast you could realize you'd said the wrong thing. Maple jumped back like she'd been hit. Jeff stepped toward Pamela. June moved between them protectively.

"I think you'd better go," June said, just as Jeff said, "You fucking bitch."

Maple spooked like a horse, then took off for the stairs. The sound of her pounding footsteps echoed over their heads.

Jeff looked after her, but didn't seem inclined to follow. "You fucking miserable bitch," he said to Pamela, "trying to break up a family because no one fucking wants you."

Pamela hated that what he said actually hurt her. It was true that no one wanted her, and although most of the time she didn't care, it would have been nice.

"Well, everyone wants you. For your money," Pamela said, although personally she thought it would be nice to have that kind of draw. Being liked for who you were put a lot of pressure on you to perform. Being liked for your money was simple, clean.

Jeff hesitated, seeming unsure what to do.

"Can I offer you a drink?" Pamela said. June exploded into laughter.

"Maple is coming with me," Jeff said.

"Well, then, go fucking get her."

Pamela gestured toward the staircase as June took another bottle of vodka out of the freezer.

Jeff just stood stupidly in the entryway, completely useless. Men were incapable of handling any situation in which they didn't have complete control, which meant they were totally incapable of handling teenage daughters.

Pamela started making cocktails. She looked up when the front door opened. Jeff had left without Maple. Pamela just turned to June and laughed.

seventy-one

MAPLE

M aple didn't know where to go. She didn't want to go back to Vida's room in tears. She didn't want to tell Vida and Effie what had happened. She didn't want them to know.

She ended up in Pamela's room. She hid in the bathroom, crawled into the enormous bathtub to cry, pausing occasionally to observe the effect of her tears on her reflection in the wraparound mirrors.

Did she look tough?

Was she a strong girl now?

She heard a car pull up outside, heard June stagger down the drive. Then the house was quiet.

Maple remembered the drawer of drugs. She climbed out of the tub and hurried toward them. All the drugs were laid out like spells in a witch's book. Maple didn't know exactly what each one did, but she had a feeling it would be magical.

"Looking for anything in particular?"

Maple turned just as Pamela walked into the bedroom. At first blush, Maple thought she was in trouble, but she was calmed by Pamela's expression, her lean attitude. Maple realized she might never be in trouble with Pamela, which made her feel unnervingly adult.

"I don't know what any of them are," Maple said honestly.

Some of the pills had numbers or letters. One was shaped like a shark. One was probably a mint.

Pamela stood in the bedroom, framed by the light from the bathroom door.

"Is it true what you said about my dad?" Maple said.

"I mean, she might not be a teenager." Pamela observed her chipped nails. "But I guarantee she's not over thirty."

That wasn't exactly what Maple had meant, but she supposed she had her answer. Her dad was still cheating on her mom. He was "working" in Amarillo all the time. And probably, one day soon, he would be gone completely.

"Do you think my parents are going to get a divorce?"

She thought Pamela would know. Pamela seemed to know everything, especially when it came to the terrible things people could do.

"Maybe," Pamela said. "I doubt your father wants to lose half of everything. California might have been a strategic move on Heather's part."

Pamela dropped onto the edge of the bed. She was so cold. Maple admired her. She hoped that she would be that cold when she grew up.

"He thinks I cut Piper's stirrup, but I didn't. I wouldn't do that. They all think I'm—" Maple huffed, trying to pull her tangled feelings apart so she could communicate them. "No matter what I do, it's never good enough. No matter who I am, they don't see me. Not the way I want to be seen."

Pamela patted the bed. Maple walked over. Pamela took the girl's hand and squeezed it, as if she was about to say something inspiring. Instead, she said, "Fuck every last one of them." And then she smiled hopefully at her.

seventy-two

HEATHER

Heather was half asleep when Jeff came in. He stood in the center of her bedroom, halfway between her and the door. She could see him in the light of the TV.

She sat up so fast her head spun. "Is everything okay?"

"This isn't working."

"What?"

She turned the TV off and switched on the lights. Her brain was soggy with pre-sleep. Why was he doing this? He'd better not be doing what she thought he was doing *now*.

Let her be dressed. Let her have her makeup done. Have the god-damn courtesy to pick a good day, not to wake her up in the middle of the night. In all the years this had been coming—because it had been coming for so damn long—Heather had given him so many more opportune moments.

"It's too much." Jeff was already backing away from her, moving toward the door, like he wanted to communicate without being present.

"What is?" She swung her legs over the edge of her bed, feeling the urge to chase him, pin him down, hold him there.

"I want to move back to Texas."

"No." Was he kidding?

"You don't have to come. But the girls might want to."

"Are you kidding?"

"No, I'm not kidding. Maple is at that woman's house right now—that Pamela bitch—drunk. Apparently, she tried to kill her sister today—"

"What are you talking about?"

Heather shook her head. He had lost his mind. He was confused, but that could be fixed.

Then the answer hit her: the stirrup leather. Maple had ridden before Piper. She had handed the horse to her sister. Was it possible that she had cut the stirrup to get back at her sister for riding the horse?

But Maple wouldn't have done that.

"You don't even know!" Jeff snapped. "That's the thing! You don't even know! What exactly are you doing at that barn all day?"

"I'm trying to support our daughters. Without controlling them." She tried to think about how Kieran would have put it. Everything made sense when he said it. "I'm there for them, but I don't know *everything* because . . . because it's their lives, not mine."

"Sure. Supporting them. Getting drunk with these horrible women. Fucking some teenage boy in Kentucky."

That was the worst thing he could think of—of course it was. The worst thing she could have done to him was exactly what he had done to her.

"I didn't sleep with him," she said. She had done one thing right at least. "If you actually care. Sometimes I wish I had, that I was a different person, more like you. But I couldn't. I wanted *this* to work. That's what I wanted."

She felt guilty for speaking in the past tense. She felt guilty for everything. For being cheated on. For being a bad mother. For having dreams that always stopped just short of coming true.

"I don't want a divorce," she said.

That caught him off guard. "I didn't say 'divorce.'"

Heather gasped, startled. She was starting to see more clearly now. "Of course not. You don't mind losing me, but God forbid you lose money." She leaned against her bedpost. "You know, I honestly think the money was the beginning of the end. You started making so much, and it was like you thought you had to have affairs, like you owed it to yourself." She could tell he didn't like the idea that he was a victim of his own wealth, corrupted. "If we weren't rich, you couldn't leave. You would have to stay. We would have to make it work."

She knew that wasn't necessarily true. People without money separated all the time. But money made it easy to live out dreams, even the ones you should have kept in the box.

"Heather, can you honestly say that you love me?" A blue vein pulsed in his neck.

"I want to love you. That should count for something."

Jeff left. Heather wasn't quite sure where he'd gone—it was hard to guess when someone could afford to go anywhere.

He wanted to take the kids back to Amarillo. Would they want to go with him? Piper hadn't wanted to come to California in the first place. Maple had her friends, but Jeff was right. They weren't the best influences.

Would Piper and Maple pick Heather? Heather couldn't imagine a world in which anyone would pick her.

She felt cold panic sweep through her. She was so empty inside already that it was easy for the chill to fill her.

It struck her that she had been afraid her whole life that she would be left. That was the reason she wanted control over every little thing. And now it had happened. He was gone. And he wouldn't come back.

She hadn't done a very good job of guarding against it. She hadn't made her husband love her. She hadn't even made her children love her enough to be sure, to be secure.

She needed her daughters. Needed them now before it was too late. Before they left her too.

She called Maple. But it was after midnight, and her daughter didn't pick up. She was with Pamela. Heather would see her tomorrow morning. She didn't need to track her down. She would pick her up early and drive her to the horse show. Heather would be the perfect mother. It wasn't too late. She would be too good to leave.

She still had a chance with Maple, and she wasn't giving up on Piper either.

Heather went to Piper's room. It seemed so far away, through the network of hallways and mostly empty rooms. The lights were out under the closed door. Heather knew she should leave it until the morning, but she couldn't. She needed to see Piper. To know she was still there.

Heather opened the door. The bed was empty, the covers thrown back. She felt the chill inside her start to harden. Where was her daughter?

She heard Jeff's words again: *You don't even know!*

Jeff had taken Piper. She had already gone back to Texas. Piper had left, and it was all Heather's fault.

Suddenly frantic, Heather called Piper's phone. She called five times in a row. Finally, Piper picked up.

"I'm at the barn!" she said as if she knew she'd been caught. "I'm walking back now."

Heather could hear the crunch of the dirt as Piper walked.

Heather should have felt calm. Piper hadn't gone with Jeff. She hadn't left.

But instead, Heather felt a growing panic, a fear she couldn't contain. She had found Piper, but was she already too late?

When Piper was a baby, Heather picked her clothes. She braided her hair. She chose her name. But as soon as Piper was old enough to express herself, she had begun firmly pushing Heather away. Heather could still feel the push of her toddler hands.

I can do it. I can do it on my own!

All of her life Heather had been trying to hold on to her, but she was always pushing her away. Until she brought her to the horses.

Heather still remembered that first day. Piper was three—far too young to be riding—but Heather couldn't wait. Ever since she'd lost her own horse, she had dreamed of the day she could give horses to her daughters. She would never do what her parents had done. She would never put her children through that pain. She would give her daughters horses, all the horses a girl could ever want.

Piper had watched out the window from her car seat as Heather drove alongside pastures where horses grazed or walked.

They had put Piper on a pony, helmet strapped tightly. She had bobbed along, her instructor leading, Piper beaming. The instructor had said she was a natural. And Heather had thought, *This is my daughter. This is a part of me I can fix.*

Heather had bought Piper horse toys every birthday and read her horse books every night. For years horses kept them connected; horses were the one sure line between them. But then Heather had gone too far, overstepped. She'd tried too hard to fix herself through her daughter's life.

"What are you doing at the barn in the middle of the night?" Heather said, unable to keep the fear from her voice—only it sounded like scolding. Her fear sounded like punishment.

"I just wanted to check on Commotion," Piper said. "I was worried, with the fall and everything."

"I'm coming to meet you," Heather said.

"Mom, don't." Piper's voice was strained. "I'm almost home."

Heather didn't care.

seventy-three

PIPER

P iper had not gone to the barn to meet Douglas. She had gone to the barn to take a pregnancy test. She had taken three, and they were all broken. They were all wrong. There was no way in hell you could get pregnant just by having sex.

Piper went to the horse. She hovered in Commotion's stall, unsure what she should do. The horse stood beside her, nuzzled into her chest, his eyes bright. He soothed her.

She didn't feel any of the big emotions—not joy or sadness or anger. She just felt the sense of her life turning over inside her, so some things—things that had once felt so important, like competing in the horse show or making friends or keeping busy—now dropped away and disappeared.

Her mind was resetting itself to a new reality, like it had when her family moved to California. *We're doing this now.* And that reality felt simultaneously cataclysmic and cooling, because suddenly nothing else mattered very much.

Piper was keeping the baby. She knew that instantly. It wasn't what she'd planned for, but it had the savor of fate. As if all of her

life experiences had been conspiring to bring her there, to that moment. As if she had been destined to move to California, destined to
find that boy, destined to have that child.

She didn't know what Douglas would do. Everything she knew
about boys his age told her that he wouldn't be happy. That he
would find a way to blame her and separate himself from her. She
imagined him shutting down, cutting her off. If he was afraid to
even like her, wouldn't he be more afraid now?

When Heather called after midnight, Piper had this horrible
sense that she knew, that the pregnancy had been telegraphed to her
in mother code.

Piper ignored the call, but Heather kept calling. Piper experienced a moment of dissociation in which she thought that one day
she would be the mother calling her child. And she felt that she was
wrong to be having a child when her relationship with her own
mother was so imperfect, as if she should not be able to become a
mother until she had solved her own mother, as if otherwise their
problems might keep zipping down the line.

Finally, Piper answered her phone. She tried to tell Heather not
to come, but as usual Heather wouldn't listen. Heather would do
only what Heather wanted to do.

Piper's first instinct was to feel angry. To feel this was somehow
her mother's fault. Not the pregnancy, obviously, but that she
couldn't tell her about it.

As sure as Piper was of keeping the baby, she was just as sure
that her mother would react badly to the news. She wouldn't be able
to help herself. And years from then, and for the rest of her life, Piper
would never be able to forget Heather's initial reaction. It would
taint their relationship. It would taint everything. Forever.

Piper walked fast to the horse trail, and then she ran. A manic
voice in her head warned her, *Don't run! You're pregnant!* She knew

that was ridiculous. Pregnant people could run. They could live and breathe and make choices.

Piper didn't have to give up college. She could live at home. She would have lots of support. All she would have to sacrifice was her whole heart.

Heather appeared on the trail in front of her. They both slammed to a stop, feet apart from each other. Flushed. Out of breath.

"You didn't have to run." Piper panted. "I'm fine."

Piper looked at her mother, at all the familiar features that conspired to make her "Mom." And she had an unexpected, overwhelming desire to tell her. Who else could she tell? All of her friends were so far away. She wanted to tell someone who loved her. She wanted to tell her mom.

"I'm glad you're okay," Heather said, as if Piper had been in danger. As if she had been, and Heather had sensed it.

"I'm sorry I didn't—"

"It's fine," Heather said fast.

It was late at night, yet she seemed wide-awake. She was sparking with worry. Was it all for Piper?

As they walked toward their house, Piper fell into step beside her mother. From the corner of her eye, she noticed Heather reach for her, but then her hand hovered and dropped.

Piper wanted to reach back, wanted to be someone who could, but the wall between them was still there. It wasn't there for anyone else, in any part of her life. It was there only for her mother, and Piper could not break it down.

"I wanted to ask you," Heather said, "if everything is okay with your sister. Your dad said . . ." She drifted off, seemingly hung up on a loose end.

Piper had completely forgotten about the drama with Maple. "The stirrup leather."

Heather paused outside their gate to punch in the code. "Do you really think Maple would do that?"

"I don't know," Piper said honestly. "I do think Vida's a bad influence. Maple acts like her. She talks like her. She's even starting to *look* like her."

"Vida's never been my favorite, but she's Maple's friend. And I think she's been a good influence, in some ways. . . ."

"I could have been seriously injured."

Knowing she was pregnant made Piper feel extra ferocious. She could have lost the baby. She could have been killed. People died in horse accidents. Douglas's mom had permanent brain damage.

"This is all about you, you know," Piper said.

"What's that?" Heather held the gate open for Piper.

"The way Maple is acting. She's trying to impress you. To get your approval. Your love . . ." Piper felt flimsy saying it, as if she still longed for those things, too.

"I love both my girls," her mom insisted.

"I'm not sure you can. You don't even see us."

"I see you," Heather said, so fast her response felt flippant.

"Do you? Or do you just see who you want us to be?"

Heather took Piper's hand, held it tight. "I don't want you to be anyone other than who you are."

"I'm pregnant."

Piper hadn't meant to say it. It had just spilled out of her. In an instant, she had recognized she would have to say it. There would never be a good time. And then she had said it, and then it was there, hanging between them. Piper needed her mom to love her no matter what, and there would never be a good time to ask for it.

Heather froze outside the gate. Piper could practically see her mother's heart pounding out of her chest.

"I took a test," Piper said. "Three tests."

"But you . . . Who's the . . . ?"

Piper watched Heather, waiting for her to ruin it, knowing she would. Waiting . . .

"It's going to be okay," Heather said, so abruptly Piper flinched. And then she hugged her. Piper felt her whole soul pinch, preparing for an impact that never came. Heather was holding her so tight. "I love you," she said, running her fingers through her hair. "I love you so much."

seventy-four

VIDA

Maple was still at Vida's house the next morning, even though she had left Vida's room after eleven. She was downstairs with Pamela making smoothies. Vida thought Maple must have slept in Pamela's room, which was so fucking weird.

Even weirder was that Maple refused to go home when Heather came to pick her up. Vida could hear Pamela talking to Heather in the entryway.

"I think she's just a bit overwhelmed. Her father came over last night and was extremely rude to everyone. Totally inappropriate!"

Carefully, Vida crept down the stairs so she could listen better. Maple was hiding in Pamela's room. Effie was in the shower.

"I'm sorry about that. I think he's"—Heather shook her head, snapping out of something—"just an asshole, to be honest."

"You seem stressed." Pamela smiled like she was happy about it.

"I'm fine. There's just a lot going on right now." Heather forced a nervous laugh. It echoed oddly through the foyer. "Family drama."

"Why don't you just let me keep an eye on Maple?" Pamela said.

"I can drive her down to the show. She's probably just reacting to the drama at home. She's a very sensitive girl."

"I don't know. . . ." Heather seemed preoccupied. "I don't think that's a good idea."

"Can I give you some advice?" Pamela said. "You can't force a girl like Maple. You're just going to push her away." Pamela rested her hand on Heather's shoulder, directed her toward the door. "We're friends, aren't we? You can trust me with your daughter."

"Okay," Heather agreed, seeming relieved. "I have to run a few errands today. With Piper. I'm not sure how long it will take. But we'll be at the horse show tonight."

"Totally fine. We'll give Maple the grand tour. Distract her with some horse show magic."

Pamela escorted Heather out the door and shut it behind her. As she turned back into the house, she noticed Vida crouched on the landing.

Vida stood up straight. "I don't understand why you're being so nice to Maple."

"I'm not being nice to her," Pamela said, checking that Maple wasn't nearby.

"Where did she sleep last night?"

"She was upset. I slept on my sofa, and she slept on the bed."

"She's not your daughter."

"I know that, sweetheart."

Vida gripped the banister. "She's my competition."

"Angel, she's not even in the same universe as you," Pamela said.

Vida wanted to feel that was true, but all she could feel was some inner chamber of her heart collapsing.

Nothing was going her way. She was a mean girl with shit horses and no father and no future. The one thing she had, the one thing she could rely on, was Pamela. So why the fuck was her mom trying to help her competition?

Maple appeared behind Vida on the landing. "I can go home if you don't want me here."

Vida rounded on the other girl. "When has not being wanted ever stopped you?" she snapped, then pushed her way past Maple to find Effie.

seventy-five

PIPER

When Heather had left that morning to pick up Maple at her sleepover, Piper arranged to meet Douglas. He had parked off the road near the horse trails, under a copse of trees.

Piper approached his truck with a pervading sense of doom. All of her life she had been led to believe that babies were prison sentences, especially for men. You were supposed to wait to have kids—*Travel! Find yourself! Live!*—before you settled into your parasite phase. Before you gave up on You and handed whatever life you had left over to the next generation, so you could blame them for fucking everything up.

Even though Piper knew that Douglas was just as responsible as she was, she hated to be the one who had to tell him. *I'm sorry, but you've been sentenced to eighteen years, then paroled for a lifetime, because we lost control in the heat of the moment. Next time, come on my tits.*

He kissed her as soon as she got in the truck. She let him. She was so nervous she felt electric. Like she might shock him if he brushed her the wrong way.

"I need to tell you something," she said when he pulled away, his fingers still knotted in her hair. She gazed into his lust-bright eyes; then she pulled the trigger. "I'm pregnant."

To his credit, he did not flinch. "Are you gonna keep it?"

She nodded, and he practically leapt across the console to embrace her. He kissed her neck and her jawbone and her cheekbone, like he was too excited to find her mouth. She had nothing to be scared of.

"I always wanted to be a dad," he said.

She thought that was a strange confession from a nineteen-year-old boy, but maybe not from a boy who'd never had one.

interview 8

DETECTIVE PEREZ

etective Perez hated Kieran Flynn immediately. He reminded her of her own estranged father.

He had a way of looking at you as if he didn't see you, a way of talking to you as if he didn't hear you. He had a way of living as if he could create his own reality.

Detective Perez spent twenty minutes trying to get him to let his guard down, trying to get him to open up and seem human. Finally, she gave up. Some people could just shut themselves down.

She asked Kieran the famous question: *Where were you when it happened?*

"Douglas Dunn said you were here with him around midnight," Detective Perez said. "You told the officers you left around nine p.m."

Kieran did not waver. "I've known Douglas since he was a baby. Great rider. Very good on a horse. Not particularly good with numbers."

"So you're sticking with nine?"

"I believe you asked me to approximate. I told you I left after dark. There are long days on this job. Time doesn't exist for horses the way it does for people." Kieran took that moment to look pointedly at his watch. "Do you have any relevant questions? I have a business to run. A lot of people—a lot of horses—rely on me." As if Detective Perez were just a cop, but Kieran was a *horse trainer*.

"We'll let you know."

"If you must." Kieran crossed the stall with an air of busy importance. He swung the door open with a practiced thrust. Then he paused. "Have you talked to the girl yet?"

"No," Detective Perez said. "There has to be an adult present."

"I'd be happy to sit in, if you can't find someone," Kieran offered, suddenly finding time. "You should talk to her. She knows what happened better than anyone."

SOUTHERN
CALIFORNIA
INTERNATIONAL
HORSE
SHOW

seventy-six

MAPLE

Maple had never witnessed horse show magic.

Pamela drove the girls to the showgrounds on opening day. The arenas were all empty: great hollow stadiums. There were aisles and aisles of temporary horse stalls, stained and dented and chewed on. An abandoned city in the cradle of the mountains.

Then the vans started to arrive. They brought tents and bunting—all in RSFE colors—to cover the old disused stalls. To build a circus in the barn aisle.

There were flower arrangements and outdoor furniture, refrigerators filled with ice-cold sodas and champagne. Next came all the tack—the show tack, which was better than the tack they used at home: polished bridles, brand-new saddle pads, sheepskin-lined leather front and back boots.

They sanitized the stalls. They filled the water troughs and set the hay nets and put down fresh pine shavings.

Then the horses came. They wore travel helmets. Their legs were neatly wrapped. Some whinnied and pranced; others were so used to horse shows that they practically put themselves away. They filled the air with horsey smells and squeals, made the grounds come to life.

Last came the riders, anxious and overdressed. Lining up for bad coffee, tooling around on golf carts that always had too many people on board.

The warm-up ring was bursting with frustration and chaos, riders calling, "Pass on the left!"

Horses got spooked, so everyone panicked, then came running to watch or help—whichever opportunity presented itself.

Everyone knew everyone. There were celebrities in that world. The best riders. The best trainers. The richest ones. But most of all, the bad trainers, the ones with reputations.

"He got disqualified for drugging a horse."

"He transported a horse that went neurological and caused that outbreak back in 2022."

"I saw him whip a horse so hard he broke the crop."

Vida had immediately commandeered a golf cart. She knew how quickly they were claimed. She drove Effie and Maple all through the grounds, pointing out all the good riders and the rich owners and the bad trainers.

Vida seemed to have accepted Maple for now. Maple had made her laugh on the car ride over, and things between them were good again.

That was what it was like being friends with Vida. She was the most acrobatic of friends. She would swing you. She would drop you. And then, at the last second, she would catch you. And you were so surprised, so grateful, that you just had to keep swinging.

Still, every time Vida and Maple's friendship broke and then repaired itself, it seemed more tenuous—as if the point would arrive when it could not be so easily fixed.

Maple's head was swimming with the horse show. It was the

perfect distraction from everything else—her fight with her father, her refusal to go home with her mother, her dread of seeing Piper again.

There were so many trainers, so many riders, so many horses, that all of Maple's problems began to feel very small, very far away.

"How many riders compete in the Little Palm Cup?" Maple asked Vida.

"Maybe forty or fifty," Vida said.

The Cup was the following day. It was held in the main arena. It was a big deal. All the best Junior riders would be competing, with all the best horses. But none of the horses were as good as Commotion.

As the girls drove around the showgrounds, Maple engaged in a fantasy in which she rode Commotion in the Little Palm Cup and won. Her mom and her dad would both be there. They would be so proud of her. The whole family would come together in the Winner's Enclosure. Maple's mother would pin the first-place ribbon onto Commotion's bridle. Her dad would hold the trophy. And they would say to her, *You're the best daughter we could ever hope for. You're perfect. You're exactly right.*

While Vida and Effie were having a lesson with Amy, Maple wandered down to the show office. She got in line. She didn't tell anyone. She didn't ask anyone's permission. That way, no one would ever see her coming.

That night, Vida introduced Maple to horse show nightlife. Nighttime at horse shows, Vida said, was the best time. There were bonfires at the end of every barn aisle. People drank and talked long into the night.

The show's location in the mountains guaranteed a vast cover of stars—Maple could even see the Milky Way. The horses stuck their sleepy heads over the stall doors. The air was dry and cold.

As it got colder, everyone moved closer to the fires, watched the flames play on faces. Everyone drank—wine and whisky and champagne. No one paid any attention to the girls, so they drank, too, at their own little fire away from the adults.

Vida took her turn on their flask. They were drinking whisky because that was all they were able to find—Dominic had hidden a bottle of Blue Label on a high shelf in the tack room. After filling her flask, Vida had topped the bottle off with water.

"He'll never notice," she said.

Maple curled her toes inside her boots. She was wearing her riding gloves to keep her hands warm. Drinking whisky on an empty stomach was making her queasy, but she felt acutely aware that both Vida and Effie were watching her, would know if she threw up, so for the past hour, she had been focused on nothing other than not throwing up.

Sometimes she would seem to turn a corner and feel *amazing*, but then she would force herself to have another sip to keep up and feel sick all over again. She could reasonably say her entire relationship with Vida was like that.

Vida was glugging whisky like a cowboy, which Maple didn't think was the best way to prepare for the Cup tomorrow. It also didn't make Vida especially nice.

She was sharpening her insults by degrees, always testing how far she could take things.

"I guess your sister's a chickenshit because she pulled out of all her classes," Vida said.

After making a big issue of riding Commotion, Piper had dropped out of the horse show at the last minute. She had been away all day with Heather. Maple figured their absence had something to do with her dad and didn't really want to think about it.

Heather had texted her twenty minutes ago to say they were finally on their way.

"Your dad seems like a total dickwad," Vida noted. She assumed a false casual pose. "You know what? It's too bad you're not good enough to ride in the Cup, because you have a better horse than anyone in the class. You could probably win, if you actually had a fucking clue what you were doing."

Maple sat up. She had reached a whisky plateau. She felt invincible for one hot, clear moment. She remembered Pamela's advice: *Fuck every last one of them.*

"It's too bad you can't afford better horses," she told Vida. "Then maybe you'd actually have a shot."

"Ooooh!" Effie perked up, bouncing in her seat.

Maple knew better than to think Effie might take her side, but right then she didn't care.

"I wasn't gonna tell you," Maple said. The truth was she had been afraid to tell Vida, but she wasn't afraid right then. "But I put my name down for the Cup."

Vida did a quick scan of their surroundings; then she kicked a log so their fire collapsed. Flames and smoke shot in Maple's direction. An ember burned Maple's wrist.

Maple jumped up from her seat. "You're a fucking psycho!"

But insults didn't work on Vida. She kind of loved them, as if she were relieved you had finally sunk to her level.

"I'd rather be a psycho than a loser."

"I don't like you," Maple said.

It was true, but she had never admitted it, even to herself. Despite everything Vida had done in the past, Maple had stayed with her, but she didn't want to stay anymore. She could stand on her own. Or maybe that was just the whisky talking.

"I don't want to be your friend anymore."

"Thank God," Vida said. "I only let you hang out with me

because my mom told me to. I never liked you. In fact, I really hate you. I think you're so fucking annoying."

Suddenly, all the cards fell into place. Maple had never been able to understand why Vida wanted to be her friend when she seemed to dislike Maple. Why she invited Maple to her pool, to her sleepovers, to every trip to the bathroom. Why she stuck to Maple like the most toxic kind of glue.

Fuck her. Fuck them all. Maple didn't need her. Maple didn't care. Then, at the peak of a whisky tower, she slipped. A wave of nausea tumbled through her, and she opened her mouth and threw up all over Vida's tall boots.

seventy-seven

VIDA

Vida started crying on the way back to the hotel. Pamela seemed horrified. Vida was a little horrified herself, but she was also really, really drunk.

"She ruined my boots! They reek! I can still smell them!"

After Maple had thrown up on her boots, Vida had raced toward the cleaning bay, with Effie trailing behind her. Vida had fought to get her slippery boots off with a jack, but she ended up tripping herself, so she fell over. The vomit-covered boots stayed on.

Effie stood by, refusing to help. "I'm sorry! But it's disgusting!"

"Get my mom!" Vida finally ordered her.

Pamela came. Working together, they managed to get the boots off. Then, with rags and saddle soap and a toothbrush, Pamela went to town on the boots, trying to get the vomit out of every crevice. But they still stank. Now, in the car, Vida could smell a horrible mix of oil and vomit that was making her stomach turn.

"What the hell were you thinking, getting this drunk before the Cup?" Pamela demanded. "You're lucky Kieran didn't see you."

"What does it matter?" Vida whined, feeling slightly energized by the melodrama of the situation. If Maple had vomited on anyone else's boots, she would have laughed. "I'm not gonna win tomorrow. I might as well just get drunk and ride in vomitous boots." She threw herself back against the seat. "And next year, I'll be in adult classes, and Kieran still won't train me, and all my horses will be *so old* and probably have injuries, and I'll just limp along until I have to quit. Go to college like a basic bitch. Work at a dental office."

"That's not true."

"Yes, it is." Vida wiped her nose, slightly sobered by the truth.

"You're the best rider," her mom assured her. "That counts for something."

Vida sat up, as if something big had occurred to her. "I've wasted my whole childhood. All I did. All I've done. For the past seventeen and a half years. I sacrificed everything. *You* sacrificed everything." She shook her head, mystified; then she dropped down in her seat, surrendering.

Vida wasn't going to win the Cup. She wasn't going to ride for Kieran. She was going to become what she had been destined to become from the beginning, from the day she was born, from the moment she had been conceived.

She caught her mother's eyes in the mirror. Her future had always been right there, watching over her. She had been raised by her own fate.

Pamela pulled over in the dark parking lot of their modest hotel. She kept the car running, but she didn't say a word for a very long time.

seventy-eight

PAMELA

P amela gripped the bracelet Vida had made her. "I thought . . . ," Pamela started, and then she stopped again. She was quiet for so long that Vida actually sat back and seemed on the verge of falling asleep. "You're right. I have failed you. In so many ways. But the worst—my biggest regret—is that I somehow convinced myself that I hadn't." Pamela turned to face Vida, who was plastered against the seat—limp, drunk, the very picture of Pamela herself when she had been that age. "I thought I was teaching you to be tougher and better, but I was just teaching you to be me.

"You're a bully. You seem strong to other people, but you're not. I know you're not, and it's because of me. Because I lied to you all your life. Because I wouldn't even tell you who you really are."

"Mom," Vida said weakly, "stop. You're being mean."

"I didn't tell you who your father was, because that was what he wanted. I did everything he wanted, because he was my trainer. And he trained me."

Vida sat up, reanimated by the revelation. "Mom, fuck off," she said.

It was nonsense, but then everything was. Pamela had told the truth, and now everything was nonsense.

"I'm telling you the truth. Kieran is your father. Douglas Dunn is your half brother."

Then Pamela laughed, because nonsense was funny.

"What. The. Fuck. Mom, stop laughing! This isn't funny!"

Pamela stopped short. She dropped her head on the steering wheel. The engine was humming. She could feel its vibrations on her forehead.

Pamela had thought that telling the truth would make her feel better, make her feel in some way released. But she just felt bad in a different way. She was still the same person, it was still the same world, whether she lied or whether she told the truth.

"Go back to the room," Pamela finally said. "Make yourself throw up. There's Gatorade in the fridge. Drink one. Take two Advil. And go to sleep."

She put the car in drive and waited for Vida to leave.

Vida slid her fingers around the door handle. "Where are you going?"

Pamela looked her daughter dead in the eyes. "I'm going to tell him. We're not keeping his secrets anymore. Okay?"

seventy-nine

HEATHER

Earlier that day, Heather had taken Piper to a doctor who confirmed that she was indeed pregnant. Then Heather took her daughter to dinner, because she didn't know what else to do. She was playing hard at being okay with this. She was playing with her whole life, it seemed.

She couldn't help thinking that the gods could not have concocted a situation in which she had less control. She tried to convince herself that Piper's pregnancy was a test, but that exercise was somewhat curtailed by the recognition that there would be a baby whether she passed the test or not.

It did occur to her that the guy had to be local, which meant Piper would stay in California with her. Unless her dad offered him money. Unless the guy wanted to try Texas. There was really no end to what Jeff could do to entice Piper, so Heather was playing very, very hard at being very, very okay with this.

"You could move into the guesthouse if you want," Heather said. "Both of you. Whoever he is."

See how okay she was? *Deliriously* okay.

The father had to be someone from the barn. Piper was friends with everyone, a part of the team. And there were a lot of male grooms, a few male riders.

"I'll have to talk to him first," Piper said.

The pronoun made Heather's back twinge.

"While we're on the subject," Piper said, "he wants to be the one to tell you. Tonight. At the horse show."

That was when Heather felt a prickle—call it a mother's intuition.

They reached the showgrounds well after dark. Piper was texting furiously, back and forth with her mystery guy. The mystery father of her child. The mystery destroyer of all of Heather's carefully crafted dreams.

Piper's face was lined with worry. Her shoulders were tense. Heather hated the guy already. It shouldn't be like this. It couldn't. There had to be some way to unwrite this wrong.

Piper looked up. "I guess he just wants to talk to you privately. I don't know. . . . That's kind of weird, right?"

That was when Heather knew beyond a shadow of a doubt that Douglas Dunn was the father. He wanted to talk to Heather alone because he was afraid of what she might say. And Piper looked pained, like she knew that this wasn't normal, like she was worried this wasn't good.

It wasn't good. It wasn't at all what Heather wanted for her daughter. What she'd dreamed of. All Piper's life, from the day she was born, not once had Heather thought to herself, *I can't wait until you turn eighteen and make me a grandma! I can't wait until you chain yourself to some horseback-riding fuck boy!*

Douglas had screwed her daughter over. He had done it in secret, and now he had ruined her life.

"No, I think it's a good idea for me to talk to him alone." Heather removed her seat belt. "Where should I meet him?"

"He's at Commotion's stall."

Of course he would use the horse as a shield. Piper gave her mother directions, watching Heather closely all the while. Heather knew Piper was waiting for her mother to screw up, holding her breath, like she knew it was coming.

Heather knew it was coming, too.

As Heather got out of the car, as she started across the show-grounds, she felt an overwhelming sense of injustice. Her daughter had been robbed. She was barely an adult, and now she was going to be a mother. Now she was going to be a partner to a guy who would no doubt cheat on her the first chance he got, who probably already had. To a guy who was no doubt using her for her horses and her money. To a guy who had almost slept with her mother.

Heather had tried to give up control, and this was what had happened. This was the consequence of her taking her hands off the wheel. Her elder daughter's life had been obliterated. Her younger daughter wouldn't speak to her. Her marriage was in shambles.

It might not have been all Douglas's fault, but enough of it was for Heather to feel good about punishing him for it.

It was almost midnight, but there was still one last fire burning coolly in the night. Heather recognized a few of the RSFE mothers hanging around with their daughters, drinking, laughing beneath the stars.

The barn aisle was dark and warm with horses. The shavings had a fresh pine scent. Heather peered over Commotion's stall door and found Douglas standing, like some kind of horsey saint, with the horse's head cradled against his chest.

Heather yanked the latch open, startling the horse and the boy. Commotion tossed his head in surprise.

Douglas crossed out of the stall and met her at the door. He kept his voice low, like he didn't want the horse to hear. "I wanted to be the one to tell you."

"You monster."

Heather felt frightened—there was an intensity to him that unnerved her. He had hardly looked at her since their trip to Kentucky, she realized. His eyes always grazed over her, past her shoulder, over her head.

Heather didn't move, although her whole being was pulsing with fear, which was spiraling quickly into anger. She waited for him to speak, but he seemed unable to say anything. He would open his mouth and then close it, like the words were sticking to his tongue.

She opened the door. That shook him loose.

"I need you to not tell Piper about Kentucky," he said, stumbling back into the stall as she came in.

She smiled, an odd reaction. "How could you do this?"

"I love her."

"That's not a good enough reason." She had him backed against a wall.

"It's not fair." His Adam's apple throbbed as he swallowed. "I didn't know she existed. I didn't even know she was possible."

"I can't promise you I won't say anything."

Heather did not want to lose Piper, but she did not want to sacrifice her either. She couldn't let him ruin her daughter's life.

Heather started to move. Douglas caught her by the wrist; he held her with gentle insistence, the way he would have held a horse.

"You can't tell her." He pulled her closer, so she could smell the lingering scent of peppermint. "It might make you feel better, but it would hurt her."

"You're using her."

"I'm not."

"You'll cheat on her."

"I won't."

"You'll leave her."

He shook his head wordlessly.

"You have no idea what you'll do," Heather said. "You hardly know her. You hardly know yourself."

"You're right. I don't know myself, and I don't trust myself either. But I do know her. She's the best person I've ever met. And that's because of you. Because you're there. Because you love her. That's all anyone really needs, to be loved by someone."

Douglas was extremely compelling at close range. He had a way of talking in breakthroughs; she remembered it from those early days of searching for a horse.

He released her arm, gazed across the stall to where the horse stood watching. His voice dropped, turned tender. "Tell her, if you need to. I hope she'll forgive me. I think she will."

He was probably right, but what he didn't say, what Heather knew, was that Piper was more likely not to forgive *her*. And what would Heather save in telling Piper the truth? What would she accomplish? It was too late to go back; for the first time, Heather knew that. It was too late to spend the rest of her life trying to go back to the point when she'd lost control.

"You really want to have a baby?" she asked him. "You're nineteen years old. You have your whole life ahead of you."

"She is my life now."

Heather thought it was such a reckless thing to say. This confession, more than anything, made her realize how broken Douglas actually was, how alone, how desperate. Maybe that was the only way to fall in love. Maybe when you stopped being desperate, stopped needing someone else *that much*, that was when love left. Maybe that was when she had lost her husband. Maybe in getting everything they'd wanted, Jeff and Heather had lost the ability to need each other.

"Mrs. Parker?"

Heather jumped a little in surprise; she'd thought they were alone. It was clear in Douglas's expression that he had, too. She turned to see Kieran on the other side of the stall door. His expression was casual. His eyes were bright.

"I believe your daughter has been looking for you. Maple."

Heather stepped forward. "Do you know where she is?"

Kieran unfastened the latch, then opened the door for her. "Last I saw her, she was sitting in the stands above the Grand Prix arena."

Heather nodded. Her eyes flicked over Douglas as she passed him, but he was back to not seeing her.

eighty

MAPLE

Maple threw up so hard her eyes burned. She even vomited through her nostrils, so those burned, too. But afterward, she felt better. The stars had come closer. She didn't feel so drunk.

The main arena curved out in a basin before her. The freshly painted jumps glowed; they were still set impossibly high from that night's Grand Prix. The darkness and the emptiness seemed to underline how hollow it all was. It was just a stage without the players.

Sobriety seemed to have arrived all at once, as if all Maple's worries had been just above her, and now they tumbled down.

Even if Maple competed in the Little Palm Cup, even if Maple won, all she would get was a ribbon. Her life wouldn't change. She would still be the same person: the victim, the friendless girl, the lesser sister. There was no way out of being herself.

"Hey." Maple turned to see Piper walking toward her. "Do you mind if we talk?"

Maple shook her head. Piper sat one chair over from her sister, as if afraid to get any closer. The worst thing was, Maple knew she deserved it. She knew she had asked for it. She had tried to change by becoming a worse person.

"I'm sorry," she told her sister. "For being such a brat—but I didn't cut the stirrup leather," she added quickly, because she wanted to make sure Piper didn't think she was apologizing for that.

"Okay."

"But I'm pretty sure Vida did. And she was my friend, so . . ."

Maple had allowed Vida to take things too far again and again. What had she expected to happen? Eventually someone would get hurt.

"She's not anymore," Maple added.

Piper sniffed. "She's not good enough for you."

Maple bit her lip, considering. She'd always assumed that no one understood her, but maybe she had never given anyone the chance to.

"But . . . isn't that how friendships work?" Maple asked. "If I waited for someone who was worthy of my friendship, I wouldn't have any friends."

"Shit," Piper swore, to Maple's surprise.

Maple tried to clarify. "You don't know what it's like—"

"No, I do." Piper's eyes were bright. "I really wish I didn't."

"Okay, but you don't." Maple was sure.

Piper had good friends back in Texas. People loved Piper, but they didn't love Maple. Maple had to settle for the mean girls and the bullies, for anyone who would take her.

Piper stood up and took the seat beside Maple. Maple felt a web of tension unwind, as if she were relieved that Piper had made the move for her.

"I do understand. I was . . . *hooking up* with Douglas. He made me swear not to tell anyone. And I knew that I shouldn't let a guy treat me like that. I shouldn't be in a relationship like that. But I felt like if I didn't compromise—always *more* than I should have—I would lose him."

"Douglas Dunn?" Maple said. If Piper wanted Maple to feel bad for her, that was not the way.

"Yeah. It's not a secret anymore, but it never should have been." Piper turned to face her sister. They were so close that Maple could see the dark spot in Piper's right eye, the one that never appeared in pictures, so you had to really *know* her to know it was there. "I do understand. I understand what it feels like to not want to be alone."

"I just want to be like everyone else," Maple said.

"You are." Piper offered a weak smile. "Everyone wants that."

"But I want to have friends."

Maple still couldn't help feeling Piper didn't quite get it, that no one did. And she still didn't know quite what to do with that. Would she feel separate forever? Would she feel different forever? Was it true that everyone did?

Piper nudged closer. "I know I'm your sister, but don't forget I'm your friend, too."

"I know. It's just . . . you're so perfect sometimes. It's hard to be friends with you."

"I may have fixed that."

"What do you mean?"

Piper sighed at the stars. "It's a long story. Let's just focus on you for now."

Maple lifted an arm as if in surrender. She felt like a dork. But Piper hugged her, and Maple hugged her sister back.

Sometimes Maple felt really lucky to have a sister, not to have to face all these fucked-up things alone. "I love you, sister."

"I love you, too."

eighty-one

PAMELA

It was late when Pamela got to the showgrounds, but she knew that Kieran would still be there. The horses watched as she walked down the shadowed barn aisles, their big eyes shining when they caught the light.

She should have told Kieran years ago that she wouldn't keep his secrets. In some ways, that realization made her actions feel limp, tired. As if waiting so long had robbed her of any heroism for doing the right thing. But she walked forward, because in her mind's eye, she had a picture of what her daughter could be.

She had an image of Vida jumping clear while silhouetted in a bright arena. She had an image of Vida free.

"So, you gonna leave?"

Pamela stopped in her tracks. Kieran's voice had sent chills from her temples to her toes. She was standing by Commotion's stall. She slipped inside to hide. The horse was still awake. He tossed his head at her, as if inviting her to play.

"We haven't talked about that yet."

The second voice belonged to Douglas. The voices were coming from the far end of the barn aisle. Pamela hadn't seen the men. They hadn't seen her either.

She tiptoed carefully backward until she was against the wall of Commotion's stall. Then she slid down, so she was seated in the shavings, where she stayed absolutely still.

"Of course you are," Kieran said. "You think that girl and her baby are gonna want to live at my place?"

Shit. Douglas had gotten a girl pregnant. Pamela wasn't exactly surprised, but she did not think Kieran would take it well.

"You gonna train with someone else?" Kieran asked.

Of course that was what Kieran would ask. *What about my horses?* "No."

"Hell, you'll have your own horses. All in the family, right?"

Douglas didn't respond.

"I never thought you would beat me at my own game."

"It's not a game to me. I love her." Douglas's voice had the quality of surrender particular to love.

"Good for you." Kieran's own voice had softened, as if it had become an echo. "It better not affect your riding. I don't want to hear *I didn't get any sleep because of the baby*, or whatever bullshit."

"No, sir."

"You'll make a good father. You've raised enough horses. Kids are probably easier."

"Probably."

"Douglas?" Kieran called, as if the boy was walking away. "You're a good kid. Probably because you're so convinced that you're a bad one."

"Thank you."

"No. Don't thank me. I only want credit for Grand Prix wins."

Pamela leaned against the wall. She felt time turn over inside her. She remembered when she had told Kieran that he was going to be a father. How he'd told her that she was on her own. How he'd walked away. As if he could choose not to be Vida's dad. Something about this moment made that moment feel worse.

Pamela felt as if she had lost something. A competition of sorts. One she had been playing for decades.

A heaviness came over her, seemed to overpower her. It was a feeling she'd had before, one that drove her to make her most terrible choices.

It was the feeling that she had made a fatal error sometime in her history, only she didn't know when or even what it was. But she could feel it, shuffled in the cards of her life, hiding, waiting to be turned over. Discovered.

Over her head, the stall door rattled. Her heart jerked. She stiffened, tried not to breathe as a pair of clasped hands appeared over her head.

Kieran was observing the horse, lost in thought.

Commotion bowed his head, then walked in their direction.

Her whole body seized in panic.

"Pamela," Kieran said, not looking at her, as if knowing she had been there all along, "what brings you here at this hour?"

She got to her feet, dusted the shavings off her pants. "So, you're going to be a grandfather."

eighty-two

HEATHER

Heather walked along the edge of the showgrounds toward the big arena. As she walked, she gazed out into the mountains beyond.

Her mind kept pulling back to what Douglas had said: that she loved her children. That simple truth might decide her entire future. Was love enough?

Was she a bad mother? Was she a good mother? Was it wrong to have dreams for her children?

Children made the most perfect vessels for your dreams. Dreams you had for yourself were always doomed to fail, because once you achieved them, you realized you weren't as happy as you thought you'd be. But the dreams you had for your children were golden, because you could feel only the achievement, none of the disappointment. You could imagine that your children were happy in a way you never could believe of yourself.

And what was the other option? To just accept her daughters for who they were? To watch Maple get run over and Piper hide at home alone? Wasn't acceptance just giving up?

Being a mother, being part of a family, entailed a great and terrible influence, whether or not you chose to wield it. You would worry and torment and impact your kids for the rest of their lives. They would blame you for everything. They would blame you for nothing. So didn't you need to do *something*?

And wasn't Heather doing her best? Having children hadn't made her a better person. It hadn't even made her a very different person. If anything, it had made Heather more of what she already was. More anxious, more worried, more loving and angry and fierce and determined.

She had expanded to encompass the needs of her babies, but she hadn't become somebody else. She wasn't a saint. She didn't have the answers. She didn't even have particularly good advice. All she had been armed with were her own experiences—her own traumas, really, because the good times didn't hand you weapons—and they were what she had wielded. The sword and shield of her own trauma to grant her babies a better life.

Still, it wasn't about her. She had been told that again and again. *You just need to love them.* That was what everybody said.

Heather was coming up the hill when she saw her daughters embracing. It stopped her in her tracks. She realized how much the hostility between them had unsettled her, scared her even. She needed to believe that there was a way she could hold on to them both, now more than ever.

Brewing with that resolution, more peaceful than she had any right to be, Heather walked up the hill until she reached her daughters.

"Girls? Is everything okay?"

"Yeah, everything's fine, Mom," Piper said, nudging a chair in her direction.

Heather sat down. Slowly she collected herself. So many things had changed. So many things were still changing.

She had a sudden memory of the first morning that Maple and

she had gone to RSFE. Piper had refused to go, but had hovered in a doorway while Maple's hair was braided.

Heather and Maple had explored the barn. Maple had been fearful, but Heather had felt almost wild with energy, with the certainty that they had found their home.

And now they were all there together, exactly as Heather had wanted. The three of them, like sisters, like the family she'd always dreamed of. Everything else might have been falling apart, but her daughters were with her now.

Heather felt dizzy. "Maybe we should just forget about the show this weekend."

Piper and Maple both looked surprised, but it was the right decision. Heather needed to tell them about their father's choice, needed to support them. They would get through this only one way: together. That was the most important thing.

"No," Maple said. "I want to compete. I put my name down for the Little Palm Cup."

"I—" Heather gasped a little, then looked at Piper for backup. She was trying to be a supportive mother, but the events of the past twenty-four hours were really pushing her limits.

"I know you don't think I can do it." Maple straightened up in her seat. "But that's okay, because I know I can."

"We can help you," Piper said, swinging her arm over Maple's shoulder.

"Both of you can do whatever you want," Heather said.

Her daughters looked a little too surprised, Heather thought.

It was so easy, once she'd said it. It was like a spell breaking. All the responsibility that she had taken for her children's lives, all its weight, seemed to lift from her, and she realized that she just had to love them. It was as simple as that.

Maple nudged her sister. "Mom's lost her mind."

"We finally broke her," Piper agreed.

They all scooted closer, so they were just one heap, one family.

Heather had never believed in happiness. She thought it was made up to convince people that they should always want more, should keep moving, keep looking ahead, always trying to be somewhere else.

But that night, sitting in the dark with her two perfect daughters, she realized that happiness was not in front of her. It was not behind her. It was that moment.

Now.

eighty-three

PAMELA

Kieran hovered in place. Pamela couldn't tell if he was shocked. He seemed, if anything, carefree. The stall door shook as he turned the latch, pulled it so he could open the door and come into the stall with her.

Pamela staggered back, hit the wall. The horse seemed overjoyed at more company, nodding his head and pacing at the other end of the stall as Kieran fastened the latch.

"You're making me nervous, Pamela," he said quietly. "I don't like to be nervous."

"I'm done. I'm not keeping your secrets anymore."

Pamela's voice had a slight tremor. She didn't know where it had come from, because she didn't feel fear.

Kieran scanned the aisleway, then walked deeper into the stall. "Sit down," he said. "Let's have a chat."

The phrase was familiar to her—the entry point to one of his stories. It was so normal that for a moment she felt relief.

She dropped to the floor of the stall. He sat beside her. He started his story, the way he had so many times before.

"Did I ever tell you about my first horse?"

She shook her head.

He took a deep breath through his nose, preparing himself, preparing her, as if the story was an obstacle they would get through together.

"I must have been twelve when my dad finally got me my own horse. Up until then I'd been riding other people's horses. He found this incredible horse, a thoroughbred gelding—back when everyone rode thoroughbreds, remember? Expertly trained. Perfectly behaved. So willing."

His eyes lit up. He was lost in the story.

"I had him for maybe six months, a year, when I started to realize he wasn't a great horse anymore. He had changed. Suddenly—it seemed to me—he'd picked up all these bad habits: balking, rearing. He used to charge me sometimes in the field when I went to catch him. I didn't understand what had happened.

"So I said to my dad, *What's wrong with him? Why is he acting this way?* And he said, *Because of you.* Horses are like mirrors. They reflect all the best parts and all the worst parts of ourselves back at us. That horse turned bad because I made him bad. I turned that horse into me."

He sighed, rubbed his hands up and down his legs, warming his muscles.

"I suppose in some way I want to protect them. Vida is the one I worry most about."

He had never talked about Vida that way, and Pamela felt her heart turn over, felt a terrible pull way down deep, where she still believed she could give her daughter everything that she wanted and everything that she needed.

"But you're around them all the time," she said. "What difference does it make whether you tell them or not?"

"If I don't tell them, I don't own them. That's the difference. They're not my horses." He always thought in terms of horses. "The thing is, Pamela, one day everything I've done and everything I am will come out. And when it does, don't you think it will be kind of a gift to my children to know they're not a part of it?"

"A part of what?"

"Don't pretend. You know me better than anyone."

That statement still had the power to bruise her heart, even as she realized the full impact of what he was saying. Pamela did know him better than anyone. And she knew his barn had been plagued by accidents over the years. Kieran's parents, for starters, had died in a gas leak on a weekend that Kieran happened to be away at a show. A man had been paralyzed. Two women had died. Then there was Douglas's mother, who had lost her helmet on a fall and hit her head. There had been some confusion over who had called the ambulance and when, but by the time the ambulance arrived, she'd been without oxygen for long enough that she never really came back.

Was Kieran to blame? He had been her trainer. He had been giving her a lesson. And by Kieran's own assertion, he controlled everything that happened at that barn.

There were accidents all the time. Horseback riding was a dangerous sport.

"Did you hire the woman with the umbrella?" Pamela said. "Did you cut the stirrup leather? You were teaching Maple that day. Did you help her adjust the stirrups?"

He didn't confirm her suspicions, but he also didn't deny them.

"But why?" she said. "Why would you do things like that?"

"I'm the coach. You don't make riders better by coddling them. You make them better by torturing them. Just ask God. He gives you trials and tribulations to make you stronger. He knows what you can handle."

The horse nodded along with Kieran.

"Adversity is good for people," Kieran continued. "You fall off, but you always get back on the horse. You know that. And look at that girl now. Look what she's accomplished. And it all started with that fall."

"How does brain damage make someone a better rider?"

Kieran didn't seem to like that question. "She threatened me. Just like you're threatening me. I don't like to be threatened."

"You're fucking insane," Pamela said.

She felt so good saying it. How had she not seen it before—or had she seen it? Had some part of her been drawn to the danger? Of riding, yes, but even more, of riding for Kieran.

"You can't control everything. You know that, right?" she said, feeling worried about Kieran—as always—when she should have been worried about herself. "Because that's what keeping it a secret is about—it's not about protecting anyone. You can't stand the thought of anything belonging to you being out of your control. But you're not in control."

Having children was all about losing control. About accepting the damaging consequences of your own choices, the power to create and destroy life all at once, all the time. It was easier to say *They're not really mine.*

"Just because you won't admit they're your children doesn't mean they're not. Just because that girl is riding in the Cup instead of lying in a hospital bed doesn't mean you saved her. You just got lucky." Pamela tried to catch Kieran's eyes, but he was gazing at the horse. "You're not God."

"Of course I'm God. I'm a horse trainer. I may not be God everywhere, but I am God here."

He pointed at the stall floor. He seemed so vulnerable to her at that moment, so like a child insisting that a fantasy was true.

She let her head drop against the wall. "You know what drives me crazy? You're a monster, but you're not all bad."

She had to admit that he was a little like the actual God. Most of the time, terrible things happened and you thought, *Why me?* But every once in a while, you convinced yourself: *If I hadn't struggled, I never would have made myself this strong.*

"No. I'm a damn good horse trainer."

Kieran put a hand on Pamela's shoulder. It felt so familiar. It calmed her, when she knew it shouldn't. How many times had he rested a hand on her shoulder just like that? How many times had he looked her in the eyes and convinced her that she could do something impossible?

He moved in beside her, slid his arm around her shoulder, slowly pulled her close.

"We made a good team, didn't we?" he said.

The horse had quieted, had cocked his foot in preparation for sleep.

"We had a good run together." He nudged Pamela playfully, as if she were a good sport. "Remember that show in Sarasota? Vida must have been about eight. What did I say to you after you won the Cup?"

Vida had been eight. All three of them had been in the Winner's Enclosure together when Pamela accepted the trophy. All three of them had held it for the picture. They'd been connected by that silvery cup, which had turned out to be so cheap.

Pamela could envision the scene clearly as his grip tightened around her. As if some part of her were still there.

"You said it was the best day of my life," Pamela said. "You said for as long as I lived, I would be looking back on that moment. So I'd better enjoy it as much as I could."

"Was I right?"

"Yes."

She could feel his breath, feel his heartbeat. She thought she should feel scared, but she didn't. She didn't feel scared at all. She just felt that she loved him still. Wanted his love still. She wanted to win for him, whatever game they were playing.

"I gave you that," he said. "The best moment of your life."

He took a needle from his pocket. Pamela recognized it immediately: acepromazine. He held up the needle, flicked it with his finger.

"I wish I didn't have to do this. But you've become a liability."

Pamela had never, in all those years, threatened Kieran with the truth. As if she had known instinctively that it would come to this. The horse world was his whole world. A magical place where he could act out control: control over enormous half-wild animals; control over people with enormous half-wild dreams.

If his secrets got out, he would lose his reputation. People would know there was something wrong about him, something off. They might even dig deeper. The truth, in fact, could crush his whole world—a world he had made, perhaps, too small.

"None of this works unless we're all united," he said.

None of it worked unless they were doing what he wanted all the time. Across the stall, the horse's eyes grew dim with sleep.

He took her arm and slowly rolled up her sleeve.

She could have told Kieran that it was too late—the secret was out; Vida already knew—but thinking about the string of bodies already connected to him, she wanted to protect her daughter.

She lifted her arm slowly, as if to help him; then she elbowed him hard in the gut.

"Oof," he grunted into her neck.

The horse spooked, rearing up. He charged in the tight space, creating enough of a ruckus for Pamela to wrench herself away from Kieran, to dive toward the door.

She staggered to her feet, then slipped on the stall mat. She grabbed at the latch on the other side of the gate. Her fingers had closed around the rusty metal when Kieran tackled her, dragged her down until he was straddling her on the floor.

She had a sick flashback of being straddled by him in the past—

and she felt a burst of regret because she should have known then. She should have seen it coming. You couldn't sleep with a monster and expect to get away. You couldn't ride with a bad coach and not expect to lose eventually. Lose big. Lose everything.

She wrenched her body beneath him, but he had her pinned down.

"Please, keep fighting," he said dryly. "I can subdue a fourteen-hundred-pound animal. You really think you stand a chance?"

The agitated horse was still pacing at the far side of the stall. Kieran watched the horse for a moment, then shook his head.

"I hope this doesn't affect his performance this weekend," he said without the least trace of self-awareness. Then he squeezed Pamela's arm until a vein popped.

"*Vida,*" she gasped as she felt the prick of the needle, watched her blood spurt into the syringe, then saw the liquid forced into her body.

Kieran stood up, dusted himself off and opened the stall door.

Pamela went to follow him, but she found that she couldn't move. She wasn't sure if it was the drug or something else, the culmination of years of neglect shutting everything down, taking everything away.

Commotion walked carefully over to her body. She felt a blast of air from his nostrils as he sniffed her. He reminded her of so many horses over so many years. She smiled.

She felt a tear slip down and burrow itself in her ear.

She thought of Vida. She thought of her daughter.

She might not have been able to give Vida everything, but she was glad she had given her horses.

eighty-four

MAPLE

Maple woke up early the following morning. The Parker women drove to the showgrounds together. Maple slipped into Commotion's stall to greet him. Piper and Heather stayed back to let her have her moment with the horse.

Commotion seemed happy to see Maple; he pushed his head into her chest. His stall hadn't been cleaned yet, and Maple noticed a strand of brightly colored beads in the shavings. She reached down and pulled out a friendship bracelet, like the one still on her wrist. It read, *Barn Mom*. Maple knew it belonged to Pamela. She never took it off. Maple was surprised that Pamela had been in Commotion's stall, but then she figured that Pamela had probably been checking his water or feeding him supplements or something. Maple slipped the bracelet into her pocket to give to Pamela later.

Maple's class was one of the first of the day. She had to hurry.

All three Parkers worked together. Piper braided the horse's mane, Maple put polish on his hooves and Heather took pictures to send to the girls' dad.

Things were not perfect. Things were not fixed. But that was what the horse world was for. To hold the real world at bay. To get lost in your horse and your shows and your barn family.

Kieran stood by Maple as she waited for her turn to compete, his hand resting on the horse's shoulder.

"How do you feel?" he asked when it was almost her round.

"I know I'm nervous, but I don't really feel it."

"Well," he said, "you may not be a great rider, but this is a great horse. All you have to do is stay out of his way."

Maple nodded and shortened her reins.

When it was her turn to ride, Maple entered the big arena. She goaded Commotion into a huge canter. With all of his show nerves, the horse didn't need encouragement. He thundered forward, faster than she had ever gone. Too fast.

Maple stood up in her stirrups. She pulled back on the reins with her whole body, all the way down to her heels, trying to slow the horse down. Commotion just twisted his head to avoid the bit and went faster.

This was a stupid idea, Maple realized, *a stupid, crazy idea.*

She was in a Jumper class on a Grand Prix–level horse. She had asked him to go fast. She should have realized that asking him to slow down would be harder. She should have realized that he might get out of control. And now she was panicking, afraid to keep going, unable to stop.

She might be able to stop him if she took emergency measures. She could try to run him into the rail, but he could easily jump it and take off with her across the showgrounds. She could turn him in circles to slow him down, but he could pivot on a dime, and she doubted she could stay with him. She could try to pull an emergency stop, but Commotion was stronger than she was.

She considered just letting him run like she had that night with

Vida. They could circle the arena until he tired himself out and finally slowed down, but that would be humiliating. It would be exactly what everyone expected. Maple, the weak one, would choke.

But they didn't know her. She didn't even know herself yet.

The buzzer sounded. She pointed Commotion at the first jump.

Commotion's stride stretched even farther, and he rushed the jump. They took off too close. He unspooled beneath her. His legs snapped up in front, then flicked up behind. She lost her breath and her balance. She was terrified.

They landed on the other side of the jump. She barely managed to stay on. He was like a tornado, completely cut free of all the organized riding she'd been doing. Her teeth were clanging. Her nerves were on fire.

Commotion catapulted around the first bend. Maple heard the crowd audibly gasp as Commotion rocketed over an oxer. She heard the whiplike swish of his tail behind them as they dived around a too-tight turn.

Her eyes hurt. Her heart was gone; it had abandoned her chest. She needed to throw up or shit. She didn't feel tough. She felt weak and scared. They flew around another corner.

Commotion came up fast beneath her; then he rushed the jump again. They were jumping badly. Everything was wild and disorganized.

Her gut clenched. Her stomach dropped. Again, Commotion flew. Every time he did, she thought they would crash; she thought they would die. But every time, he saved them, seemingly at the last second. It was all she could do to stay on him.

In her peripheral vision, she saw her mom and Piper along the rail; they were watching breathlessly. Nearly all the riders at RSFE were behind them. It was a lot of pressure not to die.

Something burst inside Maple as Commotion cut hard to the last line. The first jump in the line unseated her, but she jammed her heels down and clenched her stomach. She even tried to grab mane, but she caught only dead air, because his hair was plaited.

They hit the last fence at a bad distance, and Commotion took it short, but his legs snapped up, and he didn't so much as graze the rail.

The buzzer sounded. Maple was so glad it was over she collapsed on Commotion's neck. Seemingly recognizing that signal, Commotion finally slowed down.

Maple let the reins go loose. The horse dropped his head, then slowed to a stretchy walk.

She hugged his neck, thanking him, letting him guide her to the gate as the next horse started the course.

"You knew we could do it, didn't you?" she said to the horse, rubbing his withers.

His ribs expanded on a sigh. She laughed and held him tighter.

Her ride had been unlike anything she had ever experienced. It had been terrifying, unexpectedly violent. It had knocked all her senses loose.

She wanted to do it again.

She did, an hour later in the jump-off. She crushed it. She was the fastest. Commotion didn't so much as graze a rail.

Maple won. Piper and Heather and Kieran stood with her in the Winner's Enclosure. They all took a picture with the silver cup.

When Heather and Maple and Piper returned to the barn aisle, June Far was waiting. She took Maple's mother aside and told her about Pamela. Then Heather told Maple and Piper. Many of the staff and owners already knew, but they had been instructed by Kieran not to tell the Parkers until after the Cup. And they had listened, because in the horse world, competitions mattered that much.

"It was what Pamela would have wanted," one of the grooms insisted, but Maple didn't think that was true. Pamela would've wanted Vida to win.

Still, Maple was convinced that Pamela would have been proud of her ride. Sometimes she even convinced herself that Pamela's spirit had helped her win or imagined that she had been in the Winner's Enclosure with Kieran and the Parkers.

It was a day that Maple would never forget, for many reasons.

It was the day that she realized she didn't have to change. She didn't have to be someone else to deserve to be loved. She just had to stay out of her own way.

eighty-five

VIDA

When Vida woke up the morning of the Little Palm Cup, her mother was not in the room with her. That had never happened before.

The night before, Pamela had dropped Vida off at the hotel and then disappeared. Maybe she had done something illegal. Maybe she was in jail.

Vida tried to call her. When her mother didn't pick up, Vida got ready by herself. She had never prepared for a show alone before. It was weird and a little scary. She kept catching her own eyes in the mirror and seeing the fear in her face. Her own fear scared her more than anything.

Vida got a ride with Effie to the showgrounds. June didn't know where Pamela was either.

"I haven't seen her since last night," she said. "This isn't like her."

Vida agreed, but she didn't say anything. She was getting more and more worried that her mother had done something really bad.

When they arrived at the show barn, everything was chaos—which was normal at a horse show. Riders were preparing for their classes. Horses were being groomed. Kieran was off somewhere mysterious. Vida jumped into the chaos immediately. She didn't mention her mother, and neither did anyone else, which only made her more anxious.

One of the grooms told her, "Kieran is looking for you," but Vida was afraid to look for him.

As she worked, she considered what her mother had told her the night before: Kieran was her biological father. She knew her mother wouldn't lie about a thing like that.

Vida ran through the big moments of her life, saw them strung out before her with new motivations colored in, as if she had never understood her life before now.

She understood why Pamela wanted her to ride. Why they had stuck with Kieran even in bad times. Why they had fought so hard for his approval. Why they needed to win and be the best.

And Vida saw herself, how strong she was, how cruel. How she sometimes felt a monstrous force inside herself, a villain lodged in her gut. She had a name for it now: her father.

Vida had been at the showgrounds for less than an hour when Kieran found her. She spun around to face him and found her eyes searching for any resemblance between them. She took after her mother mostly, but she had Kieran's pores. Of all the things he could have given her, she had inherited his bad complexion.

"Come with me for a second," he said. "We need to have a chat."

That was when Vida knew her mom was in big trouble. Maybe Pamela had been asked to leave the barn. Maybe that was why she wasn't there. Maybe she was afraid to tell Vida, afraid to let her down.

Kieran led Vida to his customized golf cart. He must not have wanted anyone to hear what he had to say—which Vida appreciated but which also seemed to confirm her worst fears.

Kieran drove her way out past the parking lot. They stopped where the path ended, where no one could see or hear them.

It was hot out there. Vida immediately felt a coating of thick sweat bloom across her back.

Kieran switched off the golf cart's engine.

"What did she do?" Vida said, wanting to get this conversation over with as quickly as possible.

"She overdosed."

His answer was so unexpected that Vida did not understand it. "I don't get it."

"Your mother injected herself with a lethal amount of ace-promazine."

"Why would she do that? She knows it's not for people."

Vida was sure Kieran was kidding. He seemed to be saying that her mother was dead. But that was crazy.

"We'll never really know why she made the decision to take her life." Kieran's voice sounded oddly bloodless. "She was struggling with money, and she wanted the best for you. Sometimes that can be a lot of pressure."

Vida knew her mother better than anyone. "She wouldn't have killed herself."

Vida's eyes were drawn to the place where the mountain peaks met the sky. She had an idea that her mom was *there*, at the vanishing point. If she hurried, she could catch her.

"Vida." He put his hand on her shoulder. "Where are you going?"

Her breath felt hot inside her mouth. She was disoriented. She had a horrible feeling that she was the one who had died. Her mom had gone on living and left her behind in a dead world.

"Look at me," he said. "Take a deep breath."

Vida looked at him. His eyes were green, too. Were they the same shade as hers? Did they have the same nose? The same ribs?

He squeezed her shoulder. "You're a tough girl. You'll get through this. Someday you might find it liberating. There's no one left to disappoint."

She remembered his parents were dead, too.

Her fucking grandparents.

Her mind was firing and misfiring so many thoughts at once.

Her mother was dead.

Kieran was her father.

And he wouldn't admit it, even now, when her mother was gone. He was acting like Vida was any other student, like this conversation was slightly awkward, a burden, a bummer.

She had nowhere to go. No one she could trust.

She was in a golf cart with Kieran, and no one else was around. She felt vulnerable. She felt afraid, but she wasn't quite sure what she was afraid of.

"I just don't think she would—," Vida started, but he cut her off.

"You know, Vida, you're too young to understand the tremendous responsibility a parent feels. Your mother wanted to give you everything, but she couldn't. You're so much stronger than she ever was. I don't think you realize . . . I don't think you always realize how much you hurt people. I'm not saying you mean to, but I think your mother has always felt that she wasn't good enough for you."

It was almost like he was saying Pamela's death was Vida's fault. It was almost like he might be right. Maybe her mother *had* killed herself. Maybe she blamed herself for what Vida was. Just the night before, she had called Vida a bully, had said that she ruined her daughter. Vida had been too shocked and hurt to correct her.

Maybe Vida had broken her. It wasn't hard for Vida to believe that she could break someone. It was something she had feared all her life. She could be so mean. She could be so tough. She wasn't like other people. She had always suspected that she had the power to crush someone. But she had never, ever wanted to crush her mother.

Vida looked down at the neat sleeves of her riding jacket. She was supposed to be competing soon. She was supposed to be riding in the Little Palm Cup.

"Here's what I'm thinking. You do a few years as an Amateur," Kieran said, laying out his training plan like it was the thing that mattered. "And when you're ready, you'll go pro. You'll ride the best horses." He squeezed her shoulder again. "What do you think, kid? You want to ride for me?"

She blinked at him, dizzy with shock and confusion.

"You know what else I was thinking?" he continued. "Why don't you ride Razzle Dazzle in the Meter Ten this afternoon?"

It was like he thought he could dangle a horse in front of Vida and distract her from her mother's death.

"I think you'll have a real shot on him," he said.

The day before, that would have meant the world to her. Today, she felt nothing.

"But first, I need you to talk to the detectives." Kieran started the engine. "I think you should tell them all about your mother's history. About the financial pressure she was under. Just so they get the whole picture. She kept drugs at the house, didn't she? They'll want to know all of that."

She met his eyes—shocked, surprised—and then it hit her. Her mother's last words to her: *We're not keeping his secrets anymore.*

L ater, Vida sat in the investigation stall with the two detectives. Kieran was with her, like this was a riding lesson. Making sure she made no wrong moves.

Vida didn't know what to do. She didn't even know—really—if Kieran was her father. She had no proof he'd had any involvement in Pamela's death.

Except that he always carried Ace at horse shows.

Except that he was sitting across from her now, watching her intently.

Except that he had told her exactly what to say.

He had trained her for that moment in a dozen ways. *Don't show emotion. Keep your eyes up. Focus. Don't cry.*

It was impossible to believe that the person she had looked up to all her life was not only not who she thought he was but the worst person she could have imagined.

She didn't know how to act. She was filled with a sense of dread, as if the whole world had suddenly turned against her. Without Pamela to protect her, it kind of had.

All that remained inside her was the root will to survive, to get through this moment. She had to be smart. She had to keep moving. She would deal with the emptiness later. She would deal with the grief later. She would deal with the paternity, and the possible murder, and everything else later.

She just had to get through this.

Vida was strong. She had mostly thought that was a good thing, but it occurred to her now that strength was a little perverted, a little villainous. Because even as she knew that she had lost the only person who had ever fought for her, the only person who had supported her, the only person who had ever loved her, she knew that Kieran was right. She *could* get through this. Not every part of her maybe, but enough of her to keep moving forward, more shadow than human, into the stinging light of her destiny.

That strength made her a little delirious, a little crazed. Her eyes drifted over the other people in the room, and she thought, *I don't have anyone. Worse, I don't need anyone.*

And she knew that her mother would have been proud of that, too. Would be proud of her forever, whether she was in the room, on a cloud, or really truly nowhere now.

Vida sat back, then crossed her neat tall boots.

"Do you have a mother?" she asked the detectives.

She didn't think they could have had a mother like Pamela, but anyone with a mother would understand.

"My mother wanted to give me everything. She wanted to give me horses. . . ."

eighty-six

DETECTIVE PEREZ

Detective Perez helped clear out the stall. There would be no official investigation.

The horses watched as she and her partner, Detective Ortiz, walked down the barn aisle toward the parking lot.

"So," Detective Ortiz said. He had kept quiet most of the day. Perez was the junior partner, so Ortiz liked to step back to let her learn. "You think it was suicide?"

"Well, there's the history with drugs," Detective Perez said. "And her daughter was a little . . . *intense*. And she was under a lot of pressure financially."

Detective Perez was a mother herself, and while she didn't believe in spoiling her children, she could see the draw, feel the pressure.

No one ever really explained what you were supposed to do with children. Were you supposed to make them happy, or were you supposed to make them good? And how could you do either when you were probably not happy or good yourself?

Detective Ortiz nodded. "Suicide does seem to make the most sense."

"I didn't like that Kieran guy. He reminds me of my father."

"He was very helpful," Detective Ortiz said.

"Too helpful. All this packing away evidence, moving the body . . . but I guess it lines up with the type of person he is. He seems to think this is his domain, and we don't belong. . . ." She drifted off, thinking of her father as they approached the parking lot. "And he doesn't have a motive. From what everyone said, that woman revered him. They all do."

They reached their car. Detective Ortiz climbed into the passenger seat, leaving Detective Perez to collect her thoughts.

Way out in the big arena, under the lights, a girl and her horse were jumping over enormous fences. There were people in the stands—not many, but they gave the girl and her horse their total attention, as if riding was a matter of life and death.

eighty-seven

MAPLE

Maple didn't know how to deal with Vida after Pamela's death. Maple wanted to hate her for all the things she'd done, but now that seemed unfair. Luckily, Vida made it easy on her. She ignored her and everyone else.

Vida had moved in with June and planned to stay until she turned eighteen. Still, she hardly interacted with June or Effie. She reminded Maple of Douglas, the way she cycled through her rides like a machine: cold, implacable, a little haunted. She avoided Maple, and Maple avoided her back.

It was weeks before Maple even approached Vida, and then only because she had to. They were preparing for another horse show, and in her show jacket, Maple had found something that belonged to Vida—something that she had completely forgotten about.

She caught Vida preparing to school Cassidy Moreno's horse.

"Hey." Maple walked forward carefully. "I have something of yours. Well, not yours exactly . . ." Maple reached into her pocket and pulled out a beaded bracelet.

Vida scowled. "You don't have to give me our friendship bracelet back, stupid," she said, sounding like her old self.

"No! I wouldn't! It's not . . ." Maple pressed the bracelet into Vida's hand. "I completely forgot I had it."

Vida held up the bracelet so she could read the beads: *Barn Mom.* Maple could see the wave of shock roll through her.

Maple stood limply by. Lately she had been feeling so strong, but something about Vida brought her right back.

"Where did you get this?" Vida demanded.

Maple knew that Vida herself had made the bracelet for her mom. It had been a big deal to Pamela. She hadn't worn diamonds or silver bangles like the other moms. She had only worn the bracelet Vida made her.

"It was in Commotion's stall. At the last show," Maple said, her voice dipping on the significance of that event. "I'm sorry. I forgot about it. It was such a crazy day."

That night Kieran had gathered everyone around the horse show campfire to share the news about Pamela, even though almost everyone knew by then. He had rested a hand on Vida's shoulder and told the crowd, "Pamela was an example of the best of this barn. She dedicated her whole life to this family. She will be greatly missed. . . ."

Maple remembered feeling hollow, like a stand-in for herself. Like they had all been suddenly enlisted to perform in a play in which they would pretend that Pamela was dead. Meanwhile, Maple could still hear Pamela's words like she was standing right behind her: *Fuck every last one of them.*

"I really liked your mom," Maple said suddenly. She could immediately tell it was the wrong thing to say, even though it was what everyone said at moments like these.

"She wasn't your mom," Vida said possessively, as if she envied every moment Pamela had spent with Maple. As if Maple had stolen those moments, and now she was trying to steal Vida's grief, too.

"I know that."

"So it's not the same."

"Vida," Maple said more firmly than she had intended, "I know that."

The horse at Vida's side bobbed his head as Vida held the bracelet in her hand. "Thanks for finally giving it back, I guess," she snipped, turning back to the horse.

"No problem." Maple stood by for a second as if she should say something else, but she couldn't think of anything else to say. Finally, she offered, "Have a good ride."

eighty-eight

VIDA

Every morning, Vida felt like she had woken up in the wrong world. She would lie there in disbelief. If she shut her eyes, if she tried again, could she reset it? Go back to where she'd left herself?

It was a little terrifying how the world kept going. There had been the funeral and the move. And so many questions. Suddenly everyone had been asking her questions.

"Are you okay?"

"Do you want . . . ?"

"Where should we . . . ?"

Vida divided her life into neat tasks so it wouldn't be overwhelming. The eulogy. Going through her mother's things. The DNA test.

She had planned to collect a sample from Kieran, but when she found out that Douglas was moving in with Piper, she'd stolen his toothbrush from the suitcase in his truck bed.

She cried when she read the results. Even though she had believed her mother, it was different seeing it with her own eyes. As if her mind and the world were two different places, and now it was true in both.

She waited for Kieran to be arrested. When he wasn't, she thought her suspicions must be wrong. She was being paranoid. She was thinking crazy.

Even if Kieran had been responsible, what was Vida supposed to do? She wasn't a detective. She was an unlikable teenage girl. She wasn't the type to ask for help. She didn't even know what kind of help to ask for.

Then Maple handed Vida that bracelet.

Vida snipped, "Thanks for finally giving it back, I guess."

As she rode, she held the bracelet so tightly in her fist that the letters left marks: *Barn Mom*.

The bracelet might not prove everything, but it proved one thing. It proved a lie.

Pamela had been wearing the bracelet in their car that night. Vida had watched her play with it. The bracelet had been found in Commotion's stall, but the body had been found in Nikita's.

Kieran had moved the body.

The bracelet might not be enough evidence for a conviction, but it was enough to make Kieran suspicious in both worlds.

Vida found Kieran in his office; he was making copies of entry forms for the show. He was wearing his drugstore glasses. His office smelled like mouse droppings. Everything was so mundane, so much like it always was, that she felt a little undone.

"What's up?" he asked her.

Did he seem a little wary of her? He never had before. She gripped the bracelet in her pocket like it was the answer to a question she hadn't yet come up with.

Without Pamela there, the barn had changed. It was as if someone had let the air out, not just from Vida's dreams but from all their dreams. Pamela had believed in the barn more than anyone. Believed in Kieran. In a way, she had given him his power. For years and years.

Until that night.

Pamela had gone to confront Kieran with the truth. She had never returned. The secret that she had revealed was being kept.

Vida hadn't even told Douglas about her DNA test. She knew she should, but she had a sense of the secret's power. Her mother had revealed it, and her whole world had come crashing down.

The truth was Vida was afraid.

She gripped the bracelet tighter, and she thought about her mother. Her mother, who had loved her. Her mother, who had tried to give her everything. Her mother, who had lived for her. Her mother, who might have been brave enough, in the end, to die for her.

Pamela had said she'd made Vida just like her, and Vida hoped she was right.

"I wanted to ask you something," she said because she still didn't know the question. *I thought the body was in Nikita's stall. Don't you always carry Ace at shows? I know she was going to confront you.*

"Shoot."

"Are you my dad?" She gasped at her own question, like she had shot herself.

The color left his face. He looked older, like he did on Mondays.

"Where did you hear that?" he said, like rooting out the source of a rumor was more important than answering her question.

She still felt compelled to answer him, as if she owed him every-thing, when she might owe him only her life.

She should tell him: *My mom.*

She should threaten him: *I know.*

Because she did know. She knew because she was at least half him. All the things she had always feared in herself—her coldness, her cruelty, her power—were right there staring back at her.

She could move toward them, accept them. She could say, *This is all that is left of me.* She could believe: *This is who I am.*

Or she could forge her own path.

Beyond the dreams her mother had birthed inside her. Beyond the void her father had left.

Somewhere far, far away.

The journey would be hard, but she could make it on horseback.

"I'm leaving," she said. "I won't be coming back."

"Vida," he said, but she did not hesitate.

She did not wait for him. She did not need him. She never had.

eighty-nine

PIPER

Piper was watching *Heartland* with her sister while Douglas met with Vida. He had been overly solicitous in asking Piper's permission, as if it were a sin that he should ever be alone with another girl, which honestly made Piper more anxious than she would otherwise have been.

So when he texted I need you, she felt a hot ping of fear. She bolted from the sofa.

"Where are you going?" Maple asked. She knew Vida was there. She was just as curious about Vida's visit as Piper was.

"Douglas asked me to come."

Maple paused the TV show. "Can I come too?"

Piper debated. "Maybe not just yet. I'll let you know."

Piper hurried out across the yard, toward the guesthouse. Douglas had moved in after the horse show. Heather had insisted on it; she was being so supportive that her voice sometimes screeched with strain.

Piper had started classes at UCSD. She was surprised to find herself actually blazing with determination. She was going to be a doctor and a mother and a partner all rolled into one.

Douglas still asked her all the time if she was sure about him being there, if she was sure she wanted him, if she was *sure* it was all okay. And she was so sure, and she wanted him and she loved him so very much, that she sometimes felt tragic about it, even at the most mundane moments. As if they had cheated the world by being in love, and one day they would have to pay for it.

She didn't know why Vida had wanted to see Douglas alone. She'd assumed it was something horse related. It all seemed very heightened—as horse things did with horse people.

When Piper went into the guesthouse, she immediately saw a change in Douglas. It was as if all of his muscles and all of his nerves had been pulled too tight.

"What is it?" she said, rushing to his side.

He put his head in his hands.

"What happened?" she asked Vida.

Vida announced, like a doctor giving a diagnosis, "Kieran is Douglas's biological father. And mine."

"I just don't understand." Douglas looked searchingly at Piper, like he expected her to have the solution to that problem, too. "I don't understand why he wouldn't say."

Piper tried to get her head around it, tried to hold on to Douglas's hand as it seemed to shrink and slip from her fingers. Piper's mind was reeling.

"Does that mean Kieran is . . . ?"

If what Vida told them was true, then Kieran was her baby's grandfather. The Parkers were part of the barn family for real.

Vida just sat there with a perverse smirk, like the *Mona Lisa* of bad news. "It gets worse."

ninety

DETECTIVE PEREZ

He had driven six hours to meet her. He wasn't in riding clothes, which robbed him of some of his power, so he looked like any attractive, troubled young man.

"Thank you for agreeing to meet me," he said.

They were sitting outside a church, around the corner from the station. She wasn't actually supposed to be meeting him. There wasn't any official investigation into Pamela's death, but he had sounded desperate on the phone.

It had always surprised Hortensia Perez that as a detective, she very rarely got to offer people resolution. Her job was mostly just doing paperwork and managing the emotions of victims or perpetrators.

He took a deep breath. "I'm sorry I didn't tell you why I was there that night." His eyes were pleading, like he especially needed *her* forgiveness. "But my girlfriend is pregnant, and I was there to tell her mom, and I— No one knew. So I didn't think I should tell you unless I had my girlfriend's permission." He seemed on the verge of panic. "I left Kieran alone in the barn aisle around midnight. I didn't see Pamela, but I know he was there. I'm really sorry."

"It's okay," Perez assured him.

The truth was, none of that information was helpful. It wasn't enough that Kieran had been there—Douglas had been there, too. As had Emma Moreno and probably a number of other people. Hortensia could have told him that on the phone, but he'd insisted on speaking to her in person.

"I hope I didn't interfere with your investigation," he said.

"You didn't, Douglas. It's okay."

He met her eyes, then swallowed hard. "Kieran is Vida's biological father. Her mom told her right before she died."

Those facts certainly added another dimension to Kieran and Pamela's relationship.

"He's mine, too. I don't know if you know that—I mean, *I* didn't know that."

"I didn't know that."

His eyes had a burning sadness. "Do you think he killed her?"

Hortensia didn't know what to think. She didn't like Kieran, and his fingers were all over the investigation, but sometimes it was easier to assume that if you couldn't prove something, it couldn't be true.

"I really can't—" She stopped. "Wait. Did you say no one knew your girlfriend was pregnant?"

"No. I only found out a couple hours before. Only Piper and Heather knew. And Kieran. We still haven't really told anyone. You're supposed to wait."

"That's . . ." She cocked her head. "But *I* knew. I mean, I heard a rumor."

One of the moms had said something about Douglas getting a girl pregnant. The same one who had told her that she'd seen Douglas there alone. "Do you know Emma Moreno?"

"Yeah. She's one of Kieran's clients."

"Still?" Emma had mentioned something about switching trainers.

"Yeah. Her daughter just started training with Kieran."

The old adage said to follow the money, but with these people, you needed to follow the horses.

ninety-one

PIPER

I t was Piper's idea to go at night. They paid off Nash. They loaded up their trucks with all of their equipment. They tacked up their horses, ponied the extras. Then they rode along the darkened trails toward the Parkers' house.

The night air stank of eucalyptus and desperation. The horses fed off the riders' nerves as they traveled along the trails in the dark. They whinnied to one another, picked up a trot. Vida rode one of her mother's horses, ponied the other two. Her expression was closed and determined, like she was riding into battle.

Effie tried to keep up with her, but eventually she fell behind and rode with Maple. They giggled about something, with the teenage urge to make anything funny, especially anything scary.

Heather met them at the gate. They had spent all day getting the barn ready: new stall mats, fresh shavings, water troughs.

The plan was to keep all the horses on the Parker property for now, while they looked for a new trainer. But Piper hoped that Douglas would find the confidence to train them himself. They could start their own team, build their own barn family, safe from the world and from Kieran.

The morning after they took the horses, they were all edgy with the expectation of some confrontation. Vida had sat on a chair in front of the barn as if challenging anyone to try to take her mother's horses.

It was Piper who eventually went to her. She was the only one brave enough.

Piper knew that Vida didn't like her. Piper didn't much like Vida either. But now Vida was family: her child's aunt, maybe one day her sister-in-law.

"He won't come," Piper said, taking the chair beside her. "He's too smart for that."

Vida exhaled slowly, as if released. She was too smart not to agree.

"He's my father," she said. "He's Douglas's father, too. Don't you worry that we're like him?"

"Honestly? I don't think parents have as much of an influence on their kids as they think."

Vida held Piper's gaze for a moment, and Piper held back a shiver, thinking she saw a family resemblance. Piper forced herself to push past it, to see the good side, always.

"You know, whatever happens, you'll always have a family here. With us."

"Oh, God, no. I'm moving to Europe as soon as I turn eighteen. And I'm never coming back." Vida gripped the armrests on her chair. "And one day, I'll win the Rolex or Longines or the fucking Olympics. And he'll see me, and he'll know: I'm so much fucking better than him."

ninety-two

DETECTIVE PEREZ

As Hortensia's car wound through the roads of Rancho Santa Fe, she was cheered by the thought that she was so far outside her jurisdiction—not just in distance but in every imaginable way—that she would probably never get caught.

The houses were all set back from the road, behind bright green pastures and vineyards and orange groves. They were fashioned in the style Americans believed to be European, but they were bigger, more garish, *newer*, monuments without history.

Emma Moreno had agreed to meet Hortensia at RSFE, an arrangement that she had immediately found suspicious. She expected it was because Emma wanted Kieran to be there, possibly even to sit in on the interview, like he had with Vida—which Hortensia now believed she should never have allowed. The way the girl had acted could certainly have been a consequence of his presence.

Even without Kieran's interference, speaking to Emma again was probably pointless. She might have lied about seeing Douglas alone, but that didn't mean she had lied about anything else. And even if she had, she wasn't about to admit it at RSFE, where Kieran had the home-court advantage.

Did Hortensia really think Kieran had killed Pamela? The question had been playing on her mind since Douglas had asked it. When she thought back to that day at the horse show, she could see Kieran in everything—he was Dominic's employer, Douglas and Vida's father, everybody's trainer.

Hortensia had no sure reason to think he was responsible, but she had still driven six hours to Rancho Santa Fe on her day off.

She parked in the upper lot. As she journeyed down a stairwell, she could see that the barn was in chaos. At first she assumed it was just ordinary horse people chaos—like the kind she'd witnessed at the show—but the horses were missing. Half the stalls were empty. Owners and riders and grooms all stood in groups, not even trying to lower their voices.

"They just took them in the middle of the night."

"Vida had better not have kept the front boots I lent her!"

"Everything is gone."

Hortensia hovered on the edge of the chaos. There were times in her job when she had a sense of things falling into her lap. As if somewhere, some god actually wanted the bad guys to lose sometimes.

She listened. The Parkers and the Fars and Vida had all taken their horses in the middle of the night. Douglas Dunn had quit. And Kieran was nowhere to be found.

Eventually, Hortensia saw Emma Moreno wandering the aisle. Hortensia crossed in front of her, blocking her path.

"Mrs. Moreno—"

"Kieran's not even here," Emma said, although Hortensia hadn't asked to talk to him. "Cassidy was supposed to have a lesson with him this morning, but he's not even here!" Emma had her daughter beside her, all turned out in the cutest pink polo shirt and two neat braids tied off with ribbons. "They're saying Douglas quit. They're saying all kinds of things. And the Parkers and the Fars are gone. It's just a mess!" Emma froze in the aisle, unsure what to do.

All around them, the owners and trainers and riders were re-aligning, deciding where their loyalties lay.

"If he's actually their biological father, that's pretty fucked up."

"He's always been an abusive trainer. I've said it a million times: It's emotional abuse."

"I don't trust anyone but Douglas on my horses."

Hortensia knew that moment was exactly the right time, the most vulnerable time. If the barn was falling apart, then Kieran's power would be at its weakest.

"I would really like to talk to you," Hortensia said.

"I can't! I have Cassidy!" Emma said, spinning around so her daughter jerked like a fish on a line.

"Mrs. Moreno, this is important. I spoke to Douglas Dunn." That got Emma's attention.

"What do you mean? When?"

"He came down to the station yesterday." The easiest way to get someone to talk was to convince them that *they* were in trouble. It was a neat detective trick. "His story didn't quite match yours."

Emma blanched, then scanned the aisle. "Where's your partner?"

"This isn't an official investigation." Hortensia smiled politely. "It's just two moms talking." There was no such thing as "off the record" when it came to speaking to a detective, but two moms talking could share the darkest secrets. "About a hypothetical situation. You would have to trust me."

Emma looked into the detective's eyes for the first time. Hortensia knew immediately why she had been avoiding them—Emma wanted to tell her something. She wanted to tell her everything.

"What do you think?" Hortensia asked.

Emma took a deep breath, then glanced at Cassidy. "Sweetie, why don't you see if there are any bridles you can clean?"

Cassidy rolled her eyes and wandered off, her braids bouncing.

Emma led Hortensia out to the deserted viewing area. In the big arena, a single rider warmed up her horse alone. Emma watched. Hortensia worried that if they waited too long, she might change her mind.

"Hypothetically"—Hortensia took a seat right beside the other woman, like they were friends, just two barn moms—"you might have been intimidated. You might have been afraid of Kieran. Or unsure what you saw."

"Dominic quit," Emma said. "Did you know that? Right after the show. He moved back to Italy. He was with Kieran for twenty years."

"I didn't know that," Hortensia said.

"Then this morning . . ." Emma shook her head to clear the cobwebs of her shock. "They're saying that Douglas and Vida are Kieran's *children*. And look what happened to both their mothers. I think that's just . . . I mean, it's very dark, isn't it?"

"Hypothetically," Hortensia encouraged her.

Emma's tone changed suddenly. She sounded desperate to be believed. "Kieran told me she did it to herself."

"Let's start at the beginning," Hortensia said, trying not to sound too much like a detective. "You were near the barn aisle around midnight."

Emma nodded. The truth was in her throat now, ready to come out. "I was drinking with Tracy Hicks's team—I think I told you that. I knew Douglas was still hanging around. We'd hooked up before at a horse show. I was keeping an eye out when I saw Heather going to meet him. I followed her, and I overheard about the baby. He said he was in love with Piper, so that was hard.

"I didn't think you would arrest him or anything, by the way! When I said all that stuff in our interview," she said. "I just thought maybe he deserved to be shaken up by someone." She hesitated, stuck on the Douglas point.

Hortensia decided to help her out. "Guys are assholes."

"Absolutely!" Emma breathed, freed for a moment. "So I left. Obviously, it wasn't my intention to eavesdrop! But then, later, I just started feeling more and more angry. So I had this idea to—I don't know—confront Douglas about what he had done to me. I just wanted an apology.

"When I went back to the barn aisle, I saw Kieran and Dominic moving the—you know—*body*. From Commotion's stall. I thought that was odd."

It was very odd. A groom had found the body in Nikita's stall.

"Kieran told me to go back to the hotel. Said he would call the police. But he didn't call right away, did he?"

"He called in the morning. Around six thirty."

"I saw them just after midnight. I know because Cassidy was so pissed. She just wanted to go back to the hotel— I hope you don't think I'm a bad mother!"

"Of course not," Hortensia assured her.

She didn't. She was a homicide detective. She knew what a bad parent really was.

"I would do anything for my daughter. Sometimes that's the problem," Emma confessed. "The next day, Kieran suggested that I not mention having seen them. He said it would be bad for *Dominic*, because he didn't have a green card. And I fucking bought it. We loved Dominic. He was an amazing groom."

"He seemed nice," Hortensia said. She understood him better now.

"Kieran suggested that maybe he could start training Cassidy. I honestly was just so happy I didn't even think! I didn't really think about it! Why would Kieran kill Pamela? I mean, yes, she was kind of a bitch, but she was Kieran's top client. Everyone knew that. And we all knew about the drugs. And the daughter. And we suspected the money problems. Suicide just made more sense. But now that I've heard all this about Vida and Douglas—"

"Hypothetically," Hortensia said, trying to stay on track, "I think you should come down to the station and give a statement."

"Would I be in trouble?"

"No," Hortensia said, and she meant it.

It was difficult in her line of work to believe that people were good. She had learned that on balance, they were mostly self-serving, but that knowledge made the moments when they did things for others all the more brilliant.

"Emma?" Hortensia caught her eyes, drew them away from the horse and the arena. "Everyone will say that you're the hero."

ninety-three

HEATHER

Heather couldn't sleep. She had a feeling that no one had been able to sleep in the weeks following Pamela's death. It seemed to her that beginning on the night Pamela died—at the very moment when Heather had decided to be supportive, to let her children go—her entire world had conspired to test her resolve.

Everything was kind of a mess. Her husband was still fighting to get their children to leave her. Her elder daughter was living in the backyard with a boy Heather didn't trust. Her younger daughter had been traumatized.

Her closest friend was dead, had allegedly killed herself to avoid the same crushing pressure that Heather felt every day: the pressure to be the parent she was *supposed* to be. And now it had been revealed that Pamela might not have killed herself at all, that she might have been murdered by the trainer Heather had chosen for her daughters.

So it seemed unlikely that Heather would ever sleep again.

One night, she walked out to the barn, hoping that the horses might cure her. Hoping to feel like she had gotten one thing right.

It was cozy in the barn aisle. It smelled like fly spray and horses and pine shavings. It felt like home.

Heather startled when Douglas came out of one of the stalls. She should have expected him to be there, with the horses as always.

"Sorry," he said. "I didn't realize you were here."

"You were here first," she said.

"I'll go." He started toward the guesthouse, then stopped, seeming not to want to go home. He turned back to face her, looked at her with an expression caught somewhere between guilt and need. "Do you want me to leave? I don't mean now. I mean, do you not want me here?"

Heather was *trying*, but she hadn't exactly been welcoming. She didn't know how to be. Douglas appeared to her now to have been a bad omen, a sign that she had missed. And the latest news about Kieran had served only to underline that feeling. The mean part of her resented Douglas for it. *Really? There's more? Aren't you already bad enough for my daughter?*

Now he was asking her if she wanted him to leave. And perhaps he meant it. If she said the word, he would go. The bad luck would disperse. The wrong choice Heather had made in ever taking her daughters to RSFE would fade into the distance. The sad story that had suffused their lives would become someone else's story.

"I don't want to be like him," Douglas continued, reaching up automatically as Queenie stretched her head over the gate. He ran his hand down the horse's face. She nibbled at the hem of his shirt. "But it scares me how much I already am. Even the baby. It's . . . it's a little eerie."

He rubbed the horse's nose. Heather watched him.

He was her family now. As much as she might think she could cut him out, she couldn't. He would always be the baby's father. He might always have her daughter's heart. And he needed Heather. He needed a mother.

"You're nothing like him," she said.

His eyes lifted and landed on hers.

"You've already shown that in a million different ways, with a million different choices." She walked toward him until she could rest a hand on his shoulder. "You're going to be this baby's dad. And you're going to be the *best* dad, because you're going to love the baby all the way, unconditionally. Take the good things from your father, if you can find them. Leave everything else behind. We're your family now. Not your barn family. Your blood."

She hugged him then, held him to her heart. She finally accepted this was *right*. She felt the rightness wash over her, setting her free. This was the way it was supposed to be.

Not perfect. Not the life she chose. The life she had.

ninety-four

DETECTIVE PEREZ

That night, when Hortensia tucked her daughter in, she told the girl that she had seen horses that day.

"What kind of horses?" Estella said, arranging her dolls in a halo around her head.

"Jumping horses," Hortensia said, thinking about the gorgeous stone barn, the insanely high fences, the immaculate horses.

Estella sighed, like there was something soulful about jumping horses. She leaned back on her pillow. "When can I ride horses? When I'm five?"

Normally, Hortensia kept her answer to that question noncommittal. She didn't want to explain to her three-year-old that they had money but not horse people money. But that night, she thought about Cassidy Moreno, her braids and pink hair ribbons. Estella would look adorable in riding clothes.

Horse people were crazy, but there was something a little magical about the horse world.

And she echoed, "When you're five."

ninety-five

MAPLE

The Parkers' driver dropped Maple off in the porte cochere. She left her backpack in the car and raced toward the barn. It was freshly painted, white with green trim. Maple herself had chosen the colors.

She passed by Piper in the round pen with Douglas and one of the yearlings. Their new puppy was waiting patiently at the gate. Piper waved, and Maple waved back.

She found Heather in the breezeway, tightening the girth on her horse. "I thought you weren't supposed to run, miss."

"I wasn't running," Maple said, slowing carefully so as not to give herself away. "Anyway, I'm the teacher."

Maple had started giving Heather lessons, just in the basics. Heather didn't want to compete, but she wanted to be able to go on trail rides with her family.

They were going on one now. Maple strapped on her helmet, then helped her mother put on the bridles. They led the horses out toward the mounting block and hopped on.

As they rode along the pastures, horses greeted them, chased them along the white fences. The property held dozens of horses now. They had started a training program, and the client base was growing.

Maple rode alongside her mother, giving her pointers. "Relax your shoulders. Tighten your core. Open your hip angle."

Heather sighed, then teased, "I thought this was supposed to be fun."

They rode out onto the trails beyond their house. They had to pass by RSFE. The barn was deserted. Kieran had closed the whole place down before he was even charged. He hadn't waited for people to quit. He just stopped training.

Maple supposed he hadn't been strong enough to handle the truth. She thought it was a little ironic that he had spent his whole life teaching other people to be brave when he wasn't.

They had heard that Kieran's barn and property had been raided, that he had been charged with murder. They were in communication with Detective Perez, and they were trying to help her put together a strong case, with Emma and Dominic acting as witnesses.

Maple and Heather stayed quiet until RSFE was out of sight, and then they chatted about school, about Piper and Douglas and the baby, and about Jeff's next visit.

They rode up and down the low hills, past orange groves and vineyards and paradise.

They talked about horses. Because their new world was filled with possibilities and all the horses they could dream of.

acknowledgments

Biggest thanks to my editor, Jen Monroe, and her assistant, Candice Coote, for seeing this book through many iterations and, most of all, for trusting me to rewrite the entire book at the eleventh hour. You made this happen.

Thank you to the spectacular team at Berkley, especially Loren Jaggers, Stephanie Felty, Fareeda Bullert, Bridget O'Toole, Elisha Katz and Emily Osborne.

Thank you to my phenomenal agents, Sarah Bedingfield at Levine Greenberg Rostan and Hilary Zaitz Michael at WME.

Thank you to all the horses who left their mark on my heart: Desi, Belle Star, Pablo and, of course, my Tennessee.

Thank you to all my horsey employers over the years: North Coast Equestrian Park, Marble Mountain Ranch, Hayden Clarke Sport Horses and Enterprise Farms at the Paddock Riding Club.

Enormous thanks to all my writer friends for constant support and reassurance. I truly could not do this without you.

GIRLS
AND
THEIR
HORSES

ELIZA JANE BRAZIER

questions for discussion

1. Heather thinks she knows what is best for her daughters. Is it ever okay to push your children?

2. What do you think of Heather's and Pamela's parenting? Do you think it's helpful or harmful to their daughters?

3. Pamela allows Vida freedom to be herself, even when she makes wrong or dangerous choices. Is it possible to be too hands-off as a parent?

4. If parents don't offer their children guidance, will they seek it elsewhere through teachers, peers, or other parents?

5. The novel looks at relationships in which one living thing has influence over another. How does influence play a part in your own life?

6. Horses are so important to the main characters. Do you see any parallels with how the characters treat their horses and how the parents treat their children?

7. Why do you think Heather believes that horses can fix her relationship with her daughters?

8. Do you think Kieran is a compelling coach? Why or why not?

9. In the novel, Maple always feels like she is not as good as her older sister, Piper. Have you ever been jealous of someone close to you? How did it affect your behavior? Where do you think jealousy comes from?

10. Do you have any horse experience? If so, what is it? What did you like or not like about working with horses?

11. Do you believe that horses (or other animals) can communicate with people?

behind the book

I started riding at the age of five, but by then horses were already in my life and always would be. My granddad worked in high-stakes betting at the Southern California racetracks: Del Mar, Hollywood Park, Santa Anita. Later, when I lived in England, my boss at an accounting firm owned shares in racehorses that were stabled at Highclere Castle. My husband's cousin Paul Flynn was an Irish horse trainer and jockey who won the Hennessy Gold Cup. I even had two black horses pull my husband's casket through the streets of London after he died.

Educating myself about horses has been a lifelong journey. There is always something new to learn, a new method to try, a new way of seeing things. Working with horses has allowed me to reckon with my own flaws, my moods, my attitude. Horses have made me a better person. I have learned so much. *Girls and Their Horses* was born of that learning.

A few years ago I worked as a horseback-riding instructor in Orange County and later Los Angeles. I taught riding fundamentals to the children of the rich and famous. I was fascinated by the parent-child dynamics.

Those experiences inspired the question around which this book is based: Is it wrong to push your children? And beyond that, at what point does influencing another living thing become wrong or dangerous? *Girls and Their Horses* is filled with dynamic relationships, whether between a parent and a child, a teacher and a student, or a rider and a horse.

These relationships allow us to take a look at ourselves—if we are willing—and see who we truly are. Only in reckoning with our real effect on other living things can we become better people—if we dare.

That is the greatest challenge, and the greatest journey of our lives. And for me, horses will always be a part of that story.

reading list

Dark Horses by Susan Mihalic

The Horse Whisperer by Nicholas Evans

Horse by Geraldine Brooks

Big Little Lies by Liane Moriarty

Dare Me by Megan Abbott

The Hunting Wives by May Cobb

Read on for an excerpt from Eliza Jane Brazier's

IT HAD TO BE YOU

EVA

I've heard that killing someone is like falling in love. But I wouldn't know. I've never done it. Fall in love, I mean. That's for lunatics.

I see him on the sleeper train from Florence to Paris. He's standing there—now, right now—on the other side of the glass, trying to peer in through the mirrored window, and I think, *I wish we could stay like this forever.*

This is the exact relationship I want. I can see him but he can't see me. He's attractive, but especially attractive is the expression he wears because he thinks nobody can see him. His expression says, *It's the end of the world, this is the worst day of my life, and I'm stuck in a sleeper compartment with seven other people.*

Hard same.

I can almost see him debating, *Can I just stand for twelve hours?* Contemplating, *How did I end up here?*

No one takes the sleeper train anymore. I'm here only because it's harder to hide weapons on an international flight. Not impossible, but harder.

I could find all the weapons I want in Paris, but the longer you work this job, the more superstitious you get. I guess everyone gets superstitious when someone dies, especially when you're the one killing them.

He takes a step back. I think he might leave, walk down the aisle, maybe hang in the dining car.

It's actually me who opens the door. Sometimes I do things without thinking. Hazard of a job that's based on instinct. I want. I do. It happens. Just like that.

"Oh, I'm sorry. I didn't see you there." I've been staring at him for the past two minutes, but I'm so convincing that I half believe myself.

His face changes the moment he sees me, like I'm the whole world watching, expecting some kind of performance. Suddenly his expression is bland, almost meek. He's over six feet tall and border-line hulking, but with me in his sights, he's Clark Kent.

"Oh, no, *I'm* sorry. I wasn't sure if there was space in the car." He pushes his glasses up on his nose.

Let it be known that the seats are assigned.

I hold the door open. "We're the first ones here. But I checked the stubs; it's a full car." There are little ticket stubs above every seat, so everyone knows exactly where they belong.

He hesitates, as if caught between his performance of politeness and train angst.

"First time on a sleeper?" I ask.

"It's not that," he says.

"Anything I can help with?" I don't like to pry. It's true. I *love* to pry.

"Probably not." He has a suitcase behind him, so utilitarian that I assume he works in tech and wants people to know it.

I'm very good at reading people. This guy works out—*a lot*. He's wearing a suit he either has borrowed or can't afford to replace; it's loose and tight in all the wrong places. He probably took the train because he's actually broke. Or because he's too broad to fit comfortably in an airplane seat. He's favoring his right shoulder. He keeps his arm slightly cocked, as if bracing for impact.

He's not my usual type, which intrigues me. It's always better to choose a type that isn't yours. Call it an insurance policy.

I step back so he can move past me. He seems to think I'm much bigger than I am, because he hits the doorframe trying to avoid me, then hisses slightly through his teeth. It's obvious he's extremely uncomfortable being a human, which I find attractive.

"Do you want me to help you with your bags?" I ask.

I don't wait for him to answer. I grab the handle of his big wheeled suitcase and start to pull. It doesn't move. It's much heavier than I expected.

"I can get that," he says, but now it's a challenge.

"I got it." I engage my muscles and roll it neatly through the door. "What do you have in there?"

"Uh, computers." Called it.

He frowns at the bag like it's the bane of his existence. I can understand. If I had a bag that heavy, I'd dump it in the Arno.

"You don't want to leave it in the luggage racks?" I left all my bags on the racks—black, nondescript, with nothing in them that ties back to me, unless you recognize the custom satin finish on my Glock.

"No." He stows it neatly under the seats.

"You've done this before."

"I don't like planes," he says, pushing his glasses up again. They keep sliding down. At first, I thought it was because he doesn't normally wear them. I thought he was trying to look smarter. But I can see the variation in lens thickness—he's practically blind in his right eye—and then I realize they're falling because they're bent.

"Here." I reach for his glasses, slide them off his nose and quickly adjust them. "Everyone's face is crooked in a slightly different way."

I go to put them back on him but he is completely frozen. I can be too familiar with people sometimes. I know so much about them—heart rates and arteries and pressure points—that I sometimes feel this false sense of intimacy, as if I can wind them up like toys.

"Sorry," I say, handing him the glasses instead of putting them on his nose.

He swallows, seems uncertain. Of what, I don't know. He hesitates before he puts them on. When he does, they're perfect.

"See?" I say, as if that justifies everything.

"Thank you," he says, and then he takes the seat farthest from me. I don't think it's even *his* seat. He surreptitiously takes the tab off and lets it fall into a crack.

It's so weird how total strangers can casually devastate you. Not that I really care. I don't *really* care about anything. It's just easier sometimes to care deeply about things that don't matter.

"I get motion sickness," he says because he knows that I noticed him removing the tab. "I have to be close to the door." And it's suddenly so fucking awkward between us. It's shocking, actually, how awkward interactions with complete strangers can sometimes be.

"I don't care where you sit," I say, which only makes it more awkward. I should reassure him that I like the window. We could smile at each other, delight in our unique preferences, ruminate on our beautiful differences, but instead I just take my seat. Placating people is such a chore.

I look out the window and into the train station. It's eight p.m. and the crowd is starting to thin, get drunk and tired and hopeless. I should've just taken a plane.

"Six more people, huh?" he says. He's pacifying me, trying to smooth things over. Like the world might end if two strangers don't get along.

I sigh. Six more people. The train is almost full. I ran a check before I came to our car. There are open seats scattered here and there, but no real space. It's the law of assassins: Everything that can go wrong will go wrong. Sometimes it's fun. Sometimes it's eight p.m. at the end of a depressing weekend in Florence. Unless.

"You know," I say, "there is something we could try . . ."

He shifts uncomfortably. I'm starting to suspect he really doesn't like me. It's almost like he knows me.

I nearly say *Never mind* to let him off the hook—but why should I? I'm out here solving his problems for fun, and he's looking at me like I'm presumptuous.

"I'm sure it will be fine," he says, saintly in his repaired glasses.

The compartment door slides open. An Italian woman comes in. I'm relieved. Maybe she can break the spell. Maybe this guy and I can both stop trying to be nice to each other now. I thought he was cute at first, but this is getting too messy. I want to hook up with men who worship me completely. Otherwise it's kind of a waste of my time.

Of course this woman is the passenger whose tab he removed. It's fun watching him squirm as she looks at her ticket and the seat number—for so long, the story of it might constitute an epic—while we watch.

"I think I'm . . . ," she starts, but drifts off when she looks at him. He has a *drift off* face.

"They always bungle these things, don't they?" he says in perfectly accented Italian. I recognize his strategy immediately—blame *them*, those damn train people.

"They always do!" the woman agrees. "It took me two hours on the phone to arrange my ticket! My granddaughter had to help me! We had a ticket booked for Monday, but I need to be in Paris *by* Monday and I didn't realize I needed to book for the day before. Well, it was such a mess!"

It's a tedious story but we all listen because we're all here together for the next twelve hours. At around ten o'clock we'll pull out the beds and sleep on racks like corpses. Dead bodies are all laid to rest with strangers, too. Life is chance more than anything else. So is death.

"I'm sorry," he says. "That sounds like such a nightmare." He is using his pleasant voice. He didn't use it with me.

The woman has moved on from her problem with the seats. She realizes there is an open seat beside *him*, so maybe it's not all that bad. "I suppose I'll just sit here—what difference does it make?" She takes the seat. He shrinks in a very convincing way to make room. I bet he regrets not sitting next to me now. At least, I hope he does.

I can't help smiling as she slots in beside him, from the bottom of her thigh to the top of her shoulder. So cozy. He catches me smiling. To my surprise, he smiles back.

I feel something catch between my legs, like he's been fishing down there all this time.

He quickly stows his smile away, lest I forget I've decided not to like him.

The other passengers all come at once.

Two young Italian men. An American businessman. An older Englishman. A young Frenchwoman. A partridge in a pear tree. All in this one little train car.

Glasses Guy catches my eyes again. He is now crammed against the wall, looking exceptionally pale and miserable. Still, his eyes are almost hopeful when they meet mine. Like everything that happens from here on out is an inside joke between us. Like we are the only two people in the world who understand the absurdity of this exact circumstance. We were here first. Everyone else is part of *our* story.

It's so weird how certain people in your life just stick out. How you can go for years and years not meeting one. How you can convince yourself they don't exist. That it was something that happened when you were young. That it'll never happen again. That you were made of magic once, but you aren't magic now. And then, suddenly, you look across a train car and see someone sticking out like a page that's misaligned in the book of your life.

An Italian voice comes over the speaker system, telling us the train is about to depart. The lights flicker. There is this dragging sensation beneath our feet. He flinches. The train jerks. It rolls out of the station and into the night.

Our eyes meet every so often. He's super miserable now. He seems like he's in real physical pain . . . When the woman beside him shakes with laughter—she's talking on the phone. When the train jolts. Even when the lights flicker. Still, he seems okay with this, like he wants to suffer as much as possible. To get his money's worth.

But eventually he seems overwhelmed. He's pale as paper. His eyelids flutter occasionally. I think he might throw up, which is one way to clear a compartment. I imagine the two of us alone with his vomit. I'd stay. Puke doesn't really bother me. I see it a lot in my line of work.

Eventually he extracts himself from his seat—calmly, efficiently—and walks out the door. The train jolts. He lurches against the door-frame, then catches himself and disappears down the aisle.

Photo by Beverly Brooks

ELIZA JANE BRAZIER is an author, screenwriter, and journalist. Eliza entered the horse world at the age of five and has worked as a rider, horse trainer, and riding instructor. She lives with her horse and dogs in California, where she is developing her books for television.

VISIT ELIZA JANE BRAZIER ONLINE

 ElizaJaneBrazier

 ElizaJaneBrazier

Ready to find
your next great read?

Let us help.

Visit prh.com/nextread